The publication of Polly Courtney's debut novel *Golden Handcuffs*, a fictional exposé of her career in the Square Mile, earned Polly acclaim in the *Observer*, *The Times*, *Sunday Times*, *Independent*, *dian*, *Daily Express*, *Daily Mail*, *Evening ndard* and many other publications. Her second vel, *Poles Apart*, came out in 2008 and is an eye-opening depiction of life as a young migrant in England today. Aside from writing, Polly works on various sports-related web ventures including Girls ootball.com and is a keen footballer playing for n LFC. Polly is also part of a semi-professional g quartet, No Strings Attached, an all-girl mble that plays all over the UK. She has a ters degree from Cambridge University in neering and lives in London.

more information about Polly please visit www. ycourtney.com.

POLLY COURTNEY

The Day I Died

AVON

AVON

A division of HarperCollins*Publishers*
77–85 Fulham Palace Road,
London W6 8JB

www.harpercollins.co.uk

A Paperback Original 2009

First published in Great Britain by
HarperCollins*Publishers* 2009

Copyright © Polly Courtney 2009

Polly Courtney asserts the moral right to
be identified as the author of this work

A catalogue record for this book is
available from the British Library

ISBN-13: 978-1-84756-150-3

Set in Minion by Palimpsest Book Production Limited,
Grangemouth, Stirlingshire

Printed and bound in Great Britain by
Clays Ltd, St Ives plc

Mixed Sources

Product group from well-managed
forests and other controlled sources
www.fsc.org Cert no. SW-COC-1806
© 1996 Forest Stewardship Council

FSC is a non-profit international organisation established
to promote the responsible management of the world's forests.
Products carrying the FSC label are independently certified
to assure consumers that they come from forests that are managed
to meet the social, economic and ecological needs
of present and future generations.

Find out more about HarperCollins and the environment at
www.harpercollins.co.uk/green

Thanks to Charlotte, Natalie, Vanessa and everyone else at St Christopher's who helped me create the fictional Fairmont House and all the Dunston's characters. St Christopher's is a charity that supports and encourages children, young people and vulnerable adults to realise and achieve their potential.

Thanks also to my infallible agent, Diane, to Kesh and the rest of the team at Avon, and of course to Chris.

For mum and dad.

Chapter One

She came to with a jolt. Someone was pressing a finger against her neck.

'You're all right. Take it easy, OK?'

Her eyes slowly focused in the dim morning light and she propped herself up on one elbow. A man in a luminous yellow jacket was crouching over her.

'Steady now . . . Slowly.' He reached round to support her and shone a small torch in her face. She tried to twist away but her muscles felt all spongy. There was a noise like a hundred car alarms going off at once. And the people . . . There were people everywhere.

'Okaaaay,' he said, clicking the torch off and rocking back on his heels. 'You've had a bit of a shock, but nothing serious.' He gently hoisted her into an upright position.

'Derek, over here!' cried someone above the din.

The paramedic gestured that he was on his way and took another look at the girl.

'Here,' he said, grabbing what looked like a crumpled jacket from the gutter and shaking off the grit. 'Sit on this – you don't want any more cuts and bruises, do you?'

She allowed him to slip it underneath her, and for the first time looked down at her body. Her palms were grazed

1

and bleeding slightly, like a child's after a playground fall. Her bare feet were scratched too, probably from the shards of glass that littered the street. But it wasn't her skin she was looking at; it was her clothes – or lack of. Tugging at the stretchy material of her dress, she tried to cover the tops of her thighs, only to find that the whole garment moved down and she didn't appear to be wearing a bra.

'Once we've accounted for everyone we'll get you to a hospital and check you over properly. Can you tell me your name?'

She nodded vacantly.

The man waited a moment then repeated, 'Can you tell me your name?'

'Derek!' the voice yelled again. 'Over here, please!'

Holding up a hand in acknowledgement, the paramedic peered into the girl's face. She avoided his gaze and stared out at the mayhem. The road was strewn with fallen masonry, pieces of twisted metal and broken, blackened furniture. Parts of the street were stained with blood. But she saw none of it. She wasn't listening to the sirens or the screams. Something else was occupying her thoughts.

'I think you may be in shock,' said the paramedic, standing up. 'Put the jacket around you and I'll get one of my colleagues to check you over. Just wait here, OK?'

She nodded vaguely, continuing to stare into space as the man rushed off. The questions were mushrooming inside her head, multiplying, jostling and competing for space. Questions like, why was she here, where the hell was 'here', what had happened . . . ? But of all the fears crowding her mind, one was so immediate, so profound that it eclipsed all the rest.

She didn't know her own name.

How was that possible? And it wasn't just her name that was missing; it was her whole life: her background, her home, her family . . . Friends, lovers . . . Everything was a blank.

Ignoring the mounting nausea, she tried to focus, to force her memory back into action. She ran through as many names as she could think of in the hope that one might click. None did. Her head pounded and there was a high-pitched whining in her ears. The harder she struggled to remember, the emptier her mind seemed to be.

She shivered and wrapped the coat around her bare legs. Her breathing was shallow and her hands were shaking uncontrollably. The fear engulfed her all of a sudden. She looked around. It was as though she was scared of something, or someone. It wasn't just fear of the unknown – the unknown that was her identity – it was something dark and amorphous: a paranoia that she couldn't explain. She only knew one thing for sure: *she had to get away*.

On autopilot, she grabbed the jacket from under her and stood up. Her legs wobbled and the ringing in her ears intensified. She was half expecting a paramedic or one of the other uniformed men to stop her as she slipped away, but nobody did.

The scattered debris hindered her bare-footed progress, but slowly she picked her way down a narrow street bordered by tall buildings that seemed eerily quiet compared to the pandemonium she'd just left. She looked back. It was a nightclub, she ascertained. That explained her flimsy dress. The remains of a neon sign, bulbs half shattered, stuck out above the entrance, which was now little more than a burned-out concrete shell. She wondered

3

what could have caused the destruction. A burst gas main? A *bomb*?

She slowed down, relieved to have escaped unchallenged but still feeling tense and scared. It was partly the fear of what lay ahead, she thought, but mostly it was fear of what had gone before: the huge, gaping hole that was her past and, more specifically, the thing – whatever it was – that had caused her to run away.

The sun had yet to rise in the mottled pink sky and her dress wasn't providing much warmth. She shook the grit off the jacket and pulled it around her. Something rubbed against her hip as she tied the belt. The pocket was open and her fingertips brushed smooth leather.

Stopping in the shadows, she pulled out the wallet. 'Joe Simmons' read the name on the credit card. She leafed through the other items. Two more credit cards, one cash card, one gym membership card, a couple of other unidentifiable swipe cards, lots of receipts randomly folded up and shoved into one compartment – definitely a man's wallet, she thought – and a Post-it note covered in anonymous scribbles. Hoping that Joe Simmons was a rich man, she unzipped the notes pocket and peered inside.

Despite the anxieties, she felt a rush of excitement as she counted the eighteen twenty-pound notes. Mr Simmons *was* a rich man. And careless. Only a fool carried that much cash around with them. She slipped the wallet back into the pocket and continued walking towards what looked like a main road, wondering how it was that she could know such things as the value of money, how to read, how to add up and how to speak English, without knowing her own name. Her memory seemed to have blotted out the facts whilst maintaining the skills.

4

She stopped at the kerb and took in her surroundings. In front of her was a leafy park, a pleasant surprise after the claustrophobic alleyways and looming buildings. She darted across the four lanes of traffic, light at this time in the morning and mainly black cabs. *Black cabs*. Again, she was perfectly familiar with such things, as a concept. She knew how they worked, what the little yellow lights meant, she could imagine herself getting into one and telling the driver where to go. She knew that black cabs were a feature of London, that London was the capital of England, and that England was home of the Sunday roast and the royal family . . . But she didn't know whether Sunday roasts or royal families had featured in *her* life.

The park gate was locked. She looked around, not yet sure of her plan. A sign told her she was on Piccadilly. *Piccadilly*. That rang a bell. Piccadilly Circus. She knew the name. But then, she knew the names Einstein and Mozart and New York and Jesus, but she didn't know what they meant to her. General facts were fine; personal facts were a mystery. Had she been here before? Perhaps.

She quickened her step. There was an underground sign up ahead. Underground. Tubes. She remembered all that. Perhaps she could get on a tube and head out of London. Because that was what she needed to do. *Get out*.

She peered through the grating at the entrance to Green Park tube station.

'You all right there, love?' asked a voice.

She jumped in alarm. A man in a fluorescent yellow jacket grinned back at her, his face black with dirt.

'Er, um, I'm fine.'

'You hoping for a tube?'

'Um, yeah.'

5

He shook his head. 'Bit keen, aintcha? 'S not even four yet. First tube's half five!'

'Oh – yes, of course. Silly . . . Yeah . . .' She started to retreat up the steps. Her heart was still thumping from the shock.

'Hey. Where's you tryin'a get to?'

She hesitated. It was a good question. 'West London,' she said, plumping for somewhere that seemed sensible but not too specific.

'Tribe, us,' he said, winking.

She looked at him. 'I guess I'll come back at half five,' she said, perplexed. 'Thanks!'

'Tribe, us!' he shouted as she hastened up the steps. She was glad of the grating that separated them. 'N ninety-seven or N nine!'

It was only when she stopped to pull a piece of gravel from her heel that she realised her mistake. 'Try a bus,' he'd been saying. Of course. Nothing to do with West London tribes at all. She thought about running back to apologise, but as she deliberated a pair of bright white headlights swung into view.

She stuck out her hand as the double-decker loomed towards her – another reflex that just came naturally – and stepped back from the road. Her jacket belt came undone in the blast of air as the bus stopped, revealing her tattered dress. She caught the momentary look on the driver's face and tied the belt in a double knot as she stepped aboard.

The driver's suspicions were clearly confirmed when she reached into the wallet and brought out a crisp twenty-pound note. He raised an eyebrow, looked at her and jerked his head sharply towards the back of the bus. She tried to poke the money through the clear plastic partition but he just shook his head, checked his mirrors and pulled out. She staggered along the aisle and climbed to the upper level where he wouldn't be able to see her.

There was a surprising number of people sprawled around the top deck, in various stages of consciousness. At the front were three inebriated girls in short skirts, talking in loud voices about faking orgasms. A few rows back was a bunch of kids in hoodies, looking mean and pretending not to be interested in the girls' conversation. There were three or four lone passengers and a guy clutching a sleeping girlfriend, semi-snoring with his jaw hanging open.

It was strangely comforting to be around people – people who were too tired or too engrossed in their own lives to think about hers. Her paranoia receded a little. She slipped into a seat near the back, feeling comfortably anonymous, and wondered whether that was what she was afraid of: people scrutinising her condition, trying to force the memories back into her head. Maybe that was partly it. But even as she contemplated this, the dark, unidenti-fiable fear crept to the front of her mind, blotting out the drunk girls and the snoring man. It was more than just a fear of people meddling; it was something else.

The girls blabbered on, discussing the merits of panting versus groaning at a volume that only applied to drunk people. They had been clubbing, she thought, just as she had. But they hadn't lost their memories – or at least, not more than a night's worth. She pressed her shoulder against the window and let her head roll back.

Jane. Kate. Louise. Sarah . . . She reeled through as many names as her tired brain could muster, hoping for a glimmer of recognition. Nothing. She thought about how people saw her, as a person. Was she kind? Funny? Smart? Was she honest? Was she the sort of person to steal a wallet containing three hundred and sixty pounds? That was different, though. She'd had no choice about stealing that. If she'd handed it in she would have had to tell the police about losing her memory, and then some psychologist or psychiatrist would have asked all sorts of questions, and . . . no, it just didn't bear thinking about.

Another worry was creeping its way through her conscience. It was the fact that she had just run away from a scene where people had been badly injured – maybe even *killed*, she thought anxiously – some of whom might have been people she knew. Nobody went clubbing on their own, did they? In which case . . . She shuddered. There would be friends or a sister or a boyfriend out there. Perhaps they'd been even more badly affected than her . . . Perhaps— No. No. She forced the thoughts out of her mind.

Her eyelids dropped shut. She had no idea where the bus would take her, but she didn't care. They were powering along a main road out of London, away from the scene, away from the questions and the prying para-medics. The window juddered against her head as her brain fought a losing battle with exhaustion. Jenny . . . Lucy . . . Rachel . . . She fell into a shallow, fitful sleep.

Chapter Two

The moment her eyes fluttered open, she knew something was wrong. The bus was empty and flying along a dual carriageway through fields and forests that didn't look at all like London.

She poked the crustiness out of her eyes and ran both hands through her hair. A pain shot down her neck and spine as she pushed herself up in the seat. She tried to catch her reflection in the window, but the sun was shining fully now and all she could see was a layer of translucent grime. She staggered to the front of the bus and down the steps.

'Gad Almighty!' cried the driver as she tapped on his plastic booth window. The bus lurched a little to the left, then righted itself. He looked at her and shook his head. 'What da hell is you doin' in here?'

She shrugged apologetically. 'I fell asleep. Sorry – I . . .'

'You been on dis bus all mornin'?' he demanded, slowing down for a roundabout.

'Mmm,' she replied, flying sideways as they swung round. She wondered where they were. Not London, she was fairly sure.

'You comin' to the depot then?' he asked aggressively. 'How was you up dere widdout me seeing, eh?'

She mumbled something about being tired and glanced through the window for a clue. There was a road sign a little way off, but too distant to read.

'Where was you wantin' to go to?' growled the driver. He seemed quite cross.

'Um . . .' The road sign was almost upon them; she could nearly make out the place names. 'Well, west . . .' She strained her eyes. 'Bagley,' she said.

'Bagley?' he repeated angrily. 'Where da hell's dat?'

She glanced up as the sign flashed past. 'Radley,' she said. 'I said Radley.'

He screwed up his face and looked at her, perplexed. 'Radley's where we's at now! You was tryin' to get to Radley by gettin' on the N ninety-seven? Jeez.' He shook his head again. 'I don't know what you's playin' at, but you better get off my bus 'fore I get done for runnin' a taxi service. I'll drop you up here.'

The bus slowed down and pulled off the main road, then, to her surprise, turned a corner and weaved through a series of narrow lanes that were clearly not designed for motorised vehicles, let alone double-decker buses.

'Station's up there,' he barked, pressing a button that made the doors hiss open and watching her stumble out into the daylight. He was still shaking his head as the bus thundered off down the small country lane.

It wasn't clear whether Trev's Teashop, the greasy spoon that occupied part of the quaint station building, was open; it looked dark inside, although she thought she saw movement in the window as she approached.

She was about to enter and ask about her chances of a cup of tea when the door swung open and a ruddy-faced bald man in an apron waddled out.

'Morning!' he squawked, sounding as though his voice box was blocked – a bit like his arteries, perhaps.

She smiled and watched as he set to work winding out a frilly brown awning above them, humming tunelessly to himself.

'Hi,' she ventured, watching as he straightened out one of the tassels on the awning and stopped to admire his work.

'Yes, yes.' The man – whom she presumed to be Trevor himself – brushed his hands against one another and bustled back inside. She followed him in. 'I haven't forgotten about you. You're a tad early, though, aren't you? Not that that's necessarily a *bad* trait. I mean, early is better than late, of course. But *on time* is preferable.'

She frowned and loitered by the counter, wondering how a café stayed in business when its owner was so rude to the customers.

'Are you . . . are you open, then?'

'Nearly there, nearly there,' he muttered, switching the lights on and squeezing behind the counter to flick more switches. She waited patiently, hoping that the preparations would soon be in place for her cup of tea. 'Watch and learn, watch and learn.'

She continued to wait, perplexed as to why she should watch or learn, and irritated by the man's habit of saying everything twice.

When it was clear that the water was boiling, the mugs were in order – twice rearranged by the red-faced man – and there was milk in the fridge, her frustration began to get the better of her.

'Can I have a cup of tea?'

The man stared at her as though she'd just demanded

he hand over the contents of the till. 'What a presumptuous young lady!'

She stared back at him, mirroring his expression. She was the customer, for God's sake. She'd been here nearly ten minutes. All she wanted was a cup of bloody tea.

'I think perhaps we'll have to run through the ground rules again. Remember, I'm paying you to serve the customers here, not to sit around drinking cups of tea,' he said testily.

'I—' she started to protest and then stopped herself. The pompous man seemed to be assuming she was here to serve customers. He thought she was a waitress or something. Which might mean . . . which might mean he'd pay her. And if he paid her, she might be able to use the money on somewhere to live, which would mean that she could get a proper job, lead a normal life, do all the things that normal people did when they had a background and qualifications and experience and *a past they could remember*. In a moment of clarity, the plan formed in her mind.

'Of course, no, sorry.' She smiled apologetically, still thinking through the details. 'I didn't mean to sound rude. I was just asking whether, *in general*, I can have a cup of tea. You know, like, in a quiet moment when there's not many customers, when I've been on my feet for hours . . . whether I can have a cup of tea in that instance.'

The man looked at her, touching his shiny head and clearly trying to work something out. 'Hmm.'

He continued staring at her, his forehead deeply creased. *He knew*, she thought. He knew she wasn't the girl he'd hired.

'Well, in that instance . . . well, yes, I suppose that would be OK.' He nodded, dipping his head in and out of his multiple chins. 'Where did you say you were from, er . . . sorry, I've forgotten your name.'

She opened her mouth, hoping something would tumble out automatically. Nothing did. Her fingernails dug into the leather wallet in her pocket as she struggled desperately for an answer.

'Er, what, *my* name?'

He looked at her strangely. 'Of course *your* name.'

Then it came to her: not her name, but the closest thing to it.

'Jo,' she said. 'Jo Simmons.'

'Oh. Right.' He frowned again. 'And you're from . . . ?'

Oh God, thought Jo. Too many questions. Where on earth was she supposed to be from?

'Well, London, most recently.' At least that much was true.

'But you're *foreign*, aren't you?'

'Um . . . my parents are.' Genius. She was getting quite good at this.

'But where—'

'Could you just remind me of the hours I'll be working?'

He looked at her, smoothing the apron over his enormous belly, then finally replied, 'Well, you'll remember we settled on seven till noon because of your classes in the afternoons.'

'My classes, yes, exactly . . . Seven, that's what I thought. And I can't remember what you said about pay. Could you . . . ?'

'Thirty pounds a day, as we agreed,' he snapped. 'Six days a week.'

Jo nodded again. That was a hundred and eighty pounds a week. How much did it cost to rent around here?

'Shall I show you the ropes?'

Jo breathed a sigh of relief and allowed the bald man to give her a sweeping tour of what was really quite a basic setup: hot-water tank, toaster, fridge, coffee machine, cupboards filled with grotesque sets of matching brown and gold crockery. It was clear that the man had delusions of grandeur for Trev's Teashop.

The reference to Jo's parents had left her feeling ill at ease. It wasn't that she didn't like to lie to the man; she barely knew him, and what she did know she didn't particularly like. It was that she didn't know what the truth *was*. She didn't know where her parents were from – or where they were now. She didn't know whether they knew about the nightclub explosion, or whether they knew she'd been caught up in it. She didn't even know if she *had* parents. The chances were, though, there was someone out there who cared about her. She just didn't know how to let them know she was OK without turning herself in – and that was the one thing she couldn't do.

'I'll expect you to do most of the flitting between tables.' The man waved a stubby arm across the premises. She nodded again, wondering who had been flitting up until now. 'Now, you're wearing black trousers, I trust?'

Jo froze, suddenly remembering that she was wearing a tiny dress and no shoes underneath the jacket. 'Well, I couldn't find trousers, but—'

'Ooh, Mr Jackson! First customer!' cried Trevor. 'First customer!' he said again, ushering her towards the back of the café. 'Your shirt's in the store cupboard under the stairs. Quick, quick!'

It was with mixed feelings that Jo pulled the brown aertex shirt over her head. She wasn't keen on the embroidered

14

teacup that covered her left breast, or the fact that she had 'Trev's Teashop' plastered across her front, but she had to admit that it was more appropriate than her own attire, which she was desperately trying to convert into a knee-length skirt to cover the tops of her long legs.

Along with a trowel, a plastic rhino, a sketchbook and a rah-rah skirt, Jo found what she was looking for in the back of the store cupboard: a mirror. She peered at her reflection in the half-light.

It was like looking at somebody else. Jo pulled at her skin – young skin, she thought, probably early twenties – and tilted her head this way and that, inspecting her face. Her eyes were bottle green, with dark lashes, which were coated in heavy, day-old makeup. Her lip had been bleeding slightly. She gathered her long, knotted hair in one hand and tried to twist it into some sort of order. It was almost raven black, with a dyed red streak at the front.

She spat on her hand and wiped the worst of the dirt off her forehead, wondering how her appearance had passed without comment by the portly teashop owner. Something caught her eye in the mirror. On the back of her hand was a splodge of blue ink. Writing. 'SASKIA DAWSON,' it said.

Who was that? Was it her? Was *she* Saskia Dawson? If so, why had she written her name on her own hand? Saskia. It didn't sound familiar. But then, very little did. Jo tore a page from the faded sketchbook and scrabbled around for a pen. Letter for letter, she copied it down and tucked it into the waist of her newly formed skirt.

'Ah, Jo! Go and serve table four, would you?'

Jo quickly worked out how Trev's Teashop operated. It wasn't so much a teashop as a caffeine outlet for commuters on their way into London – at least, that was how it seemed at seven o'clock in the morning. She did her best to flit from table to table, but there was only so much flitting one could do with so few seated customers and a queue for takeaway coffee that occupied most of the shop. She marvelled again at her boss's self-delusion.

'Blasted thing,' muttered Trevor, turning purple with exertion as he tried to break his way into a new tub of coffee beans.

Jo cast her customer an apologetic look and turned round. 'Let me try.'

'Doesn't work,' he said, reluctantly loosening his grip on the tin-opener. 'The tub's got some new-fangled seal thing on it. We'll have to— Oh. Right. You've done it.'

Jo handed over the open container and got back to serving customers, trying not to smirk. It had just been a case of employing some common sense: twisting the seal, applying some pressure and then levering off the lid.

Common sense. That was something. At least she had that. And having it gave her a clue as to what type of person she was. Her brain worked in a logical way – like a scientist's, perhaps. She could think laterally and solve problems. It was true, she made a reasonable waitress, but she didn't think she'd been one before. Not properly. Maybe as a summer job a few years ago, while at school . . . School. That was another blank.

She tried picturing herself in various workplace scenarios. Sitting in an air-traffic control tower. No, too stressful. Patrolling the streets in police uniform. Too much authority. The Trevor experience had taught her that she didn't like being told what to do. Staring at a computer screen in an office. Boring. Standing up in court dressed in robes and a wig. Not unfeasible, she thought, although she was probably a bit young for that . . . Jo poured another filter coffee and sighed. She didn't have a clue.

Fortunately, Trevor seemed sufficiently unobservant to overlook his waitress's lack of footwear. Her feet were freezing and the soles were turning slowly black, but there was nothing she could do except try to keep them in the shadows behind the counter. Occasionally, he would send her to check on table ten, the little bench outside the café where a commuter would occasionally perch as he waited for a train or a friend, and every time, somehow, he failed to spot the bare feet.

It was on one of these errands that Jo found herself in the situation she'd been dreading. Another girl, about her own age and of similar build and colouring, was running up the road towards the teashop, hair flying, satchel banging against her hip. She was dressed in black trousers and a cheap polyester blouse.

Jo caught her attention and stepped out to greet her. 'Hi! You must be . . .'

'Renata,' she gasped, trying to push her way into the café.

'Yes, you were due to start work at seven, weren't you?' Jo stood in her way.

'Am so sorry,' she said breathlessly. Her accent was Polish, or something like that. No wonder Trevor had been confused by Jo's fluency. 'Bus was not come, so I walk, then bus come but wrong bus . . .'

'Oh dear.' Jo smiled sympathetically. She felt terrible for doing this, but her need to survive outweighed her remorse. 'Unfortunately, because you were late, we had to find someone else for the job. It was getting busy, you see.'

17

She gestured towards the queue snaking out of the café.

The girl's mouth fell open. Her English wasn't perfect, but she understood.

Jo couldn't bear it. 'But if you come back in three or four weeks we may well need another waitress.' She nodded encouragingly. 'Do come back, won't you?'

The girl muttered something in her own language and looked at the ground. For a moment, Jo thought she might march into the teashop and demand an explanation from the boss, but then she just turned, shook her head and walked back the way she had come.

Jo wandered into the café to help with the coffees. She was filled with self-loathing. Good people didn't behave like this. Good people didn't steal wallets. They didn't con innocent girls out of jobs. They didn't reject the help of others and they certainly didn't turn their backs on friends or loved ones who might have been hurt or even killed . . .

She stared into the frothing milk. It was a possibility – and one that left her feeling very uncomfortable – that actually she *wasn't* a good person. Deep down, with everything else erased, all that was left was this. A lying, calculating, hard-hearted thief. Or maybe she was just desperate. Maybe the terror and guilt and paranoia had made her act in this way. Maybe she was just trying to stay alive.

Chapter Three

Jo's basket was filling up quickly. She hadn't eaten since, well, sometime before the explosion, presumably. She was ravenous. Everything in the shop looked appealing: cakes, bread, meat pies . . . She even found herself salivating over the Budgens own-brand malt loaf.

The cashier girl was politely trying to extract herself from a conversation with the pensioner, but he clearly wasn't seeing the urgency.

'Well, it is August,' she said patiently. 'It gets quite warm. D'you need a hand?'

The man attempted to balance his shopping on his walking frame and started to release his grip on the checkout.

'I need new legs!' he cried as the load slipped off for a second time and he started all over again.

Jo wondered where she usually did her shopping. She had a feeling that old-age pensioners and conversations about the weather hadn't featured much in her life up until now. London, she thought. That was where she had lived. The paranoia – the ugly, dark fear of whatever it was – had originated in London.

She tried again to determine what *had* featured in her

life. Friends. A mum. A dad. Brothers. Sisters. School mates. Neighbours. Any or all of the above. They'd start missing her soon, she knew that. It was selfish to vanish without a word to any of them – but this was the problem. It seemed too daunting, too dangerous to turn herself in. She couldn't face the idea of going to the police. And without going to the police, she couldn't let people know she was OK – unless she could somehow enlist the help of Saskia Dawson without giving herself away – whoever Saskia Dawson was.

'Do you know of any B&Bs around here?'

'Any what?' asked the girl, mechanically scanning the pack of chocolate digestives.

'B&Bs. Bed and breakfasts. You know, places to stay.'

The girl looked momentarily enlightened. 'Oh, right. Um . . .' She scratched her greasy forehead. 'No. Sorry.'

'Is there another town nearby?' asked Jo. She wondered whether she'd be better off asking one of the deaf pensioners instead.

'Yeah. Abingdon. That's four pounds fifty-four.' She glanced at the growing queue.

'Thanks. Is that far? Can I walk there? Do they have clothes shops, that sort of thing?'

The girl shrugged and took Jo's crisp twenty-pound note. 'I guess.'

'Thanks.' Jo sensed that she wasn't going to get much more information out of the girl. She held out her hand for the change. It was shaking badly, she noticed, and sweating. The fear had receded a little since she'd come to Radley but it was still there, looming in the back of her mind.

'That's fifteen forty-six change.'

Jo took the money and tipped it into Joe Simmons' wallet. As she was leaving, she glanced at the shelves behind the cashier's head.

She stopped and looked harder. Suddenly, she knew what had featured in her life before now – what would cure the shaking hands, the sweating, the anxiety. She knew what would relieve the nagging sensation that she hadn't been able to identify up until now. And the revelation brought on a fresh wave of nausea.

'Sorry – one more thing.' She reopened the wallet.

The girl gave her a look that she'd previously shown the old man.

Jo picked out the cheapest bottle, paid the cashier and rushed out.

The high street was empty save for a couple of hunched-over residents shuffling from shop to shop. Jo perched on the wall by the parish hall and drained the bottle of water she'd bought, then quickly decanted the vodka. She was desperate, but she wasn't desperate enough to swig from inside a plastic bag – not around here.

She took her first sip. It burned her insides, ripping at her throat and leaving an aftertaste that was instantly familiar. The reactions of her body and mind were at odds. It was good to have fed the need, allayed those symptoms, but it was frightening to think of the implications.

OK, so she had had quite a shock and everyone knew alcohol was known for curing the shakes, but this was more than the shakes. This wasn't a taste for vodka; it was a *need*. Her body was craving the stuff.

She stared at the parish notice board, trying to make out where Radley was in relation to Abingdon and Oxford. She couldn't focus. All she could think about was this new, abhorrent revelation. She swigged and thought, swigged and thought. What did this mean? What sort of life had she been living up until now? And why was she so damned scared about turning herself in, coming clean? What had happened in her past? Who *was* she?

Jo took another swig and delved into the plastic bag. Her fingers curled round the little notebook she'd bought and then felt about for the biro she'd nicked from the cashier. That was another thing: why had stealing the pen come so naturally to her? It wasn't the incident itself that troubled Jo – the biro leaked and was worth nothing anyway – it was the principle. She was a thief. The pen wasn't the only thing she'd pinched, either. First, there had been the wallet, then the Polish girl's job . . . It was a worrying trait.

She pushed aside her concerns and glanced at the food in her bag. Drinking on an empty stomach was stupid, she knew that much. But the eating could wait. It had to. Before she did anything else, she had to straighten out her thoughts – pull together what she knew. She tore the cellophane wrapping off the notebook and started to write.

Nightclub near Piccadilly
Live in London?
Impatient, intolerant – feel wrong in small village
Thief – comes naturally. Survival?
CAN'T STAY IN LONDON – WHY?

Jo swallowed another gulp, larger this time. She knew she should probably find this Abingdon place, buy some clothes, some shoes, find a place to stay . . . but the writing was helping. It was as though, by transferring what little she knew into the pages, the notebook was becoming her. It was slowly filling up with all the details and characteristics that only a few hours ago had eluded her. Soon, she hoped, she would be able to piece together who she really was.

Alcoholic?
But healthy – slim, good skin, etc.
Going through bad patch/partying too hard?
Maths, common sense

She stared at the words and felt a twinge of resentment; it was as though this life, this personality, this *person*, whoever she was, had been thrust upon her. It wasn't fair. She didn't want to be an alcoholic. She didn't want to have this paranoia. Like a teenager taking umbrage at her parents for conceiving her, she wanted to scream: 'It's not my fault! I didn't *ask* to be the way I am!' But she had no one to scream at.

Jo closed the notebook and slipped it into her jacket pocket, willing herself to screw the lid on the bottle and think about something else. Her hands were shaking less now, she noticed. One last swig. She stood up to study the notice board. Her feet wobbled beneath her. Grabbing the hand rail, she pulled herself steady. 'Streetlighting in Gooseacre,' she read. 'Rats in Lower Radley.' 'Mahogany Dresser for Sale.' Jo squinted up at the area map.

Abingdon was a brisk twenty-minute walk, according to the directions – although Jo wasn't sure how brisk her walking would be after half a bottle of vodka. Everything around her had become fluid: the pavements, the shops, the clouds. She dropped the bottle into the bag and then turned and nearly fell down the parish hall steps.

Jo wondered how long the amnesia would last. What if the memories never returned? She reached for the vodka, then stopped herself. There was a panicky sensation inside her, the sort you got in a nightmare when you were desperate to run away but your legs wouldn't work. Perhaps she would never find out who she really was. Jo forced herself to breathe normally and tried to ignore her yearning. Actually, given what she had seen of her character so far, there was a part of her that wasn't sure she *wanted* to know who she was. And more specifically, she wasn't sure she wanted to find out why she'd run away from everything this morning.

Abingdon's selection of shops was slightly broader than that of its neighbouring village, but not much. Jo had expected to recognise some of the high-street stores – such as they were – but she felt reasonably certain that Choice Buys and Stylz weren't big names in UK fashion.

'Sorry, miss.'

Jo blinked back at the security guard whose arm was blocking her way. He shook his head at her. She stepped back, waiting for an explanation. It was four o'clock in the afternoon and the shop was swarming with people. It couldn't be closed.

Then she realised. She saw herself through the doorman's eyes. She saw the crazed expression on the dirty face, the bare feet sticking out from beneath the crumpled jacket. She smelled her breath and spotted the telltale plastic bag. *She* wouldn't have let her into Stylz of Abingdon.

*   *   *

24

The mirror in the McDonald's toilet was made of some sort of brushed metal that wasn't particularly reflective, but even so, Jo could tell it was an improvement. She had tried to simulate a shower by rubbing the accessible parts of her body with hot water and the strange foamy syrup she assumed to be soap. Her hair was still knotted and the soles of her feet seemed to be painted black, but that was no bad thing. From a distance, it almost looked as though she was wearing shoes.

An hour later, Jo had acquired a couple of nondescript cotton tops, some cheap underwear, a pair of black trousers and some shoes, all for less than thirty pounds, which seemed suspiciously cheap, even to someone half-cut. She looked presentable, if not fashionable.

She tugged at the trousers so that they covered her shoes, wondering what type of clothes she had worn before. She still had a sense of her likes and dislikes – not a memory, exactly, more a natural bias towards certain styles. Just as she'd known in the supermarket that she liked fruitcake but not mushrooms, she knew that her preference was for the bootleg cut and sleeveless tops. Today, of course, there were other constraints, like money and the requirement for her clothes to double up as the teashop uniform.

She perched on a low car park wall, allowing herself a short break but very aware that she needed to find a bed for the night. Her head was throbbing and her limbs felt heavy and weak – not just because of the vodka. It was the homelessness. It was being in a strange place. The pressure to find somewhere to stay before nightfall, the running away, the loneliness . . . These things, combined with the stress of the morning's events and all the unknowns, were weighing down on her, crushing not just her spirit but also her physical strength. Breathing deeply, she pushed herself up and followed the signs to the Tourist Information office.

She arrived just in time to see a Fiat Punto reverse from its spot in the empty car park and zoom off. Jo peered through the tinted windows of the building. The clock said one minute past five.

'Fuck,' she said out loud. It made her feel a bit better.

A young man walking past with a briefcase looked up. 'I beg your pardon?'

'Um. Hi. I just . . . I'm looking for a stace to play.'

The man frowned. 'Sorry?'

'A – a place to stay, I mean. Is there a bed and breakfast or something around here?'

'D'you know, I'm not sure!' He chuckled as though it was quite amusing that she would have nowhere to sleep tonight. 'Of course, there's the Premier Inn, but that's on the other side of town, and,' he looked her up and down, 'I think it's about seventy pounds a night.'

Jo nodded irritably. The man was offensive and useless. 'Thanks.'

'Ooh, there *used* to be a place on the way into Radley. Above the convenience store halfway along Radley Road. That's quite a walk, though, and I'm not sure it's still running. I have a feeling there's somewhere around here too – Bath Street?' He waved his hand vaguely. 'Hmm, sorry.'

The man strode off, leaving Jo squinting through the darkened glass of the Tourist Information office. She knew it was futile, but she had to make sure she'd explored every avenue. Maybe there would be a list of nearby guesthouses pinned to the wall or something. A leaflet lying open on a desk, or a phone number . . .

The walls were covered in large, laminated posters of church spires and Oxford colleges. A banner hung from the ceiling advertising guided tours of the old County Police Station and on every surface was a little plastic box containing guidebooks in a variety of languages: *'Bienvenue à Oxford!' 'Witamy, w Oxfordzie!' 'Willkommen in Oxford!' 'Bienvenido a Oxford!'*

Jo's forehead made contact with the dirty glass and she closed her eyes. Then she opened them again, realising something. She looked again at the nearest set of guide-books. *'Bienvenido a Oxford!'* she read again. *'Conozca una de las ciudades mas bellas de Inglaterra.'* Learn about one of the most beautiful cities in England.

She could speak Spanish.

Jo pulled away from the window and looked at her own reflection. It wasn't much; it wasn't a huge revelation, but it was something. She reached for her notebook and scribbled it down. Walking along Bath Street, her newfound sense of elation gradually diminished as she realised that there were no signs of hospitality in the vicinity – not unless the B&B was masquerading as a Chinese restaurant or a nightclub called Strattons.

She stopped to consider her options. The hotel was a last resort; Joe Simmons' money wouldn't last for ever and she wasn't sure when she'd get paid for the waitressing work. A bed and breakfast, or better, a youth hostel: those were her only real options. There was a remote chance that the guesthouse above the shop was still operational – if indeed it existed at all – but she knew the chances were slim.

She was obviously going to have to ask around. But how long would that take? And who would help her? The only people nearby were four lanky youths who were practising the art of suspending their trousers from beneath their buttocks.

Jo wondered what day it was, and whether the nightclub would be open later. She briefly considered the option of going out drinking, relying on meeting a guy and being invited back to his for the night. She dismissed the idea immediately. It was too risky, too ridiculous. She took a swig of vodka to help her think. She had to find people to ask. Perhaps the shopping centre would be a good place to start.

The idea of clubbing stayed with her as she hobbled back to the town centre, the cheap plastic shoes wearing away at her ankles. It was the alcohol, she thought. Her imagination was running wild. She was picturing a scene: her at the bar in a club, finishing her drink. A guy leaning sideways towards her. He was an older guy, maybe twice her age but not unattractive. It was so vivid, the scene, almost as if . . . *it was a memory.*

She was remembering something from before the blast. Jo could feel him tapping her elbow, offering her a drink. It wasn't her imagination; it had happened. And she was remembering.

Jo stopped and shut her eyes, trying to summon more. Maybe it would all start to come back to her now. She stood there, waiting for the scene to rematerialise, but it wouldn't come; she was trying too hard.

Jo walked on, distracted but with a new sense of hope. It wasn't much to go on, but it was a start. Perhaps this flashback was the first of many. She reached for her notebook and laid it against a wall, scribbling down what she'd seen.

The next two people she asked had no idea about local guesthouses and the third just looked at her suspiciously and hurried away. For the first time all day, Jo started to lose faith in herself. She had no one to call. She was alone in a strange town where nobody wanted to help her, and before long it would be dark. She had limited cash, and even if she did opt to blow seventy pounds on a hotel room, she'd have to find it first. She found herself on the road back to Radley, hoping, despite all the odds, that the man was right about the B&B. The alcohol was blurring her thinking and she could hear the blood pounding round her head.

When she reached the convenience store, she headed straight for the bottled water.

'Evening,' croaked the elderly woman behind the till. Despite the wizened face and white hair, she had incredibly sharp-looking green eyes.

'Hi.' Jo hardly dared ask the question. 'Could you tell me, is there a bed and breakfast above this shop?'

The woman looked slightly taken aback. 'Goodness! Who told you that? There *used* to be.'

'Used to be?' Jo's hopes fell away. She had walked up another dead end.

'Well, yes. About ten years ago!'

'Oh.' Jo paid her for the water. 'And are you sure it's not running any more?'

The woman laughed. 'Quite sure! It was my little business, until they made me shut up shop.'

'Oh, right.' Jo nodded and broke open the bottle of water. 'I don't suppose you know of any others around here, do you?'

The woman looked at her. Jo could feel her eyes roaming the cheap clothes and knotted hair.

'I'm new,' Jo explained. 'I – I arrived this evening. I was supposed to be staying with a . . . a friend, but that didn't, er, happen.' She could hear the lack of conviction in her voice and tried to assert herself. 'We fell out. And I've got a job in Radley that starts early in the morning so I have to stay nearby.'

The woman raised an eyebrow. Jo held her breath. She had gone into too much detail.

After a long pause, the woman spoke. 'I'm afraid I don't know of any this side of Abingdon,' she said. 'I'm sorry.'

Jo nodded and made to leave.

It was a last-ditch effort, but as she leaned on the door, she looked back at the woman. 'Who made you shut up shop?'

The shrewd green eyes narrowed for a moment. 'The council. You know: rules, regulations, paperwork, fire hazards. That sort of nonsense. They don't like me because I blocked the ringroad development going through my shop – but that's another story.'

Jo nodded, seeing an opportunity. It was a long shot, but her only one. 'Do you . . . still have the rooms and everything?'

The woman's expression slowly changed to a sceptical smile. 'What's your name?' she asked.

'Jo.'

'I'm Pearl. Pearl Phillips. Are you really stuck for some-where to stay?'

'Totally. I've tried everywhere. There's nothing this side of town – I've looked,' she gabbled. 'I can pay. I've got money. Like, twenty, maybe twenty-five pounds a night?

I'm desperate! I wouldn't tell anyone. D'you think maybe—'

The woman smiled and held up her hand. 'Calm down, Jo. Let's call it fifteen.'

Chapter Four

'Cornflakes or toast? That's all there is, I'm afraid.' Mrs Phillips looked at her expectantly from behind the kitchen counter.

'Toast, please,' Jo replied in a daze. Her head felt heavy. It was half-past six and she had slept badly, despite her exhaustion and the comfortable bed. Her mind had been racing with anxious, panicky thoughts that became less and less rational as the night wore on. Then at two a.m., having finally drifted off, she had woken with a jolt, her breathing shallow, covered in sweat, her pulse racing. The nausea had taken hold as she lay there willing her brain to shut down, ebbing and flowing for what seemed like hours. Sometime around dawn she must have dozed off again, only to be woken by the sound of birds and a blocked nose, which, on later inspection, turned out to be a nosebleed.

The landlady started ferrying jams and spreads onto the table and arranging them in an arc around her guest. Jo mumbled her gratitude, distracted by the incredible number of cat replicas that covered every shelf and surface in the room.

'You like cats, then.'

There were china cats, furry miniature cats, cat teapots,

cat postcards . . . Even the woman's slippers were shaped like cats.

Mrs Phillips looked up and smiled. 'Very observant. Yes. I'd get a real one if I knew it wouldn't outlive me.' She whipped the toast from under the grill and slid it onto a plate. 'There you go. Gone are the days when a full fry-up came as standard, I'm afraid . . . Mind you, the marmalade's home-made.'

Accepting the slightly burned toast, Jo's eye was drawn to the stack of newspapers on the table – presumably copies that would later be sold in the shop. Her stomach flipped as she considered the possibility that the explosion she'd run from the day before might warrant coverage.

'Pick a channel.' The landlady pushed the remote control over and nodded at the small TV. 'I like to see my news in print, but you probably prefer the television.' She started flicking through the first of the papers.

Jo scrolled through the stations in search of some news, eventually settling for a mindless chat show. She buttered her toast, trying to guess Mrs Phillips' age. Physically, she looked quite old, maybe seventy, but her mannerisms belonged to a younger woman. She was lithe and full of energy.

'So, what brought you to Radley?' She aligned the pages of the first newspaper and moved on to the second.

Jo jiggled her head, implying that she had too much toast in her mouth to talk. *A bus.* A night bus on its way to the depot. She couldn't tell the truth, and she'd already told Mrs Phillips about the job at Trev's Teashop. Nobody would move to Radley in order to work in a place like that.

'A friend,' she said finally. 'I, er, wanted to get out of

London for a bit – change of scene, you know.' She took another bite to buy herself some time. 'Um . . . my mate offered to put me up for a while, so I found myself a job – the job at the teashop – and then . . .'

'Then you fell out with your friend,' finished the woman, nodding. 'And this friend – was it . . . a *male* friend, by any chance?' She raised an eyebrow.

Jo looked at her. With a surge of relief, she realised that Mrs Phillips had assumed the most plausible story of all: that Jo had just split up with the boyfriend who she'd been planning to live with. She nodded.

'I see. Ooh, kettle's boiled. Tea or coffee?'

Jo opted for coffee, relieved. Mrs Phillips was a perceptive woman, she thought. And nosy, too. Jo knew she'd have to stay on the ball to avoid getting caught out by her own lies.

'Have you always been a waitress? I'll leave you to add milk and sugar.'

Jo stuffed a large piece of toast in her mouth and made a winding gesture with her hand. Why hadn't she thought about this? She should have invented a background. Sooner or later, people would start asking – of course they would. And she had to stick to a story. She'd already told Trevor her parents weren't English – what other nonsense would she come up with?

'No,' she said, still chewing. For some reason, she could only think of one possible career path that involved part-time waitressing, and she wasn't sure it would stick.

Eventually, it was time to swallow.

'I'm an actress.'

'Goodness! Really? Would I have seen you in anything? What sort of acting?'

Jo shrugged modestly. 'It's just minor parts, mainly –

nothing big.' She was trying to remember the name of a low-budget film or series that would seem plausible for a small-time actress. Nothing sprang to mind.

'Go on,' the woman goaded excitedly. 'Try me. I might've seen you in something.'

Jo shook her head. This really was testing her acting skills. 'No, really – it's been mainly screenplays and short films, like . . .' She thought frantically, trying to make up a name that sounded like a title but wasn't likely to be one already. '*The Goose*,' she said finally.

Mrs Phillips was still looking at her expectantly.

'And . . .' God, this was hard, '*Jim's . . . Secret . . . House.*' Jo poured some milk into her coffee and stirred it ferociously. She could feel her cheeks burning.

'Hmm, I'm not sure I know them,' Mrs Phillips said tactfully.

Jo sipped her coffee and reached for the remote control, hoping that the TV would stave off any more questions.

'Never anything worth watching in the mornings,' the old lady commented woefully. Jo wondered whether she was like this when she was on her own, or whether this endless chatter was simply her way of making up for her ten-year break from hospitality.

As if to prove Mrs Phillips' point, one of the presenters got up from his multicoloured couch and started enthusiastically demonstrating some sort of home steam-cleaning machine. Jo flicked to another channel, where a red cartoon character with a hook on its head was pushing a wheelbarrow across the screen.

She had nearly given up on finding anything informative when her grip suddenly tightened on the remote control. She stared at the TV in horror.

'. . . don't know any more about the motive behind the explosion, but police tell us they're pursuing multiple lines of enquiry.'

The reporter pressed on his earpiece as the studio presenter asked him another question. Jo's eyes were fixed on the screen. She couldn't even blink. A strip of red and white police tape fluttered in the breeze behind the reporter's head but other than that, the scene hadn't changed since yesterday morning. She could even see the spot on the pavement where the paramedic had left her to wait. One word was echoing round and round in her head: *motive*. Someone had wanted the explosion to happen. It had been some sort of bomb.

'Very little is known about the guests or staff present on the night of the explosion, so the death toll isn't clear. But we understand that at least fourteen people are missing, feared dead, and there are twenty-one seriously injured in hospital.'

The camera panned back to the studio.

'Thank you, Jamie, reporting from the scene of the Buffalo Club blast in Mayfair, London. And now, the renowned Turner Prize has created fresh controversy, this time not over a pickled cow but a pickled egg . . .'

Jo stopped listening and looked down at her coffee. Mrs Phillips scooped up the newspapers and prattled on about the state of modern art today but Jo could barely hear it. A bomb had gone off. A *bomb*. But bombs were what happened to other people, usually in the Middle East, not in *her* world – whatever world that was.

Mrs Phillips started making noises about opening up the shop. Jo just nodded into the steam of her coffee. She knew she should probably be leaving for the teashop, but the reporter's words were still swirling around in her mind. *Fourteen people missing, feared dead.* It was only now that the implications were starting to trickle through. People had died. They could have been her friends. Fourteen, out of ... How many did a nightclub hold? Three hundred? That was one dead in every twenty people. It was possible – probable, in fact, depending on how many she'd been out with – that not all her mates had escaped alive.

An unpleasant feeling swept through her. It wasn't just the realisation that her friends – whoever they were – might have died in the blast. It was the realisation that *she* had died in the blast; that she was one of those 'missing, feared dead'. And if she didn't give herself up soon, then she would officially *be* dead. As far as her loved ones were concerned – assuming she had loved ones – she had died.

'... I don't suppose you know yet, do you?'

Jo looked up. Mrs Phillips was peering at her.

'I'm sure everything's a bit up in the air at the moment,' she said. For a moment, Jo thought the woman might have guessed her connection to the Buffalo Club blast. Then she realised.

'Er, yeah. A bit up in the air,' she repeated vaguely. 'Not sure about anything just yet.'

Mrs Phillips nodded and started shifting all the pots and jars back onto the shelves. 'Well, if you're OK with the arrangement and you keep it all quiet, then I'm more than happy for you to stay for as long as you like.' She gave the table a brisk wipe and threw the cloth into the sink.

Jo nodded and drained her cup, still in a daze. 'Thanks.'

She should have come clean. Yesterday morning, with all the paramedics and policemen and noise, she should have stayed put, and then told someone about her amnesia.

But she hadn't. And she still couldn't. Nor could she quite fathom why, but she knew that coming clean wasn't an option – not until she'd shrugged off this horrible black feeling of guilt or whatever it was.

'Nice to have company again, actually,' said the woman, lifting the apron from round her neck and looking about the place.

You don't say, thought Jo. Then she felt bad. The woman had picked her up off the streets and offered her home-made marmalade, for God's sake.

And then it came back to her again, that sinking feeling. This wasn't the first time she'd felt bad about Mrs P. It had started this morning, when she'd woken up and seen the half-empty bottle of wine next to her bed, pieces of cork floating inside and the biro all splintered and leaking onto the carpet beside it.

She had stolen from her landlady. Last night on her way up the stairs, Jo had slipped the wine off its shelf and shoved it into her plastic bag while the woman waffled on about fire extinguishers and smoke alarms. It seemed almost surreal – as if it hadn't happened, or it had happened to someone else. She'd been drunk, but it *had* happened. Or rather, Jo had made it happen. Stealing wasn't a passive thing. It was something you chose to do. Jo had chosen to steal from the person trying to help her – again.

'You've got your door key, haven't you? Not that you'll need it, unless you're back late. You can just come through the shop. I'll be there.'

Jo nodded and jangled the keys she'd attached to Joe Simmons' wallet. She was still thinking about what she had done. And how she was starting to hate the person she thought she was.

She waved mechanically and set off down the stairs. Then she stopped and looked back. 'One more thing. I don't suppose you're online here?'

'On what line, dear?'

'Uh . . .' Jo nearly went on, but decided it was too early in the day for explaining the concept of the World Wide Web. 'Never mind.'

Chapter Five

'Afternoon! Tickets, please . . . thank you . . . lovely . . . Tickets, please . . .'

Jo's heart fluttered up into her mouth as she offered her ticket up to the inspector, her palms sticky with sweat.

'Errrr,' he squinted for several seconds and then handed it back. 'Lovely, thank you.'

Jo pushed the ticket back into her pocket with a shaky hand, trying to steady her breathing. It was ridiculous, this anxiety. She had to get it under control. It wasn't as though she'd done anything wrong; she had paid her three pounds, she was sitting in Standard Class, she wasn't playing loud music . . . But that wasn't the point.

The point was, the inspector was in a position of authority. He wasn't a policeman, but almost. He reminded her of the people she'd run away from two days before. His voice was like that of the paramedic's: firm but kind, with the propensity to turn officious. Any small reminder of that scene outside the club was enough to make her skin crawl. She alighted from the train with relief.

According to the map outside, Oxford station was a little way out of the city. Jo assessed the commotion by the bus stop – screaming brats and stressed mothers and pushchairs – and looked up at the near-cloudless sky. The walk would do her good, she thought.

She had a vague plan: to wander round town, looking at people, seeing things, trying to remember something about her life. She had come into Oxford because she needed to see something that wasn't a pensioner or a cat or a well-kept lawn, or an irate commuter on his way into London. If Jo was right about being a London girl – and she felt strangely sure she was – then the comings and goings in Radley village weren't going to be enough to trigger any memories from her past.

She knew she was being impatient, expecting things to come flooding back after only a few days. But, as she was beginning to realise, impatient was just the way she was. She hated queuing, she didn't walk slowly and she wasn't a fan of the slow pace of life. That was one of the reasons she felt so sure she'd been a Londoner before. Londoners didn't stop at the checkout to talk about yellow lines or lampposts or letter box sizes like the ones she'd seen in Mrs Phillips' shop that afternoon. Jo wanted to remember things *now* – or at least, she was pretty sure she did.

Oxford city centre was a typical mix of old stonework, sixties breeze blocks and modern, all-glass storefronts. The pedestrian zone was teeming with Saturday afternoon dawdlers: ambling couples, spotty teenagers on skateboards, bored-looking fathers with boisterous children on reins, frazzled mothers laden down with a hundred plastic bags. Jo lapped it up, inhaling the smells – jacket potatoes and coffee and sun cream – and picking out fragments of conversation perforated with peals of laughter.

Towards the edge of town, the streets turned into cobbled lanes that meandered between tall, sandstone buildings lined with bicycles and occasional students. It was August, so the undergraduates were on holiday, Jo guessed. She stopped in an archway and looked out at the vast, sun-lit courtyard that lay beyond. It was like looking through a secret door into another world: fountains, lawns, turrets and gargoyles . . . Jo watched as a pair of girls her own age wandered past, clutching folders and books, wondering whether she had seen this world before. Maybe she'd even lived in it.

'Can I help you?' A small man in a bowler hat stepped out of the shadows and smiled at her kindly.

'Oh. Um, I was just . . .'

The man continued to look at her, and from the corner of her eye Jo could see his eyebrows lift. But she didn't reply. Something else had caught her attention. Along the street, propped up on the pavement, was a small black sign: 'QUIET PLEASE. EXAMS IN PROGRESS.'

Jo couldn't breathe. She felt nervous and sick. *Exams.* It was something to do with exams, only she didn't know what.

'Are you a student, ma'am?'

'Er . . .'

'A prospective student?'

'Um . . . No.' Jo looked at the man. 'No, sorry. I was just, um, waiting for someone. But I guess they've . . . gone.'

'Right you are.' The man dipped his head politely and disappeared back through the arch.

Jo walked on, past the sign, trying to form a sensible explanation for her sudden twitchiness. She felt nervous at the idea of exams. So what? No one liked doing exams. They were horrible things. But . . . Jo tried to dig deeper, but the reasoning became flaky and brittle. She couldn't

42

draw any conclusions. Except perhaps that she had done badly in exams at some point, or cheated, or failed . . .

Jo continued her random circuit, turning left and right at will and trying to quell the anxiety inside her. Eventually, she heard the bustle of the high street and followed the sounds back into town.

In the hour that followed, Jo wandered and watched people's faces: old, young, black, white, smiling, scowling. Sometimes, someone would catch her eye. Occasionally, on making eye contact, a shudder would pass through Jo's body and she would dart into a shop or a drift of pedestrians, fearing recognition – or worse, acknowledgement. She spoke to no one.

A blackboard outside one of the large chain bookstores promised 'Half-price iced coffee and cool, comfy sofas'. A few doors down, a J D Wetherspoon advertised double shots for two pounds. Jo hesitated. Her mouth was already watering at the thought of the cold, sour liquid ripping through her insides. She could taste the vodka on her tongue.

Jo stepped past the doors of the bookshop and headed for the pub, then stopped. The special-offer bunting fluttered over the entrance, inviting her in for her two-pound shots. She tracked back and tried to feel tempted by the half-price iced coffee.

It was no good. Jo didn't want iced coffee. She wanted alcohol. She turned again and then came to another halt, feeling her addiction pulling her forwards and the reins of her willpower holding her back – a tug of war where both sides were so strong that neither could win. Then finally, her willpower gave a final tug. She spun round and marched into the shop towards the stairs that led to the second-floor café.

The 'cool, comfy sofas', it turned out, were all taken. So were all the other seats except for a couple of wooden chairs hidden amongst large family groups that looked neither comfy nor cool. Jo hovered by the window, clutching her half-price iced coffee and waiting for someone to leave.

'Wanna sit down?'

Jo realised that the bald, bespectacled man with a laptop was talking to her.

'Um . . .' She floundered. Of course she wanted to sit down; she just didn't want to sit down with him. 'Yeah, thanks.'

She perched on the vacant seat and smiled to show her gratitude. The man grinned back in a rather creepy way. She looked out of the window.

'You went for the special offer too,' he remarked in a mechanical monotone.

She nodded civilly and sipped her drink.

'Not so special, really, is it?'

Jo forced a laugh.

'You wanna know what I think?'

No, thought Jo. She looked at him briefly, so as not to appear rude.

'I think they double the price for a day, then they put it on "special offer" –' he indicated quotation marks with his pale, bony fingers – 'at the usual rate. Ha.'

Jo grunted, turning her head pointedly towards the window. The man took the hint and started tapping on the keys of his laptop. When she was sure he was fully engrossed, she reached into the plastic bag that was serving as her handbag and drew out a chocolate digestive.

It would have been nice, she thought sadly, to have someone to talk to – someone trustworthy and practical

44

and sensitive. She wouldn't feel quite so alone, so vulnerable, if there was someone else in the world who knew her secret. What would be really helpful, of course, would be a friend who had known her *before* the bomb, but of course there was no way of finding such a person without coming clean to the world.

She still wasn't entirely convinced that hiding herself away like this, pretending to be dead, was the best thing to do. There was a police station down the road; she had walked past it an hour ago. If she wanted, she could go in there and declare herself a victim of the Buffalo Club explosion. She could let them contact her family and wait while some probing shrink asked questions she couldn't answer, then she could sit in an interview room, or cell or whatever, and hear from other people what sort of a person she really was. But even as she contemplated the idea, she felt sick with fear.

Something drew her attention at the edge of her field of vision. A headline. She had seen it earlier that day, in Mrs Phillips' shop, but hadn't dared stop to read the article in front of her landlady in case she aroused suspicion. Mrs P had already caught her trawling the newspapers for clues the day before, and she'd had to invent a ridiculous story about an old acting friend.

'SINGLE LINE OF ENQUIRY FOR BUFFALO CLUB BOMB,' read the headline. The woman reading the newspaper was directly behind her bald companion, so Jo could only just read the text without letting speccy think she was trying to make eye contact.

'A group of young, radicalised Muslims are thought to be . . .' The newspaper was lowered as the reader sipped her drink. Jo drank some of hers and waited. '. . . at the centre of the only line of enquiry for the explosion that claimed fourteen lives last Thursday. The bomb, thought to have been planted in a rucksack and left in the cloakroom of the . . .' Baldy looked up from his typing. Jo gazed randomly around the café until she could hear the tap-tap of his fingers again.

She glanced at the newspaper and was perplexed to read 'GIRL RESCUED BY INFLATABLE LOBSTER'. The woman had turned the page. Jo stirred her drink. Perhaps she'd slip into the shop and grab a paper when Mrs Phillips wasn't around, or pretend to be looking for something else. Or maybe she should actually spend eighty pence or whatever and *buy* a newspaper, instead of sneaking around stealing things from people who were trying to help her. Jo sighed. She didn't want to be like this. She wanted to be honest and kind, to put others first. But it was hard to put others first when . . . well, when her own survival was at stake. She had to think about herself, to stay on her toes – that was the reason for all this deceit. Or at least, she hoped it was.

Surreptitiously, she pulled out the notebook from her makeshift handbag and jotted a couple of things down under the heading 'Bomb details'. She flicked back a couple of pages and stared at her messy scrawls from the other day. Then the typing stopped and she could feel the man's eyes boring into her again through his thick-rimmed glasses. She shut the book.

'Still using pen and paper, eh?' He glanced proudly at his silver laptop and for a dreadful moment, Jo thought he might try to show her what he was working on. 'I've practically forgotten how to write!'

Jo grunted politely and took a long swig. A vodka would

have slipped down more easily, she thought. But that was the problem. She didn't like the fact that alcohol had such a minor effect on her, that she was conditioned to use it. She hated that her body craved the stuff, that it functioned better with it than without it.

She looked out at the bustling high street below. Across the road, a middle-aged woman was standing, her handbag tucked under one arm and a giant box-shaped present on the ground beside her, all shiny red paper and curly ribbons. Anxiously, the woman looked left and then right, then checked her watch. Jo scanned the street, wondering which person or people, of the hundreds she could see from her elevated viewpoint, the woman was waiting for.

Like a character in some elaborate cuckoo clock, the woman went through her routine again. Look left, look right, check watch. Wait. Jo could see the anxiety on her face. She scanned the crowds again, then turned her attention back to the woman. Look left, look right, check watch. Wait.

Jo felt sorry for her; someone was clearly keeping her waiting, making her worry. But it wasn't pity that she was feeling, five minutes later when the woman was still standing there, her head scanning the crowds even more frantically. It was shame.

Jo was making someone worry. Jo – or whatever her name was – had let herself become 'missing, feared dead', and there were people – or at least she *guessed* there were people – who were worrying about her, waiting, hoping.

Eventually, the woman's stony face melted into a smile and even through the double-glazing Jo could hear a muffled cry as the two women threw their arms around one another. It was her daughter, thought Jo, watching as

47

the younger woman emerged from the embrace and pointed gleefully at the red shiny parcel, her stylish white coat flapping in the breeze. It was her daughter who had been keeping her waiting.

The women moved off, laughing frivolously and making animated gestures with their hands. Jo felt a fresh wave of uncertainty wash over her. She couldn't say why, but she felt quite sure that somewhere, right now, her mother was waiting for her, worrying.

She finished her drink and thought again of the police station down the road. That was the right thing to do. She had to turn herself in. She had to own up, for her mother's sake. Whatever she'd done before, whatever the reasons for the paranoia, whatever the consequences, the only fair thing she could do was walk into that police station and come clean.

Jo stood up and took one final look out of the window, even though she knew the mother and daughter were long gone. In the spot where they had hugged, a man was sitting – or rather, lying. Jo peered down at the scene. Two people in uniforms were crouching over the man, who was dragging himself along the pavement like a slug.

A clearing had formed in the crowds as shoppers gave the crawling man a wide berth. It was only when Jo saw the dog – skinny, mangy and limping – that she realised. The man was a beggar. He was being 'moved on' – only slowly, because he was drunk. Or disabled. Or ill. She didn't know, and clearly the policemen didn't care.

She watched as the man sloped off into the shadows and the crowds flowed back into the area. She picked up the pen and stared at her notebook. Yet again, she had convinced herself that coming clean was the right thing to do. She had gone right to the edge and looked over. And yet again, she was talking herself back down. She might have been right about her mum being out there, worrying. It was perfectly likely that she had family and friends who cared about her. But she'd been wrong to believe that their reunion would be like the one she'd witnessed outside.

Her role wasn't that of the daughter in all this; she wasn't an innocent latecomer. She was the tramp. She was the outsider, the one who didn't belong. Maybe she did have friends and family, but so too did the homeless guy, presumably. For different reasons, they had left them behind. Jo didn't even know what the reasons were, in her case, but she knew one thing for sure: she was on the run. And until she had worked out what exactly she was running from, she had to keep running.

Jo slipped the notebook into her bag and caught sight of the two words on the back that she'd copied from the scrap of paper. 'SASKIA DAWSON.' For the hundredth time, Jo strained to summon her memory. For the hundredth time, she drew a blank.

She bid her table companion farewell and walked out, having made her decision. It was time to put the only clue she had to good use.

Chapter Six

Jo slipped into the wobbly swivel chair and logged on. The keyboard was coated in a grey sheen and the O key was jammed with something sticky, but eventually she punched in the password and pulled up an internet browser. With much stabbing, she managed to type the search engine URL into the address bar.

She stared at the screen while the website loaded. It was obviously a slow connection. Jo frowned. *A slow connection.* How did she know that? How was it, she wondered, that she knew about website loading times and keyboard shortcuts and the differences between Internet Explorer and Firefox, when she didn't even know her own name?

The site finally loaded and Jo typed 'Saskia Dawson' into the box. Her hands were shaking – partly because she hadn't drunk anything in two days but also because she was nervous about what she might find. It was possible that Saskia Dawson would lead her to discover something about herself – or that Saskia Dawson *was* her, although admittedly Jo couldn't think of a sensible explanation for having her own name written on the back of her hand.

There were only six results, of which five related to the findings of a German professor on the subject of

Endogenous N-acetylaspartylglutamate in the *Journal of Neurochemistry*. Jo clicked on the links in case they offered any clues, but everything was written in a mixture of German and gobbledegook. The sixth hit was a Facebook profile. *Facebook*. Yet another thing she was perfectly familiar with.

Eventually, the page opened: 'Facebook helps you connect and share with the people in your life. Sign Up. It's free and anyone can join.'

Jo thought for a second. Something told her she had a Facebook account, but she didn't know her login, and the sign-up form required an email address. She opened up another browser, navigated to Google Mail – slowly and noisily, due to the letters involved – and registered for a new address. Then she returned to Facebook and set up Jo Simmons as a member.

Finally, she was in. Saskia Dawson winked back at her, all pouting and saucy and seductive. And blonde. Jo stared at the photo. It definitely wasn't her face.

She looked at the image for a while, scouring it for something she recognised. Bleached, wavy hair, plump lips, alluring brown eyes . . . Saskia was gorgeous, in a cheap sort of way. She was probably in her early twenties, like Jo, but it was hard to glean much more from the photo. Her expression seemed to imply both naïve and sophisticated at once: flirtatious, yet coy. But anyone could look like that in a photo.

After a couple of minutes, Jo had to look away. She had stared at the face for too long. It was like saying a word over and over again; after a while, you weren't even sure it was a word. Saskia Dawson could have been her sister, her friend or a complete stranger. She had no idea.

There were three options next to the profile picture: Add as Friend, Send a Message, View Friends. Jo clicked on the third link.

Saskia has 267 friends.

A long list of names appeared, each accompanied by a small photo. Jo ran an eye down the page, carefully scanning the smiles for one that resembled her own. Nobody looked familiar. Unless Jo had been one of the hilarious people who had used a picture of a washing machine or cartoon character instead of her face, then she wasn't one of Saskia's friends.

Some of the names had extra information too, like 'London' or 'Brunel graduate' or 'Jake Dickson is off to Southend' or 'Kirsty Graham is soooooooo hungover', but there was nothing useful. All Jo could glean was that Saskia Dawson had a lot of so-called friends who were all, like her, in their early twenties and that she probably lived in London. There seemed to be no link to the girl now masquerading as Jo Simmons.

Jo went back to the girl's profile page and assessed her options. Add as Friend, or Send a Message. She could send a message, but what would it say? *Hi, my name's not actually Jo Simmons, but I had your name written on my hand. Any idea why?* Jo didn't fancy her chances of getting a reply.

She needed to know more about Saskia – needed to see her full profile. Perhaps the messages and postings and other photos would give her a clue as to where she lived, where she worked, which pubs she went to, that sort of thing. Jo stared at the face for a moment longer, then pressed Add as Friend.

Chapter Seven

'Morning!' squawked Trevor, the sound grating on her nerves as it did every day.

Jo responded with her usual mumbled greeting, going straight to the back of the teashop to dump her plastic bag. She wasn't sure why he'd gone to the effort of getting a door key cut for her; he always arrived first.

She returned to the counter, ran the hot water, wiped the surfaces and brought the supplies through from the back. Her mornings had developed a kind of rhythm that was disconcertingly predictable. She could hardly believe that only just over a week had passed since she'd stumbled off the night bus into Trev's Teashop.

'I'll open up,' said Trevor, needlessly. Jo had learned her lesson on the second morning: opening up was the proprietor's job. Other tasks he would happily delegate – and generally did – but winding out the awning each day was something he liked to be seen doing. It allowed him to show the world that he, owner and manager of Trev's Teashop, Oxfordshire, was open for business. He probably thought of himself a bit like the Queen cutting the ribbon on a new institution, thought Jo, watching him sweat with the effort.

'I've got an errand for you,' said Trevor, propping the door open and waiting for her to look up. 'I need these things posting,' he said, patting a pile of letters on the counter.

Jo nodded and started to dry her hands.

'No – not now. Post office only opens at nine. You'll need to buy stamps. You can take the money from the till.' He explained this last point slowly, in case it might be too complex for her.

Jo got back to stocking the fridge, wondering again what she had done for a living before she'd lost her memory. She hoped it was something more challenging than this.

Her contemplation continued as the morning progressed. This being a Friday, the usual eight o'clock rush was less frantic than usual and spread over a longer period. She was on autopilot: taking orders, serving drinks and doing as much 'flitting' as was possible, given the lack of seated customers and Trevor's recent transition into more of a managerial role. Instead of manning the counter, he preferred to busy himself in the background, keeping an eye on Jo's handiwork, making unhelpful suggestions and trying to strike up conversations with the commuters – most of whom did their best to ignore him.

Jo handed over a double espresso and watched as the suited customer added a mound of sugar, then another, then another. She frowned. The sugar wouldn't dissolve in that small amount – anyone could tell that. But that wasn't why Jo felt perplexed. She felt perplexed because of something going through her mind, something she knew.

The man's espresso was becoming a suspension. That was the proper term for a liquid solution where not all the particles were dissolved. The man hurried out and Jo was left staring at the space where he had been. A *suspension*. Where had that word come from? And how had she known to use it?

Another customer came in and Jo found herself mechanically filling the shot-holder again, trying to work out what this new piece of information meant – if anything. Perhaps it was insignificant. It was probably something they taught in school that anybody might remember. Perhaps all this meant was that Jo had paid attention in school – which was something of a revelation in itself, but not a particularly interesting one.

Jo watched the dark brown liquid bubble into the paper cup, wondering whether coherent memories would come back to her or whether she'd have to piece things together from clues like this. If she didn't start remembering things properly, then she'd only have half the picture. She might discover what she liked, what she was good at and what type of person she gravitated towards, but she wouldn't know *why*. She wouldn't know what, in her past, had caused her to be the way she was.

She handed over the coffee, caught up in a complex internal debate about nature versus nurture and the pros and cons of remembering her past. There was still a part of her that didn't actually want to know what had happened. If they were bad memories, it might be better that she didn't have them at all. Because once they were back, there was no way of un-remembering them.

What she really wanted was the *option* of remembering. As if her memory operated like a tap, she wanted the ability to turn it on, gently, then if it started gushing out unpleasantly and making a mess, she could turn it off again. The problem, of course, was that her memory didn't operate like a tap. She wasn't in charge. Nobody was. The more she tried to remember, the more elusive the memories became. She just had to wait, and observe, and jot things down.

The media was one possible source of information. Jo had been following the coverage of the bombing all week. She was half hoping, half dreading that one day she'd return from her shift to see her face on the lunchtime news – a grainy version of a holiday snap or a Christmas family photo – with her real name and the word 'MISSING' underneath. She insisted on helping Mrs P arrange the newspapers every morning so that she could skim the pages for a reference. But there was no such reference. Every article seemed to be a rehash of the initial coverage, and even that hadn't said very much. As the week progressed, the news of the Buffalo Club bomb became less and less significant, and this morning the investigation hadn't even warranted a mention. Clearly the media wasn't going to help her very much.

There was a lull in customers. Jo distracted herself, wiping the surfaces and rinsing the milk jug, but she wasn't fooling anyone. Or at least, she wasn't fooling herself. Her hands were shaking and her eyes kept wandering down to the cupboard under the sink where six dark liqueur bottles sat, teasing her. They were supposed to be for adding to coffees, presumably, but if the crusty, sugary coatings inside the lids were anything to go by, they rarely got used. And there *were* crusty, sugary coatings inside the lids, because Jo had checked. She had opened them all, sniffed them and put them away again. About fifteen times.

The craving was stronger than ever today, perhaps

because it had been nearly a week since her last proper drink. She reached down and extracted the leftmost bottle, unscrewing the lid and preparing to duck behind the counter. Amaretto – not her first choice, but better than the other options, which all smelled rather like petrol and had unrecognisable Italian names. She glanced around, then crouched down.

Her lips made contact with the crystallised sugar and she tilted the bottle, gagging for the sweet, fiery liquid in her throat.

'Nine o'clock!'

Her head hit the counter.

'Sorry?' Jo fumbled around for the lid and replaced the bottle with one hand, holding out the other for the pile of letters. Her body was filled with unfulfilled desire.

'You hadn't forgotten, had you?' Trevor grinned at her stupidly.

Jo flashed a smile and removed her apron. The sense of anticlimax, of getting so close and then pulling away, was exasperating. 'No, just about to go,' she said, swallowing a mouthful of saliva. 'Down the road and on the right?'

'Down the road,' he motioned like an obese air steward, 'and on the right.'

The warm air felt good on her skin, and gradually, with concerted effort, Jo managed to disentangle herself from the yearnings and focus on the things around her. Birds cheeped in the hedgerow, trees rustled in the breeze and somewhere nearby, farm machinery was whirring into action. A cloud skittered across the sky, briefly obscuring the sun and then leaving it to shine, and for a moment, Radley looked like the most beautiful place on earth.

Semi-detached and set back from the road with a

pebble-dashed front, the post office looked exactly like somebody's house except for the rounded red sign on the telegraph pole outside and the billboard announcing the headline, 'VIOLIN CASE THWARTS ROBBERY'.

Not for the first time, Jo marvelled at how some things seemed so familiar whilst the details of her life remained a mystery. She knew exactly what first-class stamps looked like and how the UK postal system worked. She knew what Facebook was and how to use it. How, then, could she not name a single one of her friends?

She applied the stamps and looked at the swarthy young man behind the counter.

'I don't suppose you have an internet connection?'

He nodded over to a large, bulbous monitor in the corner of the store. It looked like a TV from the 1920s.

'Could I just . . . ?'

'One pond for fifteen minutes.'

'But I only—'

'Three pond an hour.'

'What about two minutes?' She smiled virtuously.

Reluctantly, the man smiled. 'OK, but quickly. Log in as Admin. Password is "password".'

The internet connection was even more sluggish than the one she'd used before. Jo waited for the Facebook login to appear, wondering whether perhaps, by some sort of administrative error, Radley had been left off the UK broadband rollout map.

She logged in and clicked on the Friends tab. Her face fell.

You have 0 friends.

Then she noticed the message. She clicked on her inbox.

Saskia Dawson
Today at 03.49
Who R U?
   Do I know U Jo Simmons?! I don't accept friends
who ain't got no profile pic . . .

Jo drummed her fingers against the makeshift desk, frustrated. Of course Saskia hadn't clicked Accept. The request had come from an anonymous stranger. For all Saskia knew, Jo Simmons was a dirty old pervert looking for cheap online thrills.

'Time's up,' called the guy from behind the counter.

'I've hardly logged on!' she yelled back, fingers hovering over the keyboard.

Jo Simmons
Today at 09.11
Re: Who R U?
   Hi Saskia, sorry for the randomness – I'm using an alias . . . Long story. Haven't got round to putting up a photo.
   Here's a clue – long, black hair with a red streak at the front. Know who I am? :-) xx

Jo logged off and ran through the door, the adrenalin still pumping from the brief correspondence. She was so busy devising an excuse for her boss that she slammed straight into somebody on the post office forecourt.

'I'm so sorry!'

She squatted down to pick up the letters, which had scattered in the breeze.

'No worries.'

With relief, Jo realised that the man she'd knocked

flying had not been one of Radley's aged inhabitants; in fact, the man seemed quite youthful – early thirties at most. He laughed as she handed over the gritty pile.

'I'm used to being rugby-tackled.'

She smiled. It wasn't that she was flirting, exactly, but . . . well, OK perhaps she was, just a little. The man was handsome: tall, with coiffed light brown hair and a tan. He could well have been a rugby player.

'Hope they weren't important.' She nodded at the letters as he pushed them into the post box.

'Oh, just replies to my fan mail. Standard responses, you know.'

She laughed uncertainly. Gosh, maybe he *was* a sportsman, like, maybe the captain of the England rugby team . . .

He shook his head, smiling and revealing a row of pearly teeth. 'I'm kidding. It's bills, mainly. Are you heading for Trev's Teashop, by any chance? Want a lift?'

Jo was confused again. He must have been a customer at the café. She had probably served him coffee.

'How did you know where I worked?'

He shook his head and smiled again, motioning for her to get into the passenger seat of a slick little BMW parked on the road. 'Well I wasn't *deliberately* looking at your chest, but . . .'

Jo groaned at her own stupidity. Of course. The aertex shirt.

She wasn't sure whether getting into a complete stranger's car was entirely sensible, but neither, probably, was accepting a job from a complete stranger, or a place to stay. And besides, he had an honest smile.

'It wasn't just the shirt, actually,' he confessed, pulling out and accelerating to quite a speed.

'No?'

'No. I've seen you in there.'

'What, you're a customer?'

'No. I've seen you through the window. I work from home quite a bit so I walk around town. Stops me getting cabin fever.'

'Oh, right.' Jo wanted to ask what he did for a living and where in Radley he was based and a whole load of other questions, but they were already at the teashop. 'Well, thanks for the lift.'

He laughed. 'Saved you all of thirty seconds.'

'Well, yeah.' She released her seatbelt and opened the door. Then, in a moment of boldness, she added, 'Pop in for a coffee some time. I'll give you a freebie.'

He raised an eyebrow.

'Free, er, coffee, I mean.'

'I look forward to it,' he said, winking through the passenger window. She slammed the door, feeling the blood rush to her face.

She heard the whirr of his electric window behind her as she re-entered the café.

'By the way, I'm Stu. What's your name?'

She turned back and smiled.

'Jo. See you around.'

Chapter Eight

Jo punched in her login and password and looked around the empty internet café as the page loaded up. A sign hung above her head, advertising '*FAX – PRINTING – WEB @ CCESS*' in spiky handwriting. Appended to the last point was an additional explanation: 'Check your email! Chat!' – presumably to entice the technophobic Radley residents online. Jo looked back at the screen. She had one new message.

> Saskia Dawson
> Today at 12.54
> Re: Who R U?
> Roxie?!?! Good to hear frm U hun! Bin textin U & no reply . . . Thought you was dead! Why the alias? U freaked me out xx

Jo's heart pounded against her ribcage. *Roxie.* She was getting somewhere. Saskia Dawson had given her a name – such as it was. Roxie. She rolled the word around in her mouth a few times, trying it out. It seemed . . . odd, somehow. Not what she'd anticipated.

She read the message one more time. *Thought you was*

dead. So presumably Saskia had known about Jo being caught up in the bomb blast. Which implied that Saskia had been there too . . . or maybe not. She would have to find out – but carefully. It was clear they were friends, but Jo couldn't tell what sort of friends. She didn't know how far back they went, how much they confided in one another, what she supposedly knew of the girl. She would have to trust Saskia, to some extent, but not more than she needed to. Opening up completely would leave her too vulnerable.

Jo Simmons
Today at 12.56
Re: Who R U?
   Yep it's me! Sorry I didn't reply to your texts – I lost my phone. All been a bit mad these last few days . . .
   Alias thing just a joke – I lost my fb login details (stored in my phone – duh!) so just set up a random account for now.

Jo clicked Send and looked again at the young blonde who continued to pout back from the mugshot. The face seemed more familiar now, but that was hardly surprising; Jo knew the streaks of blusher and locks of hair off by heart. She tried to remember something about the girl, or the friendship – presumably it had been a friendship – but it was just speculation, nothing more.

   The fact that Saskia knew about Jo's presence at the club that night was intriguing, but alarming too. It seemed likely that they had been out together, possibly with others. And if that were the case, Jo thought anxiously, then they probably had a lot to discuss. Which could prove tricky, although not unfeasible. Assuming Saskia was happy to converse via Facebook. That was the ironic thing about Facebook – you weren't actually talking face to face; there was always time to plan your response. Except, Jo realised, watching the page refresh, when both parties were online.

Saskia Dawson
Today at 12.59
Re: Who R U?
   U dopey cow! Want me 2 hack in2 yr fb account?
Glad ur ok – reckon most of the girls r keepin
a low profile, eh. xx

Jo frowned. It was the second part of Saskia's message that really interested her – although the first half did too. She tried to think of a way of finding out who 'the girls' were, and why they'd want to keep a low profile.

Jo Simmons
Today at 13.03
Re: Who R U?
   Hack wd be good – if you can! So have you
spoken to others recently?

She was treading dangerously, but she had to. Saskia was her only lead. Coming clean on the amnesia thing was an option, but not one she wanted to take. If she was clever, she would be able to mine her friend for information without divulging anything about her situation.

Saskia Dawson
Today at 13.05
Re: Who R U?
    Whats ur user name then – think u said
rebecca.ross99@hotmail.com? Yeah I spoke 2
Candy yest . . . She aint sayin nothin either.

Rebecca Ross. So that was her name. Roxie was just a nick-
name. Jo looked at the words on the screen. They sounded
good. Better than Jo Simmons, she thought. Although it
probably wasn't wise to embark on any sudden name-
changes in Radley. Her boss and her landlady were already
suspicious enough.

And who was Candy? What was the deal with all these
porn-star names? Jo pictured the three girls together, even
though she didn't know what Candy looked like: Saskia,
Roxie and Candy, getting ready for a night on the town.
A night in the Buffalo Club. It was like a scene from some
corny American movie.

Jo Simmons
Today at 13.06
Re: Who R U?
    Thanks mate. Yes, try that . . . Hopefully it's right –
I haven't logged on in ages so can't quite remember!

Jo wondered about asking some sort of clever question about
Candy and Saskia – something that would give more away
about their relationship, or explain why the girls were
'keeping a low profile'. It seemed odd that Saskia hadn't
talked more about what had happened in the club that night;
surely bombs didn't go off that often in London nightclubs?

65

Saskia Dawson
Today at 13.08
Re: Who R U?
    Cool – leave it w me. I'll send U a new login.
By the way, U got any work? I'm quitting the
stripping thing – gonna get a real job!

Jo stared. Then she glanced over her shoulder in case
anyone happened to be looking at her screen. She reread
the girl's words and then opened another browser.
    'Buffalo Club London', she typed into Google.
    And there it was. The Buffalo Club: Mayfair's Premier
Table Dancing Establishment.

Chapter Nine

A motorbike screeched to a halt in front of her.

'Look where you're goin'!' yelled the man from inside his helmet.

Jo leaped back onto the pavement and looked around, trying to focus. The vodka had gone to her head and she wasn't sure where she was, or where she was going.

Her heel made contact with something. She put her hand out and nearly fell over a sign advertising English Cream Teas. To her left was some sort of fairytale castle and beyond that, a black and gold sign hung over the street with the words 'Ye' and 'Olde' and something else she couldn't read. Jo held the vodka bottle up to her face and ascertained that it was indeed empty.

'Just in time for the second half,' said the barman, nodding towards the giant screen that took up most of the back wall of the pub. He had loose, wobbly jowls and a missing front tooth.

She slumped on the only available stool at the end of the bar and tried to concentrate as the barman pulled her pint. The pub was packed – or, at least, one end of the pub was packed. Like prayer mats, all seats had been turned to face the giant screen and there wasn't a man in sight not staring upwards. Jo leaned forwards on her arms, relishing the warmth and the hubbub and the shouting. There might even have been people here who were more inebriated than she was.

'Th'nil-all,' the barman lisped through the gap in his teeth. Jo smiled politely and sank into her pint.

The jigsaw was fitting together, slowly, but Jo didn't like the image that was materialising. The Buffalo Club was a lap-dancing club. She was a stripper. Less than two weeks ago, she'd been making a living by taking her clothes off for strangers. Jo gulped down more beer, repulsed. Presumably she'd been doing it for the money. Perhaps she'd been in debt. Perhaps Roxie was *still* in debt, she thought. Maybe it was a good thing she had died. It was like an extreme way of declaring yourself bankrupt – declaring yourself dead.

Another good thing had come out of this, she realised – amongst all the bad things. At least now she knew that she hadn't been partying with her mates on the night of the explosion. Jo – or rather, Roxie, or Rebecca or whatever her name was – hadn't lost any close friends after all. Unless, of course, her close friends had also been strippers. Which they might have been.

Strippers. Jo closed her eyes, picturing Saskia Dawson's profile picture: the Bambi eyes, the bottle-blonde hair, that pout. Of course. What other profession involved looking so superficial, so flirtatious? Jo wondered how close they had been. The Facebook conversation gave her an idea, but you couldn't read much into a few lines of text; after all, Jo hadn't been telling Saskia everything, so maybe the converse was true too. Maybe they'd only just met, and that was why she had Saskia's name on her hand. Or maybe they'd been best friends, chatting backstage before they went out to get naked. She just didn't know. Jo beckoned the barman over.

'Thirsty, eh?' he said, grabbing the empty glass with a look of approval and filling it up. 'There you go. On the 'ouse,' he said with a cheeky grin that might have been attractive on someone less flabby.

Jo tried to thank him and found her words came out in all the wrong order.

'I should probably be warning you of the risks of irresponsible drinking and such like,' he said.

She tried to fix him with a look that said 'leave me alone'.

'But, tell the truth, I like a girl who can sink a pint.'

Jo claimed her free drink and looked around for an alternative seat. She briefly considered settling on the carpet amongst the legs of the avid fans but decided she was marginally safer at the bar.

Perhaps she'd been a student, thought Jo. Students were always short of money. That would explain the stealing. That would explain why someone like her had turned to stripping. She swallowed more beer. What was she thinking? *Someone like her.* As if she knew what she was like. She was making assumptions about herself based on what? Gut feeling? Hope? The fact that she had a reasonable grasp of English grammar and spoke with a middle-class accent?

She reached into her plastic bag and drew out her notebook. The fact was, she didn't *know* what she was like. It was quite possible that she wasn't actually a very nice person.

Suddenly, a tremendous roar filled the room and Jo felt glad she hadn't opted for a seat on the floor. Men cheered, footballers cartwheeled and pints of beer spilled all over the place.

'One-nil,' said the barman excitedly. Jo nodded as though she cared.

> Buffalo Club = strip club
> Needed the money?
> Friend(?) Saskia

'You a journalith, then?' asked the barman, peering at the book.

Jo turned the page quickly. 'No,' she said. 'Just . . . writing a shopping list.'

She was impressed at her quick-wittedness, given the amount she had drunk. This pint would be her last, she decided.

'You causing trouble, Den?' yelled a coarse voice from across the bar. Lumbering towards her was a large man in a dirty white vest. 'Is he causing trouble?'

Definitely her last drink, thought Jo, shaking her head politely and realising that her head was actually resting on her arms. She sat up.

'She's writing a shopping lith,' explained the barman.

'Oh, very organised,' chuckled the man, leering over Jo's shoulder. 'Chips,' he said, nodding. 'My missus always forgets them.'

Jo glanced at his belly and decided he was lying. She shut the notebook and slipped it back in her pocket.

'What're you drinking?' asked the fat man.

'Hey, she'th got a pint,' said the barman. Clearly Jo didn't get a say in the matter.

'It's nearly finished,' argued vest man.

Jo looked down. It was true. She was nearly through her second pint. She had to slow down. 'I'm fine, thanks,' she tried to say, although it came out as 'phalanx'.

'Come on, let me buy you a drink,' pressed the man.

It was then, as the man leaned sideways and gave a sort of nod of encouragement, that Jo saw it again. She saw the guy at the bar. She felt him tap her elbow. She heard him ask what she wanted to drink. Only this time – and maybe it was the alcohol doing funny things with her head – it was much clearer. She could see every line on his face. She could picture the rows of expensive spirits behind the bar, even hear the throb of the music in the club. And this time, the memory didn't stop there. She knew what happened next.

'You all right?' asked the barman, squinting at her anxiously.

'Yeah,' she said quietly, trying not to lose hold of the memory, feeling the blood drain out of her face. 'Where are your toilets?'

Locked in the cubicle, slumped on the lid with her head in her hands, Jo closed her eyes. Her head was spinning and she felt as though she was on a boat in stormy weather.

She remembered accepting the offer and choosing a vodka martini – an expensive drink, as the club dictated. Wow, it was coming back to her. The man had pushed the glass towards her and then moved closer himself. He'd smelt nice. Expensive aftershave. She had smiled seductively, the way she'd learned to do, and then asked him a question. Something mundane. Nothing personal. Jo fought to hold on to the image as she marvelled at how much was coming back.

She had led him away from the bar. He'd settled in one

of the leather chairs in the corner of the club. He was shy, she thought. Probably not a regular. She'd started to dance, gyrating a little, nothing special – then something had happened.

Jo ground the palms of her hands into her head, trying to remember the details. It was hazy now, though. She couldn't picture the scene. Just voices. Shouting. And those alarms, the frantic noise. There was panic everywhere. She thought she remembered struggling with the straps on her shoes, scratching at her ankles so she could take them off and run, but it was all muddled.

'Is there someone in there?' The cubicle door rattled.

Jo flushed the toilet for effect and lifted the lid. Her thoughts swung back to the present.

'Sorry.' She brushed past the girl, falling sideways against the sink. A strange feeling of *déjà vu* came over her. She tried to summon more detail, but her brain was fuzzy. Had something happened in a toilet, somewhere, sometime . . . ?

'You want that drink, then?' asked the barman as she walked back through the pub.

Actually, Jo had been heading for the door. 'Gottago.'

'C'mon, juth one more – ooh.' The man seemed distracted. In fact, as he squinted across at the screen the entire roomful of bodies erupted like an over-shaken can of beer and the noise levels rose to deafening. 'Hey!' yelled the barman along with everybody else. 'We won! C'mon, you gotta have one more now!'

Jo said something that got lost in the din and wandered unsteadily onto the street. She didn't even know who'd been playing.

*   *   *

72

She was somewhere in West Oxford, it transpired. Out of courtesy to the helpful shopkeeper who told her how to get to the bus stop she needed, Jo purchased some crisps and a couple of cans of lager.

She ignored the scowls of fellow passengers as she cracked open the first can. It was probably illegal or something, but Jo didn't care. She had worked it out. She had discovered what made the memories come back: alcohol. Good or bad, her thoughts were flowing freely now.

Jo wondered how many people knew her dirty secret. In a way, it made things easier, the fact that she was officially dead. It meant that nobody was looking for her. Maybe there were people out there who knew that Rebecca Ross had been a stripper, but now she was dead . . . Saskia Dawson was the only potential leak, and she had her own skeletons locked away – assuming she didn't make a habit of disclosing her line of work. Jo had to hope that that was enough of a threat to keep the girl quiet.

It occurred to Jo as she fell off the bus and tottered onto Radley Road that Jo Simmons was no longer just a temporary alias. It wasn't just something she used in order to fit in. It was her name. Her new identity. So as long as she didn't draw attention to herself in Radley, she could survive as Ms Simmons for . . . well, for ever if necessary. Jo shuddered. That was a horrible idea. She couldn't just draw a line under the last twenty-odd years of her life. But at the same time, in a way, it appealed. There was something comforting and neat about the idea. Like wiping a virus-ridden computer: it was a drastic step, but it worked. And everything ran more smoothly afterwards.

Of course, there were benefits to starting again, cleaning the slate of her life and all that. But what about Rebecca?

Effectively, Jo had killed her off. She hadn't done so intentionally; it had just been a consequence of events. And now she had to decide whether to resurrect her old self or leave her behind and move on. She opened her second beer, her mind in a state of flux.

It was early evening when she stumbled into the shop. Mrs Phillips was on a stepladder with her back to the door, sliding packs of toilet roll onto the top shelf. Jo slipped past quietly. She didn't have the energy for a conversation this evening – let alone one of the landlady's interrogations.

'Nice day?' sang the woman without turning round.

Jo stopped in her tracks.

'You knocked the doorstop,' she explained.

'Oh, right. Yeah, good.' The words tumbled out like porridge: lumpy and stuck together.

Mrs Phillips got down from her stepladder and started packing it away. Jo took the opportunity to sneak out unnoticed. Unfortunately, she misjudged the angle at which she was standing and found herself walking into the dried foods aisle. The shelf wobbled a bit and a number of packets jumped onto the floor.

'Shit.' She squinted to assess the damage, hoping Mrs P hadn't seen.

'Drinking, were you?'

Jo turned to find the old woman standing right beside her. How she got there so fast was a complete mystery. 'Er, yeah. A bit. Sorry – I'll clear this up.'

'Are you all right, Jo?'

'Yeah, fine! Why?'

Mrs Phillips didn't answer, exactly. She just leaned forward and extracted some crisp crumbs from Jo's hair.

'Oh, must've . . . fallen . . .' Jo was quite surprised by the size of some of the flakes. A couple of them were whole crisps.

'Have you eaten anything today?' Mrs Phillips asked. 'Apart from these?'

Jo thought for a moment. Actually, she hadn't. No wonder the beer had gone to her head. 'A bit, not much.' She started to pick up the fallen packets of lentils.

Mrs Phillips looked down at her. 'Look, Jo. I don't want to interfere . . . I know it's none of my business, but . . . You must look after yourself. Alcohol isn't the answer.'

Jo shoved the packets back onto the shelf and scowled. It was true. This *was* none of her business. 'The answer to what?'

Suddenly, she felt angry. This woman was her landlady, not her counsellor. She had no right to preach about 'answers'.

'Well, to your problems,' said Mrs Phillips. 'Whatever they are.'

'I haven't got problems!' Jo replied, louder than she'd intended.

'No, I didn't mean that. Of course you haven't.'

Jo shook her head. Now the woman was patronising her. *Of course you haven't.* That was another way of saying, *I know you've got problems.* Well, that was uncalled for. This woman was stepping out of line. She had no idea what Jo was going through.

'Don't take the piss.'

'No, no, I wasn't.' Mrs Phillips held her hands up defensively. 'I just don't like to see people upset.'

'Upset?' Jo stared at the woman, unable to stop the words pouring out. 'I'm not fucking upset! I'm fine! Or at least, I *was* until you started telling me I wasn't!'

75

The landlady nodded.

That did it. She didn't have to stand here being nodded at like that by a woman who barely knew her.

Jo stormed through the back door and up the stairs. She stuffed her possessions – the few she had – into a plastic bag and marched out the way she had come.

'Here,' she said, stuffing some twenty-pound notes into the woman's hand. She was quite proud to have mastered the maths. 'That's eight nights at fifteen quid a night. Take it. *Take it.*'

Mrs Phillips looked shocked. Initially her fingers resisted curling round the notes, but eventually they did. Jo pushed the wallet back into her pocket and left the shop. She didn't need this. Her life was messed up enough without some meddling old cow trying to offer advice.

She strode down the path, forming a plan as she went. At six o'clock the teashop would be shut, and she reckoned there was just enough space behind the counter for her to lie flat without being seen from the road. She was resourceful. She could look after herself – which was just as well, because yet again, she was on her own.

Chapter Ten

Jo rolled over and buried her face in the pillow. Something hard dug into her forehead. She wriggled onto her back again but the light burned through her eyelids. Her feet were cold.

Gradually, consciousness took hold. She realised why her hip was jutting into something cold, why her mouth tasted stale and why her head felt as though it had been placed in a pressure cooker. She was fully clothed, surrounded by moulding, hairy blankets and coats. The teashop blinds were set at exactly the right angle to allow the sunlight to stream into her eyes.

Jo hauled herself into a sitting position and craned her neck to look up at the clock. Strange. There appeared to be only one hand. She squinted up at it for a couple of seconds, then worked it out. The hands were diametrically opposite. It was six o'clock, she deduced.

Suddenly, a long, protracted whining noise made her jump. Jo looked up at the clock again. A wave of panic rose up inside her. It wasn't six o'clock, it was five past seven. *The noise was Trevor's singing.*

She leaped up and kicked the makeshift bed to one side. She would have to somehow get everything back into the store cupboard without him noticing. Her head was pounding so hard it felt as though the capillaries were about to burst. She couldn't think. Her throat was crying out for water but she knew there were things that needed to be done before sorting herself out. She just couldn't work out what.

'Morning!' Trevor emerged from the back of the teashop with his customary swagger.

'Hi!' Jo managed with more than the usual level of cheer. *Oof.* Her head was about to explode.

'Late again?' he said, approaching to embark on his opening-up ritual. Thankfully he wasn't the type to notice details like crusty eyes or scarecrow hair.

'No, I was . . . wiping the tables.' Jo stepped backwards as he rifled through the drawer, looking for the awning key. Her foot landed on the pile of blankets.

'What's that?' he asked, following Jo's anxious downward glance.

'What?'

Trevor bent down, brow furrowed. 'It looks like a sock.'

Incredibly, he hadn't actually noticed the giant mound of linen next to the bin; he was more interested in the sock that must have worked its way off her foot during the night.

'Oh, *that.*' Her brain wasn't working quickly enough. 'Yes, it does look like a sock.'

She swooped down to pick it up whilst yanking her trouser leg down to conceal her bare foot, thankful that she'd had the drunken foresight to sleep in her uniform.

'What on earth . . . ?'

'Oh, I remember,' she said, finally thinking of something. 'It belongs to a customer. He took it off the other day.'

Trevor's frown intensified. 'A customer took his sock off? Why?'

Jo blinked back at him, wondering what had possessed her to say that. 'Oh, you know . . . He was just . . . showing me something. Er, on his foot.'

Her boss's suspicions seemed to intensify. 'My question is: why is it still there? You're supposed to sweep the floor at the end of your shift.'

Jo bent down to pick up the offending item. 'Sorry. Must've missed it. Careless.'

'Hmm.' Trevor shook his head despairingly and marched out of the shop. Jo breathed a small sigh of relief.

She waited until he was part-way through his opening-up ceremony before gathering her bedding and carrying it back to the store cupboard. Her head was pulsating. It felt as though her brain had come away from her skull and was getting more bruised with every footstep.

'Jo? Are you there? Jo?'

Trevor's voice sounded quite insistent. Jo stuffed the bedding into the cupboard and hurried out to where he was standing, shoving her feet into her shoes on the way. She would sort it out properly later – once she'd splashed some water on her face and done something about her hair and the onion-like stench on her breath.

'Look at this!' Trevor was standing outside beneath the newly erected awning, pointing at the little bench he called table ten.

She followed his finger and stared at the cheap white

surface. She couldn't see what she was supposed to be looking at.

'Look!' he said again. 'You said you'd wiped the tables!'

Jo frowned at him. The bright light was hurting her eyes. 'What?'

He stared incredulously at her. 'There are coffee cup marks all over it – and bits of food! We'll get rats. And think of the impression we're giving. This isn't some cheap fast-food outlet, is it?'

No, thought Jo. It's an over-priced fast-coffee outlet. She could just about make out a faint ring-mark on the table and a couple of microscopic crumbs. 'Sorry. Think the detergent ran out.'

'I pay you good money,' he said angrily. This was a slight inaccuracy, thought Jo, given that she was earning just thirty pounds a day and he hadn't actually paid her for this week's work yet. She was rather hoping that payday would be today, but now didn't seem like a very good time to ask.

She mumbled something apologetic and referred again to the detergent – which, by happy coincidence, had nearly run out. Trevor seemed excessively grumpy this morning.

'Well, I'll show you where the new ones are and you can do the tables again,' he said patronisingly. '*Properly*, this time.'

Jo rolled her eyes and followed her boss back inside. It was only as he threw out his hand to open the store cupboard that she realised what was about to happen. Sure enough, agonisingly slowly, the blankets and coats tumbled onto Trevor's feet and unravelled all over the floor.

'What . . . ?'

'Oh, those old things,' said Jo, feeling inspired. 'I found

them the other day. I thought they could probably do with going to the charity shop.'

Trevor poked around in the pile with his stubby foot. 'Did you indeed? And where did you get them?'

'The back of the cupboard,' Jo said casually. She couldn't actually remember where she'd found them. Last night her mind had been preoccupied and addled.

'Oh, right.' Trevor extracted a beige full-length coat from the muddle. 'So you took it upon yourself to consign my coat, along with other items you found whilst poking around in *my* cupboard, to the charity shop?'

'Er, no, well . . .'

Trevor looked furious. 'I don't like being lied to, Jo.'

She stammered some more but the inspiration had run dry.

'I should warn you that I'm seriously considering your position in this teashop. You've already demonstrated that you're lazy, careless and deceitful, and I'm beginning to think you may have an unhealthy relationship with some of my customers.'

Jo cursed herself for inventing the ridiculous story about the sock. She put on her most apologetic expression and hoped she didn't look too much like the hung-over wreck that she was.

A voice sounded from the front of the shop. 'Hey, anyone in?'

They returned to the shop like a chided schoolgirl and teacher, Jo recognising the smooth, confident tone instantly.

'Ah, hi, Jo. How's things?' Stuart stepped forward, not seeing her warning glare. 'Just popping in for my "freebie". You open yet?'

'Um, er . . .'

'I can answer that,' replied Trevor, stepping out from behind the counter. 'Yes, we're open but no, you can't have your "freebie". This teashop does not offer "freebies".'

Stuart looked a bit taken aback. 'Er, right. I see. Well, I just wanted to leave this for Jo,' he said, depositing what looked like a five-pound note on the nearest table. 'See you later.'

Like a crab, he sidestepped out of the café and disappeared.

Trevor looked at Jo. '*That* is exactly what I'm talking about.'

Jo nodded feebly. It seemed fairly pointless to protest.

'Well?' squeaked Trevor, nostrils flaring. 'What are you waiting for?'

Jo wasn't waiting for anything, but presumably that wasn't the correct response.

'I suppose I should give that table a good scrub . . .'

'You should do no such thing. Get out. You've had your last chance. I don't want to see you in here again. I'll find someone else. Someone honest. Someone who can do things properly. I should've known there'd be trouble as soon as you said you were *foreign*.'

Jo hastened towards her bag of possessions on the counter, trying to work out a line of defence but distracted by the irony of her boss's last comment. She couldn't think straight. It wasn't just the alcohol in her bloodstream or the fact that Trevor was waving his flabby arms at her, exposing his sweat patches; it was the fact that she didn't *want* to form a defence. She needed a job because she needed the money, but that wasn't enough of a reason for her to stick around.

'And because I'm an honest man,' he went on, still smouldering, 'I'll pay you for the week. It's more than you deserve.' He grudgingly handed over a brown envelope.

Jo didn't speak. She had nothing to say. With a final glance at the nasty plastic seats and the flowery café walls, she walked out, picking up Stuart's fiver as she left.

Chapter Eleven

She had walked for a couple of hours before Jo remembered to look in her pocket. When she did, despite her situation and despite her pulsating head, she smiled. It was an old five-pound note. Clearly Stuart had intended to use it to pay for his coffee. Across the front, in red biro, he had scribbled five words: 'Dinner Thurs? The Grange, 8 p.m.'

Jo didn't know whether to feel flattered by his chivalry or amused by the man's presumptuousness. Clearly, Stuart was assuming that she'd accept the invitation. There was no phone number, no alternative, no information about where The Grange was or what type of place it was. The only thing Jo could glean from the note was a confirmation of something she had already suspected: Stuart was full of himself.

She stuffed the note in her wallet, then pulled out the envelope and transferred her week's wages across. A hundred and eighty pounds. A hundred and eighty much-needed pounds. Jo still had over a hundred from Joe Simmons' original stash, but she knew how quickly it would disappear if she couldn't find somewhere cheap to live soon.

She massaged her temples, trying to alleviate the

throbbing pain. She suspected the headache wasn't just a result of yesterday's drinking. The developments of the last few hours were also partly to blame. She was homeless and unemployed – again. Being constantly on the move, or constantly ready to be on the move, was tiring, and the uncertainty of her existence was beginning to wear her down.

In a way, she longed for the stability of a 'normal' life. Every once in a while – like now – she considered turning herself in and reverting to the life of Rebecca Ross. Every time – like now – she rejected the idea on the grounds that, for all she knew, Rebecca Ross's life wasn't 'normal' at all, and even if it had been 'normal', the turmoil of transplanting Jo Simmons back into it didn't bear thinking about.

The houses petered out and she realised she was on a track that led to the turquoise lakes she had seen from Mrs Phillips' guesthouse. *Mrs Phillips*. Jo cringed. Thinking back to the scene in the shop, she wondered whether she might have been a bit harsh on the old lady. Sure, Mrs P had been meddling in something that didn't concern her, but still . . . Jo felt a twinge of guilt. Now she was sober, last night seemed like something of an over-reaction.

The lakes looked unnaturally blue, as though they'd been airbrushed for a holiday brochure. Jo guessed they were the flooded remains of a chalk quarry pit and her mind wandered to other possible industries in the area. What could she do for a living? Was she trained in anything useful? She wondered whether any skills she might have would still apply. If she could add up, could she do other things? Perhaps she was a qualified plumber, she thought, or a doctor or brain surgeon . . . Hmm. She could picture it now: walking into a hospital and offering her services as a neurologist. The irony almost made her smile.

The path veered away from the lakes and took her west in the direction of Abingdon. The sun was high in the sky now; it was probably nine, maybe ten o'clock. Maybe Stuart could help her get a job. He looked like a well-connected young man – if such things could be deduced from the cut of a man's trousers or the whiteness of his teeth. You couldn't own a convertible BMW 3 Series if you didn't know a few people, could you?

The track brought her out on a single carriageway that she took to be the Abingdon ringroad. Jo found herself weaving through a suburban maze of estates punctuated by corner shops and miniature parks.

A group of young men about her age were kicking a ball about in a small patch of grass. Jo stopped by a tree and looked on. To call it football would have been an exaggeration; this was more like watching a bunch of apes jumping around on a giant pinball machine.

'Sanjit, you fat bastard! You could've got that if you'd moved!'

The ball rolled past the goalie at a leisurely pace and came to rest a few metres from where Jo stood. The goal-keeper, a rounded young man with sloping shoulders and a Roman nose, lumbered towards it. Jo stepped forward, rolled the ball onto the top of her foot and flicked it back to the man.

It was a couple of seconds later, when the wolf-whistles from the small Asian guy in the England shirt had died down, that Jo stopped to think about what had happened. She had flicked the ball up and booted it back into the game, as if . . . as if it were the most natural thing in the world.

Surely that wasn't normal? Surely not everyone could do that – especially not many *women*?

A tall young man with a side parting and alarmingly short white shorts looked over. 'Sorry about him,' he shouted. 'Doesn't get out much.' He rolled his eyes in a way that was clearly designed to make him look more mature than his friends. Unfortunately, at that exact moment the ball came plummeting down on his head.

'Stop flirting, Henry,' yelled England man, clearly pleased with the accuracy of his shot.

Finally the ball was controlled and the game of pinball resumed. Jo stayed put for a moment, contemplating her apparent skills. She had kicked the ball. But not just in a lucky, kick-it-and-see way. She had rolled it from stationary onto the top of her foot, lifted it into the air and launched it at exactly the angle she'd intended.

The haphazard game continued, the score-line developing as predictably as a lottery draw. Sanjit was hopelessly inept at stopping the ball, despite taking up most of the space between the two piles of jumpers. That didn't matter much, though, because the guy at the other end, who was wearing what looked like a fisherman's hat, was equally lacking in skills.

There was a small amount of talent on the pitch, thought Jo, admiring the man nearest her manoeuvre around the wolf-whistler with the relative skill of a professional. He was tall, like the well-spoken guy, but with less of a belly and – if the shorts were anything to go by – more of a sense of style. He dribbled the ball up the wing and sent it straight between the legs of the fisherman, who looked as though he was sitting on an invisible toilet.

'Wanna play?' asked the scorer, jogging halfway to where

87

Jo was standing. He had spiky blond hair and chiselled features that were glistening slightly with sweat.

Jo hesitated. Running about seemed like a good hangover cure, but she still wasn't convinced by her newfound ability. It could have been a fluke. A lucky kick. She wanted to test out her theory, but she wasn't sure she wanted an audience while she did so – especially not this fit guy with his blue eyes and sexy smile.

'Come on. We're two against three.'

As he said this, the fisherman attempted a drop kick and managed to send the ball behind his head onto the main road.

Jo nodded. 'All right then.' She dumped the plastic bag under a tree and tied her hair in a ponytail. 'I'm Jo.'

'Matt,' the fit guy replied. 'You're on my team, with Sanjit.' He nodded at the rotund goalkeeper, who waved back like a clown. 'On the other team there's Raj –' he pointed at England shirt – 'Henry –' he motioned to the man in tight shorts who gave a little bow – 'and Kieran.'

Kieran came running back from the main road and attempted to head the ball back into the game. It was a reasonable effort, thought Jo, considering the hat.

'OK, ready?' yelled Raj, clearly keen to show off his footwork.

Jo found herself taking the left side of the pitch. Passing and dribbling, she and Matt worked together and quickly turned the game into an exercise of shooting practice against poor Kieran, who was still searching for a technique that worked. Henry and Raj darted about randomly, confounded by the new opposition but unable to bring themselves to admit that they were losing because of a girl.

It felt good – not just because Jo was running around, winning the ball from Raj, scoring goals and clapping hands with the gorgeous Matt. It felt good because it felt *instinctive*. She didn't have to think about it. Despite not remembering the exact circumstances, Jo knew she had been here before. She'd been a midfielder. She'd been on a team she was proud of. Football had been a part of her life.

Eventually Raj held up his hand. 'OK, next goal wins,' he yelled, and proceeded to kick the ball straight past Sanjit's stationary limbs. Jo looked across at Matt. He winked at her and smiled.

'Bravo! Good game, all,' cried Henry, clapping Raj on the back as they wandered round picking up goalposts.

Jo was nursing a blister on the sole of her foot – a consequence of playing in eight-pound Choice Buys plimsolls – when the questions started.

'So, where d'you play usually?' Matt rubbed his face with the fabric of his T-shirt, revealing a perfect six-pack underneath.

'Er . . . left wing,' she said, trying to stay focused.

'No, I meant what club – where do you train?'

'Oh, er, right.' Jo shook her sock. It was a good question. 'Well, I used to play for a team in London, but I've just moved here so I'm not really playing, er, properly.'

Henry gasped in mock offence. 'What, you mean you don't call this "proper"?'

Jo smiled and carefully pulled her sock back on. The pain shot up from the circle of exposed pink flesh.

'Thanks for the game, anyway. Ow.'

'Any time. It's nice to have someone who scores.'

Raj looked a bit put out. 'She didn't score *all* the goals.'

'Hey, you should swap numbers with one of us,' suggested Matt. 'We're here most Saturdays, sometimes weeknights too.'

There was a rustling noise as all five young men reached for their mobile phones.

Jo smiled. 'Actually, I don't have a number at the moment.'

They all looked at her as though she'd claimed to be without arms.

'I'm sort of . . . between numbers. Between houses . . .'

'Between jobs?' suggested Sanjit.

'Yeah, as it happens.'

'What field of work?' asked Matt as they headed towards the edge of the park.

Shit. Again, she was unprepared. Jo tried to think up a plausible story that wouldn't command too many follow-up questions. Using the actress line on these guys would be suicidal. Annoyingly, though, her brain was buzzing from the football and she could only think of silly responses like bull fighter and inventor and sky-diving instructor.

'Instructor . . .' she found herself mumbling. Then for some reason she added, 'of kids.'

'Isn't there a name for that?' quipped Raj. 'Aren't they called teachers?'

Jo rolled her eyes as though she heard that joke every time. 'I'm not a teacher,' she replied. 'I kind of help children . . . do stuff.'

She was desperately trying to think of something else to say when Matt came to her rescue.

'I know what you mean,' he said. 'You're a support worker, aren't you? A kind of mentor.'

'Yes! Exactly.' Jo nodded fervently, slightly concerned that Matt knew so much about her supposed career. 'A mentor.'

'I work at Dunston's in Oxford,' Matt explained. 'I don't actually work with the kids – I do the marketing and press and that.'

'Saint Matt,' muttered Raj under his breath.

Matt casually stuck his foot out and tripped him up. 'And what is it you do these days?'

'I'm an entrepreneur,' Raj replied stiffly. 'Anyway, see you next week.'

He cut down a side street at the edge of the park and disappeared with an impressively large swagger for someone so small. Matt laughed quietly.

Kieran stopped walking, all of a sudden, and stuck out his hand. 'Nice to meet you, Jo.'

Jo shook it, surprised by the sudden formality. He seemed like quite a peculiar young man.

'Where are you going?' asked Matt. 'We, er . . . we live together, don't we?'

'I need to buy some flowers,' Kieran explained.

'*Flowers?*'

'Yes. I like flowers.'

Matt looked perplexed but didn't push it. 'OK. Well, see you later then. Jo, which way are you heading?'

Jo picked a direction at random, which by happy co-incidence was the way Matt seemed to be going. They left Henry and Sanjit at a bus stop and set off up the road together.

'So, how d'you all know each other?' asked Jo, keen to keep the topic of conversation away from herself.

'I went to school with Sanjit, who knew Kieran from

uni. Raj is some sort of distant relative of Sanjit's, and Henry . . . well, he just appeared one day and started poncing around. He's all right. They call him Tim Nice But Dim.'

Jo smiled. For the first time since arriving in Oxfordshire, she was having a conversation with someone her own age – and not having to do too much lying. It might have been partly the exercise, but she felt almost relaxed around Matt.

'Watch out for Henry,' he warned. 'He's a real charmer. Got a way with the ladies . . . Or at least, that's what he reckons.'

'Mmm, must be those shorts.' Jo laughed. Talking to Matt reminded her of something. Someone.

'And Raj probably thinks he's in there too. He's the *entrepreneur*.'

'Oh yes,' said Jo, straight-faced. 'I've never met an entrepreneur before. Did you say he's related to Sanjit?'

'I don't think they have many genes in common. Sanjit's the laziest git in the world and Raj has ADHD. But then, Sanjit's dad owns the patent to some sort of satellite widget that means he'll never have to work in his life, so I guess that explains it.'

Matt reached into his pocket to pull out a set of keys, and with a sense of disappointment Jo realised they were standing outside his flat. Suddenly, the image crystallised and a scene started playing out in her mind.

She had seen fragments of it before, she realised: first when she'd run into the man outside the post office, then again when she'd gone drinking in Oxford. It could have been a daydream or some weird trick of the mind, but now she felt certain it wasn't.

She was in somebody's bedroom. Maybe hers. The details of the room weren't clear but she knew she was sitting on a bed. A guy with blond hair was standing over her, looking at her, arguing. He was crying. She might have been crying too, Jo couldn't tell. All she knew was that it was her fault. She was hurting him.

For several days now, Jo had tried to reassemble the scene, enhance the images, hear the words . . . but it was impossible. The memory wasn't clear enough. It was like trying to complete a jigsaw puzzle with only half the pieces. She didn't know who the guy was, or why she was seeing him now, so clearly.

'Where are you heading?'

Jo forced the blond guy out of her head.

'Into Abingdon.'

It was the truth. She needed to find a place to stay, and a job. It was all very well messing about with footballs, but the fact remained she was in a pretty desperate situation.

'You're going off into the outskirts – you know that?'

'Um . . .' In a moment of rashness, Jo decided to come clean. Well, nearly clean. 'To be honest, I'm a bit lost. I need to find a B&B for the night. I had a bit of a . . . a problem with the place where I was supposed to be staying.'

'So you really are between houses?'

Jo nodded.

'Tell me that's not your worldly possessions in there?' He nodded at the carrier bag, smiling.

'Ha!' Jo forced a laugh. 'No. No, the rest is with . . . with a friend back in London. This is just, er, some stuff. Toothpaste, knickers, you know . . .'

'Oh, right.' He raised an eyebrow and Jo wished she

hadn't mentioned the knickers. 'Well, I'm not too hot on B&Bs. If it was social housing you were after, I'd be full of ideas, but . . .'

Jo's expression clearly revealed her ignorance.

'Dunston's,' he explained. 'That's what we do. Get people off the streets and into housing.'

Jo closed her mouth. 'Yes, obviously.'

'Ooh, I know. What are you after, posh and expensive or cheap and cheerful?'

'Cheap and cheerful,' Jo replied quickly. She hoped she wasn't coming across as too much of a loser.

'Good. That means less of a walk.'

Matt led her up his road and along a perpendicular street where the purpose-built flats turned into tall, rambling Victorian houses that looked significantly more run-down. Jo's attempts at thanking her guide were brushed aside.

'I'm not missing much. I'd only be waiting for Kieran to come home and keep me amused with his flower arrangements.'

Jo laughed. 'He seems quite, er . . . unique.'

'He's special, that's for sure. Twenty-three, going on twelve.' Matt slowed to a halt and led her through a set of white gateposts. 'So, here we are. Don't expect too much.'

The hostel turned out to be perfectly adequate. Run like a B&B but with none of the dusty ornaments or potpourri, it was basic but clean. The man in charge seemed to know Matt and offered Jo a discounted rate of twenty pounds a night.

'D'you wanna take down my number, in case you're bored enough to want another run-around next week?'

Jo shrugged casually, wondering whether Matt was

single. Then she stopped her thoughts right there. There were so many reasons why she shouldn't let herself fall for this guy. She didn't know a thing about him, for a start, and he certainly didn't know her. And if they did ever get close then she'd either have to tell him the truth – which was way too dangerous – or live a permanent lie. And it was too soon to be thinking like that, anyway – not to mention the fact that she was seeing another man in a few days.

'Thanks,' she said, taking the scrap of paper. 'I'll call you in the week.'

Chapter Twelve

It was amazing the difference you could make using only free samples and testers, thought Jo, dipping her finger deep into the pot of lip gloss then wandering casually down the aisle. She applied the finishing touches whilst browsing hair removal creams, so as not to arouse suspicion with the Boots security guards.

According to the tattered phone book she'd found in the guesthouse, The Grange was a restaurant in central Oxford. It was tucked down a cobbled side street that Jo walked past several times before noticing. When she eventually did, it was still only ten to eight so she went for a longer walk to make herself late.

She hadn't meant to start drinking; it was just that the gaggle of girls coming towards her had looked faintly familiar and the glow of the deserted pub had seemed welcoming. And yes, her nerves were playing up too; she hadn't been on a date since . . . well, she didn't know.

Frankly, thought Jo, tipping back the glass and enjoying the familiar burning sensation in her throat, she deserved a drink. She hadn't had one in nearly a week (not counting the odd sip from the bottle of vodka beside her bed). Hunting for jobs with no qualifications and no CV was thirsty work.

Jo had resigned herself to a career as a waitress or barmaid or assistant – something involving no particular skills. But even that was proving difficult. The cafés in Abingdon were welcoming enough but they all seemed to be staffed with sixty-somethings who could (and sometimes did) serve soup and rolls in their sleep and who showed no signs of planning to move on. The sports centre, the library and several bars in town had sent her away with a smile and a patronising promise to call her if anything came up.

Jo spotted her date as soon as she crept through the doors. Dressed in a cream shirt with the top buttons casually undone, Stuart looked like an aftershave model. His hair, with its flat top and coating of gel, looked almost plastic in its perfection. Jo felt instantly ashamed of her charity-shop attire.

'Hey,' he said, rising from his seat and kissing her on each cheek. 'Fashionably late.'

Jo nodded bashfully. It ruined the aura somewhat, she thought, having someone point it out.

'What are you drinking?'

'Er . . .' Jo sat down, hoping he couldn't smell the alcohol on her breath. 'Wine? Please.'

Stuart made a hand gesture that sent a waiter gliding up to their table as though on runners.

A wine menu appeared between them. Jo made it clear that she wasn't getting involved in the decision, but that didn't stop Stuart muttering, 'Louis Latour Puligny Montrachet? Veuve Clicquot Rosé? Bestue Santa Sabina?'

Jo shrugged.

'Is red OK? Ooh, that looks good. Bodegas Luis Cañas Reserva Seleccíon de la Familia.' Stuart looked up at the patient waiter. 'Yes, we'll go for that.'

Jo watched him snap shut the menu. She had guessed correctly: he was full of himself. Sexy, but a little bit arrogant.

'So, everything going well at the teashop then?'

Jo grimaced. 'Er . . . well, no. Not exactly.'

'I didn't get you in too much trouble, did I?' He grinned cheekily.

'Well, I think I was already in trouble,' Jo replied. 'But you were the clincher.'

'Really? The clincher? Me? Oh God. I'm sorry.' He leaned back as the waiter returned with the wine and poured some with great panache into Stuart's glass. Swilling it for quite some time, Stuart took a sip and proclaimed it 'OK', without looking at the waiter.

'I had no idea I was the clincher,' he went on.

The waiter filled Jo's glass and topped up Stuart's.

'Don't feel bad,' said Jo, wondering whether he actually did. He seemed to be rather enjoying his guilty act. 'I had it coming. The boss was just telling me how he was worried about my "unhealthy relationship with some of the customers" when you walked in and asked for a freebie.'

Stuart pulled a look of mock horror. 'Oops. Oh dear. Cheers, by the way.' He tapped his glass against Jo's.

The menu was one of those cryptic ones with phrases like 'bourride of brill with rouille and Gruyère' and 'foie de volaille mousse with Madeira'. Jo decided to go by price and opt for something mid-range for each of the courses.

'You're not allergic to shellfish then,' said Stuart.

Jo laughed frivolously and wondered what she'd asked for. Allergies. That was a point. The thought hadn't even crossed her mind.

'So, what will you do now?' asked Stuart, when Jo finished explaining about the fiasco in Trev's Teashop.

The wine was slipping down too quickly. Jo tried to reduce the frequency of her sips. 'I'm looking for something else. Any ideas?' She was only half joking.

He clicked his teeth. 'Not really my line of work.'

'Oh, yeah? And what *is* your line of work?'

He waited to catch her eye. 'Have a guess.'

'Well . . . you work from home a lot and you drive a nice car . . . And you dress well . . .' She looked him up and down. 'And you're good with people . . .'

'Am I?' Stuart smiled back coyly. 'Jo, it almost sounds as though you're flirting with me.' He raised an eyebrow.

Jo looked down at her wine, embarrassed.

'I'm not always good,' he went on, unabashed. 'But then, nobody's good all the time.' He fixed her a meaningful stare. 'So, what am I?'

Jo waited for her cheeks to stop burning. She hadn't meant to flirt; it had just sort of happened.

'Jo?'

'You're a property developer,' she said, plucking something out at random that sounded suitably unflattering.

He frowned. 'Nope.'

'Um . . .' Jo shrugged helplessly, 'insurance broker.'

He looked offended this time. 'No. Try again.'

Jo smiled, lightening up again. 'Helicopter pilot. Fireman. Farmer.' This was more fun than inventing her own career. 'Hairdresser. Oh, I know, you're a stunt double!'

'OK. Now it's gonna be a real anticlimax.' Stuart allowed the waiter to present the starters. Jo looked down and saw a mass of rubber tubing on her plate. 'I'm retired.'

Jo screwed up her nose. 'What?'

'I was a trader until just over a year ago, then I quit while the going was good. Well, goodish.'

'What . . . You don't work *at all* any more?' Jo wondered how much money the man had managed to put away. Two million, she reckoned, at least.

Stuart cut into his sliver of salmon. Jo wished she'd been better able to read the menu. 'I do a bit of consulting to keep myself busy, but other than that I play golf, go to the gym, entertain beautiful ladies . . .'

Ladies, Jo noted. Plural. She wasn't sure what to make of that. 'What sort of consulting?'

'Well, people consult me to ask where they should put their money. I do a little voodoo dance, throw a few sticks on the ground and give them their answer.'

Jo laughed, pushing the chewy rings around her plate. At least the lettuce was recognisable. Stuart continued to talk, somehow making his vacuous life sound quite interesting. Jo felt like a contestant on some awful life-swap reality TV show: here she was dining with a multimillionaire while only a few nights ago, she had been sleeping on a café floor.

'Same again?' asked Stuart, holding up the empty bottle.

'How did that happen?' asked Jo, pretending to be shocked by their rate of consumption. She really had to slow down.

The main courses arrived, in Jo's case, giant prawns and some unidentifiable sea-dwelling creatures with shells, and Stuart steered the conversation back round to her.

'So, what are your prospects like?'

'Prospects?'

'Prospects of finding another job.'

'Oh. Well, I was thinking of going into financial consulting. What d'you reckon?'

He smiled, filling her glass from the new bottle. 'I think I'd have to assess your tribal dancing skills. There's more to it than meets the eye, you know.'

Jo laughed. 'Maybe later. No, actually, I'm not sure I'll find another waitressing job. There doesn't seem to be much demand for them in Abingdon.'

'Abingdon?'

'Well, Abingdon or Radley. I moved to Abingdon last weekend. My other place . . . didn't work out.'

Stuart shook his head. 'Radley's loss. So what will you do? I mean, what happens in waitressing circles? Are there agencies, that sort of thing?'

Jo knew she was being patronised. 'You know, waitressing isn't my *career*.'

'Oh?' Stuart looked intrigued. Clearly he'd taken her for a dumb, tea-serving bimbo – which, in a way, she was.

This time, Jo was prepared. 'I work in cafés to fill in the gaps. My real job is working with kids. I'm a . . . a mentor.'

At least this one she thought she could pull off without coming unstuck. It wasn't like saying she was an astronaut or a vet. You couldn't ask tricky questions about working with kids.

'Where did you train? My mate's girlfriend is a child psychologist.'

Bollocks. 'London, um . . . University . . .'

'Oh. She went to Manchester.'

Jo managed to mumble something and had another go at dissecting the creatures on her plate. They seemed to be all shell and no flesh, and the strange twisted utensil she'd been given didn't seem to help in the slightest.

'Is that where you were before, then? Try pulling the head off first.'

Jo couldn't see anything that looked like a head. She yanked the animal in half and tried to work out which was edible. 'Sorry, what?'

'London. Were you in London before you came here?'

'Oh. Yes.' Result. There seemed to be a tiny piece of soft grey tissue amongst the debris.

'So, you moved from a mentoring job in London to a teashop in Radley?'

Jesus. The meat was disgusting. Jo washed it down with some wine and tried to straighten her thinking. Her behaviour did seem a bit odd, when he put it like that.

'I thought I'd got this job sorted in Radley, so I found a place to live. Then the job fell through and I was already settled, so I thought, well, why don't I find another job?'

A piece of fishy gristle flew across the restaurant.

Stuart nodded, politely ignoring her ineptness. 'Right. And then you moved again.'

'Right.' Oh dear. This wasn't sounding at all plausible. Jo gave up on her main course and had one last go at explaining.

'I moved to Radley for one job, which fell through, but once I'd moved I thought I'd find another job nearby, so I moved again, but then that fell through.'

'The job or the place?'

'The place. No, the job.' Jo was utterly confused. 'Um, can we talk about something else?'

Stuart laughed. He speared his last mouthful of steak and offered it across to Jo. She bit into it gratefully. It tasted delicious.

'So, whereabouts did you live in London?'

Jo made the steak last as long as she could, hoping

desperately that a vivid memory of some part of London might leap into her head. 'West,' she said, when it didn't.

'Anywhere near Ealing? I used to live in South Ealing.'

Jo puffed out her cheeks as though trying to remember the local geography. 'Not far, I guess. I was a bit further out – a place called . . .' Shit. 'West Ham.'

'West Ham? That's East.' Stuart frowned.

'West Ham-*ly*', she corrected, quite credibly she thought. What was the logic behind West Ham being in East London?

'Never heard of it. Dessert?'

Jo didn't want to take any more risks with the indecipherable menu so she shook her head and finished off the wine. Stuart asked for the bill and seemed to forget all about the West Hamly thing, conveniently for Jo, who was rapidly losing track of her lies.

The waiter swooped back with the bill, then swooped off again with Stuart's card tucked neatly inside. Jo wondered how much it had come to. She probably would have got a more substantial meal in the Burger King down the road, but this had been an experience. A good experience, she thought as she set off for the bathroom. Tonight had been enlightening.

'Bit of a worry,' said Stuart, when she returned. 'They've still got my card.' He gave a look of mock concern. 'I might go and hunt down our man.'

He darted off, heading for the cluster of waiters who were doing just that – waiting.

Stuart was still complaining to the head honcho when their original waiter appeared at the table with the little machine in his hand. Jo leaned over and took a peek. She guessed it would have come to over a hundred pounds, probably nearer two hundred. But it was something else that caught her eye.

Even though her vision was blurry, Jo was fairly sure she wasn't mistaken. Embossed on the gold card sticking out of the reader were the characters, 'MR & MRS S. THO—'

Stuart returned to the table, glanced crossly at the waiter and punched in his PIN. Jo watched him through suspicious, drunken eyes. Surely he wasn't married? There must be some other explanation. Maybe he was separated and using an old card. Maybe it wasn't his card. Although, strictly speaking, that would make him a thief, which wasn't particularly reassuring either.

Jo wrestled with explanations as he fished in his wallet for the tip. She tried to cast her uncertainty aside, but it gnawed away at her. She had felt like this before. She recognised the mix of feelings: helplessness, hope, hurt, disbelief. It was all horribly familiar.

She tried to remember what had happened before. It was a man who had betrayed her, definitely. But the betrayal had hurt her more than this one. The man had meant something to her. It wasn't the blond guy from the other flashbacks; this was someone else. Someone harder. Meaner. He didn't even seem to be sorry – only angry at being found out. Jo had discovered something about him. Not another woman, she thought, something else. It was hazy, but she could see it now. They were outside. She was confronting him. All he could do was shout, in that horrible way . . . with that accent . . .

'Shall we go?'

Jo snapped to. 'Er, yeah.'

'Fancy a drink in Oxford, or d'you want to head back to the village?'

She hesitated. Stuart looked so sweet, so open, so kind. Surely he wasn't a cheat. It seemed totally implausible. But then . . .

'I wanna head back.' She got up to leave. 'There's a bus back at half ten, I think.'

'Bus?' Stuart frowned. 'God, I didn't know they still had those things.'

She followed him out. Silly Jo. Of course they wouldn't be getting a bus. Men who retired at thirty didn't use public transport.

The taxi seemed to be taking them via Abingdon, which was convenient, but Jo felt sure she hadn't told Stuart where she lived.

'What did you tell the driver?'

Stuart turned in his seat and let one arm casually drop down to behind her head. 'There's a bar just opened on the high street called Zebra. Thought we could go there for one or two. Or three. Or ten. That's where you're living now, right?'

Jo wasn't sure about this. She wanted to believe that Stuart was single, that he thought of her as something more than just a cheap date. But the credit card had thrown her. She felt drunk and confused.

'Sorry.' She shook her head. 'I think I'd better call it a night.'

'Nightcap at yours, then.' It was a statement, not a question. Stuart's arm slipped down so his hand was touching her shoulder. He moved closer, and she could see his eyes.

They were lovely eyes, she had to admit. But there was something she wasn't quite comfortable with here. And besides, showing Stuart her twenty-pound-a-night hostel bedroom with its single bed and grimy wash basin, and

105

then offering him a swig of her white label vodka, just wasn't worth contemplating.

'I can't.'

'Come on, Jo.' His hand slid up into her hair. 'Just one. I feel like we're only just getting to know one another.'

Jo slithered sideways, out of his reach. They were already in Abingdon, she realised, on a road that looked very much like the one with the hostel.

'I'll get out here.'

Stuart released his seatbelt and moved over to her side of the cab, putting one hand on her thigh and squeezing it.

'Don't. Just one drink.'

Jo tried to push him away but he didn't seem to notice. She leaned forward and tapped on the driver's partition window. 'Can you stop here, please?'

She opened the door before the cab had even stopped moving.

'I've gotta go. Sorry.' She jumped out.

It wasn't obvious which way to go, but Jo decided on left and marched off. It looked like the right road, she thought, but then one road looked much like another around here, especially after all that wine . . . and the distinctive white gateposts of the hostel were nowhere to be seen. With a feeling of dread, Jo heard a crunching sound behind her.

'Jo.'

She looked round. Stuart was catching up with her.

'I don't have your number,' he said. 'I want to see you again.'

She kept walking. Surely the hostel was somewhere along here on the right.

'Give me your number.'

Jo stopped, but only to glare at him. Nobody ordered her around like that.

Stuart stepped towards her. 'Come on . . .' He reached out and put a hand on her arm. Then quite quickly, he put his other hand on her waist and pushed her backwards against a low fence. She was trapped.

'Stuart, no,' Jo said calmly, betrayed by the quiver in her voice.

'Quick kiss good night,' he said, breathing wine fumes on her face. Close up, he seemed more drunk: swaying, eyes wandering all over her body. Jo tried to wriggle free but his grip tightened around her waist. Despite her fear, there was something else on her mind. Another memory. Indistinct though it was, she could picture a scene just like this somewhere else.

'Let go of me,' she said weakly.

'I wanna see you again.' His lips moved towards hers. 'And I think you wanna see me too.'

She shook her head, bending backwards at an unfeasible angle to avoid the kiss. As she fought, she remembered where this had happened before. It was in the club, with the man who had betrayed her. He'd been just as angry, and Jo had felt just as scared.

'I could see it in your eyes at dinner,' he slurred, bearing down on her. 'That look. That come-on. You want it too, I know it.'

Jo couldn't speak; she could hardly breathe. What look? What come-on? She forced the memory to dissolve, turning her face sideways as he made another lunge for her face. Out of the corner of her eye, she noticed something. It was on the opposite side of the road to where

107

she'd expected, but it was unmistakable. Tall and white, standing out in the darkness, were two gateposts.

For a moment she allowed Stuart's tongue to work its way into her mouth, hot and slimy. His breath stank. She felt his hands loosen around her waist, one sliding up her back and onto her neck. Then she slipped sideways and ran.

She could hear his breath and his footsteps behind her, at first in the distance but getting closer. She looked back, but her hair whipped into her eyes and it was all she could do to keep running. Her shoes were working their way undone, bringing back the half-formed memory of her escape from the club.

'Jo! Come back!'

He was only a few metres behind her. Jo reached for the gatepost and swung round it, fumbling for the key on her wallet. She felt giddy and sick. He was on the driveway. She could hear his panting get louder as she stabbed at the lock, where, thanks to a miracle, the key slid in first time and let her in.

Exhausted, she slammed the hostel door shut and caught her breath. Then she remembered something else. She'd seen it earlier but hadn't registered. As Stuart had ferreted about in his wallet for a tip, there had been something else in there. Something shiny, like a gold coin but smoother. And hollow. She'd been too preoccupied with the credit card to think about it, but now she realised. It was a wedding ring.

Chapter Thirteen

Tap-tap-tap-tap. Silence. *Tap-tap-tap-tap*. Silence.

Jo woke from a restless sleep and stared at the ceiling. The events of the previous night filled her mind almost immediately.

Tap-tap-tap-tap.

She thought about getting up and investigating the irritating noise but decided she'd rather put up with it. Running away from a married man and barricading herself in a hostel. That was how her night had ended. Jo cringed. How had she got herself into such a mess?

Tap-tap-tap-tap. It was getting louder.

She reached down the side of the bed and pulled out her notebook. Last night's entry was an almost illegible, drunken scrawl.

> Someone betrayed me – WHO? Not the blondy. Funny accent.
> Did something that hurt me.

Tap-tap-tap-tap. 'Miss Simmons?'

Jo let the book fall shut and propped herself up in bed.

Today was another day. There were other things to think about. For a start, she had to find a job.

Tap-tap-tap-tap. 'Are you there, Miss Simmons? Can you open up?'

Jo started. That was her name. She pulled the duvet up over her and looked around for her clothes. 'Who is it?' she croaked.

'It's Gaz. Hostel manager.'

His voice sounded urgent, she thought, wondering what on earth could be pressing enough for the hostel manager to wake up a guest first thing in the morning. Heavy-headed, Jo pulled on her crumpled clothes and opened the door.

'What's up?'

Gaz stepped back into the hallway and beckoned for her to follow. 'I'll show you what's up.'

Jo stumbled along the corridor after him and down the stairs, utterly perplexed.

'That,' said the man, leading her into the small open space that served as the reception area for the hostel, 'is what's up.'

Jo followed his gaze to the floor, where the sweet Slovakian girl who cleaned the rooms was sweeping shards of glass into a dustpan. A draught swept through the place and Jo realised that one of the panes in the front door was missing.

'Oh dear. Looks like you've had a break-in,' she said, not sure what this had to do with her. 'I hope nothing was taken.'

Gaz shook his head. 'No. It wasn't a break-in. It was a disturbance. Caused by you.'

Jo frowned, not liking the manager's accusing tone. 'I'm

110

sorry, I think there's been a mistake. I didn't know anything about this until now. I've been—'

'We know what happened,' he growled. 'Several guests heard the noise and saw what was going on. Your man tried to break in through the front door.'

'What? My . . . What . . . ?' Jo was confused. Gaz was presumably referring to Stuart, who might well have been seen approaching the hostel. But *breaking in*?

'Please don't argue, Miss Simmons. Several guests saw. You were having a row with your fellow outside and when you came in, he tried to follow you.'

Jo opened her mouth to protest, but realised she had nothing to say. She didn't know what had happened once she'd run upstairs to her room. It was quite possible that Stuart, in a drunken rage, had tried to punch his way in. Jo grimaced. Thank God he hadn't succeeded.

'The glass repair's gonna cost sixty quid,' Gaz told her. 'And I have to tell you, you should be in a double room if you're with someone.'

'I'm – I'm not,' she protested.

'Good, 'cause that was my next point. He's not welcome here.'

'Right, good. So . . .' Jo was trying to ask whether she was being evicted from the hostel.

'Look,' said the manager, his expression mellowing a little, 'I don't wanna kick you out. You're a mate of Matt's, so I know you're sound, but . . .'

Jo could see what he was thinking. The same thing had just occurred to her. Stuart knew where she was. He might come back and cause more trouble.

'I'll pay for the glass,' she said, trying to talk him round. But even as she said it, she knew that wasn't the point.

She had to sort this out herself. 'And for the nights I've stayed. I'll leave today. I'm sorry for all the hassle.'

Unlike the last time, Jo made no sound as she entered the little store. Mrs Phillips was serving a customer and didn't notice her come in.

Jo hadn't walked straight here; she'd made a detour via a shop she wouldn't usually have noticed but which had caught her eye the previous week because of something hanging in the window. The price had been higher than she'd expected – meaning that so far Jo's day had cost her nearly two hundred pounds, what with the broken glass and the hostel room – but she'd bought it anyway.

'Well, look who it is!' cried Mrs Phillips as the customer shuffled off. She clasped her hands together, either in horror or excitement, Jo couldn't tell which. 'It's the surly young actress from London!'

Jo moved uncertainly towards her. She'd forgotten about the actress thing.

'How are you, Jo? Sober?'

Sheepishly, Jo nodded and looked at the floor. 'I'm sorry about the other day.'

Mrs Phillips rolled her eyes. She looked mildly amused, Jo realised with relief.

'You were in quite a state.'

'Yeah.' Jo nodded. 'I'd had a weird day.'

The shopkeeper looked at her knowingly. 'I don't think you should visit him again.'

Jo frowned. 'Him?'

Mrs Phillips smiled, as if they both knew exactly what she was referring to. 'Your young man. The one you were

112

going to live with. I presume that's where you went the other day?'

'Er, yes.' Jo quickly nodded. 'Yes, that's right. Trying to patch things up . . .'

The woman shook her head sadly. 'It's not always possible to go back to how things were, I'm afraid. Sometimes you just have to draw a line.'

Jo nodded wryly, wondering how to ask the question. She reached down for the small plastic bag, which she'd tied in a knot at the top in an effort to replicate wrapping paper.

'I got you something. A sort of "sorry" present.'

'Oh, a "sorry" present!' Mrs Phillips laughed and took the bag. 'What is it?' She pulled the gift out of the plastic and gave a little squeal.

'You might hate it,' Jo warned, sceptically eyeing the cat-shaped watering can.

'Well, I don't!' Mrs Phillips cried indignantly. 'It's lovely! Thank you! I can use it out the back on my geraniums.' She reached out and opened her arms.

It was a bit like hugging a pile of Jenga bricks, thought Jo, carefully wrapping herself around the elderly frame. She didn't want to squeeze too hard in case something broke or fell off. But despite her frail physical strength, there was something very strong about Mrs Phillips. Enveloped in her skeletal arms, Jo felt like a child. It was as though this woman, despite her sharp ribs and pointy shoulder blades, had the capacity to protect her. It felt nice. After all the battles she had single-handedly fought in the last few weeks, it was reassuring to know that there was someone else on her side.

'I was wondering . . .' Jo stepped back and looked around her. 'I was wondering whether maybe—'

'Your bed's all made up,' Mrs Phillips cut in.

Jo smiled back awkwardly.

'But I have one condition.'

'OK,' Jo said quickly. She was willing to help in the shop, pay more rent, anything – she'd already thought about all that. Living with Mrs Phillips was better than any other option, by far. She was willing to pay her way.

'You're to stay off the soup.'

'*Soup?*'

'Drink, Jo. Alcohol.' She waggled a finger.

'Oh, right.'

Jo nodded slowly, realising yet again that Mrs Phillips knew more about her than she'd given her credit for. A little part of her felt angry that the old woman was trying to meddle in her life again, but that part was quickly silenced as she acknowledged something else.

Mrs Phillips was right. It was so obvious, now she thought about it – now that somebody else was spelling it out for her. *Sometimes you just have to draw a line.* That was it. She had to draw a line. Roxie or Rebecca or whoever she had once been belonged on one side of the line, with the stripping and drinking and everything else. Jo Simmons was the other side of the line. She had left all that crap behind. Jo Simmons didn't have a drink problem.

'I won't touch a drop.'

Mrs Phillips' face wrinkled into a smile and she held out a key. 'Well, go on then. You know where you're going.'

Chapter Fourteen

The rain had been hammering against the windows all morning. Jo poked her head round the door to the shop.

'Mrs Phillips? Can I use your phone?'

The woman looked up from the tins that surrounded her on the floor. 'Twenty-three. Yes, of course. How's it all going, anyway?'

'How's what going?'

'The job hunt. Or have you already found something?'

Jo hesitated. Now she felt guilty. The phone call she wanted to make wasn't connected to her quest for work – well, it was in a way, but only loosely. She had decided on a change of tack. Finding a cash-in-hand job in Abingdon was proving fruitless. If she was to succeed in starting a new life, Jo had realised, she would have to embark on a *career*. And that meant creating a CV. Which, she knew, would mean inventing a credible past.

'I've got a few options,' she lied. 'Nothing definite yet.'

As Jo climbed back up the stairs to the flat, she heard Mrs Phillips curse and mutter something about losing count. 'Twenty-three!' she yelled down.

She didn't like lying to Mrs Phillips, but it seemed unavoidable. Having set herself up as an out-of-work actress from London, it seemed implausible that she'd want to hang around Radley looking for waitressing work, so Jo had told her landlady that she was on a 'career break' and looking for short-term roles teaching drama in schools. It almost fitted with the lie she'd told the lads.

The phone rang for quite some time before a sleepy voice groaned into the receiver.

'Uyeau?'

Jo looked at the clock. Nine fifty. 'Oh, hi. Sorry. It's Jo.'

There was another grunt and Jo imagined Matt heaving his torso into an upright position.

'I woke you up, didn't I?'

'No! No, I'm awake – been up for ages! I'm . . .' He cleared his throat. His voice was unnaturally deep. 'OK. You got me. Bit of a heavy night last night. How are you?'

'Better than you, by the sound of it. Sorry.'

'Nah, don't worry about it,' he croaked. 'It's Saturday – time to run off the hangover in the park.'

'That's why I was calling. Is football happening?'

'Football always happens!' he cried. 'Ooh. Ow.'

'Have you looked out the window?'

There was a rustling noise. 'Er, oh. Right. Let me rephrase that. Football always happens when it's not pissing down.'

Jo smiled. 'So, not today then?'

'N-no.'

'Oh, well.' Jo tried to hide her disappointment. She'd been looking forward to another game – even though her thighs were still sore from the last one. She wanted a break from the job-hunting. This meant that she would probably end up spending the day in an internet café, adding fabrications to her CV. It also meant that she wouldn't get to see Matt, which, if she was honest, was the biggest letdown. 'See you next week, maybe.'

'Hang on,' said Matt. Jo waited hopefully. 'Let's meet up anyway. In the pub. We often go to the pub instead of the park, if it's raining.'

'OK . . .' She hesitated, wary of appearing too keen in case she accidentally gave off whatever vibe she'd given the adulterous Stuart. 'Which one?'

'King's Arms, opposite the entrance to the park. I'll see if the others are up for it. They'll be needing a hair of the dog if they're feeling anything like I am.'

'Cool,' she said, feeling a little apprehensive. The pub implied alcohol. But she couldn't turn down the opportunity to meet up. She'd have to force herself not to drink. 'Eleven o'clock?'

'Uh . . .' There was a crashing sound. 'Ow. Yeah. Good plan.'

Jo set off early and stopped at the café that offered free internet access to all paying customers. She settled at one of the terminals with a KitKat and a glass of tap water.

Saskia Dawson
Yesterday at 15.36
Your login
  Hey Rox! Here u go:
  Username rebeccaross99@hotmail.com
  Pw roxie
  Don't leave it on a bus or whatever u dozy bint! xx

Jo hurriedly logged out and then logged back in using her new – or old – account details. This was it. This was where she discovered who Rebecca Ross really was.

Except it wasn't.

Sure, she found out that Rebecca – or Becky, as most of her friends seemed to call her – was twenty-four years old and had a hundred and eighty-nine 'friends'. She discovered that she was a member of the London network and several football-related groups. She deduced that her favourite film was *Bend It Like Beckham* and that, if the photos were to be believed, she had a habit of going out dressed in not much more than a band of elastic and had at some point been on a holiday to southern Spain. But she didn't discover who Rebecca Ross was, because nearly all of the comments and pictures and notes on her page were over a year old. She only knew what Rebecca Ross *had been* like.

With a sense of defeat, Jo scrolled through the meaning-less messages and out-of-date events, waiting to spot a name, a face, a word . . . something . . . anything that sparked a recollection. She had hoped that Facebook would open the floodgates, set the memories flowing. But nothing inside her had shifted. It was like looking at somebody else's page.

She slumped forward, looking down, then up. Other than the profile photo, which was quite clearly Jo – smiling, looking young and excitable, and without the red streak in her hair – she recognised nothing. It was almost as if she had left all her old friends behind – for good.

She tried to deduce something useful from all the out-of-date, childish scribbles. There was nobody on Jo's 'friends' list with the same surname as hers, which implied that she had no brothers or sisters, but that wasn't neces-sarily the case. Not everyone was a member of Facebook and people got married and changed their names.

She checked the time. It was quarter to eleven. She bashed out a thank-you note to Saskia then logged off the site, still thinking about what she had seen – and what she hadn't. She went onto Google.

The phrase 'support worker' produced over a million hits, the first of which was a recruitment website specialising in careers in social services. The going rate for support work jobs, it seemed, was twelve pounds an hour. Annual salaries ranged from eighteen to twenty-five thousand – significantly more than a waitress would earn – and the contracts seemed to be full time, unlike the Spanish translation jobs she had seen earlier in the week. There were even some vacancies in Oxfordshire. It may have come about through a lie she'd impulsively told the lads – and she was aware that she was partly pursuing this line just to get close to Matt, which wasn't entirely sensible – but her fictitious profession no longer seemed like such a nutty idea.

She clicked on one of the job descriptions.

Responsibilities include:
- Working with 8–19-year-old children, assessing their needs and setting/maintaining boundaries
- Planning, delivering and reviewing support packages designed to help reduce anti-social behaviour
- Establishing links in the community to identify additional support for young people
- Writing reports for court on progress/lack of progress of young people
  It is essential that you have previous experience working with children with challenging and anti-social behaviour.

It didn't seem that difficult, thought Jo, assuming the boundary maintenance thing was explained and the support packages came prepackaged. The previous experience could prove a bit of an issue, but presumably placements and references could be faked, like everything else. She liked children, as far as she knew. How hard could it be?

She clicked on a few other links and arrived at the websites for various organisations whose primary purpose seemed to be caring for people. She recognised one of the names. 'At Dunston's we help children and young, vulnerable adults to find safety, happiness and success,' read the mission statement.

She had already foreseen the obstacle here. Faking qualifications and experience was a risky business, and one that could ultimately put lives at risk. She didn't want to do that. But the more she browsed, the more she liked the idea of working in a place like Dunston's. It sounded fulfilling and interesting – not like serving lattes and scones. Jo wondered whether her pre-Buffalo Club career had involved caring for children. There were surely positions that didn't involve high-level clearance or qualifications?

She had an idea. Opening another browser, Jo logged back into Facebook.

Rebecca Ross
Today at 10.51
Question
  Hi Saskia,
  Random question: do you know anyone who does care work? Am going for a job – thought you might know!
  Ta! Rx

Jo left the café with a fresh sense of purpose. Waitressing didn't help anybody. She could do more than wipe tables. And it seemed, from her brief trawl of the internet, that there was a variety of jobs that didn't require proper qualifications, so she might be OK. If she was careful, she could solicit the information from Matt. *Jo Simmons the support worker*. It had a nice ring to it.

Four bodies were slumped over a table in one corner of the pub. If Matt had been lying about the fact that they often came here, thought Jo, then he'd done a pretty good job of cajoling his friends into it today. He was propped up on his elbows at the bar and sprang to life as Jo nudged him.

'Sorry! Miles away.'

She smiled. His eyes had dark shadows around them. 'Tired?'

Matt straightened up. 'Nothing a pint can't sort. Oh, I got you the same – that OK?'

'Er . . .' Jo had thought about this on the way here. But she hadn't considered the possibility that the drinks had already been purchased. 'I'm kinda off alcohol for the month.'

'What?' Matt's expression was half-smile, half-frown. 'Some sort of new season resolution?'

Jo nodded. 'Something like that. It's a . . .' *A promise*, she nearly said. But she lost the thread of her sentence.

'A what?'

Jo sniffed the air, trying to work out what had thrown her. She looked over to where the barman was preparing a hot drink and sniffed again. It reminded her of . . . something.

'Sorry.' She leaned across the bar and caught the young man's eye. 'Can you tell me what that is?'

'What, this?' He lifted the brew and more potent vapours wafted over. It was exactly like . . . something. Jo couldn't think what. 'Specialty.'

'Specialty?' echoed Jo, perplexed. Matt was looking at her, equally perplexed.

'Special,' said the man, slowly, as though Jo was a bit dim, 'tea. With whisky, ginger wine and cinnamon. Staves off the autumn lurgy.'

'Oh.' Jo watched as he carried the steaming drink away, inhaling the last of its scent and desperately trying to work out where she'd smelled it before.

'Shall we . . . ?' Matt was motioning for them to carry the drinks over to the lifeless wrecks in the corner.

Jo gave up and switched on a smile. 'Yeah. Sorry.'

She slid the beers across to Henry and Raj, and tried not to watch as they took their first sips. The orange juice tasted weird without vodka and she could feel her intestines rebelling. She forced herself to take a deep breath and turned her attention to the lads.

'So where did you go last night?'

'Good question,' mumbled Henry, supping on his pint. 'Where were we?'

'*Where am I?*' came a muffled cry from the depths of Sanjit's lap.

'We went to Oxford,' explained Matt.

'What was that club?' asked Raj. 'With the dancers? They were *fit*.'

Henry shook his head. 'They weren't *fit*, Raj.'

'And they weren't dancers,' added Matt. 'You had your beer goggles on.'

'They were sixteen-stone drunken munters on a hen do.'

Raj glared at Henry, then Matt. 'They were fit. And I was well in with that blonde one.'

The lads spent some time trying to piece together a unified version of events, but inevitably they all had their own ideas. Everyone perked up considerably as the beers went down, with the exception of Sanjit, who lay with his head on his hands, surfacing occasionally, walrus-style, to slurp his pint.

It was bearable, Jo decided, not drinking. Not easy, but she'd make herself do it.

'It was your break-dancing that got us kicked out.' Matt looked at Kieran.

'No way. Everyone was *loving* my moves.'

'So, what about you?' Matt looked at Jo. 'What have you been up to?'

Jo pretended to think through all the things that had happened in the last week. Actually, what she was doing was wondering how close Matt was to the hostel manager, Gaz, and whether he knew about the incident with Stuart.

'Well, I moved into my new place,' she said, testing the water.

'Oh, yeah? Did Gaz drive you mad at the hostel?'

Jo thought she was probably safe. 'Oh, he was lovely. But it was only ever temporary. I was waiting for this other place to become available.'

'Where is it?' asked Henry.

'Above the little shop on the way into Radley.'

'Great if you get the munchies late at night,' remarked Sanjit from his sleeping position.

'Are you still between jobs and houses and phones and that?' asked Raj.

'Well, sort of. I've got a few options.'

'I can get you one.'

Jo hesitated, wondering what connections Raj had in the field of support work or housing. 'Really?'

'Yeah, like the latest Sony Ericsson with 3G and everything.'

'Oh! Er . . . Could you?'

'Like, unlocked so you can put any SIM in it. I can get you a SIM too, but you'd have to pay for it – but, like, only a fiver or something.'

'How generous,' Matt muttered into his beer.

'Careful,' warned Henry. 'He's only doing it so he can get your number.'

'Fuck off.'

'That's really kind,' said Jo, not seeing much need for a mobile phone but not wanting to offend the guy. 'I might take you up on that.'

'Where are your options?' asked Matt. 'For work, I mean.'

'Oh,' Jo waved a hand as if there were too many to mention. She hadn't done enough research to know the names of any organisations other than his. 'All over. Shall I get a round in?'

She didn't really want to pay for six drinks but she couldn't think of another way to deflect the conversation quickly enough. As it happened, though, she needn't have worried.

'I'm off,' mumbled Sanjit, letting out a loud belch. 'Back to bed. This daylight's not doing me any good.'

Henry nodded. 'Yup, I'm gonna crawl back under the covers too.' He looked around awkwardly. 'Er, *different* covers, obviously.'

'I've gotta go and make a few calls,' said Raj, who was

already looking irritatingly perky. 'See a man about a dog.'

Matt rolled his eyes. 'Lightweights.'

Jo smiled, feeling strangely excited about staying on for another drink with Matt – even if it was an orange juice.

'I'll have another one!' a voice piped up from under the table. Kieran emerged, rubbing his head. 'Just wondering where it was made.'

Matt shot Jo a look that said, *Don't ask.*

'You know, lager is better for the heart,' Kieran pointed out helpfully as Jo set their drinks down on the table.

'Juice is better for the head,' she retorted, secretly proud of her self-restraint.

For a while, the conversation revolved around the seemingly endless supply of idiotic trivia that resided in Kieran's head. Then, just as it seemed they were engrossed in an argument about carbon-based life forms, Matt looked at her. 'You never finished telling us,' he said. 'Where might you work? Not Dunston's?'

'Oh, come on,' whinged Kieran. 'You can't just change the subject! Admit it, I'm right.'

Matt shrugged. 'OK. You're right.'

Jo watched as Kieran tipped back his pint and slammed it down, then stormed off like a sulking child.

'Is that . . . normal?' she asked when he'd gone.

'Normal for Kieran.'

'Right. Um, so, yeah. Nothing from Dunston's, but a couple of other places around Oxford.' Jo waved a hand vaguely, hoping Matt wouldn't ask where.

'Where?'

'Oh . . . Well . . .'

'Did you try Dunston's?'

Jo squinted into the corner of the room. 'No, I don't think so.'

This was exhausting. No sooner had she fended off one question, another was coming at her, full pelt.

'You know we're recruiting? The kids' homes are desperately in need of support workers – especially Fairmont House, where I work.'

'Really?'

'Yeah. Low-clearance ones too. I mean, I'm not sure what qualifications you've got, but . . .'

Jo mumbled something into her glass.

'I could get you an interview tomorrow, if you wanted.'

'Really?' Jo looked up. 'Um, I mean . . . Maybe not that soon,' she said, worrying about her lack of CV and preparation time.

'I didn't mean literally.'

'Oh, right. Well, yeah. I'd love to interview. Is it . . . ?' She tried to think of an intelligent way of asking what a support worker actually *did*. 'Is it a fairly standard role?'

Matt laughed. 'Is there such a thing?'

'Well, quite!' She was none the wiser.

'How about you meet with Geoff, the guy who runs Fairmont House? He's a bit of a dick, but he'll answer all your questions.'

Jo opened her mouth to reply, but nothing came out. She was being handed an opportunity. Matt was showing her the short cut into the career she needed – and wanted. Part of her felt like reaching out and grabbing it with both hands, throwing herself into the rewarding work and enjoying the stability of a full-time job. But the more cautious part of her knew that this was like a lobster trap. Once she stepped in, it would be very difficult to extract herself. Whatever lies she told Dunston's she'd have to tell Matt too, and stick by them for ever.

Matt was looking at her, clearly wondering why such a simple question took so long to answer.

'Er, yeah,' she found herself saying. 'That would be great. Thanks.'

Chapter Fifteen

'So your name is Lindsay McDermott, but you go by the name of Jo Simmons?'

Geoff Ramsay reminded her of George Bush. It was the grey sculpted hair and clumsy awkwardness, and the way his mouth hung in the half-open position when he wasn't speaking.

'Yes. Er . . . a childhood thing, you know . . .' Jo waved a hand vaguely. She was beginning to doubt whether she'd gone about things the right way, using Saskia's dubious connections to get her a name that came with real references. When she had initially agreed to apply for the job, she hadn't envisaged committing identity fraud.

'How strange,' said the woman, leaning forward with a disconcertingly knowing smile. Sue Meads was a wholesome-looking woman with unkempt, fuzzy brown hair that was at odds with her steely tone of voice. 'People don't usually change their *surnames*, as well as their first names.'

'Oh!' Jo gave a nervous laugh. 'No – my surname only changed later. That's a maiden name thing.'

'You mean you're married?' asked the woman, glancing down at Jo's ringless finger.

'No, er, my *mum's* maiden name,' she said, thinking on

the spot. She hadn't anticipated this part of the interview lasting so long. They were six minutes in and still talking about her name. 'She remarried when I was little, so our surname changed to McDermott . . . But then when she split up with him, um, I reverted to my real dad's name. Unofficially. Which is Simmons.'

'Right,' Sue Meads nodded. Geoff Ramsay smiled moronically.

Jo fingered the buttons on her cuffs under the table, anxiously hoping they could now move on. The shirt had been purchased especially for today, but she was getting the distinct impression, looking at Sue Meads' tie-dyed frock and Geoff's Dennis the Menace tie, that her look was too formal for Dunston's.

'Break-ups,' muttered Sue, shaking her head sadly. 'Complicated things . . .'

Jo sat there feeling guilty and wondering what the truth was about her parents. Then finally, Geoff picked up her CV.

'So you went to Manchester and studied . . .'

'Philosophy.' She smiled at the droopy-faced man. The university course had been the work of several hours' thought. A degree was necessary, she felt, because it was an easy way of explaining away three years of her life. Plenty of people went to uni and remembered nothing at the end of it. Philosophy was ideal because it involved lots of free-thinking and not too many facts; there was no way of getting caught out.

'Ah, yes.' The man nodded and tapped the CV in front of him. '"I think, therefore I am." Who said that?'

'Very good, ha!' Jo nodded conspiratorially as though they both knew the answer but didn't need to spell it out.

'Er, so anyway, I've been working at the GDA School in Haringey since then.'

Jo's heart was still fluttering when Geoff asked the next question and she realised she'd got away with it.

'. . . You just fancied a change of scene, did you?'

'Well, yeah,' Jo said casually. She had practised this one. 'To be honest, I'd had enough of London: the noise, the dirt, the stress . . .' It hadn't proved difficult to think up some plausible reasons for leaving the capital city. 'Pollution, knife crime . . .' she went on, reeling off a list of things she'd seen on the tabloid website.

'Were you a victim of knife crime?' asked Sue, blinking at her with a look of horrified concern.

'Er, well, no,' Jo faltered. As far as she knew, she had only read about it on the internet. 'But I was in one of those areas . . . you know. Gangs, rough kids.'

The two interviewees glanced at each other.

'Ha – not that rough kids are anything new to me,' she added hastily.

The woman smiled, which made Jo feel worse. 'Tell us about GDA in Haringey. What was your role there?'

They were back on safe ground. Well, safe-ish. Jo rattled off her description of Lindsay McDermott's job in Haringey, hoping she had picked up all the details from Saskia and her internet research had been up to scratch. She felt awful for lying, but she was in deep now, and there seemed to be no way out except to keep on swimming.

'Well it sounds as though you have all the right operational experience,' said Geoff when she finished outlining how she had improved the lives of a group of young teens with dependency problems. 'And I know Matt will vouch for you as a person.'

Jo nodded, wondering what Matt had told them about her, and whether someone who'd only met her twice could realistically act as a referee. She sensed there was a 'but' coming.

'My only concern is that some of our kids are very . . . how shall I put it? *Unfortunate*. They've been through a lot. Hearing them talk about what's happened to them, it can be quite . . .'

'Harrowing,' Sue Meads put in.

Jo nodded.

'A head-fuck, is what I was going to say, actually,' said Geoff. Jo was beginning to see what Matt meant about the man.

'I think what Geoff is trying to say,' Sue went on, speaking directly to Jo and ignoring the centre manager, 'is that we have to be sure that our employees can cope with what they're dealing with on a day-to-day basis. We look after our staff.'

Jo nodded again. She didn't need any looking after.

'Let me give you an example,' said Sue. 'One of our boys. He's not actually living at Fairmont but he comes to the centre for activities. Twelve years old, he is. His mother is twenty-eight. She's a recovered heroin addict. The father – not his real father – is thirty-six and has just come back from doing two years for GBH. He used to use his son as a punch-bag when drunk. Unsurprisingly, the little boy sees violence as a part of his everyday life. He's been excluded from all four schools in his area for the threat he poses to other pupils. Consequently, he can barely read or write. Do you think you can work with a child like this?'

The woman's watery eyes suddenly looked stern. Jo swallowed.

'I . . .' She was trying to pull together a sentence about how her previous experience would stand her in good stead, but all she could think about was that twelve-year-old and his horrible childhood. 'I think so,' she muttered weakly.

A punch-bag. The woman's words echoed around her head. Surely nobody could do that to a kid. And yet . . . Sue Meads wasn't lying. It was Jo who was lying by nodding and trying to claim she had seen it all before. A sudden fear took hold. She was in way over her head now.

'Good,' said Sue, her face mellow again. 'Because the new activities coordinator may well have this particular boy in his or her group.'

Geoff Ramsay looked at her. 'Forewarned is forearmed,' he said, as though the whole situation was grimly amusing.

'I should probably say,' ventured Jo, 'that I haven't had much experience in dealing with violence.'

Sue smiled sweetly. 'That doesn't matter. The kids' problems aren't physical. They're—'

'They're up here!' Geoff whispered, leaning forward and tapping his head.

Jo noticed Sue shoot him an irritable glance. It seemed incredible that someone so insensitive could be in charge of a place like Dunston's.

'Violence isn't something you should have to deal with in your role,' she went on. 'But if you do ever feel you're in a situation that's beyond your control, you only have to shout. There's a whole network of support. You should never feel alone.'

Jo nodded. She was beginning to like Sue Meads, even though she was slightly scary.

'The way we work—'

'Sue would be your line manager,' Geoff interrupted, raising his eyebrows meaningfully.

Another cross look flew sideways before Sue went on. 'You would report to me on a regular basis so you can share any thoughts or concerns you may have. We're a very open organisation. We want everyone to feel challenged but supported – staff and service users alike.'

Jo nodded. In theory, it all sounded fine. She could do all the things she had read about on the websites in the last few days. She could work in a challenging, supportive environment. She could help children and young, vulnerable adults to find safety, happiness and success. The problem was, when she was actually *in* that environment, when she *met* those children and young, vulnerable adults with their violent tendencies and terrible pasts . . . Could she do it?

'Do you have any questions for us at this stage?' asked Geoff.

Jo managed not to emit the whimpering noise that she could hear inside her head. Suddenly, she really didn't want this job after all. It was too risky. If a week ago, she had been able to leap into the future and see herself now, sitting in this office spouting lies and pretending to know what she was letting herself in for, she would never have entertained the idea of becoming a care worker. It was the children she worried about more than herself. What if she put them at risk with her incompetence?

'Well, you can always ask them as we're going round,' Sue suggested, rising to her feet.

The whimpering noise got louder. It became apparent that Jo and Sue were about to embark on a tour of Fairmont House, which implied, rather frighteningly, that she had cleared the first hurdle. Geoff started muttering about paperwork and assessments, and then abruptly stuck out his hand.

'Nice to meet you, Jo. I'm sure we'll see one another again.'

A fresh surge of anxiety ran through her; she still wanted the job, in a way, but she really wasn't sure she could do it.

George Bush waved them out of his office, still grinning inanely.

'We may as well start here,' said Sue, bustling towards the main entrance.

Fairmont House was a large, brick building that looked from the outside like a Victorian mansion. Inside, it was completely modernised with wide, open corridors and lots of white paint. It would have felt clinical, thought Jo, were it not for the children's creations that hung off every surface. *My New Mum* was the title of one colourful, blobby creation that looked like an oil spillage with a big, happy face in the middle. A canvas stretched almost from floor to ceiling and was covered by what looked like graffiti, but Jo realised was actually a poem. 'I was hurt but scared to talk,' she read as they hurried past. 'They gave me somewhere safe to walk . . .'

Sue stopped just before they reached the entrance hall and opened a set of double doors on the left. 'This is the lounge.'

The noise hit Jo first. Yelling, laughing, wailing, whimpering. They stepped into a room full of beanbags and sofas and brightly coloured furniture where a dozen kids were clustered in one corner.

'They like the wee,' Sue said. Jo's confusion must have shown on her face. 'Nintendo Wii,' she explained.

'Oh, yeah.' Jo nodded keenly. 'Good game.'

'Did you have one at your old place?'

'Yeah, the kids all loved it.' Jo smiled fondly at the non-existent memory.

'Which were the popular ones there?'

'Er . . .' There was more than one? 'Well . . .'

'The kids always go for the games that involve guns and cars,' Sue said ruefully. 'We've tried to get them into the sports but boxing is about as close as we've come to that.'

Jo rolled her eyes empathetically.

'Oh, and there's a little garden out there.' Sue pointed to the curtain that had been partially drawn to create shade for the games consoles. 'Good for the occasional barbecue.'

Just as Jo started to worry that Sue might introduce her to some of the kids – who would undoubtedly be too absorbed in their games to care – a shrill noise started up elsewhere in the house. Jo followed Sue along the corridor to the source of the sound, which showed no sign of abating.

'What are you doing?' demanded Sue, addressing a young black girl who was sitting cross-legged on the floor, screaming her heart out.

The noise continued.

'Stop it,' Sue said, quite calmly considering the state of the girl. 'Lillie, will you stop that?'

A few seconds later, more out of curiosity than obedience, it seemed, the girl stopped and looked up.

'Now, let's go back to your bedroom and talk. This is Jo. Say hello to Jo.'

Jo found herself grinning madly at the girl in an effort to make her smile back.

The girl bawled louder, resuming her position on the floor and turning a worrying shade of purple.

'It doesn't help, making that noise,' Sue said above the din. Turning to Jo, she added quietly, 'It's nothing personal. She doesn't like strangers. She was raped by her uncle for two years before she came in.'

Jo thought she might have misheard, but there was no opportunity to find out. Sue had already scooped up the little girl and waddled off, resuming her guided tour as they whizzed through the corridors.

'This is one of the residential floors. There are two. One for the under-twelves, one for the twelve-to-fifteens. Every room is different. We encourage the children to make them their own. They can change the wallpaper, the layout, that sort of thing – well, to a point.'

They arrived at Lillie's room – a typical little girl's bedroom with shades of pink and yellow and a bedspread that depicted some kind of magical princess. Jo was struggling to believe what Sue had said. *Raped by her uncle.* The girl couldn't have been older than eight or nine.

In the course of about four minutes, Sue somehow transformed the angry, distressed little bundle into a happy cherub who was quietly humming as she turned the screws on her flower-press.

'And Jo might be coming to run the activities here,' Sue concluded, rising to her feet.

The girl didn't seem to care one way or the other – which was progress, Jo supposed.

'Are you going to make me a nice flower arrangement?'

Lillie looked up. 'No, I'm squashing them,' she said, as though Sue was stupid. 'They're dead.'

'Well, yes, I suppose they are . . .' Sue backed towards the door. 'Well, I'm sure it will be very pretty, anyway. Say goodbye to Jo now.'

The girl wrinkled her nose in Jo's direction.

'Bye,' Jo whispered as Sue pulled the door shut and marched back down the corridor.

'There are twelve bedrooms on each floor,' she said brusquely. 'Twenty-four children in all. Obviously more at times, when the foster kids come in for activities.'

Jo nodded and tripped down the stairs after her. *Activities.* Even the word scared her now. How would she cope with a roomful of Lillies? Or worse, a roomful of *teenage* Lillies?

'The kitchens,' Sue pointed out, stopping briefly for Jo to peer in at the rows of stainless-steel surfaces. A man with a ponytail looked up from his frying and waved.

'And, last stop, the offices.' Sue held open a door that led to a chaotic arrangement of desks, toys and piles of paper. The walls were similarly adorned to the rest of the house. Beneath the muddle were about half a dozen computer terminals, three of them occupied. At the end of the office, a couple of kids were jumping up and down beside a man with his back to Jo and Sue.

'Put it on! Put it on!' yelled the kids.

Sue smiled. 'This is where the *hard work* happens,' she said pointedly. The chubby woman nearby put her head down and started frantically typing.

'This is Clare,' she said, waiting for the woman to stop bashing her keyboard. 'Clare's the assistant manager. Over there is Bob, who does our accounts, and—'

'Ha! He's wearing it! He's wearing it!' screamed the children, yelping as the young man they'd been pestering slowly turned round, his face obscured by a pink, conical mask that looked like a pig's snout.

Jo laughed as the cardboard nose was thrust this way

and that for the benefit of the whooping children, accompanied by boar-like grunts. Then the mask slipped off the man's face and rolled onto the floor.

She looked at him, not sure what to say.

Matt stopped, mid-snort. 'Ah. Hi.'

There was a brief silence while everyone looked from Matt to Jo and then back again.

'I'm just . . .'

'Testing out a new marketing tool?' Jo suggested.

'Yeah.' He nodded with sudden conviction. 'That's right.'

Chapter Sixteen

'Come on in,' Jo sang, trying to hide the shake in her voice. 'You must be . . . Kyle, yes?'

The boy grunted something unintelligible from under his hood and lumbered towards the far beanbag.

There was an awkward silence.

'So I guess that just leaves . . . Nadia.'

'Oozat?' asked one of the kids, shifting the armchair away from the semi-circle Jo had created.

'Nadia? She's new. She might be moving into Dunston's in the next few weeks, so it seemed like a good idea to have her along. No, don't switch the Gameboy on.'

The eleven-year-old snorted incredulously. 'Gameboy! She called it a Gameboy!' He turned to the back of the room where the newcomer was slumped, staring up at the ceiling. 'Kyle! Did you 'ear that?'

Jo wasn't sure whether she misheard Kyle's reaction, but it certainly sounded like the C-word.

'Can you bring the chair back, please, Jason?' She glanced nervously around the broken semi-circle as her command was completely ignored.

The sullen redhead on the edge of the group was staring straight ahead with an expression that somehow portrayed a combination of boredom and complete, utter hatred. Charlene, supposedly twelve but with the piercings and attitude of an eighteen-year-old, clearly wasn't the joining-in type.

Every second that passed seemed to last longer than the last. Jo forced herself not to look at the clock. The instructions from Sue had been quite direct: get to know the children and let them get to know you. That was it. For a first session, that was enough. It didn't seem very 'active' for an 'activities' session, thought Jo, but her line manager had been quite insistent. 'The first session will shape what you do in the following weeks. Running around can wait; you'll have plenty of time for that later.' Jo didn't know which was more daunting: the idea of running around with these youngsters or trying to get them to talk for two hours.

'Nadia!' cried Jo, her relief all too evident. A skinny brunette tiptoed into the room. 'Take a seat. Jason, come away from the . . . corner. Kyle, are you with us?'

She knew she was coming across like a stressed-out school matron; she just didn't know how else to be. Eventually, Jason abandoned his electronics and Kyle dragged himself across the room to fill the last seat. Five pairs of eyes bored menacingly into hers.

'Well, thanks for coming, guys.' *Guys.* Oh dear. Now she sounded like some sort of physics teacher-soccer mom hybrid. 'I know some of you have been to a few activities sessions before, but I think these will probably be a bit different . . .' She lost the trail of her thought as Kyle started stroking what looked like a knuckle-duster on his right hand.

'So.' Jo found herself being swallowed by the beanbag. 'I'm the new activities coordinator for Fairmont House.'

She hoisted herself into an upright position. Kyle said it again. This time she definitely wasn't mistaken.

'My name's Jo, and I know I'm not the only new person around here, so I wondered whether it might be useful to go round the group introducing ourselves . . . ?'

Nobody said a word.

'I'll start then,' she said, finally. 'I'm Jo, I'm twenty-four and I've just moved here from London, where I was working at a school in Haringey. Tim? Your go.'

The smallest and youngest member of the group glared back at her through narrowed eyes.

'Go on,' she urged, matron-style.

He shrugged. He was just shy, Jo told herself.

'I dunno,' he mumbled eventually.

'Well, start with your name,' suggested Jo.

'It's Tim, innit!' roared Kyle, whacking his forehead to imply that Jo was mentally deficient. 'You just said it!'

'Um, well yes. But I thought Tim should probably—'

'This is wank,' Kyle declared loudly.

Jason sniggered. 'Wank.' He gestured towards Jo and then sniggered again as though for Kyle's approval.

Jo sighed. She was despairing but also slightly angry. 'Kyle, shut up. You too, Jason. Tim's talking.'

'No he ain't!' Kyle retorted, leaning across and punching the little kid in the arm. 'He ain't talkin'!'

Jo leaned across. 'Kyle, stop it. Tim, tell us something about you.'

It was unfortunate that she had forgotten to relax her tone for Tim's instruction, and the fear showed in his expression when he finally spoke up.

'I'm at Dunston's for a few months while they find me a foster home,' he muttered, looking at the floor.

141

'I was living with me mum, but she wasn't . . . she couldn't—'

Kyle jumped in. 'She was a—'

'Not now,' Jo put in quickly. 'Thanks, Tim. Charlene?'

The redhead sighed irritably and played with the silver stud in her tongue. 'Yeah,' she said reluctantly. 'I'm here 'cause I don't 'ave anywhere else to live. I couldn't stay with my mum 'cause we was, like, arguing all the time, an' I ran out of places.'

'OK . . . Jason?'

The boy turned up his nose and looked at her as though this was all highly unnecessary. Jo wondered what Sue had had in mind when she'd suggested the introductions. Perhaps she had known it would be this difficult to extract responses from the kids, and this was why she'd advised her to set aside a whole session for saying hello.

'Yeah, well . . . I just come here 'cause . . . 'cause of stuff that was happening at home, innit.'

Jo nodded. She felt completely out of her depth. 'Nadia?'

The girl looked down at her shoes. She really was painfully thin, thought Jo. Anorexic or even malnourished, perhaps. 'I'm thirteen,' she said, sniffing, 'an' I might be comin' 'ere to live – depends on my assessment.' Another sniff. 'I been livin' on sofas an' stuff, but I need, like, a proper place.' She sniffed again from behind the wall of black hair. Jo suspected the gaunt look and the sniffing might be related.

'So!' Jo turned to Kyle and hoped for the best.

'Fuck off.'

'Come on,' she goaded, pleased to get any response at all. 'When did you come to Dunston's? Have you been here a while?'

'I ain't *at* Dunston's! I just come 'ere for activi'ies, don't I? 'Cause I ain't in school.'

Jo nodded. This was good. They were almost having a chat. 'And how long have—'

'Why d'you need to know that? You doing some sort of survey? Tryin' to get all our information? I'll get you done for identity theft!'

'Ha – identity theft,' echoed Jason conceitedly.

'Why d'you care how long I been comin'?' Kyle demanded.

Jo closed her eyes momentarily. They were all difficult kids, but she reckoned she could cope with most of them, if she played her cards right. But Kyle . . . he wasn't difficult; he was impossible.

'I don't need to know,' Jo said softly. 'I just thought it would be nice for us to—'

'Nosy bitch.'

Jason guffawed. 'Nosy bitch.'

Jo sighed. At least one thing was making progress: the minute hand on the clock. 'So now we all know each other—'

'What's *your* story?' Kyle interrupted. 'Why are *you* here?'

'Well, I work here.'

Kyle sighed loudly and looked around at the others. 'Yeah, obviously. I mean, why are you *here*? You're like, posh. You ain't never been homeless, innit. Why you working 'ere?'

Jo braced herself, wishing she could tell the kids the truth: that she *had* been homeless, only a few weeks before. 'People aren't always who they seem, Kyle.'

They all looked back at her blankly. She decided they were owed an explanation – even if it wasn't going to be entirely truthful.

143

'I grew up in London with my mum and dad – fairly standard, really.' She faltered. 'I mean, well, standard by some people's, er, standards. Anyway. I went to university and did . . .'

Jo lost track of her sentence. Something had just occurred to her. She remembered something she'd done at university, and it wasn't Philosophy.

Maybe, subconsciously, she was trying to get close to these messed-up young teenagers. Or maybe at the back of her mind, buried in the blankness, was a fragment of memory. Either way, the word that slipped out of her mouth clearly shocked her more than it shocked any of the kids.

'Drugs. I was hanging out with the wrong people, and because of that I fell out with my mum . . .' She stopped again. This wasn't part of the script. Maybe she *had* fallen out with her mother. It would make sense, if she knew anything about the spectacular failure that was Jo's life. She shelved the thought for later contemplation and went back to her made-up past.

'I was in a lot of debt, so I had to get a job.'

The new girl said something so quietly that Jo had to ask her to repeat it.

'What were you taking?' she whispered.

'Oh . . .' Jo's answer tripped out automatically. 'Cocaine.'

'*Cocaine?* Since when? For a moment the skinny girl seemed to hang on to her response, searching for something. Then she looked away.

'Horseshit,' muttered Kyle under his breath.

Jo ignored him. 'A job came up at a school in Haringey. That's how I got into this.'

She wondered how her story had come across. Did

children have a sixth sense for lies, like animals did for fear? They certainly seemed to pick up on insecurity. She looked around. The kids stared sulkily back at her. The only movement was from Kyle, who was idly rolling a joint between his fingers. She wondered what the rules were on that. Shit, she really wasn't qualified for this.

'OK!' Jo glanced at the clock and was relieved to see that another fifteen minutes had passed. 'So, what I need to get from you is an idea of what you want from these sessions.' She looked around for some sort of reaction. There was none. 'Is it to learn new skills? Make friends? Learn things? Tell me why you've chosen to come along.'

'I ain't *chosen* to,' Kyle said sullenly. 'Wouldn't be 'ere if I didn't 'ave to.'

'Right.' Jo nodded. Of course. That was stupid. Most of them probably didn't want to be here. 'Well, given that you're all signed up – for whatever reasons – let's try and make it as enjoyable as possible.' Nobody could say she wasn't trying. 'So. What might you gain from these sessions?'

Another sullen silence, in which she almost longed for the days of frothing cappuccinos in Trev's Teashop. Then inspiration struck.

'We'll do it this way.' She got up and grabbed a large sketchpad and some pens from a shelf. She tore out a sheet and ripped it into small pieces. 'Here. Everyone take a pen and some strips of paper. There you go. Take some, Kyle, go on. Now, on separate pieces, write one or two words that describe what you'd like to get out of these sessions.'

Miraculously, the kids started scribbling on their scraps of paper – with the exception of Kyle, who tried to set his on fire with a cigarette lighter.

'OK, put them in a pile on the floor here when you're done,' Jo instructed. 'Kyle, put the lighter away.'

A dozen screwed-up pieces of paper landed at her feet. Kyle finally wrote something on his charred scrap and made a show of tossing the screwed-up ball at Jo's chest.

'Right,' she said, ignoring the missile. She was beginning to feel quite proud. They were having a productive session after all. 'Let's open them up.'

Predictably, most of the scribbles were related to Jo's prompts about skills and learning, but she feigned excitement all the same. 'Do good stuff, OK . . . Make things, mmm, nice one. Oh, what's this?'

Jo's face fell. On Kyle's crumpled piece of paper was a picture of a penis.

'Hmm. OK. So, Kyle, I'm thinking this means . . . what you want out of our sessions is *this*?' She held up the image for all to see. There was a quiet ripple of laughter. 'Yes?'

'Fuck off.'

'Is that a yes? Because that's what you've put on—'

'I said fuck off!' he yelled. Kyle leaped to his feet, looked around and grabbed the nearest item of furniture: a plastic coffee table. He lobbed it at Jo, who managed to bat it away as he stormed out.

There was a moment of silence. Then Jason muttered something that she didn't quite catch.

Jo was wondering whether she ought to go after Kyle or stay with the group. 'Sorry?'

'He can't write. Or read.'

'Can't—'

Slowly, it sank in. Jo replayed the last five minutes in her mind and realised what she had done. Deliberately, she had humiliated Kyle to try to make the other kids laugh, to get them on her side. And she had succeeded. She had succeeded in doing the worst thing anybody could do to a vulnerable twelve-year-old boy.

She collected the pens and set off in pursuit, wondering how Sue Meads would react to the news of her first session – and of her subsequent resignation. Then, suddenly, the penny dropped. Kyle was the boy Sue had mentioned. He was the kid who'd been excluded from every school in the area because of his violent behaviour – behaviour that stemmed from a childhood of abuse at the hands of an alcoholic stepfather who was doing time for GBH.

She closed her eyes and felt the guilt slowly smother her. She was not a support worker. She needed a job, but not this one. Jo Simmons was not cut out for this.

Chapter Seventeen

Clare, the assistant manager, was the only one in the office when Jo poked her head round the door.

'Morning!' She looked up briefly while her podgy fingers continued to thump the keyboard.

Jo crept in, not sure whether to wait or to come back later. She wanted to give Sue as much warning as possible, but knew she owed it to her to do it in person.

'Can I help you?'

Jo moved closer, running her nail round the corner of the envelope. 'I'm looking for Sue. Is she in?'

Clare stopped typing and smiled. 'She was expecting you.'

'She – she was?' Jo's heart started pounding. Sue must have had a complaint about the kids' first session.

'Yeah. She thought you'd probably come in yesterday. To hand in your notice.'

Oh God. The session had been so bad that everyone was expecting her to quit.

'Well, I'm here now. Here's my letter.'

Clare shook her head, still smiling. 'Don't bother.'

'You mean . . . ?' Jo swallowed. They must have already sacked her. It was too late for her to resign.

'I mean, she won't let you.' Clare waddled over and pulled a stray sheet of paper from inside the printer. 'Bloody thing. Always jamming.'

Jo was still not clear where she stood. 'Did Sue say . . . ?'

Clare pressed a button on the machine and waited for a response. 'Everyone tries to quit after their first session – well, nearly everyone. Sue told us to make sure you didn't hand in your notice.'

'No.' Jo shook her head. There was a misunderstanding. She wasn't quitting in the way that other people probably wanted to quit when they first started working here; this was different. She was quitting because she really, really wasn't up to the job. 'I can't do it.'

After some growling and thumping on Clare's part, the machine whirred into life. 'Finally! Yeah, you can. You just have to get used to it.'

'No, no, really. It's not that. It's not that I'm out of prac-tice or the kids are hard work. It's . . .' Jo couldn't summon words that were strong enough. She wished she could explain about her fake qualifications and lack of experi-ence. 'They *hate* me. Seriously. And it's fair enough, because I was useless with them. Unprofessional. It was a disas-trous session.'

Clare whipped the printed sheets off the machine and sighed loudly – either at the page formatting or at Jo's whinging, she wasn't sure which.

'Can't have been that bad,' said Clare. 'Nobody's complained.'

'Really?' Jo wasn't sure. She couldn't believe Kyle would have passed off the opportunity to expose her incompetence.

'I'm sure you did fine,' she said, shrugging.

No, thought Jo. No, no, no. She hadn't done fine. They would realise soon enough. She was a fraud. An unqualified, inexperienced impostor who had conned her way into this job and who couldn't be trusted with the children. Jo had spent most of the night awake, arguing with herself over whether to push on with her disastrous career at Dunston's in the hope that she would improve or to do the honourable thing and resign. She felt so guilty for being here at all – but then, she also felt guilty about the idea of quitting so soon. In the end, though, with all things weighed up, there was only one course of action. She *had* to hand in her notice.

'Will Sue be in later?'

'Not sure,' said Clare, waving her hands over the jaws of the printer like some sort of urban snake charmer.

'If I leave it on her desk, will you tell her it's here?' Jo was hesitant to do so in case it went astray and they claimed it had never existed, but she had to get it to Sue somehow.

'She won't read it,' Clare warned, grabbing the sheets and kissing them. 'Hallelujah! At last.'

'Well . . . can you let her know, anyway?' Jo propped the letter on her boss's keyboard.

Clare nodded. 'But turn up to your session on Friday, won't you?'

'Mmm.' Jo cringed at the thought. She was contractually obliged to turn up, of course, because of her fourteen-day notice period.

'Oh, by the way, Matt left this for you,' Clare said, reaching across the desk and passing over a small yellow Jiffy bag. 'He wasn't sure you'd cross paths.'

Jo took the package and left the office, head bowed. Two more weeks. Eight sessions. God help her.

Seated at the back of the bus, she scratched off the tape that held the bulbous parcel together. Something small and heavy was nestled inside reams and reams of bubble wrap. She emptied the contents onto her lap.

Raj had done well. Jo didn't know much about mobile phones, but it was clear that this shiny device did more than just make calls. With no instruction manual, she could only marvel at the array of buttons, shutters and microphones – and hope that she wasn't going to be arrested for handling stolen goods.

It took most of the journey for the phone to boot up but when it did, even the pensioners at the front looked round in alarm. It was as though a brass ensemble was tuning up in her groin. Jo smothered it and glared at the man next to her. As she got off the bus, a different but equally loud fanfare followed her out. She pulled out the phone. An envelope symbol was flashing on the screen.

Hi Jo, Hope u like new
phone. SIM cost £5 – guessin
thatz ok. Laterz. Raj

Jo smiled at his lack of shame and his peculiar use of the letter z. She hadn't really felt the need for a mobile phone up until now, but it was probably sensible to have one, really, especially as she would soon be looking for another job. People didn't exist in this country unless they had a phone number and an email address – and a bank account, as Jo had recently discovered. Persuading Dunston's to pay her in cash had provoked more than a few raised eyebrows.

Something unpleasant occurred to her as she walked along Radley Road, trying to work out how to reply on the high-tech device. She realised that to all intents and purposes, Jo Simmons *didn't* exist. It was true that she had most of the technical elements required for everyday living: a name, an address, a job – although the latter not for long, admittedly – and a couple of people who might vouch for her as a person . . . but that was all. It wasn't an identity.

Everything about her was superficial. She had friends, but none she had known for more than a few weeks. She had bogus qualifications and professional experience that only existed on paper. She had skills and a personality, but she didn't know how they'd been derived. It was as though she was hollow; from the outside she seemed just like everybody else, but if anyone were to take a proper look – not that she'd let them – they would find out that it was all a façade.

The fanfare happened again as she was contemplating an attempt at replying.

It's Matt. Hope u don't mind –
I nabbed your number. Don't
worry about Raj's money – I paid.
Tight git. Fancy watching the
game round ours fri? Matt

Her smile widened as she pictured Matt unwrapping the phone, making a call, capturing the number and wrapping it up again. She didn't want to read too much into it, of course, but it did seem like a lot of effort to go to – and paying for the SIM was a nice gesture. Jo wondered what match he was referring to. She'd look it up and reply later.

'You look chirpy. Morning going well?' asked Mrs Phillips.

Jo shrugged noncommittally. Actually, aside from the message from Matt, the morning was not going well. She had traipsed all the way into Oxford to resign, only to be told that her boss probably wouldn't read the letter and even if she did, nobody would take it seriously.

'How's the new job?' asked Mrs Phillips, leaning forward in a way that suggested Jo wasn't going to slip away for a good few minutes.

Jo couldn't be bothered to lie. 'I've quit.'

'But . . . You only just started.'

'I know. But I couldn't do it. The kids were too . . . too much.'

Mrs Phillips frowned sympathetically. 'Are you sure you gave it a proper go? You can be quite . . . impulsive.'

Jo shook her head impatiently. Mrs P didn't get it, of course.

'I'm out of my depth. The children need someone more . . . experienced.'

'You're experienced, aren't you?'

'Not in the right way.'

Jo wished she could open up completely. It was so tiring, living a lie.

'If you say so . . .'

Mrs Phillips sat, nodding gently with a faraway look in her eye. Jo wondered whether she was even thinking about her tenant's plight or something else entirely. It occurred to her that she knew almost nothing about the old lady.

'Have you always had the shop?'

Mrs Phillips blinked. 'The guesthouse came first. I ran it while my husband looked after the shop.'

Like a goldfish, Jo opened and shut her mouth. *Husband.* She had never stopped to think about a Mr Phillips.

'Then when Ted was gone I was doing both, for a while.'

Gone. Gone to heaven or gone elsewhere? Gone off with another woman? Jo glanced at Mrs Phillips' hand. There was no ring. 'Wh – when was that?'

'Oh, years ago now.' The woman brushed it aside. 'It didn't work, doing both. Someone needed to be in the shop at all hours and that meant nobody was doing the beds . . . I was giving myself a nervous breakdown. One of them had to go.'

Jo nodded, remembering something she'd learned on her first night. 'And the council dictated which one?'

Mrs Phillips nodded sadly.

The door jangled and a customer walked in. Mrs Phillips straightened up and sang a cheery greeting and then she turned to Jo. 'So what are your plans for the rest of the day?'

Moping. That was how she had intended to spend the day. She had planned to slope off to her room and stare at the scribbles in her notebook, wallowing in self-pity, vodka bottle in hand, trying to make sense of the disjointed set of notions that constituted her past: her inexplicable paranoia, her drink problem, the cocaine thing that had surfaced the other day, her sordid career as a lap-dancer, her apparent inability to hold down a job, her compulsive lying . . . But something had changed in the last few minutes. She no longer felt so despondent.

It wasn't just the message from Matt. It was talking to Mrs P. The woman was ancient and her husband was 'gone', yet she still got out of bed each morning and managed a friendly smile for her customers. She didn't much *like* sitting behind the till scanning groceries; she wanted to be upstairs cooking fry-ups in her cosy, cat-adorned eaves. But she got on with it. She didn't mope.

'I'm gonna sort myself out,' Jo said. 'Get a job I *can* do.'

Chapter Eighteen

'Ooh. Hello.' Kieran stood in the doorway looking quite surprised to see her. He was wearing an apron that looked several sizes too small and bore the slogan 'Kitchen Princess'.

'Hi.' Jo waited to be invited in, but Kieran seemed to be waiting for a prompt. 'Can I . . . come in?' Jo wondered whether she might have misread the kick-off time on the website. 'I think Matt said you were watching the game?'

'Oh, right. Yeah. We are.' Kieran finally seemed to understand. 'Come in.'

Jo followed the peculiar young man into the flat, which smelled slightly of old socks and pepperoni. In a way, she thought, Kieran was more like a teenager than a twenty-three-year-old. He was kooky and sulky and had very few social skills in the normal sense. But at the same time, there was something middle-aged about him too. He was like the eccentric, embarrassing father who took pride in wearing Christmas jumpers and silly hats in public, just to embarrass the family. Only in Kieran's case, there was no family – only a very tolerant flatmate.

'Jo's here!' announced Kieran, clearly expecting Matt to be as surprised by the news as he was.

Matt looked up from poking around in the oven and

smiled. He jumped to his feet and then made as if to kiss her cheek, but at the last minute clearly decided that was too formal and clapped her on the arm instead. 'Good to see you.'

'You too.' Jo smiled awkwardly. 'I brought some beers.' She lifted the carrier bag and ended up swinging the cans into Matt's genitals. They both pretended they hadn't noticed.

'September resolution over then?'

Jo grimaced and pulled out a bottle of Coke. 'Not yet.'

In a way, she wished that she could break her pact with herself – with Mrs P – just this once. She wanted to relax with a beer and watch the football, like a normal person. It would also make things easier later on when she broke the news to Matt about her leaving Dunston's, having a bit of alcohol inside her. But she was standing firm. She wouldn't drink.

She watched as Matt poured the glass of Coke and broke open a can for himself. She suspected he might take it quite personally when she told him about her resignation. He'd been instrumental in getting her the interview and he'd probably see himself partly to blame for her failure. He wasn't, of course. But she couldn't explain properly why not without unravelling too many essential fabrications.

'Will we have enough pizza?' asked Kieran, scratching his head as though the sums were too complex.

Matt went over to the sink. 'Well, we wouldn't have if I'd left you to it, Kitchen Princess.' He picked up a circle of polystyrene and waved it at Kieran. 'You're supposed to take these off.'

They moved through to the lounge, where piles of magazines, a bench press and lots of wiring connecting various pieces of equipment confirmed that the place was very much a boys' flat. The walls were a myriad of colours, one dark orange, one brown, the others varying shades of yellow as though the owner couldn't decide which tin of Dulux to go for, and everything seemed to be slightly off-kilter: the doorframes, the staircases, the furniture . . . they all leaned or tilted or sagged.

'Sorry about this,' Matt said, shifting the most obstructive piles of clutter to the corners of the room. 'It just sort of –' he dipped his head towards Kieran – 'happens.'

After a good deal of button-pressing on several remote controls, three suntanned men appeared on the giant TV.

'. . . and we know how inventive they can be with the ball, but it's fair to say their performance of late hasn't been up to much. I think a lot of people will be wanting to find out what they're capable of tonight.'

The men nodded in earnest agreement and took it in turns to say the same thing using different words. It was quite an art form, thought Jo.

'Hope they do better than last time,' Matt remarked, taking a swig of his beer. He was next to Jo on the sofa but they were separated by a laptop and a tangle of cables.

'Yeah.' Jo nodded as though she remembered *that* time all too well. She had done some considerable research online in the run-up to tonight. She knew that the teams playing were Arsenal and Tottenham Hotspur and she had learned a couple of players' names on each side just in case she needed to sound knowledgeable. In fact, some of the names had sounded vaguely familiar in the way that Henry the Eighth rang a bell, but she had no idea who Rebecca Ross had supported – if anyone. Facebook hadn't shed any light on that one.

'Did you watch that game?' asked Matt.

Jo pretended to think back through the football fixtures. 'Er, no.'

'Fucking disaster.' He shook his head. 'I dunno whether it's better or worse with the new management.'

She nodded grimly, willing the game to start.

The commentators' faces were finally replaced with shots of the stadium and Jo sensed that she was out of the danger zone. Soon, play would commence and she would be able to gauge from Matt's reactions which team they were supporting. Then Kieran piped up.

'Which manager would you say was better?'

With dismay, Jo realised that the question was directed at her. 'Oh, er, well . . .'

Matt too was waiting for her response. Jo had no idea how to answer. Clearly there had been some sort of management change on one of the teams, but she didn't know which and she couldn't remember any names. 'I guess . . . Ooh! Look!'

And there, racing across the pitch behind the rows of players just close enough for the camera to catch, was exactly the distraction Jo needed. All eyes turned to the screen, where a middle-aged man – naked except for a pair of white shoes – was being smothered with a blanket by security guards. Immediately afterwards, to Jo's relief, the whistle blew.

It may or may not have been thanks to Kieran's solid advice that the reds were one-nil up after fifteen minutes. 'Cross it, you prat!' he shouted. 'Use the wing!' Once or twice, having ascertained which team it was they were with, Jo ventured some guidance of her own, but didn't really feel she could take credit for the lead they were taking over Spurs.

She tried to relax, but all she could think about was the fact that she still had to tell Matt her news. There just didn't seem to be a natural way of saying it.

'*I've quit my job.*'

'Why did you do that? He was free in midfield!'

'*I can't work at Dunston's any more.*'

'Too late! Should've moved for the free kick!'

By half-time, nearly a litre of Coke later, Arsenal were winning two-one and Jo was feeling jittery with all the caffeine. She still hadn't told him.

'I wonder why football shirts are always just one colour,' said Kieran, frowning at the TV screen.

Matt looked across. 'You mean, like, not patterned with flowers or polka dots or pictures of fruit?'

'Well, maybe not *fruit* . . .'

Matt shot Jo an apologetic glance. 'I think the idea of kit is to let players see quickly who's on their team. If they had to squint at the shirt and work out whether the shape was a star or an orange, it would kinda defeat the purpose.'

Kieran didn't seem satisfied. 'But . . . what about jockeys?'

Matt opened his mouth to speak, then thought better of it and walked out. Jo seized the opportunity and followed him through to the kitchen. The pizzas were smelling rather well done.

'Mmm, crispy.' She smiled as he slid some blackened remains from the top of the oven.

'No need to be polite. It looks like charcoal.'

Jo laughed. 'Don't let Kieran hear you say that – he'll be on about carbon-based life-forms again. The ones underneath look OK.'

Matt gave her a knowing look.

As he carved up the pizzas, Jo forced the words out.

'Matt? You know Dunston's . . . ?' Well, they were almost the words.

'All too well.' He reached into the fridge for more beers.

'Well . . .' Jo stopped hacking the pizza for a second. 'I can't work there.'

'What d'you mean? Another?' He held out the bottle of Coke.

She shook her head. 'I'm not experienced enough to be the activities coordinator.'

He frowned. 'No need to worry now. You've already got the job.'

'I know, but I've quit.'

He reeled round and stared at her. '*Why?*'

Jo tried to outline the reasons in a rational way that still managed to express the severity of her incompetence. 'I'm not used to dealing with kids that are so . . .'

'Fucked up?'

'Well, yeah.' She wouldn't have put it like that, but Matt had hit the nail on the head – albeit crassly. 'I just . . . don't know how to deal with them. That first session . . .' She thought back to the scene on the beanbags and cringed. 'I can't describe it.'

'Well, try.' He looked serious.

She remembered that time in the office with Matt and the mask. It was obvious that he had a natural way with the kids; they'd been whooping and screaming with delight, while Jo had only succeeded in making them jeer and swear and clam up.

Matt was leaning against the kitchen work surface, waiting.

'Well, for a start, they didn't want to talk to me.'

161

'They don't wanna talk to anyone,' he said. 'Of course they don't. They don't have any trust.'

'But then when they *did* talk, I didn't know how to react. I mean . . . Do you ask questions? Do you just stay quiet, wondering what they mean? And how much do they all know about each other? What if I made someone say something that was supposed to be confidential?'

Jo fixed her gaze on the wonky kitchen units, wishing she could tell Matt the truth about herself. It would make things so much easier.

'Anyway, the afternoon turned into this hideous get-to-know-each-other session where nobody wanted to get to know anybody else, and I came up with this stupid idea for making them tell me what they wanted from the sessions. I got them writing it on bits of paper. Only one of them can't read or write. So I embarrassed him in front of everyone.'

Matt seemed to be waiting for some sort of climax.

'It was awful,' Jo said. 'Disastrous.'

He cocked his head to one side. 'Doesn't sound it.'

Jo wrung her hands uncomfortably. Perhaps she hadn't explained it very well. She had missed out the bit where Kyle threw a coffee table at her face, and she hadn't described the looks on the kids' faces. 'Well, it was.'

Matt frowned as though unable to make sense of something. 'You've worked with kids like this before, haven't you?'

Jo nodded hesitantly. This was the crux of it. This was what she really needed to explain, to get her message across.

'So you know what it's like? Maybe you've just forgotten how hard it is at the beginning. You were probably close to the other kids by the time you left. It gets easier, doesn't it?'

She didn't reply.

'Look, I know I don't work directly with the children, but I do see them every day. I know them. I know what they can be like.'

·Jo shook her head. He wasn't getting it. He was assuming she had the gift that he had with the kids – and why wouldn't he? She was a qualified care worker, as far as he knew.

'Especially Kyle,' he added.

Jo's head shot up. 'How did you know it was him?' The paranoia kicked in. The kid must have lodged a complaint.

'Kyle Merfield makes everyone want to quit.'

Jo looked at the floor. For a very brief moment, she considered the possibility that she might have resigned too hastily, that she hadn't given herself a chance in this role. Then she remembered the look on Kyle's face and came to her senses.

'Look, there are lots of reasons, but . . . the fact is, I'm not right for the job. I just wanted to thank you for getting me the interview.'

Matt turned round and tipped the pizza slices onto a tray. 'No worries,' he said quietly.

Jo bit her lip. He looked hurt. She wished she could give him a better explanation.

They returned to the lounge in time for the start of the second half and another useful observation from Kieran.

'If the football's pumped up enough it can explode – no, implode – at kick-off.'

Matt didn't bother to comment. He was staring at the screen, pretending to watch the game. Jo suspected his thoughts were elsewhere – and not on exploding or imploding footballs.

The second half was uneventful and the final whistle blew with no change in the score. Frankly, Jo hadn't been

163

concentrating on the game. Out of the corner of her eye, she'd been watching Matt, whose attention hadn't been fixed on the TV either.

'At least we won,' he said flatly as the commentators started agreeing with one another again. 'Even if we did make a meal of it. Hey, we're out of beers.' Matt looked at his flatmate.

Kieran seemed to be in his own little world, frowning intently at his big toe.

'Mate? Beers?' prompted Matt.

Eventually, Kieran understood. 'Oh, you want me to go and buy some more.'

Matt nodded meaningfully.

Kieran looked out of the window where darkness had almost set in. 'Ah, I can't be bothered.'

'We need milk and washing powder and stuff, too. It's your turn to go to the shop.'

Jo glanced sideways at Matt. She wasn't certain, but she thought he might have been hinting that he wanted to be alone with her in the flat.

'I'll go tomorrow.'

Matt stared at him, his eyes wide. 'You must've run out of underwear by now.'

'I have,' Kieran replied proudly. 'I'm doing the inside-out trick.'

Matt shook his head. 'Dirty bastard.'

They had reached stalemate.

Jo had an idea. 'I'd better go now anyway.' She looked at Matt. 'Why don't you buy the stuff? I'll walk with you.'

He leaped to his feet and then checked himself. 'All right,' he said casually.

The night air was cool on their skin but not cool enough

to warrant a jacket. They walked to the sound of their footsteps and the distant hum of the A34. Jo was wondering whether to broach the subject of Dunston's or just to thank Matt for a lovely evening and slink off home.

'Jo,' he said eventually, stopping outside the little store and turning to face her. 'I don't think you should've quit.'

She sighed and looked back at him. The glow of a street-lamp was casting a shadow across his jaw. 'Look . . . I know you've helped me and you feel a bit responsible for me working there, but—'

'No, it's not that,' he said. 'It's nothing to do with me. It's to do with the kids. And you. You're being too hard on your-self. And, well, I realise I don't really know you that well, but . . . it seems like you're giving up too soon.'

Very briefly, as Jo looked at Matt's eyes and then down at the ground, she considered explaining to him why she'd really left Dunston's. Then the moment of insanity passed and she shrugged.

'I know it's a bit of a nutters' asylum,' he went on, step-ping closer. 'And it's not the easiest place to work, but . . . at least give it a proper go.'

They were standing only inches apart now. Jo looked up again, just as Matt's hand touched her shoulder. She raised her face and felt his lips gently crush hers.

'Um . . . good night,' Jo stammered as they pulled apart.

'Good night.' Matt smiled. 'Think about it, won't you?'

Jo had forgotten what she was supposed to be thinking about, but nodded anyway.

'I will.'

Chapter Nineteen

'So!' Sue blinked at her across Geoff's cluttered desk. 'Our first get-together.'

And sadly our last, thought Jo, nodding politely.

'How d'you think it's gone so far?'

Jo faltered. *So far*. It was as though Sue was referring to something ongoing, something that was worth evaluating for the purpose of future improvement; not something that was about to end.

'Um . . .' There was no point in skirting around the point. 'Did you get my letter?'

'Letter?'

'My resignation letter.'

Sue rolled her eyes and laughed. 'Oh! Gosh, yes, sorry I didn't get back to you on that.'

'So . . . You know I'm leaving.'

The woman looked at her, brow furrowed. 'But surely you've changed your mind?'

Jo hoped that her hesitation would speak for itself. In truth, she had done a lot of thinking since she'd dropped the letter on Sue's desk. Several times, especially after her encounter with Matt, she had considered the possibility of staying on at Dunston's, trying to start again, to make a real go of it. But then something would happen in one of the sessions, usually involving Kyle Merfield or his sidekick, Jason, and she'd shrink away from the idea.

'Jo . . .' Sue sighed, leaning back in Geoff's office chair and staring up at the ceiling. 'Jo, Jo, Jo. Tell me why you want to leave.'

'Well,' Jo tried to think of a succinct way of putting it that would leave Sue in no doubt. She could tell her about Jason's attempt to strangle Tim with the games console power lead and her failure to intervene. She could describe how two days ago, Nadia had arrived completely off her face, and how Jo, instead of talking to her about it, had sat her in front of *The Simpsons* and told her to drink lots of water. She could recount any one of the Kyle-related incidents. It should have been obvious to Sue why she had to leave.

'I'm a liability.'

Sue let out a hoot of laughter. '*You're* a liability! Ha – and you think that makes you special around here? OK. Moving on. How did you find today's session?'

Jo didn't know what to say. They were moving on. Moving on from the small matter of her leaving Fairmont House. Moving on from the issue that rendered their one-to-one chat rather pointless. She had to get her point across.

'How did the car-wash go? Did the kids behave?'

Jo shrugged helplessly. 'Not really. Kyle nearly walked out, Jason poured water *inside* one of the cars, nothing really got washed – unless you count Charlene, who was wearing a white T-shirt so she got drenched by Kyle, who wanted to see her nipples. Oh, and Kyle stole the proceeds.'

Sue nodded grimly. 'Sounds like quite a good session.'

The thing about Sue, thought Jo, was that she was so

167

bloody *nice*. She smiled at you with those badly painted lips and tired eyes, and you couldn't help feeling, well . . . *loved*. And guilty, of course, for not being as nice as her. Jo didn't have the heart to bring the conversation back round to her resignation.

'I should imagine it did good things for community relations, anyway!'

'I'm not so sure,' Jo said tactfully.

'Oh?'

'Well . . . I think it was going OK when Charlene was knocking on doors, but then Jason and Kyle had a go.'

Sue grimaced. 'What happened?'

'Well, I guess they're just not very good at articulating themselves, you know . . . And I don't think the balaclavas helped.'

'Oh. Oh dear. Well, let's just hope the papers don't get hold of it this time.'

'The papers?'

'Hmm.' Sue's expression turned sour. 'There was a lot of bad press about Fairmont House when we moved in. That's what we're trying to counteract.'

'What sort of bad press?'

'Unjustified bad press,' Sue spat, visibly bristling. 'It started even before we'd arrived. Basically, the council didn't tell anybody in the area that the house was going to be turned into a home for disadvantaged kids, so when the neighbours found out about it, they were outraged. There were headlines in all the local papers. "Delinquents Invade Oxford", "Primates Run Wild in Fairmont". Honestly, it was a hate campaign.'

Reluctantly, Jo found herself being drawn in. Fairmont House was a refuge for young kids escaping lives of misery.

What did these people know about the lives of Kyle and Charlene and Jason?

'They're no angels,' Sue conceded, 'but I won't have them insulted like that.'

No, thought Jo. No, *she* wouldn't have them insulted like that either. Kyle was disruptive, but he wasn't a primate.

'What happened?'

'Charlene wrote them a letter. A very articulate letter. She posted a copy through all the neighbours' doors and sent a copy to every newspaper. It described how Dunston's had given her a home when her alcoholic stepfather had started beating up her mother and she'd had nowhere else to go.'

Jo swallowed, thinking about the surly redhead with the attitude problem. 'I didn't know.'

'About Charlene? Well, of course. She doesn't talk about it much.'

This was all too much. Jo's guilt was mounting with every new revelation, and instead of it making her want to walk out, it was simply making her feel bad for wanting to abandon them. She couldn't win. She *wanted* to help them, to be on their side. But it was impossible because she didn't belong here. Jo Simmons was a sympathetic voyeur, nothing more. That was all she ever could be: an onlooker.

'So,' Sue said brightly, 'let's talk through the activity plan you put together.' She opened up the notepad and revealed a page of unintelligible squiggles.

Jo wasn't aware that she had pulled together any such thing. In passing, she had talked her boss through a few ideas she had had for her remaining sessions with the kids, but that was all. Clearly Sue had noted them down and turned them into something far more grand.

'Barbecue, gardening, car-wash – oh, you've done that one. Painting, muesli – er, no. What does that say?' Sue squinted. 'Oh, mural. Yes, lovely idea. Which wall were you thinking of?'

Jo shrugged. She hadn't been thinking of any wall in particular. She had seen the idea on TV. Her intention had been to take it one session at a time. Now the car-wash was done, she would start worrying about the barbecue. And then in a week, she would leave.

'Hmm, maybe the one by the patio,' Sue mused, staring at the notepad. 'Do you know what? Something's just occurred to me.' She looked up. 'Some of these ideas would be great PR opportunities.'

Jo raised an eyebrow as though she could see what the woman was thinking.

'Yes, we've always said that we should try and use everything we do as a marketing tool – especially events and things run by the kids. Some of your ideas would work well in delivering the see-how-we-help-the-community message.'

'Oh. Right. Well, that's good.'

'Yes, yes,' Sue looked quite animated, all of a sudden, her fuzz of hair bobbing all over the place. 'We could do this one around Hallowe'en and make it a trick-or-treat night, and maybe your play could be some sort of Christmas pantomime . . .'

Jo didn't like to point out that actually by 'play' she had meant just that: playing. She also neglected to mention that she wouldn't actually be *at* Dunston's for Hallowe'en or Christmas. Although, thought Jo, it was almost a shame she wouldn't be around to witness the public relations challenge of letting Kyle Merfield loose on the neighbourhood for trick-or-treat.

'Let's discuss them with Matt, our PR – oh, of course, you know Matt.'

Jo managed a nod as she followed Sue out and down the corridor towards the office. Yes, she knew Matt – knew him better than Sue realised. But she really didn't want her next encounter with him to be a discussion about a Christmas pantomime.

'Have you got a moment?' Sue swooped down on Matt's desk, tapping him on the shoulder. 'Jo has some ideas about events for the kids that we might be able to PR if we're clever.' She beamed sideways at Jo.

Matt looked up. 'Oh, hi.'

If there was a hint of embarrassment, she thought, it passed very quickly. Matt was smiling coolly, as though three nights ago they hadn't been kissing outside the convenience store like a pair of fourteen-year-olds. Jo decided to try and match his level of composure.

'Yeah, I've just, well, I kind of thought, if I was going to run more sessions . . .' The sentences weren't flowing as she'd hoped. 'Um, Sue's written them down, anyway.'

Matt leaned over and looked at the notepad. He started nodding. 'Looks like fun.' He said the last word very deliberately, looking at Jo.

Sue nodded. 'Yes, and we thought we could probably do this one at the end of October, you know, in the local area, and maybe turn this one into a scavenger hunt around Oxford . . .'

The suggestions reeled forth. Jo had no recollection of suggesting any cake stalls or household junk collections – she was fairly sure this was a council obligation anyway – but she let the woman go on.

When Sue finished, she looked expectantly at Matt.

'What d'you think? Generally PR-able? No need to go into the details at this stage, obviously. But ball-park, d'you think so?'

Matt didn't reply directly. He was looking at Jo.

'So you're staying, then?' he asked. Just like that.

She became aware of several heads turning in the office around her. Sue was blinking at her, eyebrows raised. Matt's gaze didn't leave her face.

Jo focused on a floor tile. The guilt reared up again inside her: guilt about the lying, guilt about wanting to leave, guilt about whatever it was she had done in her past. She tried to stifle it all, to think about the issue in hand. She was being given a second chance. Matt had shown her the short cut into Dunston's, and now he was helping her again.

She was grateful; a fresh start was exactly what she needed. But she had to think about the kids. A hundred scenes flashed through her mind. Kyle's table-throwing tantrum, Jason's surly explanation, Charlene's sulk, Sue's over-optimistic encouragement . . . She felt like the victim of a conspiracy. But a well-meaning conspiracy. And just at that point, as she summoned her voice, it seemed perfectly obvious what she should do.

'All right,' she said. 'Yeah, I'm staying.'

Chapter Twenty

'Do you ever take any time off?' Jo asked as Mrs Phillips zipped along the row of tins, striking the price label machine against each one. It was exhausting just watching her.

'I get my Sundays. Blast. I knew that would happen.'

'Shall I get another roll? Where are they kept?'

Mrs Phillips tilted her head to one side and sucked on her cheeks. 'Are you ill?'

Jo feigned offence and then laughed. 'I can be considerate sometimes. But if you don't want my help . . .'

'Sorry, I didn't mean to be rude. I'm just intrigued. You're not in love, are you?'

'No!'

Mrs Phillips smiled. 'They're on the second shelf down in the right-hand cupboard at the back. Thank you.'

Jo darted off, blushing slightly. *In love*. Really. Of course she wasn't. She was just trying to show her gratitude. It was only now, now that she'd been at the guesthouse for a couple of months, that she realised the full extent of her landlady's generosity, and she was trying to give something back. Mrs P had been like a grandmother to her – or a mother, thought Jo. She swept aside the now-familiar feeling of guilt as the nebulous image of Rebecca Ross's mother flashed before her. Now wasn't the time for thinking about things that were the other side of the line. She was moving forwards now, not dwelling on her unknown past.

'Thank you, dear.' Mrs Phillips took the roll and expertly fed it into the machine. 'So, who's the man?'

Jo snorted indignantly. 'What man?'

'Well, you've been walking on air for the last few days and that smile has barely left your lips. I'm assuming it's a man – or a woman?'

'Very open-minded of you. No, it's not a woman. And it's not a man, either. I'm just pleased to have got the job thing sorted.'

'The job you were trying to leave?'

'It's . . . different. Better.'

Mrs Phillips nodded knowingly. 'Right.'

'You never answered my question,' said Jo. 'When was the last time you actually took a day off? A non-Sunday, I mean.'

Mrs Phillips let out a puff of air. 'Well, I don't know. Sometime when I had Katie, I suppose.'

'Who's Katie?'

'Oh, a girl who used to help out in the shop. Four or five years ago. Just after Ted left.'

Left. That implied voluntary exit. Jo tried to think of a polite way of probing, but there didn't seem to be one.

'Can't you get another assistant?'

Mrs Phillips finished administering the labels and ripped the long tail of waxy paper from the machine. 'I can't afford to pay one – not since the big Tesco opened in Abingdon. Everyone goes there now. This shop takes a fraction of what it used to.' She waved a hand over the aisles of produce. 'Might as well just sell milk, bread and eggs. That's all people buy here. Top-ups.'

Jo didn't know what to say. She had taken the little shop to be some sort of a nest-egg for Mrs Phillips. She had assumed that it made thousands each month, that Mrs P only worked this hard to keep herself busy. 'I'll help,' she found herself saying.

Mrs Phillips shook her head and bustled back to the till. 'You've got a job.'

Jo followed her. 'That's only a few hours a week. I get lots of free time. Like now, for example.'

The woman shook her head. 'Don't be silly, Jo.'

'I'm not. I'm being serious.' And she was. Now that Jo Simmons' life was beginning to take some sort of shape of its own, now that she no longer had to use all her energy just to keep herself afloat, she was beginning to think about the lives of other people. 'I can do odd days, at least.'

Mrs Phillips looked at her. 'You have to plan your sessions, though, don't you?'

'Yeah. And I've planned next week's so now I can take over. Come on, show me how this thing works and you can have the afternoon off.' She muscled into the checkout area and peered at the till setup.

'I . . . I'd have to pay you,' Mrs Phillips mumbled.

Jo rolled her eyes. 'That rather defeats the point of me helping, doesn't it? You can't afford to pay someone, which is why I'm offering. So, how do I put an item through the till?'

It was a somewhat drawn-out tutorial, made harder by

the fifty-year age gap and Mrs Phillips' illogical methodology, but they got there, slowly.

'So if it's a banana, I ring it up as an apple, then add five pence per item?'

'That's right.'

'Why don't I just ring it up as a banana?' asked Jo.

'Bananas haven't been entered into the system.'

'Why not?'

'We weren't selling them fifteen years ago.'

'So does that mean your stock is limited to items that were around in the early nineties?'

Mrs Phillips looked at her as though this was an absurd suggestion. 'No, of course not. I just ring things up as the closest item, then add or subtract a few pence.'

'OK.' Jo still wasn't entirely convinced. 'So do customers get receipts saying "tinned peaches and spam" when they actually bought a nectarine and steak?'

The woman's look told Jo she was pushing it. 'Actually, they don't get receipts. The printer broke last year. But listen,' she pointed a finger in mock accusation and Jo detected a faint smile on her lips, 'nobody has ever complained about the service or produce they get from this shop.'

'Well, good,' replied Jo, grinning back. 'So what are you waiting for? Leave it to me!'

It took a while to extract the shopkeeper from the cashier's seat. As her archaic stock-pricing system demonstrated, Mrs Phillips didn't like change.

'What am I supposed to be doing?' she asked, returning from the living quarters carrying a mackintosh and handbag, as instructed. She didn't seem the least bit enthused by this free time idea.

176

'Whatever you want to do! Go for a walk. See a friend. Go to the zoo. Do some shopping.'

'OK,' she said uncertainly. 'And if there's a problem at the shop . . .'

'Then I'll deal with it! I've got my mobile if you need to call me. Now go.'

'Your *mobile*,' Mrs Phillips repeated suspiciously.

Eventually, she left the premises.

Jo propped herself against the checkout desk and switched on the radio, wondering how the old woman had maintained such good health after years of perching on such an uncomfortable stool. One of the legs was shorter than the others, making it necessary to hover, rather than actually sit.

The door swung open again.

'What are you doing back here?' Jo demanded, turning the music down in case Mrs P didn't approve of AC/DC.

'Well . . .' Mrs Phillips was standing in the doorway, her eyes twinkling. She seemed animated. 'I had an idea. I thought of something I could do. As compensation.'

Jo groaned exasperatedly. 'I told you, I don't want compensation! And I don't want you to spend your afternoon off wondering how to repay me for your afternoon off!'

'Yes, well, OK. But I thought . . . How about a dinner?'

Jo looked up at the ceiling. Clearly the old lady was not going to relax until she had found a means of thanking her. 'That would be lovely. Thanks. But please don't make a big fuss or anything.'

'Lovely. I'll do that. And . . .' Mrs Phillips hesitated. 'Bring your new man, won't you? I'd like to meet him.'

Jo tried to object, but didn't have the energy. 'OK. Thanks, I will.'

Mrs Phillips was smiling as she left for the second time. Jo pulled out her mobile phone.

Do u fancy dinner round
here sometime? The old
lady insists. Jo x

She rearranged herself on the wonky stool and turned the radio up. Her first experience with the bizarre pricing system turned out not to be too traumatic, as every item in the elderly customer's basket happened to have existed before the end of the previous century.

The radio DJ started prattling on about the type of cheese he'd had in his sandwich for lunch that day. Jo scrolled through the frequencies until she heard a tune. Then she froze. It wasn't just her hand that froze; it was her whole body.

The band members were yelling furiously into their microphones, something about 'an angry mob'. It was the Kaiser Chiefs; she recognised it. The tune was basic, the whole song driven by a repetitive, thumping beat. Even with the volume turned down, Jo could feel herself getting agitated. But she also felt . . . well, it was hard to describe. It was as though the song had associations; it made her think of something else. Some other time, someone, something – she couldn't put a finger on it.

Still listening to the song, her stomach knotted with tension, Jo pulled out her notebook and jotted down the words of the chorus. Then, as the tinny chant of a teenage girl band took over the airwaves and her angst receded, she flicked through the pages of the book, looking at her own handwriting and trying to draw something out of the notes.

Buffalo Club = strip club
Needed the money?
Friend(?) Saskia
Speak Spanish
Went to uni?
Science/maths
Exams?
Mum? Dad?
Non-club friends?
Drugs – where? Who with?
COCAINE?
Football – playing it, loving it
Special tea – cinnamon?!

Jo sighed, frustrated. It was more questions than answers. Facebook and Saskia had helped to fill in some of the gaps, but the flashbacks remained patchy and random, some of them having no place, as far as she could tell, in Rebecca Ross's life – assuming her profile page was to be believed. And as for the stupid half-memories, like the Kaiser Chiefs song and the smell of the special tea . . . well, they weren't helping at all.

She had been an educated, sporty, middle-class girl. She had nearly two hundred friends – assuming she hadn't just invited all and sundry to join her on Facebook – and she vaguely recalled the feeling of being popular, the taste of success, the ease with which everything happened . . . But if that was the case, she thought unhappily, then why would she jack it all in for the life of an alcoholic, coke-snorting stripper?

Jo had wrestled with this question again and again, never reaching a satisfactory conclusion. Under what circumstances would a girl like Rebecca turn into Roxie?

There were still too many unknowns. She needed more information, or more memories. Rebecca's old friends were a possible way in, but she needed more than a profile photo to go on. Without disclosing to these people that Rebecca Ross was alive and well, living a new life with a new name, she had no way of finding any clues.

There were bigger questions, too, thought Jo as she blindly turned the pages: questions about what type of person she had been, either as Rebecca or as Roxie, and what, *what*, had made her so desperate to flee the scene of the blast and retreat from her previous life.

The door opened and another pensioner walked in, this one more sprightly than the last. Jo recognised him as one of Mrs Phillips' regulars.

'Hello dere!' he cried. 'Where's de ol' girl?'

'Hi, Mr O'Connor. She just popped out.'

'Tought she was a goner!' He chuckled. 'Dat toyme of year . . . Everyone popping deir clogs!'

'Ha!' Jo pretended to laugh and watched the old man head for the spirits aisle.

It occurred to Jo as she rang the Scotch through the till that she hadn't thought about alcohol – hadn't needed it – in over a week. In fact, she hadn't really thought about it since she'd started working at Dunston's. Since she'd had bigger things to worry about. That was one good thing that had come out of all the trauma.

'You tell de ol' girl to be back in tamara, eh!'

'Will do.' Jo smiled and waved him off.

The notebook fell shut in her lap and she felt something lift inside her. Things weren't so bad for Jo Simmons.

She was still living her life on perilously thin ice – getting thinner with every lie she told, every step she made into this new existence – but she hadn't fallen through it yet.

Two words stared up at her from the back of the book. 'SASKIA DAWSON.' Her cyber friend would probably have the answers to a lot of her questions, if she dared ask them. But she had opened up to Saskia too much already. And besides, she wasn't sure whether she really wanted to know the answers. It almost felt better not knowing the source of the paranoia, assuming there was a source. It was like waiting for exam results: she wanted to know, but not if it was bad news.

Her phone buzzed against her leg.

Name a date. Would love
to see your 'old lady'. Mx

Chapter Twenty-One

Perhaps, thought Jo, she had been over-ambitious. The examples of murals she'd printed off from the internet depicted wild storms, idyllic islands and colourful, animated God-like creatures breathing fire down onto the world. It had been foolish of her to assume that these adolescents would create such scenes on the Fairmont House lounge wall.

'What's that, Tim?' She peered over the ten-year-old's shoulder, congratulating herself for having had the foresight to get them to sketch their ideas on paper first.

His beady eyes narrowed suspiciously. 'A car.'

'Oh, yes. Of course. Ooh, lots of cars.' Jo realised that the squiggles she had taken to be background shading were in fact other cars. They weren't brilliantly drawn, but they were unmistakably hundreds and hundreds of identical vehicles in various sizes.

'You like cars, do you?'

'It's a Ferrari FX,' he replied, as though he didn't expect Jo to understand.

'Oh, right. I guess that's quite an expensive one.'

'You can't buy them,' the boy explained patiently. 'There are only a few and they're all in museums now. But I made one once.'

'You *made* one?' Jo frowned. She couldn't help doubting that the ten-year-old had been involved in the manufacture of a million-pound supercar.

'A model,' Tim said quietly. Then he froze, all of a sudden. Jo saw his grip loosen on the pencil. It rolled off the sketchpad and onto the floor.

'What did you make it out of?'

'Card.' He was looking at the ground now, not blinking. 'Card from my Weetos box. It took me a whole week.'

Jo waited to find out more about the Ferrari FX, but Tim seemed to have stalled. He was staring at a spot on the floor, not moving.

'I bet it looked amazing,' she said, wishing she knew how one was supposed to react when a kid went all quiet like this. She was out of her depth again.

Tim didn't seem to hear her. 'Mum broke it. She put her foot on it and it all fell apart.'

'Oh, no! Well I'm sure she didn't mean to . . .'

'She did,' said Tim, so quietly Jo barely heard him. 'She'd taken too much medicine. She came into my room and pushed all my toys off the shelf. Then she trod on my car.'

Jo swallowed. She didn't know what to say. There was no point in trying to console the boy about his Ferrari. That wasn't the point. In fact, none of what she said to these kids was the point. She was missing it every time – deliberately. Because the point, whatever it was, scared her shitless. Jo wasn't qualified – or worthy – to deal with the point.

'Maybe . . . Maybe we can make model cars here one day,' she said weakly.

Tim didn't answer.

'Well, your part of the wall will look great,' she said,

183

hating the false gaiety in her voice. Despite being twice the boy's age, she felt immature in his presence.

Eventually, he picked up the pencil and drew another car. 'What's that, Charlene?'

The girl was hunched up on a beanbag, her body rocking violently with every stroke of the pencil. A silver stud protruded from the corner of her mouth and her eyes were narrowed in concentration.

'Anger,' she replied.

'Oh, right. Can I have a look?'

After a couple more jerky movements, the girl unfurled and revealed a picture that was, Jo acknowledged, a heart-wrenchingly accurate portrayal of the emotion: lots of straight lines and solid blocks with explosions and rip-marks and flames.

'It'll be better in colour,' she said.

'I bet.' Jo nodded, pushing aside her concerns about Charlene's state of mind and wondering how she was going to manage the integration of the various concepts into one mural. She ran the risk of turning the lounge wall into something akin to an act of vandalism. 'Are you gonna include other feelings too, or just anger?'

Charlene tapped the stud against her front teeth and shook her head. 'Just anger.'

'Right. Well, it looks great. Jason, can I see?'

Jason had spent most of the first thirty minutes throwing pencils at the floor and trying to make them bounce and now he was attempting to lever the lid off a paint pot with his nails. His sketch was lying face down on the floor.

'It's shit.'

'Oh, I'm sure it's not.' Jo picked it up.

'No – this whole thing. It's shit.'

'Oh. Well, I'm sorry you feel like that.' Jo looked at the page. It was certainly minimal. In the middle was a single shape that looked a bit like a tomato with a line through it. 'What is it?'

He shrugged. 'My tag.'

'Your *tag*?'

Jason groaned, long and loud. It was Kyle who spoke up – Kyle, who'd been uncharacteristically quiet all afternoon. 'His graffiti tag,' he explained, as though speaking to someone hard of hearing.

Jo's concerns mounted. 'Oh, OK. And is that . . . is that all you want to put on the wall?'

There was a grunt, which Jo took as affirmative.

'How're you doing, Nadia?'

'All right.' She moved her sleeve.

Jo stopped and stared. A swathe of what looked like marijuana leaves engulfed in ribbons of smoke crowded the page. It wasn't exactly what Jo had had in mind when she'd suggested the mural, but she was willing to forgo her lecture on the harmful effects of smoking weed because of the quality of the sketch.

'Wow, Nadia! This is amazing!' Then Jo saw the magazine. 'Oh. Right. You've copied it.'

'Traced,' the skinny girl corrected.

'Oh, OK. Well, still.' Jo looked from one to the other. 'You've traced it very well. Does it represent—'

'Drugs,' said Nadia.

Jo nodded slowly. She had actually spotted this theme and had been enquiring about the girl's personal circumstances. 'Right,' said Jo, losing the nerve to dig any deeper. 'Well it's really good.'

'Fanks.'

Despite their differences, thought Jo, there did seem to be something of a bond forming between her and the kids. OK, maybe bond was too strong a word. Maybe it was just a lack of the revulsion that had been so evident when she'd first arrived. They were never going to be buddies, exactly, but at least they didn't hate her either.

'Fuck off.' Kyle leaned over so Jo couldn't see his work.

Perhaps there was still a bit of hate.

'Can I have a look?'

Kyle snarled at her. 'Not finished.'

'Yeah, I know, but can I just see?'

'No.'

'Kyle,' Jo sighed. She was really hoping that this piece of art would not have a phallic theme – particularly given the amount of effort he seemed to have invested in it today – but there was only one way of finding out. 'Everyone else has shown me their sketches.'

'Well, I ain't gonna show you *mine*, all right?'

'You can't hide it for ever,' she said. 'It's going up on the wall.'

Kyle snorted, moving his arm slightly so that the corner of his sketch was half visible. 'Horseshit.'

Jo suppressed a smile. She had learned a lot in the last few weeks, not least how to interpret what came out of Kyle Merfield's mouth. He spoke in a language that was intended not to be deciphered by people like her, as did Jason and most of the others, but Jo was beginning to crack parts of the code.

When Kyle said 'horseshit', Jo had come to realise, it wasn't just an abusive phrase like 'bullshit' or 'bollocks'. It meant he felt secretly proud or embarrassed or affectionate or any of the other emotions that twelve-year-old kids

186

couldn't bring themselves to admit they were experiencing. Jo looked at him and waited for his eyes to flicker up to hers.

'Come on, Kyle,' she said light-heartedly. They were mates now. Well, almost. 'I just need to check that you're not drawing penises again.'

His face turned thunderous.

'Fuck off!' he yelled, jumping to his feet, throwing the sketchpad on the floor and looking around furiously. The other kids looked as scared as Jo felt. She hadn't foreseen this reaction.

'Kyle . . .'

Her plea went unnoticed. The boy seized the nearest object, which happened to be a stepladder, and made to hurl it at Jo.

Then something happened. Instead of flying across the room, the metal ladder dropped to the ground with a clatter that paled into insignificance compared to the deafening, wolflike howl that was coming from the skinhead's mouth.

Doubled over, elbows out, Kyle rubbed one hand against the other. Then, when the immediate physical grief had worn off, Kyle remembered his self-respect and staggered through the door. Jo followed, leaving a vague instruction for the others to, 'Er, carry on.'

'Kyle, come back. What happened?'

She knew what had happened, of course. She had pissed him off and he'd tried to throw the stepladder at her but his fingers had got caught in the closing jaws. What she really wanted to ask was, 'What are you feeling?' and, 'Why do you get so aggressive?' But to ask those sorts of question would only have made him more angry.

They got all the way to the main door of the house before Jo caught up with him.

'Kyle, please.' She gently put an arm out to guide him away from the door. To her surprise, he didn't resist. 'Let's go into the kitchen and get a cup of tea.'

A cup of tea. That would solve all his problems, wouldn't it? Abusive stepfather, uncontrollable temper, illiteracy, aggression . . . Why hadn't she thought of that before?

Inexplicably, Kyle seemed to be following her.

'Ooh, there's a choice. What sort of tea d'you want? Earl Grey or normal?' She pretended not to hear Kyle's muffled sniffs, hoping they might dry up so that she wouldn't need to confront the cause.

'Don't drink tea.' He sniffed again and looked down at his lap, where one set of fingers was wrapped around the other.

'Oh right. Orange squash? Water? I guess there must be milk – oh my God.'

Kyle unfurled his nursing hand, revealing four fat, purple knuckles.

Jo abandoned her tea-making. 'Kyle, that looks horrible. You might've broken something. Can you move them? Try waggling them, like this.'

He winced. 'Hurts.'

Despite his shaven head and sullen eyes, Kyle had a very expressive face. He probably didn't even realise it himself, but he gave away a lot, and Jo was beginning to know what his various scowls meant.

His default expression was a standard scowl, and that was what he wore most of the time under his hoodie. It simply said *life is shit*. Then, there was a lop-sided snarl that meant *you're a fucking idiot and I don't have*

188

time for you. He generally used that on Jo when she was suggesting 'fun' activities. But there was one particular look she'd seen a few times now: a narrowing of the eyes, a tautness in the upper lip. She was beginning to recognise it.

The first time, when he'd picked up the coffee table and hurled it at her, Jo had mistaken it for hatred. But now she knew what it was. It wasn't hatred or anger, or 'pure evil', as some newspapers liked to imply. It was pain. And that was the expression he was wearing now.

She watched as slowly, the fingers curled up and back again. She had no idea where her medical knowledge originated or whether it was any more sound than her belief in the healing powers of tea, but buried deep in Jo's subconscious was a theory that if the fingers moved, they weren't broken.

'I think you're all right. I'll get some ice.'

With a bag of frozen mixed vegetables hooked over his hand, Kyle seemed to relax a little. The sniffing subsided and his shoulders came down from around his ears, although his hood remained up. Jo tried to think of a cheery, neutral subject. Unfortunately, though, everything she came up with was linked to something controversial or unpleasant. She couldn't ask about his family, as his father had spent most of Kyle's childhood serving time for grievous bodily harm. She couldn't ask what he was up to this weekend, because it either wasn't legal or wasn't fun. She couldn't ask what he was doing at school, because he didn't go to one.

'So . . . how did you get involved with Dunston's?'

'Social services.'

'And you just come along for the activities, do you?'

He nodded, not looking at her.

There was a silence. Jo's mind raced to think of something else to talk about. The harder she thought, the emptier her brain became. She fetched him a glass of water, just for something to do.

Deep down, she knew the reason for the mental block. She knew why she was struggling to make conversation. It was because, for once, she was trying to say something meaningful. Up until now, she had survived at Dunston's by making small talk and laughing off any potential issues. But this wasn't small. She couldn't laugh now. She wanted to tell Kyle that she was here for him. She wanted to explain that he wasn't the only one with problems, and that it was OK to admit to having them. She wanted to talk about why he bottled up all his feelings, and to suggest that once in a while, he let them out by talking to someone, so that he didn't find himself exploding with the pressure of keeping it all in.

'Look, Kyle,' she said, waiting for him to look up. But she couldn't say the words. What she wanted to tell him . . . it all seemed too deep, too weird. If she started going on about bottled-up emotions, he would probably never speak to her again.

Reluctantly, Kyle made eye contact.

'I know my sessions aren't great, but . . .' She tried to find a way of reaching him, getting close to him, without sending him back under his hood. 'I'm trying my best.'

Jo wasn't sure whether she imagined it or saw it, but she thought there was a slight shift in the boy's expression before he looked away.

'You have to try too, Kyle.'

He nodded, but Jo could see that the armour plating

was slotting back into place. She leaned forward and peeled the frozen vegetables off the boy's hand.

'The swelling's gone down. Are you left- or right-handed?'

'Right.'

'Well, that's good then. You can still draw. Shall we go back?'

Rather than object, or swear, or say something abusive, Kyle slithered off the kitchen stool and followed her out.

'How's everyone doing? Ready to start painting?' Jo looked around.

It wasn't exactly a jubilant response. Nobody shouted, 'Yeah!' or clapped their hands, but nobody objected either.

It was only once the wall had been divided into zones and the kids were busy scribbling all over it that Jo had another go at seeing Kyle's sketch. This time, coyly, he tilted it towards her.

Jo lunged forward and grabbed it from his frozen clutches.

'Kyle!'

It was incredible. Sketched in a sort of cartoon style was a street scene with a hundred different things going on at once. Kids were playing hopscotch outside a shop, a guy was running past with a dog, girls in miniskirts stood smoking on the street corner – looking rather like prostitutes, but still – and a woman loitered with a pram while the litter swirled at her feet. It was like watching high-definition TV in slow motion.

'This is *brilliant*.'

The boy's mouth twitched slightly.

'It's amazing. Really.'

Kyle turned back to the wall. 'Horseshit,' he muttered.

Jo knew that she wasn't supposed to see, but she did. As he turned back to paint his first brushstroke on the wall, there was an unmistakable dimple in his cheek. He was smiling.

Chapter Twenty-Two

'Have some more, Matthew,' offered Mrs Phillips, tipping the enormous casserole dish towards him.

Jo pinched his thigh under the table as he politely explained that four helpings was enough.

'Keep it for your lunch,' Matt suggested, shielding his plate with a hand as the remaining portion floated dangerously close. 'You can put it in the microwave.'

Mrs Phillips looked at him sternly.

He nodded as a smile played on his gorgeous lips. 'Or oven, obviously.'

The dinner had gone better than expected, thought Jo. Mrs Phillips had stayed true to her word and cooked a not-too-fancy chicken hotpot and Matt had proved popular by eating about five times his recommended daily allowance and agreeing with everything she said. Somehow, to Jo's relief, they had also avoided the subject of her former acting career.

'So you're a support worker too?' asked the woman.

'No. I don't actually work with the kids. Unlike Jo, I don't spend my time vandalising walls.'

'We're not *vandalising* it.'

Matt turned to Mrs Phillips, smiling mischievously.

'They're vandalising one of the walls in the house – in the name of art.'

The woman gave a doubtful nod.

'It's a mural,' Jo explained. 'The kids get to express themselves as they decorate their own lounge.'

Matt smiled and mouthed 'vandalism' to Mrs Phillips. 'I work in PR and marketing. Raising the profile of the charity,' he said. 'It's a bit of everything really. Community work, journalism, schmoozing with wealthy donors and quite a lot of web design.'

Mrs Phillips looked impressed, probably picturing Matt sitting in a studio designing cobwebs. 'I think it's lovely what you do,' said Mrs Phillips. 'Both of you. And it's good that you're enjoying it more now, Jo, isn't it?'

Jo nodded, feeling the first flutter of anxiety. It sounded very much as though Mrs Phillips was about to refer to her shift in career. If she did, Jo's story about teaching in Haringey would fall apart. A few weeks ago, she might not have felt so concerned about the prospect, but now – perhaps because of what had happened with Kyle, she wasn't sure – the idea of life away from Fairmont House seemed empty and futile.

'It's a great place to work,' she said quickly. 'Just teething problems, I guess. You know . . . getting to know the children and that. Hey, I saw this TV programme the other day about a school. This class of kids . . .' She frantically tried to create an interesting punch line. 'They were terrible!'

Her listeners nodded slowly, clearly trying to work out what made the reference worth mentioning.

'I think you made a very charitable decision,' Mrs Phillips ploughed on. 'It's not often—'

'Ha!' cried Jo, before her landlady could get on to her break from acting. 'Well, Dunston's *is* a charity! Although it's a bit of a madhouse too, isn't it, Matt? A madhouse run by an idiot. Oh, Geoff Ramsay . . . Did I tell you about Geoff, Mrs Phillips?'

The woman seemed a little taken aback by Jo's sudden bout of verbal diarrhoea. 'Er, no, I don't think you did.'

'Oh, well, he's the man in charge. It's amazing someone like that is allowed to be in charge of a children's home, isn't it, Matt?' She waited impatiently for him to nod. 'But Sue's really sweet. She's helped me a lot. It's thanks to her that I feel so at home there now. She's my line manager.'

'Is it very different from your last place?' asked Matt. He too was looking mildly baffled.

'Huh – my *last* place!' Jo looked at Mrs Phillips, who was presumably thinking of her role in *Jim's Secret House*. 'That was very different. Different people, different jobs, different place, obviously . . .'

'And no children to look after,' Mrs Phillips put in, rather unhelpfully.

Jo let out a peal of laughter. 'I wish!' She glanced at Matt with an expression that said, *She's mad*. 'D'you want to pass me your plates? Are you expecting us to eat dessert, Mrs P?'

'Well, I have an apple pie in the oven,' she replied, rising to her feet. Crisis averted, thought Jo. 'Would you like some?'

The look on Matt's face answered her question. 'Sorry,' he said. 'I'm stuffed.' Jo nodded in apologetic agreement. 'Something else for your lunch tomorrow.'

Jo's offer to wash up was met with a cry of horror. 'What sort of a thank-you dinner would it be if you had to wash your own dishes at the end?' The old lady turned to Matt conspiratorially. 'She gave me an afternoon off, you see.'

Matt looked suitably impressed. Jo had already explained that she had merely sat behind the cash register for a few hours the previous week.

'No, you two go off and do what you want.' She ushered them out of the kitchen. 'Leave this to me.'

They wandered off in the direction Mrs Phillips had indicated. Jo suddenly became aware of how the kids in her sessions probably felt when she jovially instructed them to 'have fun'.

She led the way to her room, not because she had any particular plan but because there weren't many alternatives in the guesthouse. Unless they were going to sit back down at the table and watch Friday night TV on a screen the size of a credit card, the only other option was the bathroom.

It was a clumsy entrance. The door opened inwards and Jo stepped back to let Matt walk through, but then at the last minute barged in herself to check she hadn't left any knickers or bras lying about, which meant that Matt had to leap into the doorframe and banged his elbow.

The room was free of stray underwear. In fact, it was free of most things, she realised, seeing the room through Matt's eyes: free of clothes, free of books, free of photos, ornaments, posters, clutter. It looked like the living quarters of someone with severe OCD.

'It's, um . . . quite tidy,' she said, motioning for Matt to sit down on the bed. 'I've still got most of my stuff in London.'

'Right,' he nodded. 'Still living out of that plastic bag, eh?'

196

'Yeah!' Jo laughed. Her head was hurting with the stress of keeping track of all the lies, and she could feel her cheeks glowing. 'I'm just gonna . . .' She tried to think of an excuse for popping out and splashing her face with water. 'Get us a drink.'

'Good idea.' Matt smiled. Despite the sterile surroundings, he looked as relaxed as a man on the beach. 'The perks of living above a shop, eh? So you're back off the wagon?'

Jo smiled. Actually, she was still very much on the wagon, but she thought that tonight, briefly, she'd hop off it – just for a couple of hours. 'Beer or wine?'

Matt grinned at her like a naughty schoolboy. 'Beer?'

Jo looked around the room as she left, trying to find something to keep Matt entertained. 'Make yourself . . . Er, I won't be long.'

She grabbed a pack of cold lagers from the fridge in the store and left a ten-pound note on the kitchen table, ignoring Mrs P's wary look. She'd be OK. Everything was under control. She was with Matt. She wouldn't drink much.

She stared at her face in the bathroom mirror. Having invested some of her first pay packet in makeup, her lips looked pinker than usual and her eyes more exotic, but the stress of all the lying was taking its toll. Jo let the cold water run down her waxy cheeks and tried to force her brow out of its frown. It was fine. The dinner had gone well, and now she was going to have a sensible amount of beer with Matt.

She dried her face, wondering what to do about the auburn streak that was starting to grow out. Had the old Jo dyed it herself using cheap chemicals? Or had she gone to a stylist and paid hundreds of pounds to get it redone every month? She thought probably the former.

'Heineken OK?' she asked, returning to find Matt sitting on the bed, hunched over something.

He looked up, straight into her eyes, not replying. He seemed distant or confused. Jo glanced down at his lap and then froze. Suddenly, she understood. She stood there rigidly, feeling all the energy drain from her body.

'What's this?'

Her legs started to shake.

'Is it yours?'

She couldn't answer.

'Who's Saskia?'

Jo felt like an animal on a main road. The headlights kept coming. She knew she couldn't stay here; she had to cross, but she couldn't.

'Jo?'

Matt's brow was furrowed. He'd read her notes. All the details of her former life, everything she'd collected, it was all there in the book on his lap. What could she say?

He stood up and moved towards her, dropping the note-book on the bed.

'Ideas for a screenplay you're writing?' He smiled meekly, then his expression turned serious. He knew it was more than that.

Jo's head was spinning. She couldn't think straight. There were questions going through her mind – questions she needed to ask Matt, like how much had he seen? What did he really think? But like a punch-bag, the realisation kept coming back to her, hitting her in the face: Matt had read her notes. Maybe he didn't know what they meant right now, but he'd guess, later on. He would find out about her past – or lack of. He'd know about the Buffalo Club, the new life, the lies . . . With dismay, Jo found her lower lip starting to quiver. Tears were welling up in her eyes.

'Hey, it's OK.' Matt stepped forward and wrapped his body around hers. 'I don't know what the fuck's going on here, but I'm sure it'll be OK.'

Jo sniffed against his chest. She couldn't see anything now through the tears. For a moment, she stayed in Matt's arms, engulfed, supported. If she closed her eyes and tried to forget, she could convince herself that she was safe, that it *would* be OK, that Matt was all she needed.

Then reality reared its head. Matt *wasn't* all she needed. Matt had just read the one thing she never wanted anyone to read. What she needed was to redo the last ten minutes of her life. She turned away.

'I'm sorry,' she said, wiping her bare arm across her eyes. The mascara was all over her face now but she didn't care. 'I'm sorry.'

Matt tried to face her. 'Why? What's going on?'

'Just . . . go,' she said, pressing her fingers into the corners of her eyes. 'Please.'

Matt didn't move. 'You can tell me,' he said quietly.

She nearly did, and then she thought better of it.

'Please, Matt.' Her voice cracked on his name. 'Just go.'

Without even looking at him, Jo could picture his face: an expression of confusion mingled with hurt. A part of her wanted to retract her request and to run back into his arms, to sob against his chest and tell him everything. But that was the one thing she couldn't do. She stared at the floor, wishing that she could relive the last five minutes of her life.

She knew this would happen, at some point. It was all turning out too well: the job, the guesthouse, Matt . . . Her carefully constructed house of cards had been too precarious. It had been only a matter of time, she knew, before it came crashing down. And now it had.

Without another word, Matt walked out.

Chapter Twenty-Three

The room seemed empty without Kyle. It wasn't just his cussing and swearing that was missing; it was his presence. His energy. Coupled with Jo's melancholy mood, the atmosphere was very flat.

'OK. We may as well get going,' she said. 'Jason, come away from there. We're not painting the wall today.'

A look passed between Charlene and Nadia. 'Why not?' they chimed in unison.

Jo sighed. Everything seemed like a lot of effort today. She should probably have felt pleased that the girls were so keen to partake in an activity that had been her idea. Instead, she just felt irritable. 'Because I want us to get started on something else.'

'It looks crap,' declared Jason, nodding at the half-painted wall.

'It'll look great when it's done,' Jo said, not very convincingly. In fact, the only part of the mural that Jo had any pride in was the cartoon scene along the bottom: Kyle's part. 'Right. Gather round.'

Her phone buzzed in her back pocket. Jo left it to buzz. She knew what it was: another message from Matt. Another hollow reassurance that things would 'B OK'. She hadn't replied to a single one. She wanted to; she just wasn't sure how to. At some point, of course, she'd have to confront the situation, tell Matt the truth, or something like it, and apologise, try to explain . . . But right now she didn't have the courage.

The project she was about to propose was high risk, Jo knew. Either it would be a roaring success, bringing unity and a newfound sense of camaraderie to the Fairmont House kids, or it would be a high-impact flop, pushing their collective self-esteem to an all-time low.

'Who here has ever played football?' she asked.

Nadia and Charlene exchanged another unimpressed look. Tim and Jason nodded warily.

'Well, I know this may sound a bit mad,' she ventured, 'but we've got an opportunity to play in a five-a-side tournament in London, and I think we can do it.'

'What, with *girls*?' Jason's mouth hung open in disbelief.

Jo had anticipated this response. 'It's a mixed tournament, so, yes, with girls. Nadia, Charlene, what do you think?'

Charlene shrugged as though this was just one more of life's obstacles that someone was putting in her way.

Nadia hid behind layers of dark hair, looking scared. 'Ain't never played before,' she said timidly.

'See?' said Jason, as though this proved his point. 'She never played before, innit.'

Jo nodded wearily. 'That doesn't matter. It's a Christmas tournament, so we've got two months for training.' Jason didn't seem at all convinced. 'All the teams have to have at least two girls. We'll be in the same boat as everyone else.'

'I ain't playin' football in no boat,' said Jason. 'Why don't we just enter in a guys' tournament, anyway?'

Jo sighed. It wasn't Jason's attitude that was worrying her; it was the expressions on the two pale, pretty faces that were staring at her as though she were the devil.

'It's a tournament run by a charity called Centrepoint in London,' she went on. 'It takes place every Christmas somewhere near their headquarters on Tottenham Court Road. Have you heard of Centrepoint?'

'Sounds gay,' muttered Jason.

Jo ignored him. 'It's a place very much like Dunston's, and every year they organise a big fundraising event that involves—'

She turned round as the door clicked behind her and Sue Meads' fuzz of hair poked in. 'Can I have a word?' she whispered hoarsely, as though somehow this was more discreet than just speaking normally.

Jo's heart started pumping extra fast. Sue knew what had happened; Matt had told her about the notebook. She knew about Jo's lies. This was the end of her career at Fairmont.

'Er, just have a think . . . about the tournament.'

Jo followed Sue into the corridor, trying to decide on her line of defence. Perhaps she could deny it, say that Matt was making it up. Or perhaps she should own up and try to persuade Sue that qualifications weren't that important. Or . . . oh God, she needed more time to prepare.

'Sorry to drag you out,' said Sue, still talking in a stage whisper for no apparent reason. 'I just heard some news.'

Jo tried to swallow but her throat was like sandpaper. This was it. This was where her career was wrenched from under her.

'I just spoke to Kyle's mother.'

Jo looked at her. What on earth did Kyle's mother have to do with her situation?

'It's standard procedure,' Sue explained, seeing Jo's confusion. 'When a kid doesn't turn up, we call home.'

'Yes . . . Right.' Relief flooded Jo's veins, and then guilt. This wasn't about her at all. As if she needed any more proof that she didn't deserve this job, here it was. A child was missing, and all she could think about was herself.

'What did she say?'

'Well, that's why I pulled you out. She said he was *here*.'

Jo frowned. 'Well, he's not. Did the taxi arrive to pick him up and everything?'

Sue tutted and bit her lip thoughtfully. 'I think there's more to it than that. You see, his mother was in quite a state. Drunk, I think. She was saying something about Kyle running off and being with *you*, Jo.'

Jo frowned. 'I haven't seen him since the last session.'

Sue nodded slowly and started to walk away. 'Hmm. OK. Leave it with me.'

Jo followed her as far as she dared, not wanting to enter the offices in case Matt was around. For now, as far as she could tell, her secret was safe.

'Do you think he's OK? Has he done this before? Where d'you think he's gone?'

Sue switched on a motherly smile. 'I'm sure he's fine. Probably a family row. Nothing to worry about.'

Jo nodded and drifted back to the lounge. There wasn't nothing to worry about. There was plenty to worry about – and for a change, she was thinking about other people's problems, not hers. Jo braced herself for another barrage of abuse about the tournament and threw open the door.

'So, what do you all think?'

'Wank,' said Jason, under his breath.

'Thoughts from the rest of you? Charlene, you've been a bit quiet. How d'you feel about playing football?'

Charlene glowered up at her. 'I'll be crap, won't I? I never played it before.'

'Well, you might be surprised when we get out there and train.' Jo wasn't actually too confident about her skills as a football coach, but that was a bridge she would cross later on. 'The most important thing is that you *want* to play. The day itself should be really exciting – lots of teams from all over the country. But I don't want anyone to feel they're being forced into it. Nadia? What d'you reckon?'

The new girl looked at Charlene and then back at Jo. 'I got asthma.'

'OK,' said Jo, not surprised to hear that the girl who had apparently chain-smoked marijuana for over two years suffered from breathing difficulties. 'Well, maybe you can go in goal or something. We'll see. But in principle, are you up for it?'

Presumably unable to think of another excuse quickly enough, Nadia shrugged. Jo couldn't help feeling that enthusiasm for the project was somewhat lacking. She wondered how Kyle would feel about it. She wondered where he was.

'Anyway! What I thought we could do to begin with—'

She broke off as the door opened again, this time not with a click but with a bang as it flew back and hit the bookshelf.

'Where is 'e?' yelled a woman that Jo didn't recognise. She was about thirty, with straw-yellow hair and inch-long black roots.

Sue Meads crept in behind her and mouthed an apology in Jo's direction.

'Where is who?'

'Kyle.' The woman glared at Jo.

'Let's all calm down, shall we?' Sue smiled placidly. 'I don't think we should be conducting this conversation in front of—'

'Shu'up.' The woman turned back to Jo. 'Where's Kyle?'

Jo caught Sue's cautionary glance. 'Shall we go to Geoff's office?'

The four teenagers gawped up at the women. Jo had never seen them so animated.

'How about . . . how about, Jason, you explain the offside rule to the others?'

Sue nodded approvingly and led them out. Not content to wait until they were seated, the woman tottered along beside Jo in some loud, plastic heels, yapping at her like a deranged puppy.

'Where's Kyle? Where's my son? Where is 'e?'

'OK,' said Sue, taking control as they reached the privacy of Geoff's office. The only downside was that Geoff was in it. 'Let's talk this through sensibly. I believe you've met our centre manager? Geoff, this is Kyle's mother.'

Geoff looked up and mumbled something, then got back to peering gormlessly at his keyboard. He was wearing a gaudy blue tie that was embossed with an embroidered sheep.

The woman ignored his greeting and turned to Jo. 'It's you I'm here to see.' Her teeth were almost as yellow as her hair, Jo noticed, wondering where the mad accusations stemmed from. 'Where's my son?'

'Let's start from the beginning,' said Sue. 'Why don't you tell Jo what you told me over the phone?'

'She knows all that. I just wanna know where she lives. I want my son back.'

Jo frowned, slightly alarmed at the reference to her home.

Sue sighed. 'OK, allow me to paraphrase what you told me earlier, Mrs Merfield. Your—'

'Lake,' the woman cut in.

'I'm sorry?'

'Mrs *Lake*.'

Jo made a mental note. She was glad Sue had made the slip-up, not her.

'OK. Mrs *Lake*. So, your son left the house saying something about going off to live with Miss Simmons here.'

'*What?*' Jo stared at her boss in amazement.

'And you haven't seen him since,' Sue went on calmly. 'But you didn't think to call us when he walked out.'

'Didn't need to, I fought. You's supposed to look *after* the kids, aintcha?' The woman's eyes were wild and wandering.

Jo tried to interject but she didn't know what to say.

'So Kyle walked out . . . when, exactly?' It was incredible. She could have been asking about the weather.

'Like . . . this morning. Well, last night. Late.' The woman seemed confused. 'Like, three o'clock, four . . . Summink like that.'

Jo didn't dare ask what a twelve-year-old was doing awake at three or four o'clock in the morning. She was still trying to work out how she was being implicated in all this.

'So he walked out in the early hours, claiming to be heading where?' asked Sue.

Her composure was clearly starting to annoy Kyle's mum. 'I dunno! Her place!' She lunged and pointed at Jo.

Jo opened her mouth to protest.

'Anyone for a cup of tea?'

The three women looked at Geoff, then turned away again. They watched as he took the opportunity to leave the room. Really, thought Jo, the centre manager could show a little more concern over a missing child.

'So Kyle actually said that he was planning to go to Jo Simmons' house?'

Jo tried to protest but the woman was yelling again. 'Said 'e knew where she lived an' was gonna leave 'ome again! Fuckin' bitch. She knows where 'e is.'

'OK, calm down, Mrs . . . Mrs Lake. Jo, can you shed any light on this?'

'No,' she replied in a deliberately measured tone. She looked at Kyle's mother. 'As far as I'm aware, Kyle has no idea where I live, and he hasn't made contact with me since the last session.'

'Liar!' yelled the woman, her dilated pupils boring into Jo's eyes. 'He's my *boy*. Tell me where 'e is.'

Jo felt a rush of fear, not because of the woman's tone or her accusations – which were unreasonable, and clearly Sue could see that – but because of something else. *Déjà vu.* She had argued like this before with another woman. Another mother. *Her* mother.

She couldn't say how her brain made the leap, but something in Mrs Lake's tone had set bells ringing. Jo had argued with her mother. She didn't know why; it was all hazy. There had been anger and resentment and hatred and rage, but also, guilt. She had let her mother down.

'Jo?'

Jo blinked. 'I'm sorry . . .'

Sue Meads was saying something about reporting Kyle as missing and making statements. Jo tried to focus. It was there, the memory, just out of reach.

'. . . Then we'll call the police.'

The door opened at exactly the moment Sue picked up the receiver. It was Clare.

'Sorry to interrupt,' she said, glancing around and then looking at Sue. 'I've got a boy in the office. Name of Kyle?'

Chapter Twenty-Four

'I . . . I honestly don't know,' stammered Jo. Because she didn't. She didn't have an answer for why a twelve-year-old boy would claim that she had something to do with his night-time disappearance when they had barely exchanged more than a dozen words since they'd met.

'Sometimes this happens,' Sue said gently. 'A member of staff gets close to a service user and the relationship has become too . . . personal.'

Jo stared at her line manager, horrified at what she seemed to be insinuating and glad that Kyle's mother wasn't around to hear the accusation. 'No! No, Sue, really, it's not like that!'

Sue shook her head quickly. 'No, of course. I didn't mean like *that*. I just meant—'

Jo was a bit lost in the riddles. 'I mean, it's not even like . . . I *didn't* get close to him. The relationship *wasn't* personal.'

Sue nodded and locked her fingers together like a praying nun. Her face was a picture of understanding, which was ironic, thought Jo, because she didn't seem to be understanding this at all.

'Look,' said Jo. 'Here's a summary of my contact with

Kyle. He came along to my first activities session and stormed out because I asked him to write. He came to the car wash session and stormed out because I told him off for messing around. He was there at the first mural-painting session and stormed out because I teased him about his drawing. That's when he hurt his hand. Since then, he's been painting the mural and doing quite well, and I've been encouraging him . . . But really, I wouldn't say our relationship was *personal*.'

Sue nodded and unclasped her hands.

Jo watched her, waiting, hoping. She had to prove she was innocent. Dunston's had become an important part of her life; she couldn't let Kyle's mad, yellow-haired mother mess things up for her.

'It sounds as though he's just trying to make trouble,' Sue said eventually.

Jo nodded, overcome with relief. 'I think he's a bit confused.'

Sue laughed. 'To put it mildly!'

Jo didn't like to make light of the matter, but she could see why Sue did it. They all did it at Dunston's: joke about dire situations in a way that would horrify an outsider. Now they knew Kyle was safe, it was OK to laugh. As Matt had said the other day: you've got to laugh or you'll cry.

Matt. Jo wished she hadn't reminded herself. She rose to her feet, thinking about the scene with the notebook. That was something else she'd have to resolve.

'We should keep a close eye on him,' suggested Sue, opening the door.

Jo tried to shove the image of Matt to the back of her mind and think about Kyle.

211

'He's not on the at-risk register, but he seems to be running away from something. That's not a good sign.'

Jo nodded as though she'd been thinking the very same thing, and tried to focus her thoughts. Sue was right. Kyle was running away from something. That was his solution. When something didn't agree with him – a comment, another kid, a class, a school – he ran away. It wasn't exactly unprecedented teenage behaviour. Kids threw tantrums all the time. But they didn't usually run away from the place where they were supposed to feel safe. They didn't flee their homes at three a.m.

'You're OK, aren't you?' asked Sue.

'Yeah, fine!' Jo realised she'd been scowling. The thought of Kyle's problems, coupled with her own and the situation with Matt, were weighing heavily on her mind.

'Good.' Sue smiled and walked her to the front door. 'It gets to some people,' she whispered.

Jo stepped out as breezily as she could. 'I'll be fine.' She waved. 'See you Wednesday.'

The streetlamps were already starting to flicker into life as she walked to the bus stop. Grey clouds rolled overhead, ruling out any chance of a last-minute glimmer of sunshine. Jo stood at the bus stop and waited.

A minute later, she was walking again. Not in the direction of Mrs Phillips, but back towards Oxford. She needed to move, to try to work things out. A change of scene. That was the answer. There were too many thoughts floating around in her head, too many unanswered questions. She couldn't deal with them whilst cooped up in her tiny bedroom. Jo strode up Park End Street and headed for the town centre, looking forward to losing herself in the rush-hour bustle.

Kyle's issues played on her mind as the rain started falling. He had obviously made a conscious decision to drag Jo into his family problems by implying she'd had something to do with his early-morning escape. The fact that he'd opted to do that was strange, but it wasn't what was bothering Jo. If anything, she was flattered that he'd deemed her familiar enough to be involved. Perhaps she had got through to him after all, that afternoon when he'd hurt his hand. No, the concern, as Sue had pointed out, was that he was running away at all.

She had seen it again, that expression, when Kyle had been marched through the building and into Geoff's office, to be greeted by his demented mother. The slit-like eyes, the pursed lips – she could tell he was hurting. And from what she had seen, Jo sensed that Mrs Lake wasn't offering much in the way of support.

The houses gave way to college walls and multi-storey car parks and the pavements became nicely crowded. Jo wondered whether she had ever experienced pain like Kyle had. She'd pieced together enough to know that her life hadn't exactly been full of joy: a disagreement with her mother, a spell doing drugs, a break-up with the blond guy, some sort of altercation with another man . . . But none of it, she thought, compared to what Kyle was going through – or any of the other Dunston's kids.

A team of men were stringing up some sort of lattice above the street that looked suspiciously like Christmas lights. Jo stopped for a moment and looked up. It was October.

'Mind your backs!' yelled one of the men in fluores-cent jackets, reversing into her.

Jo leaped sideways and made to confront the clumsy

man. Then she lost her nerve as she realised that he was not a complete stranger.

Kieran blinked for a few seconds, looking as confused as Jo felt. 'Hello.'

'What are you doing?' asked Jo, because she couldn't think of a better way of putting it.

'I'm coordinating the Christmas light erection,' he replied proudly. Then he blushed. 'Um, I mean, Christmas light putting-up-of . . .'

Jo smiled. 'I know what you mean. But . . . how did you get involved?'

'Oh, I head up the Seasonal Decorations Sub-Committee. HIGHER! HIGHER!'

The men on either side of the street were raised to an absurd height by yellow crane-like vehicles.

'So you work for . . .' Jo trailed off as the men were hoisted into the atmosphere. Kieran appeared to have overlooked the fact that there were no streetlamps or windows to hang the lights from at that elevation.

'The council. OK, GUYS, I'VE JUST THOUGHT OF SOMETHING!'

The mist cleared.

'I'd better leave you to it,' said Jo, waving goodbye.

'Hang on, Jo,' said Kieran, holding a hand up. 'COME DOWN A BIT – THERE'S NOTHING TO TIE THEM ON TO UP THERE!'

Jerkily, the men were lowered and the lattice fixed between the eaves of opposing three-storey buildings. Jo ducked as the crane swung dangerously low over the pavement, then looked at the head of the Seasonal Decorations Sub-Committee.

Kieran's expression was uncharacteristically serious. Jo

stood there facing him, feeling her heart pounding against her chest. She could only think of one possible explanation for the sudden sincerity.

'It's . . . it's about something Matt said.'

Jo swallowed. No. Surely not. Matt couldn't have told Kieran about the notebook.

'What did he say?' she managed to squeak.

'Well,' Kieran looked left and right, as though he suspected one of the workmen might overhear. 'He told me what happened the other night.'

He had. He had told Kieran. Jo couldn't believe it. She didn't want to believe it. Matt had betrayed her trust and told his eccentric flatmate about the notebook.

'MAKE SURE IT'S NICE AND SECURE!' yelled Kieran, blinking up at his team's handiwork. 'But just so you know, I won't tell anyone.'

Jo nodded blankly. Looking at Kieran's earnest expression, she thought he probably meant it, although she was rapidly losing faith in her judgement of character.

'Thanks, Kieran.'

'OK, LET'S TEST THE LIGHTS!'

Jo could see that his attention was elsewhere, but she wanted to be sure.

'Kieran, I know you wouldn't, but can you just *promise* you won't tell anyone? Not even the lads?'

Kieran looked at her, wide-eyed, as though he had just become involved in a very exciting, elaborate plan. 'Not a soul,' he said. 'I promise.'

Chapter Twenty-Five

Jo drained the can, crushed it in her fist and chucked it across the room. Her head rolled back against the headboard and she felt another tear of frustration trickle out.

It was too much. All the lies and unknowns and revelations and disappointments . . . and now the fact that Perfect Matt was not fucking perfect at all; he was untrustworthy, like everybody else. She didn't know what to do with it all. It was too much for her brain to process.

Jo thought about creeping downstairs to get some more booze, and then hated herself for even considering it. She hadn't even noticed it happening, but she had fallen back into her old ways. She was drinking and lying and cheating again, and rejecting the people who were trying to help her. Jo Simmons was turning back into Roxie.

There was a knock on the door.

'Everything OK, dear?'

Jo closed her eyes and let out a long, shaky sigh. Mrs Phillips. One of the people trying to help her. *No*, she wanted to say. *No, everything was not OK. Everything was crap and she didn't know what to do.*

'Fine,' she grunted.

There was no sound. No patter of footsteps. Mrs Phillips was still there on the landing.

'Just . . . wondering what all the clattering was about.'

Jo ground the heels of her hands into her eye sockets and blinked several times.

'I'm fine.'

She should have known that something as noisy as throwing beer cans around the room wouldn't pass unnoticed by her vigilant landlady.

'Are you drinking?' she asked, so softly that Jo could barely hear it through the door.

The creeping around was pissing her off. 'Open the fucking door if you wanna talk!'

As soon as the woman edged in, Jo regretted her choice of words. Mrs Phillips hated swearing.

'Sorry,' she said quietly, swinging her legs down off the bed and burying her face in her hands. 'Sorry.'

Mrs Phillips perched on the bed next to Jo.

'Has something happened?'

Jo groaned. *Had something happened?* Where would she start?

'Something to do with Matthew?'

And the rest, thought Jo.

'I'm sure he'll be back,' Mrs Phillips said cautiously. 'He's a nice young man.'

Jo shook her head and stared down at the carpet. The woman had no idea.

'He likes you,' she went on. 'I can tell.'

Jo was trying not to get annoyed with Mrs Phillips, but right now, filled with all this confusion and hurt, her fuse was short. If she said one more thing about Matt . . .

'You seemed very well-suited, actually.'

That was it. Jo couldn't contain herself any longer. The anger gushed out of her like steam from a hot vessel. 'Shut up! Just . . . shut up! It's nothing like that! It's . . . something else!'

Mrs Phillips looked slightly put out at being told to shut up, but no less intrigued. 'What?'

Jo shook her head and buried her face again. There was nothing more she could tell Mrs Phillips without giving herself away. She couldn't talk about the notebook because then she'd have to explain what the notebook contained, and that would involve coming clean on the whole Rebecca-Roxie-Jo Simmons thing.

'Nothing.'

Mrs Phillips sighed, shook her head and wrapped an arm around Jo's shoulders. Instinctively, Jo leaned sideways and collapsed onto the woman's collarbone. She was crying properly now: tears of frustration and pain and anxiety and confusion, all mixed in together.

'It's not nothing, is it?' said Mrs Phillips, gently stroking Jo's hair.

Jo didn't answer. Of course it wasn't nothing. It was the fact that she wasn't really Jo Simmons, that she was a girl called Rebecca who called herself Roxie and danced naked for a living and took cocaine and had a drink problem and didn't know who her parents were. It was the fact that she'd spent the last two months living under a cloud of guilt and paranoia, for reasons she still didn't know. And it was the fact that adorable, witty, good-looking Matt, with whom she was apparently 'so well-suited', had spilled her biggest secret to his flatmate and God knew who else.

She couldn't do it any longer. She couldn't hold it all inside her. The secrets and lies were weighing too heavily

218

on her mind and Jo felt as though if she didn't tell someone soon, she might actually burst.

'I'm living a lie,' she said.

Mrs Phillips didn't react; she just held her and waited.

Jo sat up, took a deep breath and started relaying her story. She told her landlady everything: about Rebecca Ross and Roxie and how she had crawled away from the explosion, about how she had set herself up as Jo Simmons and fallen into this new life in Radley, about inventing her career to get the job at Dunston's and fabricating the other career in acting because . . . well, because it had seemed like a good idea at the time.

'Well,' said Mrs Phillips. Then she just sat there in silence.

Jo's relief was overwhelming. It was as though all the lies had been simmering inside her for weeks, getting thicker and darker and now, suddenly, Mrs Phillips had come along and lifted the lid.

The problems were still there, of course. She was still worried about the source of the paranoia and scared that Dunston's would find her out. She still wished that Matt hadn't turned on her and that she hadn't actually worked in the Buffalo Club. But it felt as though now someone else knew these things, she wasn't quite so alone.

'I did wonder.'

Jo frowned. 'What?'

'Well, I wondered about your background. You're a hard one to fathom.'

Jo smiled meekly. That was true enough. She'd spent the last two months trying to fathom herself. What sort of person was a lap-dancing footballer?

'You didn't seem to have any friends – or *things.*'

Jo nodded. She might have known Mrs Phillips had picked up on her oddities.

'You seemed very able, but very . . . restless.'

Jo nodded again. Mrs Phillips was spot-on. She felt restless.

'Which I suppose makes sense, given that you don't know who you are.' Mrs Phillips shifted a little and looked at her. 'So is that why Matthew isn't talking to you? Because of all the lies?'

Jo grimaced and shook her head, wishing it was that simple. 'It's the other way round. I'm pissed off with him. He went and told his mate about the notebook. I don't even know how much he saw, but he went and blurted it to Kieran before I'd even explained.'

'So . . . He doesn't know everything you just told me?' Jo shook her head.

Mrs Phillips let out a long sigh. 'Oh dear . . .'

'It's a mess, isn't it?' She smiled faintly.

Mrs Phillips squeezed her shoulder. 'You're a resourceful girl. You'll work it out.' She eased herself up from the bed and moved towards the door.

Jo suddenly had a vision of Mrs Phillips telling all her customers about her lodger's secret past as they paid for their milk in the morning.

'Don't say anything to anyone, will you?'

Mrs Phillips frowned. 'And why would I want to do that?'

'I just . . . Sorry. I'm just being paranoid. I don't want people knowing, obviously.'

The woman nodded. 'Even yourself.'

'What?'

'Well, I can understand your not wanting to tell Matthew

220

or anyone else you've met recently, but don't *you* want to know about your life, Rebecca?'

'I . . .' She thought about the name on the back of her notebook. That was one lead she could follow up today, if she wanted – if she trusted Saskia Dawson. 'I don't know.'

Mrs Phillips looked back at Jo, her green eyes standing out from the sagging skin around them.

'You don't want to stay dead for ever, do you?'

Chapter Twenty-Six

Jo squeezed between two double pushchairs, the contents of which were happily squirting lurid pink juice at the bus window while the mothers chatted about fake nails. She hopped onto the pavement.

'Sweeeeet potty-toes!' cried an old man with dreadlocks, waving what looked like a plump carrot in her face. 'Tree for a pound!'

Jo weaved through the colourful stalls, mesmerised by the sheer volume of stuff that was crammed into such a small space. Unidentifiable vegetables were piled up in stacked pallets alongside batteries, mobile phones and cheap perfume. The air was heavy with the smell of tobacco and fried potato and traffic fumes. She turned the corner and checked her phone one last time. Her hands were shaking – this time with nerves, not cravings.

Hey Roxie lets say
12 in Juans Cafe
Southwk Br Rd. CU
thr x

Jo deduced that Elephant and Castle was one of the cheaper areas in London. The café, cowering in the shadow of a monstrous tower block, had a metal grille across the lower part of the window and a sign forbidding hoods and spitting. On the way into town, Jo had wondered whether, perhaps, this trip might trigger her memory. But looking around, she felt quite certain she hadn't been here before.

Like a beacon, the shock of blonde hair guided Jo towards the back of the café. The girl was sitting with her back to the door, flicking through a magazine. She looked exactly like her profile picture: pretty in a Barbie doll sort of way.

'Hi,' said Jo, creeping into her field of vision.

'Roxie!' Saskia's face lit up as she leaped to her feet and threw her arms around Jo. 'How you doin'?'

It was even weirder than Jo had anticipated. Saskia was treating her like an old friend. Jo had a vague feeling of recognition, a sense that she'd seen those round, brown eyes before, but now her memories were all mixed up with the Facebook photos and she wasn't so sure. She smiled and offered the girl a drink.

The café was decorated like a little corner of the rainforest. Plastic greenery hung from the ceiling, mottled bark clung to the walls and there were colourful animals scattered about the place. It was tacky but homely – a far cry from the false grandeur of Trev's Teashop in Radley.

'So!' Jo set the cups down on the table alongside the slab of free fruitcake and two forks. The seats were made of padded fake leather, once red but now brown with dirt. She tried to relax. 'How are you?'

Saskia shrugged. 'Broke. Single. Nothin' new.' She laughed flippantly. 'What about you?'

Jo sipped her coffee. This was going to be tricky. From what she could tell – piecing things together from notes on Facebook and the magazine lying open on the table – Saskia was one of those sweet but shallow people who thought that serious conversation meant talking about Katie Price's latest boob job. She didn't seem the type of girl who would understand the subtleties of having amnesia or running away and starting a new life.

'I'm OK, I guess.'

'You guess? So, what, you often go around pretending you's dead, do ya?'

Jo grimaced. 'It's complicated.'

'You don't say.'

'I kinda need you to promise you won't tell anyone about this.'

Saskia made a 'phhh' noise and carved off a slab of cake. 'Who's there to tell?'

The police, the press, the authorities . . . 'Just promise.'

Saskia shovelled the forkful through her well-glossed lips. 'Yeah, 'course. I swear. Fuckin' hell, Roxie, what is this? Government secrets? You workin' for the CIA or somethin'?'

Jo didn't point out that the CIA was actually American. 'Sorry. It's just it's . . .'

'Complicated, yeah, you said.' She waved her fork in a loop, speaking through a mouthful of currants. 'We're goin' round in circles.'

Jo nodded. It helped that she had been here before with Mrs Phillips only a few days before, but this felt different. She still wasn't sure she could trust the girl sitting opposite. Eventually, she couldn't put it off any longer.

'I lost my memory.'

Saskia frowned. 'What d'you mean?'

'The night the bomb went off. The only thing I remember – well, remember properly – is coming round on the pavement outside and running away. I don't know anything that happened before that.'

Saskia nodded casually. 'That happens, dunnit. It's the shock. Your mind blots out, like, a few hours of your life. Or somethin'.'

Jo shook her head as Saskia slurped on her coffee. 'No – not just a few hours. Everything. I mean, *everything* before that point.'

Saskia lowered her cup uncertainly. 'Everythin'?'

Jo nodded.

'Like, everythin' in your life?'

Jo nodded again.

The girl recoiled slightly. 'Shit, man. That why you needed your Facebook login? 'Cause you didn't know nothin' about yourself?'

'Yep.'

'So . . . you didn't know, like, where you lived, an' stuff?'

Jo watched Saskia's reaction. It was as though she were watching a freak show; she knew it was wrong to gawp but she couldn't help herself.

'So, like . . . You don't know who won the last *X Factor*?'

It wasn't clear whether Saskia was joking. 'Well, no, but I'm not sure I ever—'

'What about . . . The prime minister? D'you know who that is?'

Jo tried to explain that facts and figures weren't problems; that it was only personal memories that remained hazy, but Saskia wasn't listening.

'Brad Pitt? Madonna? What about . . . Beyoncé?'

225

'Look,' Jo sighed. 'I remember general "stuff", I just can't remember things about me. My life.'

Saskia opened her mouth to list another celebrity, then thought better of it and cut off another piece of cake with her fork.

'That's why I need you,' Jo explained. 'I want to find out what happened.'

Saskia screwed up her face. 'Like, everything that's ever happened to you?'

Jo thought about prompting her with an explanation of the dark, inexplicable fear that had lingered over her since she fled the scene of the blast, but decided that mentioning dark inexplicable fears at this point would probably make her look slightly unstable.

'Whatever you know.'

Saskia lightened up a little. 'OK. Well, I gotta admit, we ain't *that* close.'

Jo lifted her shoulders as though it didn't really matter. 'Just tell me what you can. D'you know where I was working before the club?'

'You was a student,' she replied. 'Somewhere in London. A university, I guess.'

'D'you know what I was studying?'

Saskia stared into her cup, then shook her head. 'Nah, sorry. You never said. Don't fink you liked it. You quit.'

Jo waited, her hands clasped tightly around the cup.

'Dunno why,' said Saskia.

Jo's shoulders fell. 'Did I ever moan about it? Did I mention any names? Was there anything . . . ?'

Saskia pushed out her bottom lip. 'You was messed up about somethin'. I dunno what. I fink . . . I fink you just didn't give a shit any more. You was hangin' out wiv Poncho an'—'

'Who's Poncho?'

Saskia drew a breath, then – and it was only because Jo happened to be looking up that she noticed – stopped herself. 'Some guy you was seeing.'

'What, a boyfriend?'

'Yeah,' Saskia replied breezily. 'I called 'im Poncho. Real name was Pancho or something. Poncho, like the raincoat – get it?'

Jo sighed, frustrated. There were so many questions she wanted to ask – more, now this new name had cropped up – but she knew that Saskia didn't have all the answers. She would have to be patient. If she came away with a couple of gaps filled then that was progress. Some pointers – that was all she required, then her mind would do the rest. Already, there were memories that hadn't existed a month ago. She just needed something to go on – a hook.

'D'you know anything about Pancho? Did you meet him?'

There was only the smallest of hesitations. 'No.'

'Did I . . . ?' Jo was embarrassed to ask. 'Did I drink a lot?'

Saskia smiled and looked up at the ceiling. 'We all did, Rox. God knows, you 'ave to, if you're gonna get on that stage.' She tipped back her head and finished her coffee, then devoured the remains of the cake.

Jo wasn't convinced her question had been answered. 'I mean, a lot? Did I need it, d'you reckon?'

'I dunno.' Saskia looked slightly uncomfortable.

Jo nodded and asked another rhetorical question. 'Did I do drugs?'

Saskia's hesitation was as good as an answer.

'Cocaine?'

'We all did. You, me, Candy . . . all the girls.'

Jo wasn't thinking about all the girls. She was thinking about herself. It seemed that all the misshapen, disjointed pieces of footage in her head were beginning to converge. Like a Tarantino film, they weren't in the right order and they didn't quite make sense, but at least now there was something linking them together.

She had been a university student. Playing football, having fun, seeing that blond guy . . . That much she felt reasonably sure of. Then something had changed. This was where the film skipped ahead. She'd failed her exams, split up with the guy and been dropped from the squad. Things had turned sour. She'd quit uni. There had been arguments – arguments with the guy, with the university, with her mother. She'd started working at the Buffalo Club. Drinking too much, snorting too much . . . Maybe Pancho fitted in here.

The gap troubled Jo. It was the same unanswered question that had been playing on her mind for months: why would Rebecca, the girl who seemed to have everything, leave it all behind and drop out?

She still didn't know. Jo had been overly optimistic to think that Saskia would have all the answers. Clearly they hadn't been close – except in the sense that they'd seen each other naked and had probably snorted adjacent lines of coke. Saskia hadn't known Rebecca, only Roxie. And as for the other question on her mind – the source of the mysterious paranoia – well, maybe nobody could help her on that one. Maybe there *was* no source. Maybe the paranoia was just a symptom, like the amnesia.

'Don't fink I know any more.'

'Maybe it's for the best,' Jo replied with a wry smile. 'No, you've been really helpful. I guess I kinda knew most of it already . . . I just needed confirmation, you know?'

Saskia nodded, although she looked rather perplexed. 'What you doin' now, anyway?'

Jo hid her face in the depths of her coffee mug and waved a hand as though it was too boring to explain. 'This and that. Just getting back into things, to be honest.'

For some reason, she didn't want to tell Saskia about her new life. It was something to do with the line she had drawn. Saskia belonged one side of it, with Roxie and the lap-dancing and the coke and the drinking; Matt and Mrs Phillips and Dunston's belonged on the other, with Jo.

'How about you? What are *you* up to?'

Saskia pulled a face. 'Not much.'

'Where are you working?'

'I'm not.' Saskia's pretty face turned sour. 'I'm tryin' to get a proper job, innit, but I ain't got no recent experience. Doesn't 'elp, 'aving a two-year gap to explain.'

Jo nodded sympathetically. *Try a life-long gap*, she nearly said. 'You'll have to lie.'

'Yeah, obviously.' Saskia's eyes brightened again. 'Hey, I'll be fine. Don't worry about me. You got enough to stress about.'

They rose to their feet.

'Thanks again,' said Jo as they stood outside the café, shielding their eyes from the weak autumn sunshine. She was wondering whether she should repeat her plea for secrecy.

Saskia grinned. 'Don't worry, goldfish-brain. I won't say a word.'

Jo looked at her big brown eyes and hoped they were trustworthy. That was the last thing she needed, people from her old life crowding round like vultures, all wanting a piece of the amnesia girl.

'Thanks.'

'Fuckin' hell, Rox. Will you stop thankin' me? I ain't done nothin' except eat cake an' tell you what you already knew, innit!'

They hugged and set off in opposite directions.

Jo had nearly reached Southwark Bridge when her phone started vibrating against her hip.

'Missing me already?'

'I just remembered!' cried Saskia excitably. 'I dunno why, but I just remembered the name of your boyfriend!'

'What boyfriend?'

Jo knew, even as the words left her lips, which boyfriend it was. Only one guy had featured in her hazy memories, and if she'd mentioned anyone to Saskia, it would have been him. It was the guy in the bedroom – the one with blond, spiky hair, whom she had hurt.

'Well . . . I dunno. I just remember you talkin' about him once. Anyway. Luke. That was his name.'

Jo pushed the phone back into her pocket. *Luke*. The blond guy was called Luke.

Chapter Twenty-Seven

'Everyone over here!' Jo yelled into the wind. The park was empty except for a couple of elderly dog-walkers who had spotted the commotion and made a diversion from their usual circuit.

Nadia and Charlene wandered over, hugging their bodies for warmth. Neither of them looked exactly sporty in their pristine trainers and velour tracksuits, but at least they were making an effort. In a funny way, Jo was looking forward to this session.

'Right,' she said, when the boys eventually joined them. She wasn't exactly sure how it was going to work, but she wouldn't let her tone betray such concerns. 'We've got a new member of the team! Has everyone met Taiwo?'

The tall, gangly black kid looked down at his feet.

'Gay-o,' Kyle muttered from under his hood.

Jason laughed and repeated the insult a few times.

'Shall we just introduce ourselves?' suggested Jo, talking over the insults. She hadn't spoken to Kyle since his running-away stunt and up until this point, she'd been wondering whether he might have matured a little in the last few days. Now she wasn't so sure.

Reluctantly, the children took turns to mumble their

names as the new boy continued to stare at the grass. There was a glimmer of interest from Charlene as the kid introduced himself – he had an exceptionally deep voice for a thirteen-year-old – but from the rest of the group there was just mild hostility.

'So, I know some of you have done a bit of training for the Centrepoint tournament,' she said, knowing that only Tim had touched a football in the last seven days – or possibly ever. 'But I thought it'd be a good idea for us all to come out here where there's more space.'

Authoritatively, Jo explained her intentions to get them doing basic drills, then group exercises, followed by a three-a-side game.

'With *girls*?' grunted Kyle, nodding at the shivering adolescents.

'And *gays*?' added Jason, not quite brave enough to look at Taiwo but nudging Kyle for moral support.

'Stop it, both of you.' Jo turned to the rest of them. 'Right. Get into pairs.'

The ball-kicking exercise turned out to be more complicated than Jo had envisaged. While Tim and Taiwo trotted off and started passing impeccably between them as though the ball were on rails, Kyle and Jason interpreted the exercise as a challenge to see who could kick the ball furthest, quickly sending theirs into the woodland nearby. The girls refused to play.

'Stand a little further away, Charlene,' she said, just as Nadia lit a spliff. 'What was that, Jason?'

'It's gone!' the boy yelled, flinging his hands in the air. 'We lost it!'

'Have another look! Nadia, put that out. Come on, Charlene, just try kicking it.'

'Ow! Fuckin' hell – my toe!' Charlene hopped onto one foot and grabbed the other as the ball remained stationary.

'We're bored.'

Jo looked round. Tim and Taiwo were standing either side of their ball looking rather glum.

'It's gone!' yelled a voice coming from the woodland. Jo squinted at the swaying trees. It was becoming apparent that she should have brought more than three balls.

'I'm not playin',' declared Charlene, limping towards her friend who was sucking like fury to keep the embers alive on her roll-up.

Jo tried another tack. 'It keeps you fit – helps you stay slim.'

Nadia chucked the remains of her spliff on the grass. 'So does smokin'.'

'Jason's stuck!' Kyle lolloped towards her, hands in pockets, hood up.

'Stuck where?'

'Up the tree.'

By the time she reached the woodland, Jason was already writhing about in a foetal position on the ground, clutching his knee.

'Get up.'

'Fuckin' hurts!'

'Well, whose fault is that?'

'Yours. You made us come out.'

'Jason, you sound like a girl.'

He was on his feet within seconds, following Jo back to the clearing where Kyle was poking Taiwo and Tim with sticks.

'I'm not playing wiv him.' Jason pointed at Taiwo.

Jo ignored him and tried to think of an exercise that

233

involved four people standing a long way apart. For some reason, she couldn't concentrate. Jason's petulance had triggered something in her mind. His rejection of Taiwo, flippant though it was, had reminded her of another rejection. *Her* rejection. She had been pushed away, left out, kicked off – and she thought it was something to do with football too. Jo looked away, trying to summon more details, but all she could remember was the feeling of shame and the sense that she had let herself down.

'OK!' she said, pushing the thoughts from her mind. 'Here's the plan. Stand in a square . . .'

Kyle was unusually quiet today. His insults were less venomous and as far as she was aware, he hadn't used the C-word yet. All afternoon he'd just loitered, hood up, mouth shut. Jo wondered whether this was a sign of progress or problems.

With the boys working on their dribbling, she returned to find Nadia crouching on the ground, convulsing in an uncontrollable coughing fit. Charlene was leaning over her, patting her back.

'Is she OK?'

'She's asthmatic!'

Jo waited for the spluttering to subside, feeling rather helpless.

'Fuckin' *sport*,' panted Nadia, rising to her feet and coughing up the last of the phlegm.

Jo didn't like to point out that she hadn't actually been *doing* any sport, or that the attack was more likely to have been brought on by the chemicals that were choking her lungs. 'Shall we do something that doesn't involve too much running?'

The girls both glared at her.

She was persevering. If they were to play in this tournament – which, worryingly, they were now committed to doing – then they needed at least two girls on the pitch at any one time.

Given that they only *had* two girls, that meant that Nadia and Charlene were essential members of the squad. No pressure, then.

'When it comes to you, stop it like this,' she advised, demonstrating the most basic skill of all: sticking your foot out.

Surprisingly, when she passed the ball gently to Nadia, the girl did exactly as she'd been told.

'That's it! Now pass to Charlene.'

The exercise continued, despite Charlene's melodramatic limp and Nadia's gasping, until Jo happened to look over to where the boys were playing. Except 'playing' was the wrong word.

'Guys, stop it!'

She rushed over to the source of the grunting and tried to work out what was happening. Kyle had Taiwo in a headlock and was dragging him across the grass by the neck. Meanwhile, Jason was hacking at Taiwo's legs, which were stubbornly wrapped around the football. Tim was just waiting for it to be over.

'Stop it.' Jo walked up to the fight and stood there awkwardly. 'I said, STOP IT.' She started to panic as she realised the boys were beyond hearing her. 'Kyle, let go. Please.'

'It's *our* ball,' he growled through gritted teeth.

Taiwo's arms were flailing wildly, trying to grab on to something to lessen the strain on his head.

'That's enough!' Jo stepped in and attempted to unclamp

one of Kyle's arms. Taiwo caught hold of the nearest thing, which happened to be Kyle's hoodie, and hauled himself up.

All at once, Jo saw the look in Taiwo's eyes – a mixture of hatred, fear and sadness, as though he was all too familiar with this situation – and Kyle's expression: that look of anguish she'd seen before. But it was the other thing that made her gasp. Suddenly, it became clear why Kyle had been wearing his hood up all afternoon.

The marks were dark and ugly. There were four of them, each a finger-width apart on the side of his neck.

'Kyle, come back!'

He took flight, pulling his hood up as he ran.

Jo glanced around. The girls were loitering, vaguely curious about the noise, while Jason and Taiwo glared at each other like fighters in a ring. She looked at Kyle, who was running towards the gates of the park as though his life depended on it. With a vague word to the others, she set off after him.

Yelling and gasping and screaming his name, Jo followed in Kyle's dewy footsteps, finding with dismay that the gap between them was widening. He was quicker than she was. All sorts of thoughts zipped around in her head as she sprinted, like what she should do when – or if – she caught up with the boy, and what a professional care worker would do about the fact that his stepfather was hurting him, and what to tell Sue and—

With horror, Jo realised that she wasn't the only one chasing Kyle. At the edge of the park, near the gates, was a man dressed in jeans and a T-shirt. He appeared to be blocking Kyle's way. She screamed as the man reached out and pinned Kyle's arms to his body, then crouched down and looked right into his face.

'Get off him!' She swooped down on the boy, breaking him free from the man.

Kyle grunted and wriggled out of her grasp, then stood between the two assailants, looking from one to the other and shaking his head.

Then Jo understood why. The young man pushed up from the ground and rearranged his T-shirt over his muscular shoulders.

'Oh.' Jo caught Matt's eye. 'Right.'

The other boys arrived on the scene, closely followed by Charlene and a very breathless Nadia. Jo gathered herself together.

'I think . . . we should probably head back,' she suggested. 'Kyle, we'll talk later, OK? Don't run off again.'

''Cause she ain't quick enough to catch you,' Taiwo added.

'Yeah.' Jason sniggered.

Jason and Taiwo appeared to be friends now. Jo watched as the boys set off up the road, taking turns to kick the football at passing cars and lampposts and unsuspecting pedestrians, almost as if five minutes ago they hadn't been trying to beat each other into a pulp. She wished things in her life would blow over that quickly.

Matt said nothing, hanging back as they waited for the girls to pass. Jo tried to decide what to say to him. He'd caught her off guard, turning up like this. She had been planning to confront him in her own time, on her own terms, and she certainly hadn't intended for there to be children present when she did it.

'Good session?' he asked, smiling.

Jo glowered at him. Really. He was supposed to be a sensitive guy, and here he was making light of the situation.

'Hope I didn't mess up your training schedule. The

office was dull and I thought you might've bitten off more than you could chew, so—'

'Shut up!'

Jo hadn't meant for this to be her first contribution to the conversation; she just couldn't stand any more of his jovial flippancy. They had such important things to discuss – not least, the bruises on Kyle's neck, but also the notebook and the fact that Matt had discussed it with one of the least appropriate people Jo could think of. This was like chatting about the weather on board the *Titanic*.

'Sorry.' He pulled a mock-apologetic face.

She shook her head, trying to find the words to describe how hurt she felt.

'D'you wanna talk about it?' he asked, softly this time. 'The other night, I mean. The notebook thing.'

She stopped walking and reeled round to face him.

'Yeah,' she growled, the words coming to her all of a sudden. 'Why don't we? Let's talk about it! Because it looks like you already have with everyone else! So why not? Maybe we could borrow a megaphone and have the conversation through that!'

He stared at her. 'What?'

'Don't look so confused. I met Kieran the other day.'

Matt held up both hands and reined his head back. She had to hand it to him, he was good at playing innocent.

'He told me he knows.'

'Knows what?'

'About the notebook and the amnesia!'

'Amnesia?'

Jo bit her lip, suddenly realising the extent of her paranoia. She had been so wrapped up in her own anxieties that it hadn't even occurred to her that Matt didn't *know* what the lists in the notebook meant. He was probably still as confused as he had been that night in the guesthouse. Telling Kieran had just been his way of trying to work out what it was all about. And now, unintentionally, she had gone and given him his answer.

'That's what the notebook's for,' she said peevishly. 'I've got amnesia. It's my memories.'

Matt didn't reply; he just looked at her.

'Come on.' Jo nodded towards the kids, who were fast disappearing up the street. She couldn't cope with any more of his incredulous, pitiful staring.

'What sort of amnesia?' Matt called after her.

Jo wasn't sure she wanted to be drawn into this conversation. She had intended for this to be about them, and the fact that Matt had betrayed her confidence, but it seemed to be turning into another confession altogether. If she told Matt the whole truth, then that would be the end of Jo Simmons.

'It doesn't matter.' She shook her head and picked up the pace.

He grabbed her arm. 'Yeah, it does. You've got amnesia and you're upset about something and I don't understand what.'

His blue eyes were watering slightly in the breeze as he scanned her face.

She sighed irritably and walked on. 'You told Kieran, Matt.'

He didn't reply.

'I know you were only trying to work out what was going on, and that's partly my fault for not explaining, but I didn't expect you to go blurting my innermost secrets to your barmy flatmate!'

Matt jogged a few steps to keep up.

'What did I blurt?'

Jo rolled her eyes. She wanted to believe in his innocence, but she'd heard Kieran say it. And people like Kieran didn't lie; they didn't know how to.

'I didn't say a word to Kieran about the notebook thing, if that's what you mean. I don't think he knows anything about what's happened between us except . . .'

'Except what?'

'Well, I told him about the kiss.'

She looked at him. Suddenly, something occurred to her. *What happened the other night . . .* That was how Kieran had put it. He hadn't actually said, in so many words, that he knew about the notebook.

'I'm sorry, I would've kept quiet about that but he kept going on and on about how we were so well matched and how he'd read some bollocks somewhere about how two people who both—'

'No, it's OK.' Jo looked at him, realising how wrong she'd been and how it must look from Matt's point of view. 'I think I owe you an apology.'

'Uh . . .' He looked at her uncertainly. 'An explanation will do.'

Jo smiled faintly and thought about where to begin. Matt was right. She owed him an explanation.

'OK. So . . . I'm sorry. I thought you'd gone and told people about what you saw in the notebook, but I didn't realise that you hadn't actually seen what was in the notebook, or at least, you hadn't worked out what it meant . . .'

Matt cocked his head to one side. 'Jo, are you gonna tell me what the fuck's going on?'

Relief washed over her. Matt hadn't betrayed her.

'OK.' She took a deep breath. She was going to tell him what the fuck was going on. 'So I've got amnesia. That's why I've got the notebook. To write things down when they come to me. But the thing is . . .' she looked up at the kids to check they were all out of earshot, 'I'm not who you think I am.'

'So . . .' Matt looked worried.

'You know the bomb that went off in London? The one in the strip club?'

Matt nodded uncertainly.

'Well, I was there. I was . . . one of the dancers.'

Matt stopped walking. '*What?*'

'I'm supposed to be dead. I ran away straight after – it's a long story – but the thing is . . . I've got no memory of the explosion or anything that came before it. Well, I mean, hardly anything. It's something called post-traumatic dissociative amnesia or something. I looked it up.'

Matt exhaled and nodded slowly.

'So . . . are you like . . . one of those people who can't remember their own name?'

Jo nodded, watching his reaction.

'So you mean . . . ?' Matt frowned.

'Jo's not my real name, no.' She finished his sentence. 'It's Rebecca Ross. I found out the other day. I was Roxie to people in the club. Jo Simmons is made up. So is everything else about me.'

'What, like, *everything*?' Matt blinked at her.

'Everything from my past,' she clarified, not wanting Matt to think she'd been faking her feelings for him.

'So . . .'

This was it, thought Jo. This was the end of her career at Dunston's – the end of everything as Jo Simmons knew it.

'I'm not really a support worker. I invented my CV to get this job. Made up all that stuff about working in Haringey. I don't think I've ever worked with kids in my life. That's why I'm shit at it.'

'But . . .' Matt glanced at the scruffy teenagers up ahead, who were trooping into Fairmont House. 'You're not.'

Jo rolled her eyes. 'Come on, Matt. You saw me just now. I don't have the faintest idea. I realised that on day one. That's why I tried to quit.'

'But that's not true. I don't know why you keep saying that. The kids like you – well, as much as they like anyone.'

Jo shook her head, not even bothering to reply. He was just being nice.

Matt ran a hand over his face as though he were grappling with something. 'So you've started a completely new life? From scratch?'

She nodded.

'Don't you know *anything* about your old life?'

'Well,' Jo wondered whether to tell him about her Facebook espionage and her meeting with Saskia. She decided it would just complicate things. 'Bits and pieces. That's where the notebook comes in.'

Matt smiled. 'You remember the football.'

Jo nodded, hoping Matt hadn't read any of the notes about the blond guy whom she now knew was called Luke.

'But, Jo,' he looked serious again, 'does this mean everyone assumes you're dead? From your old life, I mean. Won't there be people missing you?'

She didn't answer. It was true. She had thought about this a lot. There were probably friends and parents and maybe a brother or sister out there who were mourning her death. It was cruel to let them suffer, she knew that.

'Don't you *want* to see them again? Don't you want to know who you are?'

Jo sighed. Somehow, Matt had got straight to the point that she'd been avoiding. She did want to know who she was – desperately. But it wasn't that simple. How could she explain to Matt about this horrible, nagging paranoia that was making her shy away from the links to her past? And how could she describe the repulsion she felt at the idea of having strangers wrap their arms around her and claim they were her friends? How could she convey her fear of the unknown?

'I dunno.'

Matt looked at her as though he sensed there was more to it than that. 'Fair enough.'

That was it. The conversation was over, and so was her career in care work. Jo watched as, up ahead, Taiwo and Jason started playing volleyball over Geoff Ramsay's car outside the house. She would miss all this.

'Did you see Kyle's neck?' she asked anxiously.

Matt nodded.

'What do we do?'

He looked at her, first incredulously and then tolerantly, as if mildly amused by the stunt she'd pulled off. 'We tell Sue, who tells Social Services. Then they try and figure out who's been beating him up, and find him a foster family or get him brought into Fairmont.'

Jo nodded. 'Right.'

They approached the car park and watched as the kids scampered inside, having lodged the football under the front of Geoff's car.

'Are you OK?' Matt asked, poking the ball out and lingering outside the main door.

She nodded sadly. This was possibly the last time she'd ever walk up these steps.

'You're not gonna do anything stupid, are you?'

'Like what?' she asked, savouring the feel of Matt's body next to hers and wishing they were somewhere else.

'Like, resign.'

Jo gawped at him. 'But . . . they'll sack me! As soon as—'

'As soon as what?'

Jo laughed drily. 'Oh, as soon as they discover I faked my qualifications, I invented my experience, I forged—'

Matt pulled her towards him, looking left and right just to check they were out of sight.

'Shh,' he said, quickly pressing his lips against hers. 'They don't need to know, do they?'

Chapter Twenty-Eight

'There you go, half burnt, just how you like it.' Mrs Phillips slid the toast onto Jo's plate and pushed the grill shut.

Something of a routine had developed in the Radley guesthouse. At exactly six fifty a.m., the kettle would click and Mrs Phillips would make two instant coffees. Jo would stumble in, switch on the television and collect plate, knife, butter and one of the many pots of home-made marmalade from the kitchen. Mrs Phillips always made more toast than she could eat, but throwing a couple of slices into the bird-bin was all part of the schedule.

'Doom and gloom, as usual,' the landlady muttered, flicking through her first newspaper.

Jo buttered her toast and stared moronically at the TV. It was too early to think. In some ways, she felt it was silly to get up so early just for the benefit of some idle chit-chat and charred toast. She could sleep in and start the day a couple of hours later, once Mrs P had gone down to the shop. But she liked the routine, and she had a feeling her landlady enjoyed her company.

'House prices, unemployment, inflation . . .' Mrs Phillips whipped over several pages in quick succession. She was one of those people who liked to be seen tut-tutting over a broadsheet headline but secretly enjoyed browsing the inner gore of the lower-brow tabloids.

'How ridiculous!' cried Mrs Phillips, shaking her head. 'A German scientist claims to have "cured the disease of ageing", it says. So we're all supposed to take a pill in our mid-teens and stay looking like that for ever? Where will that leave us? Full of seventeen-year-old lookalikes, the world amok with paedophiles . . .'

Jo was about to mumble something in half-hearted agreement when the woman drew a sharp intake of breath. Her face looked pale, all of a sudden.

'What is it?'

Mrs Phillips didn't meet her eyes. She just slid the newspaper sideways, still reading it herself, and pointed at the headline above a large image of a semi-naked girl wrapped around a pole. 'STRIPPER RETURNS FROM THE DEAD WITH AMNESIA.'

Jo's body started trembling and her throat tightened. She forced herself to read on.

LONDON – A girl thought to have died in the explosion at the Buffalo Club in August has reappeared, safe and well but with no memory of what happened or who she is, according to sources.

Rebecca Ross, who was known as Roxie to clientele in the Mayfair gentlemen's club, apparently went missing on the night of the blast, leading fellow dancers to believe she was dead.

Sources claim that Ms Ross panicked and fled the scene of the bomb when she realised she was suffering from amnesia and has since set up home outside London using a new identity. She is thought to remember only fragments of her former life.

The bomb, which went off on August 2 at 3 a.m., was thought to have claimed thirteen lives and caused multiple injuries as well as extensive damage to surrounding buildings. Many victims are thought to have evaded medical attention to avoid association with the blast.

Rebecca Ross, whose new identity has not been disclosed, is said to be in good health, despite not remembering many key facts about her own life. Her family is thought to be unaware of her new existence.

Jo skipped through the last few paragraphs, which compared her story to various other examples of amnesia and detailed the medical facts behind the condition. She couldn't speak.

'Oh dear.' Mrs Phillips shook her head at the page.

Jo couldn't speak. She felt suffocated, as though a blanket had been placed over her face, preventing her from breathing, from seeing, from screaming. Her eyes blindly roamed the room. *Who?* That was the question. Who was the source?

Jo forced herself to think rationally, despite the emotions clogging up her brain. Only three people knew about her situation, as far as she knew – only three up until this morning. The figure was probably nearer three million now. Mrs Phillips, Matt and Saskia. They were the only possible leaks. One of them had sold her story to the press. Or one of them had told someone else, who had spread the news.

Jo glanced at her landlady, who was leafing through the

remaining newspapers, presumably looking for other references to the story. No way, thought Jo. Mrs Phillips hadn't sold her story.

She thought back to her last encounter with Matt, remembered the way he'd held her, reassured her, kissed her. He wouldn't tell a soul, she knew that – not after the Kieran débâcle. No, there were a million reasons why it wasn't Matt.

That left her cyber friend and ex-stripper, Saskia. Jo closed her eyes, letting the facts fall into place. Of course it was Saskia. She already knew that. How could she have been so stupid? They weren't good friends. Saskia had no reason to do her any favours. She was broke. She was savvy enough to know that tabloids paid good money for gossip like this. She had enough information about Jo to make it a juicy enough story.

Jo planted her elbows on the table and buried her head in her hands. 'Shit.'

Mrs Phillips was looking at her, biting her lower lip.

'Fucking shit.'

Jo was aware of her landlady recoiling at her language but she didn't care. This was a catastrophe. This undid all her hard work. All the effort she'd put in over the last few weeks to build up a life – such as it was – had gone to waste.

'Maybe it'll blow over,' suggested Mrs Phillips, timidly.

Jo shook her head. She knew that the opposite was true. This was just the beginning. There would be a witch-hunt to find the back-from-the-dead stripper, then everyone from her new life would be horrified to find out the truth and everyone she had once known would hound her – not to mention the press.

'Oh, Jo . . .' Mrs Phillips moved over and laid a hand on her shoulder.

Jo shook her head, too appalled to respond.

'You know, this may be a blessing in disguise,' said the woman, moving back to the papers and neatening the stack.

Jo looked up. 'What?'

Mrs Phillips picked up the pile and hugged it against her bosom. 'Well, somewhere out there you've probably got family and friends and people who care about you.'

Jo watched as she moved towards the door – almost smugly, she thought.

'Don't you think they'll be pleased to read the news today?'

The door closed softly, leaving Jo alone with the TV. She didn't like what was going through her mind. It seemed implausible, she thought, but possible, that Mrs Phillips, out of some misguided sense of righteousness, had sold her lodger's story to the press.

Jo pushed back her chair. She felt disorientated. Maybe Mrs Phillips hadn't looked smug – maybe Jo was imagining signs that weren't there. She closed her eyes and tried to remember the expression on the woman's face, but all she could see was the headline, dancing boldly in front of her eyes: 'STRIPPER RETURNS FROM THE DEAD WITH AMNESIA.'

She was running out of places to hide. If her theory about Mrs P was correct – and she was in no state to decide what was correct right now – then she couldn't stay here. There was only one place she could think of to go. One person she could trust. Or at least, she hoped she could trust him.

Chapter Twenty-Nine

Jo's tears mixed with the icy raindrops and streamed down her cheeks. She fought her way through the downpour, barely able to see, and turned into Jackman Close. The door swung open before she had even pressed the bell.

'Oh, hi, Jo! Gosh, I didn't expect to see you there!'

Jo leaped backwards as Kieran bounded down the steps dressed in Lycra shorts and a running vest that clung to his skinny chest. She tried to pull her mouth into a smile, but her raw-looking eyes probably gave her away. 'I know it's early.'

'Are you after Matt?' Kieran asked, winking. He started jogging on the spot and pumping his knees ridiculously high, apparently oblivious to her state. His hands were wrapped in red mittens with yellow polka dots.

Jo nodded, sniffing away a fresh batch of tears. Kieran had no idea. He was still under the impression that he was part of a covert operation to get Matt and Jo together.

'I think he's up. Go on in. Oh, are you wondering why I've got socks on my hands?'

'Is that what they are?' Jo took a closer look. They were indeed socks.

'Cheaper than gloves,' replied Kieran. 'It was three pairs for a pound. See ya!'

Jo ventured into the flat, wondering whether she should have rung the bell as a precaution.

'Matt? Are you there?'

The sound of running water was coming from one of the bedrooms. Jo waited for it to stop and then called out again.

'Matt? Are you there?'

'Uh?' He opened the door with a white towel round his waist, a toothbrush sticking out of his mouth.

'Uh!' he said again, retreating to spit out the toothpaste. 'Sorry!' There was a clattering noise and then Matt reappeared in the hallway. Jo couldn't help glancing briefly at his torso. 'What are you— Oh my God.' Matt stepped closer and looked at her eyes. 'Are you OK?'

Jo sighed shakily and nodded despite everything. 'Sorry it's so early.'

'Nah, don't worry about it! I always get up when Fairy Lightfoot goes running. What's up?'

She pulled the piece of newspaper from her inside jeans pocket. Unfolding it, she allowed Matt to guide her into his bedroom. He shut the door and sat down beside her on the bed.

Slowly, he read the damp cutting that lay between them. He didn't react until he'd reached the end.

'Woah.'

Jo nodded. An unexpected feeling of relief enveloped her, just as it had done when she'd come clean on who she really was. The article wasn't her problem any more; it was *their* problem. Matt would help her get through it.

They sat in silence for what seemed like minutes. Jo knew

that once she started talking, she wouldn't stop. And then she'd probably burst into tears. Finally, she plucked up the courage.

'I think it might've been Mrs Phillips.'

'What d'you mean?'

'The source.'

'Um . . . why?'

'Well, she found the article, for a start.'

Matt tilted his head. 'Yeah, but she does read every national newspaper every morning, doesn't she?'

Jo screwed up her nose. Maybe it was Saskia after all. 'I dunno. She had this weird look . . . She said something about it being "for the best".'

Matt nodded, slowly.

'You think I'm wrong, don't you?' Jo doubted herself again.

'I don't know. But I think she's right.'

She looked at him. 'What d'you mean?'

'I mean, she's right. Perhaps this is a good thing, this article.'

Jo looked at him in horror. 'Don't you realise what's gonna happen now?' Matt started to nod calmly but Jo went on, the panic mounting in her voice. 'My whole life's gonna unravel! Everyone who knows me as Jo is gonna find out who I really am! Like, Sue Meads and Geoff Ramsay and Raj and Sanjit . . . and Kyle and the other kids . . . God, they'll sack me within seconds – and then what about all the people who knew me as Becky?'

A droplet ran down Matt's forehead from his hair. 'Calm down. Who are you really worried about here? Is it the Dunston's lot? Because if it is, I can explain things to the management before they find out from the press, and it will be fine. They might think you're a bit strange for lying, but you're good, so chances are they won't sack you. Your job's low clearance anyway. And if it's the kids you're stressing about, well, I think your story pales into insignificance compared to theirs.'

Jo broke his gaze and looked at the floor. It was true.

'And if it's Kieran and Sanjit and the other idiots . . .' Matt laughed quietly, 'don't waste your energy. They won't give a shit that your name's not Jo.'

'But—'

'So it's the others, the people from your past, that you're worried about, isn't it?'

Jo considered his words. Matt was right, or as right as he could be, given what he knew. It was Becky's life that she was worried about. Of course, she was frightened of losing the life that Jo Simmons had painstakingly built, and she didn't relish the idea of explaining all her various lies to the people she'd come to know, but her fear of confronting Geoff Ramsay and Sue was inconsequential compared to the terror she felt at the idea of meeting those strangers who would call themselves her friends. And then there was the other thing – the thing she had done, or hadn't done, that had left her feeling so petrified on the morning of the explosion. What if that all came out now?

Jo tried to explain, but the words wouldn't come out. There was something blocking her throat.

'I'm sorry,' said Matt, moving the newspaper cutting from between them and putting an arm round her shoulders. 'I didn't realise. I thought you wanted to remember stuff from your past.'

Jo nodded. She wanted to remember at her own pace, not have it spelled out by the national press.

'You need a cup of tea.'

Jo turned to face him and managed a faint smile through the tears. 'Tea solves everything, eh?'

Matt smiled back. 'OK. Something stronger.'

He'd probably been joking, thought Jo, but her reaction must have been transparent. Alcohol was exactly what she needed.

'One vodka, coming up.' He sprang to his feet and grabbed one of the bottles from a bookshelf devoid of books.

Jo glanced around the room, registering her surroundings for the first time. Matt's bedroom was tidy but, like the rest of the flat, very clearly a man's lair. Hi-fi equipment, weights and crumpled T-shirts littered the floor, boxes were piled up haphazardly in one corner and there was no mirror.

'Here.' Matt pushed the glass into Jo's hand.

Jo did feel a hint of embarrassment about drinking so early in the day and for a moment she wondered whether Matt might have guessed about her drink problem. But her thirst outweighed her shame.

'So why doesn't Becky want to find out about her past?' asked Matt as she tipped back her head. The vodka was clearly expensive; it slipped down easily.

Jo waited for the fire to subside in her belly. She could feel her muscles relaxing like springs uncoiling inside her.

'I . . .' She put the glass on the carpet and tried to formulate a sentence that explained how she felt. 'It's hard to explain.'

Matt was looking at her, waiting, listening. She had to tell him.

'When I came round outside the club, I had this awful

feeling, like . . . like a paranoia, I guess. I didn't know what it was, but it felt like . . . like I'd done something really bad and I had to escape. So I did.' She shrugged. 'I just ran away. That's how I ended up here – I was trying to start afresh.'

'A paranoia?'

'Well . . .'

'Like the sort of thing you get after taking—'

'No.' Jo knew what he was going to say. 'No, it was worse than that.' She crossed her legs then uncrossed them again, considering yet again the possibility that it had just been a very bad come-down. 'I think.'

He looked at her. 'So what was it? What had you done?'

'I don't know.'

'Oh.' Matt nodded slowly.

'But anyway, the point is, whatever I did, or didn't do, there are people out there who knew me in that life, and they remember more about me than *I* do. It's not that I don't *want* to know . . . It's just . . .' She shook her head, unable to explain.

'You're scared of what you might find out about your-self,' finished Matt.

Jo looked at him suddenly, thrown by the accuracy of his words. '*Exactly*. That's exactly what it is.'

He was staring at the floor with glazed eyes – not glazed in a bored way, but mesmerised. Lost.

'How – how did you know?'

He was silent for a while. Then when he spoke, his voice was unusually quiet.

'It's really important to know who you are.'

Jo waited. He didn't seem to have answered her question.

'I thought I knew who I was,' he said eventually, 'until I learned that my mum wasn't actually my mum.'

'What?' Jo realised she knew almost nothing of Matt other than what was apparent from the outside: his wit, his looks, his way with children . . . She knew nothing about his background.

'I've never told you how I ended up working for Dunston's.'

Jo shook her head, not believing what she thought she was about to hear.

'Well, I lived with my mum until I was fifteen. We never got on – we were totally different. Then I found out why: she wasn't my real mum. She got drunk one night and told me I was adopted. I went mental 'cause she hadn't told me before. Ran away from home. I stayed on mates' floors for a bit, but then school finished and I was on my own. I got in touch with Shelter, who put me onto Dunston's. I lived in for a bit, but kept running off. No one knew why.'

Jo stared at him.

'Then, in the end, the thing that grounded me was finding my real parents. Sounds weird, I know, especially as I've hardly seen them since that first time. But I know who they are. I know who I am. A few months after finding out, I got my own place and started doing general office crap at Dunston's. They realised I could work a computer so offered me the thing in PR.'

Jo looked at him. It didn't seem possible.

'Believe me,' he smiled faintly, 'I know all about being scared to hear the truth.'

She nodded, still looking at him. Yet again, she felt terrible. She had become so self-obsessed recently; it was only when other people spelled out their problems in words of one syllable for her that she gave them a second's thought.

'Maybe I should thank whoever leaked my story,' she said lamely.

Matt smiled. He was the sexy young man again, not the messed-up, adopted tearaway. 'Maybe you should.'

He moved closer to her on the bed – so close that Jo could smell the shower gel on his skin. What happened next was as unexpected as Matt's life story had been. His hand moved up over her body and rested on her neck. She closed her eyes, still reeling from what she'd just heard. He cupped her face in his palm and slowly, his lips touched hers.

The emotions were all jumbled up inside her, swirling and churning, fuelled by the vodka and the scent of Matt's body: an intoxicating cocktail of fear, lust, hope, distress and anger left over from before.

She felt herself falling backwards on the bed, Matt's arms supporting her, his chest pressing down on hers. Jo wrapped an arm around his neck and felt his tongue slip into her mouth. She could feel him, hard, through her clothes and his towel.

It was eight o'clock in the morning and Jo had had vodka for breakfast and Matt was due at work in an hour. She didn't care. They rolled over so that she was straddling his waist and he slid a hand up her thigh towards the buttons on her jeans. She could hear her breathing quicken. Matt kissed her more passionately, one hand tangled up in her hair. Then the towel fell away and soon the knickers were gone too.

It was spontaneous, but it felt real. And for once, thought

Jo, her fingers digging into Matt's back and her body arching against his, she was doing something that wasn't a lie. For a few, blissful minutes, she could forget about everything else in her life.

Chapter Thirty

Jo pulled the buzzing phone out of her pocket. It was an Oxford number. Sue, calling from home, probably. She would have read the news by now. Jo dropped it into her lap and let it ring out.

Of course she felt guilty for not turning up to work. She wasn't ill. She knew the kids would be disappointed – not that they'd let it show. Jo hadn't warned anyone that she'd be hopping on a train and spending the day in London – but then, she hadn't warned anybody that she wasn't actually called Jo Simmons or that she wasn't the least bit qualified to work at Fairmont, either.

Jo slid her cup to one side and leafed through the final newspaper. It didn't take long to find the article. Occupying the lower half of page six, it was typeset around a photo – the same one that they'd used in the *Guardian*: Jo in football kit, looking back at the camera, smiling, hair blowing all over the place in the wind. It was better than the tabloids' equivalents, which all depicted Jo in barely there party dresses, looking drunk or stoned. Presumably they'd all been submitted by the same sources that had provided the quotes: university friends, school friends, ex-boyfriends. *Friends.* Yeah, right. She ripped the page out and put it with the rest of them.

Her phone gave an additional whirr to inform her of a voicemail. Reluctantly, she lifted it to her ear.

'Jo, it's me.' Matt's voice sounded hollow. 'I've . . . I've just seen the papers, er, so yeah, I guess you were right – it's turned into a bit of a circus. I assume you've seen it? D'you wanna talk? Um . . . Oh, and I had to explain things to Sue – hope you don't mind. Thought you'd prefer it coming from me than the press. She's . . . well she's worried too. And Geoff's yelling all sorts of crap about you, but I think he'll calm down. Just—' There was a pause. 'Gimme a call, Jo.'

She deleted the message and slumped back in the chair. *Matt.* Lovely, thoughtful Matt who, just over twenty-four hours ago, had been on top of her, touching her . . . oh God, and now her next conversation with him was going to be about the contents of these bloody clippings and what she was going to do next and whether they'd sack her at Dunston's and how her life had just been turned upside down, or inside out. This was not the morning-after conversation she had intended.

Jo held out her empty cup for the pink-haired waitress, turning over the top page to hide the image of herself. That was all she needed: people recognising her, press hunting her down, paparazzi setting up camp outside her house . . . OK, maybe she was getting carried away. She had to calm down, try to think rationally.

'D'you want another?' asked the punk, expressionlessly. She had so many piercings that her face looked like some sort of pincushion.

Jo shook her head, wondering how long it would be

before some bossy manager came over and demanded that she make another purchase or get out. There was more pressure in London. She could feel it: pressure for time, pressure for space, pressure for getting things done.

It was ridiculous. She was learning about her own life from newspaper journalists. It probably wasn't even accurate, what they'd written – in fact, in the case of the *Mirror*, it almost certainly wasn't accurate. (Roxie was not an anagram of 'Becky Ross' and she felt sure she hadn't enjoyed dancing naked as a child – other than perhaps as a two-year-old, which was surely excusable.)

The tabloids all focused on her so-called career as a stripper and what they termed her 'succession' of boyfriends, which could have meant anything, really – or nothing. There were brief references to her Chemistry degree at UCL and her 'straight A' student days, but these were eclipsed by long narratives about her sordid night-time profession. Jo reordered the pack and tried not to think about how she must look to the average tabloid reader.

Chemistry. That's what they claimed. Yet again, Jo found herself wondering what sort of a girl this Rebecca Ross was. Every new piece of information she unearthed came as another surprise. Football. Lap-dancing. Drugs. Chemistry. What next? Farming? Magic tricks? Painting and decorating? Perhaps she was an actress after all, in her spare time.

Jo glanced around the café. A gaggle of girls in blue hoodies were slurping milkshakes near the door, hockey sticks slung over the backs of their chairs. Two Chinese girls huddled over some papers in the corner and a group of pasty teenaged guys were ogling over a copy of *Nuts* by the serving hatch. Maybe someone in here was a Chemistry student. It was quite possible, she thought, given their proximity to the college. She might even have overlapped with one of them during her time there.

She reread the *Guardian* article, which appeared to be the most comprehensive and well researched.

Rebecca Ross is thought to be suffering from dissociative amnesia, having been close to the source of the explosion on 2 August. She was reported as missing and feared dead by relatives and friends. Rebecca's mother, who lives in northwest London, has appealed for her daughter to come forward . . .

Two things were troubling her. *Dissociative amnesia*. That was the first thing. How did they know that? Saskia would almost certainly not have used such a term when she first leaked the story. She wouldn't have been able to pronounce it. Possibly the *Guardian* journalist had looked it up and made some assumptions about her state, thought Jo, but otherwise . . . No. No, it wasn't logical. It must have been Saskia.

Rebecca's mother. That was the other thing. Not parents. *Mother*. There was no reference to her father, either in this article or any of the others. Surely, if she had a father, he would have put out an appeal – either with her mother or separately. And if he'd made such an appeal, it was almost certain that one of the newspapers would have referenced him in some way.

Jo tried to put herself in the shoes of a journalist and tested out various scenarios. If they knew that her father was alive but that he hadn't got in touch, then that in itself was a story – especially with the tabloids' powers of distortion. *Rebecca's father has made no attempt to contact his daughter* . . . She could see it now. And if the press had discovered that her father had died or moved away or disowned Rebecca long ago, then ditto, they would have mentioned it, even if only for the extra human-interest angle. So, all Jo could conclude was that they didn't know. The papers didn't know about her father, and neither did she – which was incredibly frustrating.

In a way, it was good to have her life story documented like this. It clarified some of her hypotheses, allayed a few fears. Her memories, such as they were, fitted into the plot. And as yet, there had been no mention of any event or action that could have triggered the paranoia – another indication that she might have overreacted; that she had simply been on a cocaine come-down. But at the same time, she felt disappointed. The articles confirmed that it was all true. Rebecca really *had* messed up everything in her life.

Two years earlier, she had been on track to get a first-class degree from University College London. She had done well at school, breezed through exams, surrounded herself with friends and devoted every spare minute to playing football or some other sport. That's what the papers claimed. Jo believed it, too. She remembered that feeling of success.

Then something had happened. Jo went 'off the rails', as nearly all the newspapers put it. Cocaine and alcohol – that's what they claimed. She had started relying on those for her kicks and had turned her back on the sport, the degree, the friends. Actually, one of the newspapers put it more bluntly than that: 'Advised by the University to repeat her final year, Ms Ross found herself heading in a destructive downward spiral.'

She'd been removed from the football squad, abandoned by friends and told to drop down a year. Those were the facts. Rebecca Ross was a failure. But it didn't seem to make sense. Jo stared at the blotchy newsprint, thinking about the black hole that was her previous existence and willing the memories to return. It was like looking at a friend's CV – a very poor CV. She knew bits of it already, but hadn't ever seen it all laid out like this. Feeling empty and sad, Jo picked up the bundle and stuffed it into her bag.

She left the café, head down. There were things she needed to do, like call Matt and have an awkward post-sex, post-revelation conversation; call Sue to be removed from her post; call Saskia and let rip. But first, she needed to remember. She couldn't just learn all these facts about her life without remembering something for herself.

It was surprising how different the university was from the rest of the city. Following the signs, Jo turned a corner and found herself in a quiet, picturesque one-way street. The looming glass tower blocks gave way to low, white-washed Georgian terraces and the roar of Euston Road became a distant hum.

Two gatehouses marked the entrance to the campus. Standing between them was a man in a yellow jacket, his feet set apart, his face a picture of tedium. The bulbous nose looked vaguely familiar, thought Jo, but she couldn't be sure. This visit was like a taste test; her brain was programmed to remember things now that she knew she had been here before, just as it would automatically opt for the more expensive wine in the test.

The man's eyes followed her across the threshold and into an enormous courtyard with what looked like a Grecian palace at its centre. His stare made her wonder whether she was doing something wrong – like, maybe not showing her student card, or not saying hello, or walking on private land or something. She glanced back and realised he was just looking at her bum. Jo pretended to know where she was going and headed for the far corner of the courtyard where students were pouring both ways through a door.

She envied them, those gaggles of jeans-clad twenty-somethings who brushed past her, laughing and chatting and clutching lecture notes as though the only thing that mattered in the whole world was passing this year's exams – along with animal rights and human trafficking and domestic violence and saying no to war, of course. They didn't need to worry about who they were; they already knew. They had pasts all laid out, neatly committed to memories, available for retrieval at any time. Jo didn't have any such pathway laid out. She didn't know where she'd come from; she had to piece it together as she went along.

The Chemistry block was listed on the signpost along with all the others. Jo stood there, staring up at the directions but not taking them in. She didn't need to. In her mind, she was already seeing the route down the polished corridor, through a courtyard and then over the road. The sign didn't give that much detail but she felt quite sure. She just *knew*. It was a relief, after all the guesswork and deduction she'd had to do in the last few weeks, that finally her memory seemed to be playing a part. But it was also slightly unnerving.

Jo nearly broke into a trot when she saw that the marble-floored corridor opened onto a small grass courtyard. She was right: this was exactly as she'd envisaged. Yes, brick buildings, ugly benches, some sort of oriental sculpture . . . This was her old route through the campus. She wasn't making this up. She was *remembering*. Then she stopped.

She was bounding down the steps that led to the cafeteria and beyond when another image materialised: her walking up the same steps, coffee in hand, shaking with the alcohol in her system. Someone was saying her name. She turned round. Professor Latham, her tutor – oh, and she could even remember his name – was looking straight at her. She could picture him now, his awkward stoop, his grey upper lip, his hairy nose.

'Rebecca, we need to talk,' he had said. Those had been his exact words. She remembered the horrible, sickly feeling inside her. It was partly the alcohol, partly the implication. That had been the beginning of the end of her time at UCL.

Jo didn't stop at the café. She walked on, past the notice board where squash courts and fencing and ballroom dancing were advertised in lurid colours. She crossed the car park and emerged at street level, remembering the glass-fronted theatre café and the rusty bicycles lined up outside. Even the numerous zebra crossings and the po-faced traffic wardens on Gordon Street looked familiar.

She had arrived. Jo looked up at the stacks of glass containers and the orange rubber tubes that were visible through the windows of the five-storey monstrosity opposite. It was completely familiar to her – almost as though coming here was still part of her daily routine.

But that wasn't what brought on the surge of emotion that came as she stared up at her old department.

The tears that threatened to escape as she stared at the brown-stained building were caused by other memories. Happy memories. Memories of classmates larking about with pipettes, of guys making test tubes explode, of her lab partner setting fire to her overalls and getting soaked as they put out the flames . . .

Her lab partner. Jo tried to remember her name. *Blank* and Becky. Becky and *blank*. The girls at the back. No, she was trying too hard now. The details were missing. It didn't matter though; the important thing was that she was remembering things at all. She felt strangely confident that more would come back to her now she knew a few facts.

Jo dried her eyes and from memory made her way to a small private park at the end of the street. Students were huddled on benches wearing gloves, poring over papers, sipping steaming drinks out of paper cups. She had been here before. In the summer. The lawn had been covered in skimpily dressed students, not piles of brown leaves, as it was today. She'd been with someone. The boyfriend. Luke.

Jo wandered over to one of the benches, teasing out the memories and trying to build up a clearer picture. Then she realised her phone was ringing. She dived into her bag, feeling guilty for not calling Matt back sooner.

It wasn't Matt. In fact, it took two rings for Jo to realise the significance of the name on the screen.

Three rings. Jo wondered what she would want. Surely, having sold Jo's story to the national press, she didn't have the nerve to come back asking for more?

Four rings. Jo's finger hovered over the Answer button.

It wasn't so much that she was angry for the damage Saskia had caused – because actually, some good had come out of the whole situation – it was more that she had betrayed Jo's trust.

Five rings. Jo considered what she'd say to the girl. Something harsh. Something that told her how angry she was.

'Hi Saskia.' Jo silently cursed her own weakness.

'Alright hun, How's it goin'? I saw the fing about you in the paper today. You alright?'

'Oh, I'm great, never better,' Jo replied tightly. 'Happiest day of my life, having everyone read about my life as a stripper as they eat their cornflakes.'

'Are you being sarcastic?'

Jo sighed heavily. 'Yes, Saskia, I'm being sarcastic. How would *you* like it if all the shitty, stupid things you'd done in your life got exposed to the nation?'

'I guess you're a bit upset about it all?'

There was clearly no point in being subtle. 'Yes! Yes, I'm upset! Of course I'm upset! Who wouldn't be? I was a fucking *stripper*, for fuck's sake. And now it's common knowledge – and you know what? That's not the worst thing.' She paused for breath. A pair of dreadlocked students glanced sideways at her as their paths crossed.

'What d'you mean?'

'The worst thing is that this didn't *need* to happen. It all came about because someone – someone fucking *selfish* – decided to make a bit of cash selling the story to a newspaper, without even thinking about what it would do to me!'

There. She had said it.

'Shit. Who did that?'

Jo half laughed, half snorted. She couldn't believe the girl's audacity. Not only had she called on the pretence of worrying, she now intended to deny her part in the proceedings.

'Oh, fuck off, Saskia. I'm not stupid.'

'What?'

As the phrase about being stupid came out, it occurred to Jo that Saskia might not actually be capable of pulling off such a scam. She pushed her doubts aside. Of course it was her.

'You were one of the only people who knew, Saskia.'

'What?'

'Look, this is getting boring. Why don't you just stop saying "what" and tell me what you want? And if you just called to piss me off, then you can put the phone down right now and I'll happily never speak to you again.'

'What?'

'OK, I'm hanging up.'

'No – wait!' Saskia yelped. 'I just meant . . . So . . . You fink it was me that went to the papers?'

Jo sighed again, exasperated. 'Yes.'

'What?!'

Perhaps she had underestimated the girl's powers of persistence, thought Jo. 'Why did you call me?'

'Fuck you!' cried Saskia with newfound volume. 'I called to see if you was OK, an' now you go accusin' me of shit! Fuck, Roxie, I fought we was friends.'

Jo hesitated. Her convictions were weakening. 'Are you saying you haven't told anyone about me?'

Saskia tutted sulkily. 'Not a single fuckin' person.'

'Oh.' Jo let the news sink in. Reluctantly, she was coming round to the idea that Saskia might be telling the truth. 'Right.'

A horrible blackness was descending on her. There were only two other people in the world who could have let her down, and neither option seemed plausible. But of the two, at least one was almost certainly out of the picture. Which meant . . . She didn't like the idea, but it was seeming increasingly likely that Mrs P had let her down.

'Don't bother apologisin' or nothin', will ya? I don't mind bein' accused of stuff I ain't done – I don't give a shit if my mate says I've—'

'OK, I'm sorry!' Jo suddenly felt overwhelmed with guilt. She could see how it looked from Saskia's perspective: as a friend, she had guarded the secret of Roxie's reincarnation, she had called to check that Jo was all right in the face of the press bombardment – a result of somebody else's intrusion, not hers . . . 'I'm so sorry. I just . . . I didn't know who else it could be. Sorry. And thanks for calling.'

Saskia huffed a little and then seemed to come round. 'Yeah, well. 'slong as you're OK, I guess, innit.'

Jo apologised some more and agreed to meet up with Saskia again once the press thing had died down, but she was no longer thinking about the accusation she'd wrongfully made. She was thinking about the one she was going to have to make.

Her phone buzzed as she lowered it from her ear. She had another voicemail.

'Hello, this is a message for Ms Rebecca Ross. It's Detective Inspector Michael Davis here from the Metropolitan Police. I'd appreciate it if you could give me a call back, urgently, in relation to the Buffalo Club explosion.'

Chapter Thirty-One

'Hey!' Matt looked pleased to see her. 'Didn't think you were coming!' He jogged over to the tree.

'Sorry,' said Jo, because she couldn't think of how else to begin. She had rehearsed this conversation so many times on the way here that she was completely confused about how it would go.

'Why?' Matt wiped a hand across his forehead. He was sweating, despite the October chill.

Jo's face broke into a smile; she couldn't help it. 'Because . . . I didn't return any of your calls.' Or texts. Or voicemails. And because as far as she knew, it was customary for people who had had sex to exchange at least a few syllables after the event.

Matt waved a hand. 'You've had other things on your mind.'

They looked at each other. Jo wondered whether Matt was going to mention the events of the other morning. She thought about how to begin. Then the moment was lost as Henry bounded towards them and booted the football in their direction.

'You chaps playing, or what?'

'I'm not really dressed for it.' Jo dipped her head apologetically. Football wasn't on the agenda today.

The other lads wandered over and started hurling abuse at Matt.

'Come on, you poof! You just gave away two goals!'

'No interest in football now *Jo's* around . . .'

'Can't you just finish the game, *then* go and shag?'

Jo hoped Raj's reference to shagging was just a co-incidence.

'I'm sure you can manage without me,' Matt smiled.

'Fine.'

They walked off. As she watched them, Jo heard Sanjit mutter something to the others, then Raj looked back at them.

'Nice to see you, *Roxie*!' He wiggled his hips in a move that wasn't the least bit erotic.

Jo looked away, but not quickly enough to miss the apologetic look on Kieran's face. She wondered what they'd been saying about her back at the flat.

'Sorry about that.'

She shrugged as though it didn't matter. 'I'd rather people say it to my face.'

Matt motioned towards the road. Jo nodded gratefully and they set off. She wondered how to broach the subject, and whether it should come before or after the other things she needed to say.

'Why the enormous bag?' he asked, nodding at the sack slung over her shoulder.

Ah. So this would have to come first, thought Jo. She tried to think of an easy way of saying it. There didn't seem to be one.

'I moved out. I'm . . . I'm homeless again.' She looked at the pavement.

Matt winced. 'Why?'

'Well . . . I was right. It was Mrs Phillips who went to the press, and I can't live with her any more.' Jo shifted the bag onto her other shoulder, glancing at Matt's face. 'I don't trust her,' she added, trying to convince herself as much as Matt that her actions were justified.

He grimaced. 'Did you talk to her about it?'

'No,' she said sheepishly. 'I just left a note on the table with my rent money this morning. Haven't seen her in days, anyway. She must've guessed that I knew.'

Jo knew she'd gone about things the wrong way; she just hadn't had the nerve to confront Mrs P. She felt so angry at the woman's betrayal she didn't trust herself to keep her temper under control.

'But,' Matt was frowning, 'is it so terrible that she told the press? I mean, I thought you agreed it was a good thing that someone had?'

They reached the road and by mutual consent, turned right, towards Matt's flat.

Jo faltered. In theory, he was right. She did see it as a good thing that someone had leaked her story. If it hadn't happened, she wouldn't have known about UCL, wouldn't have gone there and remembered those things, wouldn't have spent the last few days scribbling in her notebook as the memories trickled back. But that didn't negate the fact that her landlady had gone against her wishes. There were other ways of achieving the same thing – ways that didn't involve sneaking around behind her back.

'It was the fact that she . . . she just took things into her own hands,' Jo tried to explain. 'She could've tried talking to me, or persuading *me* to go to the press, but no – she just waded in and announced to the national press that I was a stripper!'

273

'Well, I'm not sure those were her exact words.'

'Well . . . whatever.'

'And would you really have agreed to talk to the press yourself? At least this way, people know you're alive.'

Jo didn't reply immediately. Matt was right, but that wasn't the point. 'She didn't go about things the right way.'

'No, I guess not,' Matt conceded unconvincingly. 'Fair enough. So . . .'

Matt was clearly trying to ask her where she was intending to live now.

Jo knew what she wanted to say, but the idea of coming out with it suddenly seemed too daunting. Of all the things you could do to wreck a relationship, she knew, asking to move in together after a single shag – not even a night spent together – was way up there near the top. She didn't need personal memories to know that. She would have to find another place to stay.

'You could stay with me and Kieran.'

Jo laughed at his joke. He wasn't foolish enough to suggest that she moved in with him.

Matt was looking at her, deadpan. 'If you want to, that is.' He stopped walking. Then he caught Jo's hand and pulled her towards him, slipping one arm around the small of her back.

She wanted to. Of course she wanted to. Jo couldn't think of anything she wanted to do more. She looked up at Matt's eyes as he squeezed her towards him. 'Really?' she said, softly, because his lips were already touching hers. Jo felt a shiver run through her. She remembered it all from the other morning: his smell, his taste, his body sliding against hers.

They pulled apart and stood for a moment, just looking at one another. Maybe this was an exception to the rule, thought Jo. In this instance, maybe the decision to live together would not be a relationship-wrecking one. It might even bring them together.

'I'll take that as a yes,' he said.

Jo smiled.

'Hey, you were right,' she said. 'About knowing who you are and stuff. I went back to my old uni. And . . . it was weird. Things came back to me. I mean, not everything. Just bits and pieces. But details I couldn't remember before. Like chemistry experiments and people in my class, and nights out and lectures.'

Matt looked at her. 'Did it help?'

'Yeah.' Jo thought for a second, then realised just how much it had helped. 'Yeah. It helped. I mean, there are still gaps, but I feel like I'm beginning to know where I came from.'

They turned into Jackman Close.

'So, are you gonna find out more?'

'What d'you mean?'

He looked at her as though it was obvious. 'The news-papers. Are you gonna call them and find out who left their contact details for you?'

'N-no.'

Actually, it hadn't occurred to Jo that the newspaper thing could open up a two-way dialogue. The idea that *she* could initiate contact with people from her previous life wasn't something she'd considered – or dared to consider.

'Why not?'

'Well—'

Because it scared her senseless, the idea of approaching these strangers, opening up to them. It was exactly what she'd been avoiding for months. She didn't *want* her memories to be forced upon her. And she really, really didn't want people connecting Jo Simmons to Becky Ross. Jo was a new person: innocent and untainted. Becky had all sorts of dirt in her past.

'I don't know if it would help.'

Matt looked at her. 'Going to your old university helped.'

'That was different. It was the *place* that made me remember, not the people.'

'Hmm.' Matt nodded as though he didn't follow her reasoning.

He wasn't the only one who was unconvinced by Jo's argument. The possibility of reinitiating contact with people in Becky's past hung like a cloud in her mind, infiltrating her thoughts, dampening her mood. She wished in a way that Matt hadn't suggested the option of contacting the newspapers. Up until now, she had felt invisible and anonymous as Jo Simmons. There had been no alternative way of existing. Now she had a choice – assuming anybody had left their contact details for her, of course.

Maybe lurking in Becky's old haunts, waiting and hoping for scraps of memory to return, wasn't the most effective way of remembering anyway. Perhaps Matt was right, and the best thing would be for her to confront the people, let them ram things back into her head from before. It would come to the same thing, eventually; it was just a choice between doing it on her own or accepting help – and the consequences of whatever she'd done in her previous life.

'Well?' said Matt.

Jo jumped and tried to break free from her thoughts.

'I guess we're home.' He pulled a bunch of keys out of his pocket and held them out to Jo. 'After you.'

Chapter Thirty-Two

'And how are you faring?' asked Sue, her brow furrowed in sympathy.

Jo shrugged and tried to get comfortable in the old office chair. She really hadn't prepared for this meeting, other than to down some cheap vodka before coming out.

This was her first trip to Fairmont House since the news had broken. Sue had been cagey about the purpose of the meeting, but Jo could guess. They couldn't have a failed chemistry student with no suitable qualifications or experience looking after their children.

It felt like her first interview all over again: Sue looking frumpy and kind and saying sweet things, Geoff staring moronically into space, making occasional pointless interjections and wearing a Donald Duck tie.

'It's all a bit of a shock, I expect?' Sue prompted, blinking rapidly at Jo. 'I suppose your memory's only just starting to come back?'

Jo nodded, her eyes wandering to the swathes of purple silk around the woman's neck. She knew that at some point she'd have to say something; she just wasn't sure what it would be. The alcohol had reduced her anxiety but it had also reduced her ability to speak.

'So.' Sue leaned forward on the desk. 'How about we give you an update on where *we* are, what we're thinking and so on, then you can tell me where *you're* coming from?'

Jo nodded blankly, wishing she hadn't succumbed to the vodka. In the last few weeks, she'd barely touched the stuff. But there were moments when she just needed to take the edge off things, and this was one of them.

'So Matt gave us a heads-up on what happened – how you'd been involved in the explosion and lost your memory—'

'And came to us with fake qualifications,' Geoff inserted.

Jo nodded shamefully and mumbled an apology. She couldn't tell whether her words were actually coming out slurred or whether they just sounded that way in her head.

'Well.' Sue opened up her hands as if to say, *these things happen* and glared at Geoff. 'You wanted the job, I suppose.'

Jo didn't say anything. She hadn't actually wanted the job that much, at the time; she'd just wanted *a* job, but it didn't seem sensible to point out this difference.

'Now, obviously we have some concerns about the lying,' Sue said softly, 'but—'

'As will the members of the public, when they find out,' added Geoff, swivelling his head between his colleague and Jo as though this was something they Ought To Consider.

Sue looked at him. 'Yes, that's a possibility, of course. We all know how the media reacts to child-care stories at the moment, so we'll have to have a good think about how to handle that.'

'I guess so,' Jo nodded, still not sure where all of this was leading. The slurring wasn't just in her head, she decided. It was quite audible.

'The fact is, of course, Dunston's did all the necessary background checks required; it was just that—'

'You pulled the wool over our eyes,' finished Geoff, tilting his head at Jo, the naughty child.

'Well, that's true,' Sue conceded, turning to the centre manager. 'But we have to remember that the role of activities coordinator is very low clearance. Jo didn't actually need any qualifications to get the position, so the fabrications are pretty much immaterial.'

Now you say, thought Jo, wishing she'd saved herself a lot of trouble by leaving her CV blank – just a name, address and phone number.

'Nothing's immaterial in the press,' retorted Geoff, waggling his finger as though this were an ancient proverb.

'Of course not,' Sue said brusquely, 'which is why we'll have to handle the media carefully, as I said. But the chances of them seizing on this as a story are really quite small, wouldn't you say, Jo?'

Jo sensed a tone of expectation in the woman's voice and nodded appropriately.

'I see it's all died down, anyway.'

Jo nodded again. It was true. Thankfully, the story had all but blown over. Rebecca Ross was old news. Nobody, it seemed, really cared about a London stripper who was temporarily assumed to be dead.

'Now, I don't know what you know about how we explained the situation to the children . . .' Sue raised an eyebrow questioningly.

Jo dipped her head ambiguously. She had no idea.

'We decided to tell them the truth.'

Jo swallowed. *The truth.* She tried not to think about how Kyle and Jason had reacted to the news that, a few weeks before, their activities coordinator had been earning a living by waving her tits in businessmen's faces.

'We thought it was probably better than them reading about it in the papers,' Sue explained.

'OK.' Jo took in the news. 'How did they take it?'

'Oh, not too badly!' Sue fiddled with the tassels on her scarf.

Jo glanced at Geoff, hoping that his expression might shed some light on the truth. He was staring out of the window, mouth half open.

'Really,' Jo looked again at Sue. 'Tell me.' The vodka was making her bolder than usual. It hardly mattered, anyway. Jo would probably never be allowed to see the kids again.

'Well, you know how they are.' Sue pulled a silly face.

Jo closed her eyes. She could imagine.

'They're very excited about their football tournament.'

Another lie, thought Jo, wishing Sue would just get to the point.

'They all practised in the yard when you weren't here.'

Jo frowned suspiciously. 'All?'

'Uh, well, some. I wasn't there. Clare took the session. She certainly mentioned Tim and the new boy . . .'

'Taiwo.' Jo secretly hoped that Clare hadn't managed to get all six of them playing football together in the yard. She didn't want to know that the assistant manager had succeeded where she herself had failed.

'That's it, yes. And I think she told them about your plans for the Hallowe'en outing next week.'

Jo nodded silently. They weren't her plans, they were Sue's plans. And they were ridiculous plans at that. The idea of a Hallowe'en outing next week (as if anyone had time to plan a kamikaze expedition like that in a week!) was absurd.

'Look, Jo, from our point of view it's quite simple. There are a couple of "ifs" but essentially, we feel that you're good at your job and we want you to keep doing it. The "ifs" being: if you're up to it, if we can have your word that you'll be honest and open with us in future, and if we can make sure Dunston's doesn't suffer through any bad press. So. What are your thoughts?'

'I . . .' What *were* her thoughts? She was confused, first and foremost. Sue seemed to be implying that she could have her old job back again. Just when everything seemed to be collapsing inwards on her, this pillar was remaining upright. Against all the odds. She had assumed that today would be the last time she set foot in Fairmont House, and now this woman was expecting her to start planning pumpkins and ghost costumes. Geoff had stopped gazing through the window and was looking at her, waiting for an answer.

'I think . . . I need some time.'

Sue nodded and looked at Geoff. 'Of course you do.' She pulled her mouth into a we'll-get-through-this-together sort of smile. 'In fact, I was going to suggest that. How about a fortnight's compassionate leave?'

'Um . . .' Jo noticed Geoff glance crossly at his colleague as she tried to form a response.

'Fully paid, obviously,' Sue went on. 'We can reassess the situation after that, and you can either come back or take a bit more time off.'

Jo didn't know what to say. This was an insanely generous offer and one that she really didn't deserve. She wasn't that good at her job, as far as she knew.

She was . . . well, better than she had been on day one, but that wasn't saying much. And yet they were bending over backwards to keep her on the payroll.

'Sounds good,' she mumbled, in a daze.

Sue rose to her feet, looking pleased with the outcome. Geoff stayed in his chair and started spinning a biro around on the desk, lifting a hand briefly in Jo's direction.

After a few muttered goodbyes, Jo walked with Sue to the main exit in silence. On the way out, Sue laid a hand on Jo's arm and looked straight into her eyes.

'Are you OK?' she asked. 'You seem a bit . . .' *Drunk*, Jo nearly interjected. '. . . distant.'

Jo shrugged lightly and concentrated on getting her words out with gaps in between. 'I'm all right,' she said. 'Considering.'

Sue seemed to accept the response, even if she didn't believe it. 'You know I'm here, if there's anything I can do.'

Jo smiled and thanked her boss. The problem was, there *wasn't* anything Sue could do. This was something she had to sort out on her own. The confusion over what she should do, who she was, who she wanted to be . . . it was all in her head.

She wandered through the car park of Fairmont House, thinking again about what Matt had said. It was true, she wanted to find out about Becky Ross. Maybe now was the time to stop creeping around out of sight and confront her old self.

Jo pulled out her phone and dialled the number for Directory Enquiries.

Chapter Thirty-Three

'Can I get you anything? Tea or coffee?' Jo flapped her hands nervously as she led the way through the messy flat.

'A glass of water, please.'

DI Michael Davis was tall; so tall, in fact, that he had to bend over to avoid banging his head on the wonky doorframe. He had a bland face – mid-thirties, Jo guessed – and sandy hair, what was left of it. The rapid promotion to detective inspector had clearly taken its toll on his follicles.

Jo ran the tap. He was making her twitchy. It wasn't anything he was doing – he was just stooping in the doorway, clutching a notebook, waiting for his water – it was the fact that he was a policeman. She couldn't pinpoint the source of the unease, but his presence set her nerves on edge.

It was silly, really. Up until a week ago, it would have been understandable, this anxiety. Touching knees with a policeman would have been out of the question back then, in case he somehow found out that Jo Simmons was Rebecca Ross, or that Jo Simmons wasn't Lindsay McDermott the support worker, or that Rebecca Ross was Roxie the stripper. But now the whole world knew all that.

Thanks to the media, she had no secrets at all – or at least, none that she knew of.

'Thanks.'

She motioned for them to sit on the sofa, the only raised surface that wasn't piled high with papers, tea towels, bicycle wheels and plates of old food. Jo had tidied the previous day, but somehow in the last twelve hours, the junk had grown back, re-emerging from cupboards and drawers, spreading across every surface like fungi.

'As I explained on the phone, I just need you to answer a few questions. Questions we asked all the survivors at the time of the explosion.' He looked at her. 'Back in August.'

Jo nodded anxiously. There was something unnerving about Detective Inspector Michael Davis. It was his eyes, she thought. They seemed to linger suspiciously, as though he were trying to decipher her body language or something.

'We don't usually have to read about our witnesses in the press before questioning,' he added, whipping open his notebook and looking at her again.

'I suppose not!' Jo laughed frivolously, then wished she hadn't. DI Davis clearly wasn't the frivolous type, and he probably *was* quite cross that he'd had to go to such lengths to track her down. 'Actually . . . I was wondering,' she ventured, 'how *did* you get my number?'

He looked at her as though she should have known better.

'I can't answer that, as I'm sure you're aware, for confidentiality reasons.' He paused, as though deliberating over whether to say more. 'Suffice to say, it was probably the same person who leaked your story in the first place.'

Jo nodded, her misgivings confirmed. Mrs Phillips had handed her over.

'So, the basics to begin with: your name and age, please.'

'Rebecca Ross, twenty-four.' She swallowed. Thank God for Facebook.

'And your nationality?'

'Er . . . British?' Jo wasn't actually sure, but all the evidence seemed to point that way.

'OK. Now a few questions about the club itself. How long had you been working there?'

Jo shrugged, disappointed. She had hoped to be able to answer a few more questions before drying up.

'Any idea at all? Months? Years?'

It occurred to her that she could probably work this one out. The newspaper articles had said that she'd been at UCL two years before, and she hadn't read anything about any other jobs.

'Just under two years, I reckon.'

DI Davis nodded expressionlessly and jotted it down.

'Now. Friends and acquaintances at the club. Could you tell me who else you remember? Management, bouncers, other, er . . . dancers?'

Saskia Dawson. That was the only person she knew.

'No one, I'm afraid.'

'No one at all?' He looked at her doubtfully.

Jo looked at the floor. 'No.'

She wondered whether detective inspectors had special powers to detect lies and, if so, whether something was twitching right now. Saskia had begged Jo not to mention her name – unsurprisingly, given her recent career history and habits. Her phobia of the authorities probably ran as deep as Jo's.

'OK.' The policeman raised both eyebrows and scribbled something on his notebook.

Jo's stomach lurched. She couldn't see what he was writing, but surely it didn't take that long to write the word 'none'?

'Well, that rules out all the next section.' He sounded half pleased, half sceptical. 'Oh, and the one after. You don't remember the manager or any other staff?'

'No.' He was clearly trying to trick her in some way, by asking the same question twice.

'So, you'd worked there for nigh on two years. Would you say you were fairly familiar with the setup in the club?'

'The setup?'

'The way things worked, who did what, where things went . . .'

'Oh. Um, I don't know.'

'You don't know the setup?'

'No, I don't know whether I knew the setup. I can't remember.'

'Hmm.' He wrote something else. 'So d'you think you would have noticed if anything was amiss?'

'I don't know.'

'So you'd worked there for two years, but you don't know if you'd—'

'I can't remember. So I don't *know* whether I would have noticed.'

He seemed to have forgotten that she had amnesia. Maybe he didn't believe that she had it.

'Right.' He noted it down, took a sip of water and flipped over the page. Then he turned the next page, and the next one. 'Doesn't apply, doesn't apply . . . OK, so. Personal questions, I'm afraid.'

Jo braced herself. It didn't help that Inspector Davis now clearly thought she was making the amnesia thing up.

'At the time of the explosion, was the Buffalo Club work your only source of income?'

Jo shrugged helplessly. 'I guess.'

'I don't want guesses, I'm afraid. Do you know the answer?'

She looked at him, wide-eyed. 'No.'

'You can't remember anything about any other jobs?'

'No.' Jo held out her hands. It was impossible to *prove* that she didn't remember.

'Your political views?'

Jo screwed up her nose. What did that have to do with anything?

'I'm assuming you can remember *them* . . . ?'

She looked at him imploringly. 'I don't have any.'

The eyebrows lifted again, this time accompanied by a little shake of the head. He obviously thought she was wilfully obstructing his inquiry – which she wasn't; she just didn't really know which way she voted.

'Actually . . .' She scrabbled around mentally, trying to assemble some sort of political stance. 'I'm quite left wing.'

'Are you?' One eyebrow relaxed, the other remained arched. 'And you're British born. Have you lived in Britain all your life?'

'Think so.'

'Yes or no?'

Jo shrugged. She wasn't going to fall into his trap by claiming she could remember her whole life.

'OK . . . Have you travelled anywhere that might—'

'I don't know.'

The detective sighed and whipped over a page in his book.

'Has your family ever—'

'I don't know.'

'You might want to listen to the whole question before you—'

'No,' she said, looking him in the eye. 'Because I don't know who my family are.'

He was silent for a moment. 'OK.' He nodded. 'Very well.'

Ha, thought Jo. And then she felt ashamed. It wasn't so much of a conquest; it was an admission of her own cowardice. She didn't know who her family were. Perhaps Matt was right. Perhaps – now the whole of the UK was aware of her new identity, now she had nothing to hide – perhaps it was time to confront Rebecca's past.

'Do you, or does anyone you know, have any associations with any known terrorist groups?'

Jo rolled her eyes. Really. What a ridiculous question. *Oh, yeah, I often pop round to see my mate when he's wiring up explosives in his garage.* 'No.'

'We have to ask. So, last section.' He drained his glass of water. 'On the night of the explosion, what time did you start work?'

Jo sighed. 'I don't know.'

'Did you notice anything unusual that night? Different guests, new staff, any—'

'I can't remember the *usual*,' she pointed out, willing for him to understand.

The detective nodded, slowly. 'Fair point.' He ran his eye down the page, presumably scanning it for questions that Jo might actually be able to answer. 'So you don't remember which staff were working that night?'

She just looked at him.

'No, OK . . . So, is there *anything* you remember from that night, Ms Ross?'

Jo thought about what she had seen in the flashbacks. Yes, there were things she remembered: the layout of the club, the bottles behind the bar, the nondescript man who had bought her a drink and paid for her lap-dance – the same as any other – then the strap of her shoe coming off as she fought through the rubble in the dark . . . But they weren't things that would help Detective Inspector Michael Davis find out who had planted the bomb.

'No.'

'And there's nothing else you can tell me that you think might be useful?'

He clearly wasn't holding out much hope, thought Jo, watching him tidy his papers and put away his pen.

'Sorry, no.'

'OK, well, thank you for your time.' He stood up. 'I suppose it might be a bit late now, but if you need any counselling or if you want me to put you in touch with a psych—'

'No,' Jo said too quickly. In her mind, she was seeing couches and hypnotists and inquisitive shrinks in furry cardigans. 'Thank you. I'm fine.'

He nodded and made his way across the room. 'Very well.'

Jo followed him, determined to ask her question. 'How's it going, the investigation?'

He frowned briefly. 'Fine, thank you.'

She had been hoping for a more informative answer,

but the man's expression suggested she wouldn't be getting one. She tried again. 'Any new leads? D'you have an idea about who planted the bomb?'

Detective Inspector Davis ducked under the doorframe, turned to face her and reversed onto the lower step so that his eyes were level with hers.

'I'm sure you read the papers,' he said, with a hint of weariness in his voice.

Jo nodded. Of course she read the papers. That was why she was asking. She needed to know whether the newspapers had got it right. If, as they claimed, the police were following a single line of enquiry that centred around a group of young, radicalised, 'viciously anti-Western' fundamentalists, then Jo could put to rest one of the blimp-like fears that had been hanging in her mind ever since she came round from the blast. She would know that she hadn't been involved.

'Well, there you go.' The inspector smiled curtly.

'But . . .' Jo wasn't quite done. She wanted to hear the man say, in his own words, that the papers had reported the findings correctly.

'Look, I'm sorry, Ms Ross. It's confidential. The investigation is still underway. I can't tell you any more than we told the hacks at the press conference.'

Jo nodded again. 'OK. But it's true, is it? About the line of enquiry?'

She was really pissing him off now, she could tell. But she just wanted to hear him say it. Or see him nod. Or something.

He sighed. 'What we tell the press is true, yes. Now, I have to go. If you do remember anything you think might be useful,' he fished around in his breast pocket, 'here's my number.'

Jo took the little grey card. 'Thanks.'

She shut the door and leaned back on it, letting the relief gently sink in. The ordeal was over. And although nothing was certain in the erratic life of Jo Simmons, she felt reasonably sure about one thing: she wasn't a member of any radical anti-Western group. Of all the anxieties competing for space in her head, at least one could be firmly ruled out. She had had nothing to do with the Buffalo Club bomb.

Chapter Thirty-Four

Jo stared at the page in disbelief. It was absurd. The last time she'd checked, her Facebook profile had been a year out-of-date. Like latter-day Pompeii victims, the images and comments and scribbles had been preserved in their exact former state and had lain untouched for months. Rebecca Ross had disappeared from cyberspace as she had disappeared from life. And now, this.

She drew the laptop across the kitchen table and planted her elbows in front of the screen. There were ninety-seven messages in her inbox. Two hundred and sixty-one people had requested to be her 'friend'. Those who were already 'friends' had clearly spent a good deal of time on Facebook in the last few days. Her 'wall' was plastered with so many comments it took about five minutes for Jo to scroll to the bottom.

There were comments and alerts and reminders and links and notes . . . too many words to read, too much information to take in. Jo got the gist. In general, people were wishing her well. In amongst the updates and the invitations to join strange-sounding groups like the David Hasselhoff Appreciation Society and the We Love Soft Cheeses club, there were messages of elation and disbelief.

People were happy that she was alive – even though they hadn't been aware of her supposed death.

Most of the comments were along the same lines: 'Hope you're OK. Can't believe what happened.' A couple were cheeky: 'Always knew you liked getting your kit off!' with some verging on rude: 'You slapper!' Some, Jo was alarmed to note, read almost like eulogies: 'I'll always remember your smile on the pitch when we won.' Jesus Christ. It was as though some of her friends had only read half the story and hadn't got to the bit that mentioned she *survived* the blast.

She extracted the scrap of paper from her pocket. Three names. Three numbers. She turned back to the laptop and searched for the first name.

There was one occurrence.

Oh my God, Becky, you're even more crazy than I thought! Hope you're OK, it all sounds a bit mad. Call me any time – you should have my number now but it's below, just in case.
Lots of love, Gill XXXxxx

Jo smiled. Gill. That was it. Her old chemistry lab partner. She looked down at the piece of paper and did another search.

Hope everything isn't too awful for you. Call if you need anything and TAKE CARE. Luke

Her smile faded. She wasn't sure what to think. Luke had made contact, both on Facebook and via the newspaper. She had two ways of contacting him, but she wasn't sure about using either. She didn't know enough about him. All she remembered were the feelings of togetherness and attachment – the bond they had shared – and then of separation. She had hurt him. She couldn't just pick up the phone and say hi.

The last search proved fruitless, as she had expected. Her mum wasn't on Facebook. Jo stared at her messy, slanting handwriting. The word looked like a row of zig-zags: *Mum*. What about *Dad*? Jo let the paper flutter onto the table and ran her fingers through her hair. There were still so many gaps, so many questions.

Her mother would be frantic with worry. First, she'd lost her daughter to cocaine and alcohol and lap-dancing – and she might not have known at the time, but she knew now – and then she'd been told that her girl was 'missing, feared dead', and now, having ascertained that she was alive after all, she had tried to make contact and heard nothing back, after more than a week. It was enough to give any mother a breakdown.

Jo picked up her phone, then put it back on the table. Then she picked it up again and slowly punched the numbers into the keypad. She stared at the device, not quite ready to press the Call button.

The phone started ringing and she nearly dropped it. *Withheld number.* Jo hesitated, feeling suddenly paranoid that just by logging into Facebook she had somehow opened herself up to the world. She looked at the screen. No, she was being stupid. There was no way anybody could have got her phone number.

'Hello?'

'Ah, hi! It's Dave here. Is that Rebecca?'

Jo faltered. Nobody who knew her number called her Rebecca.

'Wh – which Dave?'

There was a lot of background noise at the other end: chattering and whirring and talking.

'Dave Chan. How's things?'

Jo didn't reply. Something wasn't right. Dave Chan sounded like a bad actor, saying his lines. She quickly thought through her options. 'I think you've got a wrong number.'

'Oh. Oh, I'm sorry. Are you not Rebecca Ross? I just wanted to—'

'No.'

He was still talking as she put the phone down.

With a shaky hand, Jo clicked on All Friends and looked down the list. 'Dave Chan,' she read, 'is about to cross the Thai border.' Updated twenty-three minutes ago. She looked at the picture: an Asian guy with a rucksack and walking boots, standing on a boulder overlooking some tropical forests. It didn't make sense. Why would Dave Chan want to call her from his travels in Thailand? And how had he got her number?

And then it did make sense. It made complete sense. The man had not been calling from Thailand. He had been calling from an office in London. A newspaper office. He wasn't Dave Chan at all.

She hadn't given them her phone number, but she hadn't hidden it from them either. They must have taken it down when she'd called the editorial department to pick up her messages. Knowing that she wouldn't want to speak to a tabloid journalist, they had posed as one of her Facebook friends – except they hadn't done their homework. Jo shook her head, staring at the lush Thai landscape and wondering how many more crank calls she'd receive, now her secret was out.

The number winked up at her from the piece of paper, taunting her, reminding her of the call she still hadn't made. She felt even less certain about making it now. It was one of those nagging, gnawing doubts that emerged from nowhere and ate away at you. Like guilt.

She wondered how much her mother knew about the shadier parts of Rebecca's life, and whether that might have been what was causing this angst. That was it, she thought. It wasn't guilt; it was shame. She had been a disappointment. Like a child who'd stolen a penny sweet and was too afraid to face the consequences, Jo couldn't bring herself to own up. She couldn't make the call. She knew she'd have to at some point, but, well, she was wondering whether one of the other two numbers might be an easier option to start with.

It was ringing again. Another withheld number. Jo's grip tightened on the handset. She was ready this time.

'Hello?'

'Hey! Is that Rebecca?'

It was a woman this time, but the background clatter was the same.

'Sorry, no.'

Jo pressed the red button. Then, slowly, she dialled the number in front of her.

Chapter Thirty-Five

Jo picked up her pint and then put it back down. She had to slow down. A month ago, she would have been able to sit here with an orange juice and not feel too jittery, but the events of the last few weeks had eroded her self-control.

The doubts were really starting to set in: doubts about whether she should have just stayed incognito, about whether she should have made the call after all. Perhaps this wasn't the best way of piecing together her past. Perhaps she could just get up now, change her phone number and hide until the memories returned of their own accord. She forced herself to stay put and drank another slug of lager.

The bar was filling up with after-work drinkers, most of them young men in suits. The women were fewer in number, but easy to spot. Without exception, each was dressed in a tight-fitting blouse and starched trousers or skirt, with pointy shoes to match. Gulping her beer, Jo shrank back in the chair and tried to hide her long, jeans-clad legs under the table.

Ten minutes later, the pint glass was empty and Jo was about to walk out. Then a mousy blonde emerged from the sea of suits and tottered towards her, white wine sloshing over the sides of her glass.

'Becky! Good to see you!'

The woman conformed to the local dress code in her knee-length black skirt and pink shirt. From a distance, the outfit, the cropped hair and the heavily mascara'd eyes didn't ring any bells. But as the girl got closer and clutched Jo's shoulders, grinning madly and not letting go, she recognised the face; it was just that Jo knew it bare of makeup and framed with longer, messier hair. She had seen it on Facebook, but she thought she remembered it from her old life, too. It was unmistakably her old lab partner, Gill.

'How *are* you?' she asked, eyes wide open like a child's in a Christmas television ad. 'Oh my God, I can't believe what happened! Are you OK? I mean, obviously things are all a bit . . . weird, but are you doing all right? Oh my God, we've got *so* much to talk about!'

'Yeah,' Jo smiled, motioning for Gill to take the seat next to her.

'I don't know what to say!' Gill took a sip of her wine and then quickly contradicted herself. 'Where are you living? What are you doing at the moment? Oh my God, do you remember anything yet? Do you remember *me*?'

Jo couldn't help laughing. Yes, she remembered Gill now – bits of her, anyway. She remembered her face and her mannerisms – like the way she said 'Oh my God' at least once in every sentence – and she remembered her energy: boundless, excessive energy like a tornado whipping through the room.

'It's all coming back,' said Jo, sounding more confident than she felt. She didn't want Gill to make a drama out of her amnesia.

'Oh, good. What a relief. I thought you might not

remember anything at all. When I read that article . . . oh my God, Becky. It was such a shock. They said you didn't even know your own name.' She shook her head and took another mouthful of wine. 'That wasn't true, was it?'

Jo gave a little shrug so she didn't have to reply. She had expected this when she'd arranged to meet up. She knew that in order to get some answers, she'd have to give something in return – she just had to be careful about what she said. This was a girl she had known in her old life. Becky's life. The other side of the line. She was leading Jo's life now.

'It must've been so scary, Becky, being there when a bomb went off. I mean, you're lucky to be alive!'

Jo nodded. 'Yeah, I know. I saw it on the news.'

'Did you?' Gill leaned forward in her chair. 'Like, you saw yourself on the TV?'

'No, just the . . . the aftermath.'

'You saw yourself on TV!'

'No, I didn't actually—'

'Oh my God, I don't know anyone who's been on TV! You're like . . . a celebrity!'

Jo thought about getting another beer as Gill continued to express her amazement. It was getting harder to hear one another above the pumping music and the drunk men in suits.

'It's all kinda blown over now, anyway.'

Gill shook her head and exhaled through puffed-out cheeks. 'Oh my God, Becky. That's so crazy. I bet your mum went mental when she found out?'

'She doesn't, um . . .'

'Oh my God, Becky.' Gill blinked at her, mouth hanging open. 'You have spoken to her, haven't you? You have told her you're OK?'

Jo let the hesitation speak for itself.

'Oh my God! Why not? I mean, I know you never got on that well, and since the split you—'

'The what?'

Even as she said the words, Jo was beginning to answer her own question. *The split.* Her parents had split up. She fought to make sense of the concept, to build up her own memories around it. Faintly, she thought she remembered. Not the intricacies of who did what to whom or why, but she was aware of how it had made her feel. She remembered the shock and the denial and the rage and the guilt and the belief that somehow, perhaps, it was her fault. And then she remembered the sickening, uncontrollable fear as everything spiralled out of control.

'You do remember the divorce, don't you?'

'Well . . .'

'I mean, it's not the sort of thing you'd—'

'Look, this is where I need your help.'

Gill frowned. 'My help?'

Jo nodded slowly, her head still spinning from the new revelation. She really, really needed another drink.

'Ah, no, hang on.' Gill shook her head emphatically. 'No, you're not gonna get *me* to break the news to your mum. No way. I mean, we're friends and everything, but seriously, Becks, I can't—'

'No,' Jo cut in. 'No, that's not what I mean. I . . . I need your help tonight. I need . . .' This was the bombshell. 'I need you to tell me what you know about my family. Me. My life. The papers were right. I can't remember much.'

Gill's wine glass was midway between the table and her lips, and it stopped right there. 'But I thought . . .' Gill looked at her. 'Shit, OK. What *do* you know?'

Jo was still thinking about the divorce. It was so obvious, now Gill had said it. It was a part of her background, a fact, just like the fact that she had dark hair or she liked drinking beer. How could her brain have obscured such an important piece of information?

'Becky?'

Jo snapped to. She gathered her thoughts and then, gradually, she told Gill everything she could remember. She recounted the flashbacks from her university years, the fragmented memories of the Buffalo Club, the faint, misshapen recollections of her relationship with Luke and the break-up and the images of someone else – that other guy.

'Oh my God,' said Gill, predictably. 'So not much, then?'

'No,' Jo replied faintly. She was suddenly feeling incredibly lukewarm about the whole idea of learning more about her past. Gill was about to fill in all the gaps. She was no longer sure she wanted to hear them, but it was too late to turn back now.

'So, first year uni. We were the only two girls on our course, so we kinda hit it off from the start.' Gill smiled nostalgically. 'We had such fun, we did – messing around in the lab, burning holes in things, cable-tying Jimmy Waddle to his stool . . . d'you remember him?' Jo shook her head, but Gill didn't seem to notice. 'We nearly got him drinking sulphuric acid at one point.'

Jo smiled obligingly. She had no recollection of a Jimmy Waddle or of any of the other people Gill proceeded to talk about.

'. . . and we lived near each other in Campbell House – d'you remember that?' Gill's questions had become rhetorical. 'We went out *all the time*. Remember the Horse

302

Shed? We were in there every Thursday night with Gav and Ali and that, and Barney's every Tuesday . . .'

The good thing about Gill, Jo was beginning to realise, was that she required very little in the way of stimulus to keep going. A tiny nod or a laugh was enough. Some of the things she recounted caused a faint stirring in Jo's subconscious. She thought she remembered a Gav and a girl called Ali, and she remembered a time when deciding what to wear on a Thursday night had been the most taxing part of her week. She remembered the ease with which she coasted through life, the carefree triviality of it all.

'That's how you got into football,' Gill went on, having talked at length about some guy who worked behind the bar in some club where one of their friends used to DJ. 'You were mad about it – are you still? Captain of the UCL ladies, you were. You used to skip lectures to go to team practice – and that was saying something, as you were a right swot.'

'Was I?'

'Oh my God, yeah! You got top marks in everything! That's why it was so weird when you went . . . um . . .' She trailed off. 'D'you want another drink?'

There was a brief pause in the narrative while Gill marched up to the bar for refills. Jo checked her phone, wishing her friend would just tell her straight what she'd done. She knew she'd gone 'off the rails'; the news reports had all told her that. She wanted the details.

Not sure how well yr
temp. replacement @
Fairmont is coping –

303

apparently she still
smells of eggs frm
Hallown outing . . .M x

'What's with the massive grin?' Gill returned to her seat, sliding the drinks onto the table.

Jo tucked her phone away and waved her hand, sipping the head off her fresh pint. It calmed her a little. 'Oh, nothing. Thanks.'

'Hey, I realised I missed something. D'you remember how you met Luke?'

'No.'

She had told Gill about the break-up scene that kept replaying in her head and the vague recollections of walking through campus, talking, arguing. But she had no idea how they had met.

'Oh my God, it was so funny. We were second years, and you bought him at an auction.'

'I bought him?'

'Yeah. It was one of those charity things at the union where students offer their services and skills and stuff, and people have to bid for them. We were all plastered, and you liked the look of the guy who was offering himself as a naked waiter for the night. So you bought him.'

'Really? I wish I remembered.'

'It all went from there, I guess. You two became like the Posh and Becks of the college – the Brangelina. Everyone knew you. You were together until, well . . .'

Jo cringed, feeling slightly dizzy. She had climbed so high, and then fallen all the way down again.

'You and I were both gonna go into the city when we

304

graduated. D'you remember? All the science jobs were too dull.'

Jo dipped her head evasively. She remembered the ambition, if not the detail.

'But most of the banks had a recruitment freeze around internship time so we kinda changed tack and – well, I did. I went into management consultancy. Hence,' she looked down at her well-fitting suit. 'Ta-da. But you . . . well, you were kinda drifting at that time.'

'Gill.' Jo looked at her, unable to contain the unease any longer. 'Just tell me straight. Don't skirt around. What happened?'

Gill took a large gulp of wine and set the glass down on the table, more carefully than before. 'OK. Well, I can only tell you what I know, so it won't necessarily . . . make sense.'

Jo nodded. She was as prepared as she ever would be.

'Well, we were in our final year and we were both on track to get firsts – you easily, me borderline. Then in October, when we'd just started our third year, that was when your parents announced they were separating.'

'Did you know my parents? What they were like?'

This was the haziest part of her memory: her childhood. A few recollections had floated back to her, but only recollections of emotions – happy emotions. She had a sort of gut feeling that she'd been a happy child with supportive parents, but there were no specific memories to go on.

'I only know what you said about them – I never met them. They seemed nice. The type of parents to take you to football practice after school, help with your homework, that sort of thing. Typical middle-class parents, I guess.'

Jo nodded.

'Anyway, you seemed OK about the separation to begin with. Your dad was gonna move to Spain, your mum was gonna stay on in Finchley Road. You were quite close to your mum, I think. You called her practically every night when you first started uni.'

Jo closed her eyes for a second, feeling the anxiety return. *Finchley Road.* That was where she'd grown up. She couldn't remember the area or how to get there, but she could picture the street: a wide, tree-lined avenue with large houses on one side and flats on the other. There was a small children's playground in a clearing behind the railway where her mother had taken her as a child. Gill was right: she *had* been close to her mum.

'Then . . .' Gill lifted her wine glass and twisted the stem round in her hands, 'you found out that your mum had been having an affair.'

Jo stared into her pint glass. An affair. Jesus. Even with only a vague memory of her parents, it seemed implausible. Wrong. She didn't remember the revelation from the first time, but she could imagine how it would have made her feel.

'A guy at her work, I think. You went ape-shit. I mean, properly mad – at your mum, but also at the world in general.' Gill put back her glass. 'You started skipping lectures and going out drinking on your own. Half the time we didn't know where you were. We were living together at the time, but I hardly saw you. I didn't know what you were up to or where you were sleeping.'

'Shit.' This was Jo's attempt at a belated apology for being such an irresponsible, thoughtless friend. She couldn't believe Gill was referring to *her*.

306

'When you were around, you weren't much like the Becky we knew; you'd just lock yourself away and listen to your angry music at top volume, drinking and doing God knows what to yourself.'

Jo closed her eyes. The chorus of the Kaiser Chiefs song she'd heard on the radio started playing on loop in her head, and suddenly she remembered how it felt.

'We were all quite worried about you,' Gill went on. 'Especially Luke. He didn't know what to do. You'd stopped playing football. Well, they'd kicked you off the squad, I think. And you never hung out with us. Luke tried to help you, we all did, but you just pushed everyone away. It was as though . . .' Gill shrugged, 'as though you *wanted* to ruin things for yourself.'

Jo shook her head. This was like being forced to sit through a bad film when someone had already spoiled the ending.

'So what happened?'

'Well, you were never gonna pass your finals at the rate you were going, and Professor Latham – remember him? He basically gave you an ultimatum: pull your socks up, or repeat the year.'

'What did I do?'

'You walked out.'

Jo sighed, disappointed all over again with herself.

'We barely saw you after that. You just disappeared. I heard on the grapevine that you were working at the Buffalo Club, drinking too much, doing drugs . . . but that was all I knew. You weren't returning my calls and I didn't know where you were living. You finished with Luke, obviously.'

Jo flinched.

'Anyway, next thing I know, you're turning up in the papers as the stripper who rises from the dead!'

Jo smiled reluctantly.

By mutual consent, the conversation turned to lighter matters such as which of the suited clones at the bar were worth fancying and where city boys went when they turned thirty-five. (They retired, Jo explained, recounting her experiences with two-timing Stuart.)

'We should definitely meet up again!'

'Definitely.' Jo nodded into her shoulder as they hugged outside St Paul's. 'And don't forget what I said about keeping quiet.'

'What? Oh, yeah, of course!' Gill stuck her arm out for a passing cab.

Jo hoped she'd stay true to her word. If the conversation tonight had been anything to go by, she thought that she probably would. They'd been close friends. Although, the tabloids would clearly try anything to get a couple of juicy titbits about the girl who had come back to life.

'Which reminds me,' sang Gill, waving her hand as a cab roared past. 'Bastard. I guess you've got other people to meet up with, haven't you?'

Jo watched as a taxi pulled up, thinking anxiously about the call she still hadn't made.

Gill raised an eyebrow. 'Like, your *mum*?'

'Yeah. Yeah. I know.' Jo forced a smile and they went their separate ways, just as they had done, in another sense, a few years before: Gill speeding off through the city, Jo sloping off under ground.

She thought about her friend's parting remark. One phone call. That was all it would take. She knew her mother was desperate to hear from her. She knew they'd been close. But it wasn't that easy. In many ways, if Gill's explanations were to be believed, her mother had been responsible for much of what happened. If she hadn't had an affair then there might have been no call for divorce. If the divorce hadn't gone ahead then Jo might not have been so intent on rendering every part of her life beyond salvation.

Jo passed through the underground barrier, suddenly filled with shame and remorse. Who was she kidding? She couldn't hold her mother responsible for Rebecca's downfall. It was true that the split had probably detonated something inside her; she wouldn't have charged off the rails without reason, and her mother had provided her with a reason. But Jo knew, deep down, that she had to take some of the blame. She just wasn't sure about going ahead with the confrontation. It seemed too daunting.

Soon, thought Jo. She would make the call, but first she had to get used to who she was. Who she had been. Who she *wasn't*. She wasn't a successful management consultant like Gill – whatever that meant, anyway. She wasn't a graduate, an upwardly-mobile Londoner with lots of money and happy memories. She wasn't Becky. Or Roxie. She didn't know who she was.

Chapter Thirty-Six

Matt's hand was working its way up the inside of her thigh as Jo woke up. She rolled over to face him and smiled.

'Shouldn't you be getting ready for work?'

'Yeah, I suppose I should.' Matt watched her reaction as his hand slid up to its destination. Jo lay there, naked and helpless while he teased and then pulled her gently on top of him.

Perhaps because their first encounter had been pre-breakfast, sex had become something of a prerequisite for starting the day. Jo's concerns about moving in with Matt so early in their relationship had proved unfounded. The fact that they now saw each other morning, evening and weekend was turning out to be a positive thing. They shared showers, watched films, teased Kieran together. Matt cooked them all pizza, Kieran kept them amused and Jo fought in vain against the expanding empire of clutter.

'Seriously,' Jo gasped as they lay there minutes later, staring exhaustedly at the ceiling, 'you'll be late.'

Matt looked at the time and swore quietly, jumping off the bed and into the shower. Then, dry and dressed, he bent over her to kiss her goodbye.

Jo heard the door slam and propped herself up in the bed, allowing herself a moment's contemplation. She still had issues: memory blanks, questions, concerns over what she'd done in the past . . . But she had a lot to be happy about too. Becky might not have made much of her life, but Jo was certainly giving it her best shot.

'Morning!'

Jo leaped backwards, securing the towel around her. Kieran was standing in the middle of the kitchen wearing what looked like an orange sheet.

'What . . . ?' Jo sniffed a couple of times. The air smelled strongly of coconut. 'What are you doing?'

She knew, even as the words left her lips, that she probably shouldn't have asked.

'It's Diwali.'

'It's what?'

'Diwali. Hindu Festival of Lights. Haven't you heard of it? Oh, maybe you've forgotten.'

Jo smiled. 'I don't think I ever knew.'

Kieran had a very sweet but slightly annoying way of dealing with the issue of her memory loss. The fact that her general knowledge and brain processing power had been unaffected by the condition just didn't seem to get through to him, no matter how many times Jo explained. Very often their conversations would degenerate into painful question-and-answer sessions with Kieran verifying Jo's knowledge of every word or statement issued.

'We're putting on a celebration in town,' he said, setting light to a piece of string that was dangling over the edge of one of the many small, shallow cups all over the kitchen. 'I'm testing out my lamps. Oh, no, don't make toast!'

'Why not?'

'You can have these special Indian sweets. I made them. Prototypes for the festival.'

'Mmm,' grunted Jo, feigning enjoyment. They looked and tasted a bit like flecked carpet. 'Carrot. Yum. So, when's the festival?'

'Well, it starts next week but we've got to get all the preparations done by tomorrow.'

'Right.' Jo nodded. It still amazed her that Kieran was in any position of authority in Oxford Council. These sweets could cause mass indignation among the Hindu population if he got them wrong – which she thought he probably had – and possibly indigestion too.

'And we've had Harvest Festival and Hallowe'en, and there's Remembrance Sunday – loads of things happening around this time of year.'

Hallowe'en. Jo thought about Kyle and the Dunston's kids, and wondered who had organised their Hallowe'en outing in her absence. She felt guilty for abandoning them. A part of her wondered whether she should forfeit her last few days' compassionate leave and go back to work. After all, things had improved a lot since she last saw Sue. Her notebook had filled up with facts and memories after her meeting with Gill, and the brief foray into her old life had helped to consolidate her thoughts. But she still had more thinking to do. The gaps were closing, but the confusion remained over who exactly she was, and who she wanted to be. Maybe she did need the full fortnight after all.

'Have you always worked for the council?'

'Since uni, yeah. I did an Astronomy degree and then realised there weren't many jobs that required detailed knowledge of the cosmos.' He looked at her hesitantly. 'You know . . . you know what I'm talking about?'

Jo smiled patiently. 'I've told you, Kieran, having amnesia doesn't make me stupid. I still have a reasonable grasp of the English language.'

'Must be weird, though,' said Kieran, tucking into his Indian delicacies. 'Like, remembering some things but not others.'

Jo nodded. Kieran was being surprisingly perceptive. 'It's frustrating. Everyone else has this bank of personal memories to look back on and I have . . . well, I have random flashbacks. Makes you realise how much you take for granted.'

'Hmm,' Kieran nodded thoughtfully. 'I read a book about that once. Well, actually it was about a Martian who landed on earth and met a woman who had no memory, but then she turned out to be a witch.'

'Right.' Jo thought about making some toast. She felt slightly sick.

'Sounds like the newspaper article did the trick, though! I hear you met up with an old friend the other day?'

Jo's hand hovered above the toaster, her grip loosening on the slices of bread.

'Did the trick?' She turned slowly, watching Kieran's face. 'What d'you mean?'

She wanted to hear him reply with one of his ridiculous, nonsensical remarks that explained why he'd chosen those particular words. But Kieran's eyes were darting about like a trapped rabbit's.

'Er, I didn't mean . . . Obviously no one knows why, er, someone . . . wrote in.'

'No, hang on, Kieran. You said "did the trick". How did you know it wasn't just someone trying to make some cash?'

Jo stared at him, desperately willing him to come up with an innocent excuse. She was as nervous as he was, hoping he could dig himself out of this hole. If he couldn't, then that would imply . . . No. It just didn't bear thinking about.

'Well, I just . . . I assume someone wrote in to get you to . . . find out more about what had happened. So I guess his plan worked. Or her plan, obviously,' he stuttered.

Jo stared at him, feeling her mouth go dry. Kieran was talking as though it was common knowledge that someone had contacted the press with her story *for her own good*. The only explanation she could come up with was one that made her want to scream.

'Kieran, just tell me.' She continued to study his face, which was becoming increasingly blotchy. 'Was it Matt?'

He shrugged nervously. 'I – I don't know. He didn't – I didn't—'

Shakily, Jo stood up. One thought occupied her mind. Everything else was squeezed out by the sheer size of the revelation. Kieran was still jabbering, but she couldn't hear him properly. She could barely force her limbs to take her out of the room.

It was Matt. That was all she could see. *Matt had sold her story to the press.*

Chapter Thirty-Seven

'Oh my God! Hello again! How are you? Knackered, I bet. Where did you travel in from? Oh, is that all you've got? You do travel light. Come in, come in.'

Jo wasn't sure which question to tackle first as she was ushered through the oak-panelled hallway.

'It's so good to see you again! Just dump your stuff in the hall for now. I'll show you to your room in a bit. Excuse the suit – just got home. Oh, this is such perfect timing! Did I tell you my flatmate's in India for two months? So you can have her room.'

Jo reiterated her profound gratitude and looked around. They were standing in a spacious living room with cream carpets and high, sculpted ceilings. The flat was bathed in a warm, yellow glow that came as a welcome reprieve after the icy November rain.

'Sit down,' ordered Gill, sweeping her hand over the various white leather options. 'Let's open some wine. I know you're a beer girl but the shop round the corner doesn't sell cans – can you believe it? That's Notting Hill for you.' She rolled her eyes and darted out of the room.

Yes, Jo could believe it. This was indeed chichi Notting

Hill, and from what she'd seen so far, she could imagine the local shop selling nothing but champagne and caviar. Even though she had walked from the tube in near-darkness, the streetlamps – authentic-looking, mock-gas streetlamps – had illuminated a part of the world that Jo felt sure she had never come close to inhabiting. The pavements were lined with valeted sports cars and four-wheel drives, and every couple of blocks there was a small, perfectly tended private park.

Gill whooshed over to the sofa and planted herself next to Jo, carrying two giant wine glasses and a bottle of Something-or-other Premier Cru. Jo eyed the glasses apprehensively. She could do this, she thought. She could drink slowly. She wasn't addicted any more.

'So! Things not going so well?'

Jo nodded grimly. That was all she'd told her so far. It was a testament to Gill's loyalty – a loyalty that had survived, despite the trouble Jo had caused years before – that she had opened up her flat so readily and at such short notice with no more information than that.

'Well, this ought to help.' Gill pushed the arms of the corkscrew down and yanked out the cork with great panache. 'Sorry about the state of the place.' She poured nearly half the bottle into each huge wine glass. 'I decided to cut back and tell the cleaner not to come while Mimi's away but it turns out I'm not so tidy after all!'

Jo looked around, confused. The place was spotless. 'What d'you mean?'

'Well, look,' Gill flung her hand over a neat pile of magazines on the coffee table and motioned towards the row of shoes by the door.

Jo frowned. 'Gill, this is not a mess. I've been living with two guys for the last couple of weeks. Now *they* know how to make a mess.'

'*Two* guys? How . . . ? Oh my God, you've got so much to tell me!' Gill motioned for Jo to take one of the drinks. 'Cheers.'

Jo wasn't sure what they were celebrating, but chinked glasses anyway and felt the wine slide straight from her mouth to her belly. To homelessness, she thought sardonically. And my second abandoned career. And my disastrous love life.

'It'll be fun,' said Gill, grinning as she tucked her legs up underneath her on the sofa. 'Living together again after all these years.'

Jo smiled. It hadn't actually occurred to her, in all her gloom and self-pity following Matt's betrayal, that Gill's offer could be anything more than a rescue operation. It was a favour. A roof over her head. But maybe Gill was right. It was certainly more than a roof, for a start. Nobody could argue with two months' free accommodation in this plush Georgian mansion in Notting Hill. And maybe, once she'd got over the fact that her life in Radley had fallen apart, once she'd put Matt and the guesthouse and Dunston's behind her, then she could think about having fun.

'I really appreciate this,' she said. 'It's a gorgeous place.'

'Ah, don't worry about it! Mimi's paying the other half of the rent, so nobody's losing out.'

'So it's rented?'

Gill looked at her as though she'd just asked if it were made of marshmallows. 'Of course it's rented! You think I could afford the mortgage on a place like this, at twenty-five?'

'Well, I did wonder . . .'

'I might be doing well at TWC, but not *that* well.'

Jo wanted to ask all sorts of questions, like: what did Gill actually *do* at TWC? Who did she hang out with now? What had happened to all the old uni crowd? Who was this Mimi character? She felt rather lost, all of a sudden – as though she'd turned up at the wrong party.

'How much d'you remember of London?'

Jo shrugged. 'Bits and pieces from uni days. I walked round the campus the other day and remembered quite a lot. But the rest . . . Well, I went to Elephant and Castle and didn't recognise anything.'

Gill hooted with laughter. 'Not surprised! What on earth were you doing there?'

Jo thought about lying, but forced herself not to. 'I was meeting a girl from the Buffalo Club. She lives around there.'

'I bet she does.' Gill knocked back a large slug of wine. 'Lovely part of the world. So where have you been staying, since the blast?'

'Long story,' she said, thinking about the various beds and floors she had slept on in the last few months. Like a dream, it had made perfect sense at the time, but now it all seemed quite surreal.

On the way into London, Jo had made a decision. She would stop lying. This time round, there would be no fabrications. The web of lies she had spun around Jo Simmons had got her all tangled up – so tangled, in fact, that she couldn't even see her way through them herself. She had trusted all the wrong people, lost her sense of direction, set off in search of something that didn't exist. She had believed her own lies – lies that were meant for Matt, for Dunston's, for Mrs Phillips . . . *Mrs Phillips.*

The woman who had taken her in, who had befriended her . . . She had rescued Jo. And what had she got in return? An angry letter of blame for something she hadn't done. Jo cringed and vowed to make it up to the woman.

And so she explained. She told Gill about the bus on its way to the depot, the job at Trev's Teashop, the defunct, cat-ridden B&B, the job at Dunston's, Sue, Kyle, the newspaper leak and, of course, Matt.

'Oh my God,' said Gill, for about the hundredth time, when she had finished. Gill shook her head slowly. 'That's amazing. And I can't believe that guy – what a wanker!' She made a gesture with one hand. 'I mean, of all the things he could've done.'

Jo wasn't sure how she felt as Gill continued to slate Matt's exploits. Clearly, she was playing the role of Good Friend – the one who turned all the shades of grey into black or white and then outlined why white was right and black was wrong. The way Gill was talking, it was as though she should have felt liberated, vindicated and proud. She had walked away from the life of Jo Simmons and all the complications that went with it. She had returned to the world of Rebecca Ross where, if she took Gill's lead, she could make a success of herself. She needn't have worried about coming back to London; the nagging fear, whatever it was, had amounted to nothing – even after her face had been splashed across the national papers. But for some reason, she didn't feel liberated or vindicated or proud. She just felt sad.

'. . . but instead of *involving* you, instead of confronting the issue and *talking* about it, he just muscled in there and did what *he* thought was right.' Gill tipped back the remains of her wine. 'Typical bloke. And I mean . . . a tabloid? I thought you said he worked in PR – couldn't he have at least gone for a broadsheet?'

Gill ranted on. Jo tuned out, trying to make sense of her emotions. The facts – and Gill – quite clearly indicated that she was in the right here. There was no doubt that Matt had turned against her. All that sweetness, that sensitivity, that I-know-what-it's-like bollocks – she'd bought it, hook, line and sinker. He had duped her into trusting him. *Loving* him, even.

Jo closed her eyes, remembering the feeling of Matt's arms around her that first morning when she'd needed him most. He had dropped in that stuff about him being adopted with impeccable timing and she'd opened up – metaphorically *and* physically, she thought, shuddering – all because of something that was his fault in the first place.

She was glad she had walked away. Walking away from Matt and the whole charade that was Jo Simmons' life was the right move. But at the same time . . . She couldn't pinpoint the feeling, but something didn't feel quite right. There was a doubt hanging over her that she wasn't able to identify. Perhaps it would make more sense after another glass of wine.

'There's more in the fridge – I'll get it,' said Gill.

Jo checked her phone while Gill rummaged about in the kitchen. There were four more missed calls and two further text messages. That made it seventeen missed calls, four voicemails and five text messages today. Most of the calls had been made from a withheld number, implying that Kieran had told Matt about his blunder as soon as Jo had left the flat and he was ringing from Dunston's. Reluctantly, she opened the messages.

Jo, please call me.
I know ur angry but
I can xplain. Really.
I did it 4 u. Mx

Jo pressed Delete. It was virtually the same as all the others. She clicked on the latest one.

Jo, I love you. Please call.

She stared at the pixellated letters, rereading the line, her thumb hovering over the Delete button. Matt had never told her that before. She wasn't sure how she felt. The anger was still there, but also something else – something a bit like regret.

'Copious messages from the remorseful ex-boyfriend?' Gill surmised, returning with a fresh bottle. 'You need a new phone.'

Jo looked up, barely registering. 'He says he loves me.'

Gill rolled her eyes and wrenched the cork from the bottle. 'Don't they all? When they need to. Never when things are hunky-dory. It's like the ace of spades – they store it up and then only pull it out when they know they *really* need to win – when nothing else will do.'

Jo switched her phone off and pushed it back in her pocket. Gill was right, of course. Matt had never claimed to love her when things had been going well – not that they'd been together that long. In fact, how *could* he claim to love her after such a short relationship? He barely knew her. It was a lie that he loved her – it had to be.

'I bet he's good-looking,' Gill smiled questioningly.

Jo broke free of her thoughts. A fresh glass of wine was being waved in front of her. 'Thanks. Yeah. He is.'

'Ha – you always fell for that!' Gill shook her head admonishingly. 'You were a sucker for the lovely eyes or muscly arms or nice hands.'

Jo forced a wry laugh. 'Matt has all the above.'

'Oh, really?' Gill sounded intrigued. 'Where did you find him?'

'In a park, playing football.'

Gill shook her head. 'Unbe-fucking-lievable. You found someone who had all that *and* who played football. No wonder you were smitten. Even Luke only *watched* football.'

Jo looked at her, wondering whether to quiz her on Luke.

'Uh, sorry.' Gill stuck her face into her wine, embarrassed. 'Anyway!' She emerged from the glass. 'Was he an Oxford boy then, this Matt?'

'He went to a school near Abingdon.'

'I meant uni – was he at Oxford?'

Jo shook her head. 'He didn't go to uni.'

'Oh.' Gill seemed perplexed. 'Right.'

Inexplicably, her response annoyed Jo. It was as though his lack of degree put him in a different category in Gill's mind. He *had* been interesting, but now he was simply odd or stupid. Matt was neither of those things. Jo sipped her wine, confused by her unexpected switch of allegiance.

'So what was it like, working with . . . ?' Gill made an indecipherable gesture with her hand.

'With vulnerable kids?' Jo finished the sentence emphatically, enjoying the look on Gill's face. She thought back to the story Sue had told her about the newspaper hate campaign and wondered how the residents of W11 would react to a place like Fairmont House on their doorstep. 'Quite fun, at times.'

Gill pulled a face. 'Really?'

Jo shrugged. Actually, it hadn't been fun, for a lot of the time. It had been bloody hard work. But she wanted to prove a point, to explain to Gill that there was life outside London, that vulnerable kids weren't all gun-toting, hoodie-wearing criminals, that there were careers that involved more than sitting on a swivel chair staring at a computer screen.

'I'd faked my whole CV, though, obviously, so I was pretty useless with the kids.'

Gill nodded in awe. 'Sounds scary. I think you're brave, even trying it.'

Jo shook her head. It wasn't true. She hadn't been brave at Dunston's. Brave would imply that she'd actively sought challenges, not just walked into them by accident. And as things had turned out, when she'd stumbled into the first one, she had tried to stumble straight back out again. The only reason she'd stayed was because they wouldn't let her leave. She wasn't there through bravery; only through a need to survive.

'Bet you're glad you've left it all behind, eh?'

Jo didn't reply. In many ways, she was glad that she'd left the disruptive Kyle and his associates behind. She wouldn't miss Charlene's surly remarks or Nadia's addiction-related sniffing, per se. But when she thought about some of the kids' responses to her over-zealous suggestions . . . when she remembered the looks on their faces when she said something pompous or stupid . . . it was hard to describe. She felt sort of *left out*, now she wasn't there.

It didn't entirely make sense, even to her. It was something to do with the idea that life at Fairmont House went on without her. She was no longer a part of it. Someone else would be supervising the painting of the living-room wall. Some other poor sod had taken the kids on their Hallowe'en adventure. Someone else would be coaching them football for the tournament that she'd pushed for them to enter, she realised with a pang of guilt. She had made herself surplus to requirements.

'How are you managing for money?' Gill asked delicately.

Jo smiled drily. 'I looked in my old bank account – it's practically empty. Don't think Roxie was too good at saving.' She pulled a face. 'I'll find myself a job.'

'Any idea where?'

Jo puffed out her cheeks and shrugged. In keeping with her resolution to lead an honest life, she had decided to find work in a field that she was qualified to do – which meant, basically, something that required no qualifications. 'I guess I'll do some shop work, or waitressing. I seemed to do OK in the teashop.'

Gill screwed up her face. '*Waitressing?* For God's sake, Becky, you were on track to get a first from one of the top universities in the country!'

Jo faltered. Her friend didn't seem to have grasped the complexity of the situation. '*On track* to get,' she pointed out. 'I didn't actually *get*. Look,' she said, softening, 'don't you worry about me. I'll be fine.'

'Oh my God! I know!' Gill planted her wine glass on the table and turned to Jo with a manic grin. 'I can get you a job!'

Jo eyed her friend suspiciously as she continued to flap her hands.

'Seriously, Becky. I can get you a job that earns *proper* money – I mean, maybe not a TWC salary, but like a decent graduate starting salary. Maybe twenty-five K or something. More than waitressing, anyway!'

'I'm not going back to stripping.'

'NO!' Gill shook her head wildly, not getting the joke. 'There's an agency that places graduates in temporary roles – I used them in summer before I started at TWC.'

'Yeah, but I'm not actually a—'

'Flying High, it's called. Gav used them too and I think that's how he ended up getting his proper job through them – he's at Anderton's you know. They have amazing firms on their books!'

'But I don't—'

'Oh my God, you'll fit so well! They'll love you. We can make something up about your degree – say you had an accident or something. An accident – yeah. Hey, that's almost true! I can recommend you, or Gav can, and they'll place you in no time! This'll be brilliant. Perfect . . .'

Jo wasn't so sure. It was all very well, Gill waving her well-manicured hands about in her plush Notting Hill apartment, talking about jobs at TWC and Anderton's and Flying High, but she was living in a parallel universe. A place where you only had to waft your degree certificate in the air and companies came begging to pay you twenty-five grand. A place where waitresses and vulnerable kids were just topics of conversation that cropped up occasionally over dinner. Gill was living, she realised, in the universe Becky Ross would have inhabited, had things turned out differently.

'What sort of work would I be doing?' she asked, when Gill had run out of positive adjectives.

'Oh!' Gill waved a hand vaguely. 'I don't know ... operational stuff, consultancy, corporate strategy ...'

'I don't have the foggiest idea what any of those things are.'

'Oh, nobody has! Don't worry about that.'

'No, really, I—'

Gill swept her protests away. 'Becky, leave this with me. I'll get their details. Seriously, this is perfect for you. I can see it now. You're gonna be back on track in no time. I swear. Let me give them a call?'

Jo looked at the floor, sensing Gill's excited gaze on her face. *Back on track*. That was what she was after, wasn't it? She needed to forget about Matt and Dunston's and Radley, to jump back to the path she'd been on before, as Rebecca Ross. Jo shrugged uncertainly, unable to push out the feeling that she might be leaving something behind.

Gill grabbed her hand, willing Jo to look into her eyes.

Eventually, she fought off the doubt. 'OK,' she said. 'I'll give it a go.'

Chapter Thirty-Eight

'Another round!' cried the birthday girl, her eyes glistening with drunken excitement.

Gill was waggling her tongue about like a dog that had been duped into eating hot food. 'Ali, please . . .'

'Hey,' the girl went on. 'Let's make it flaming *tequila* this time! Does that work? You should know; you're the chemists.'

Without waiting for a response, Ali leaned over and started waving madly at the barman. Several heads turned as the girl's breasts lapped against the edge of her low-cut dress.

'Oh, *boring*,' she muttered as the barman persuaded her that tequila would not catch fire. 'Make it slammers then. Ten, please.'

Jo obediently licked her thumb and held it out to be doused in salt. She wasn't complaining about the compulsory drinking. Anything that eased the awkwardness of tonight was a blessing, as far as she was concerned – and if someone else was paying for the over-priced spirits then so much the better.

'Everyone ready?' Ali looked along the row of shot glasses. 'Go!'

Jo downed the shot, wondering whether she was the only one relishing the warm, fuzzy numbness spreading through her body. She doubted that anyone here – even the gangly-looking physicists from Ali's course, who were huddled in the corner – felt as nervous as she did about tonight.

Gill had done her best to help. She spent much of the evening pointing out and reintroducing people that Jo ought to have remembered and steering conversations away from the subject of her memory loss. In fact, Gill's deflections had been so well administered that, at times, Jo had wondered what on earth they were talking about.

At one point, a guy had tried to catch her out by asking whether she'd been to Barbarella's before. Jo had shrugged and mumbled something about coming here 'ages ago', upon which the young man had cried, triumphantly, that it had only opened a week before. Gill had quickly jumped in to clarify that Jo had been here *before it was Barbarella's*, which seemed like a perfect explanation until the guy told them that the place had been a slaughterhouse before.

'Ugh.' Gill grunted, pulling the lemon slice out of her mouth and spitting the pips into her hand. 'Gross.'

'Let'sdoanother,' slurred Ali, not focusing on anyone in particular.

The guy next to her, whom Jo vaguely remembered as Gav – now another successful, high-flying city type – held an arm around her waist for support. 'Maybe later, eh?' He smiled at the others and pocketed the twenty-pound note she was trying to wave at the barman.

'Some things never change,' said Gill, rolling her eyes and then looking awkwardly at Jo. 'Er, well, not in Ali's case, anyway. How are you doing? You OK? Is it weird?'

Jo smiled forgivingly. She knew that Gill was trying to make things easier for her. 'Not as weird as I'd thought, actually. I remember the faces. It's all sort of there, at the back of my mind, but just none of the details.'

'D'you remember Ali's drinking?'

Jo nodded as if to say *all too well*. In truth, she didn't remember the drinking. She recognised Ali's face, and she had a vague sense that they'd been acquainted in a social capacity, but beyond that, she didn't know. It was the same for most people here. The faces were familiar – partly through Facebook, Jo suspected – but she couldn't place them in her life. They could easily have been her old postman or a waiter or someone who'd served her in Tesco.

It was disappointing and frustrating. She had hoped that by coming here tonight, by being in London, immersing herself in Rebecca's old life, the memories would all come gushing back. Instead, they were trickling, bit by bit. She was being impatient, of course. But that was just how she was.

'D'you remember him?' Gill nodded at a tall, handsome stranger at the other end of the bar. He had floppy dark hair and exotic, slanting eyes. A chunky gold watch hung ostentatiously from his tanned wrist.

'No,' she said reluctantly.

Gill smiled dreamily. 'Mmm, Charlie Cooper. Isn't he gorgeous?' Then she rolled her eyes. 'Oh! Of course you don't know him – he was a few years below us. We only got to know him in our final year, when you were . . .'

'Fucking about as a coke-head stripper?'

'Well,' Gill looked bashfully at her drink. Then, decisively, she took Jo's hand. 'Come on, I'll introduce you.'

Jo allowed herself to be pulled across the dance floor,

where, disconcertingly, there were already a few drunken revellers throwing their limbs about to the tune of Beyoncé's 'Crazy in Love'.

'Charlie!' Gill descended upon the young man. 'How are things? It's been ages! Meet my friend Becky.'

The young man flashed a smile and held out his hand. It all seemed a bit formal, thought Jo, remembering how she'd first met the football lads and picturing Kieran's awkward handshake. Everything was very different. But then, maybe Charlie Cooper wasn't like any of the football lads. In fact, maybe nobody in this room was like the football lads. Perhaps her days of hanging out with clowns like Kieran and Sanjit were over.

'Enchanted,' he uttered, bringing her fingers towards his lips and kissing them. *Kissing them*, for God's sake.

'I don't think I've seen you since uni days! How're you doing? You look well. You must've graduated this summer, is that right? Hey, Becky was at UCL too.'

Charlie frowned at Gill, then at Jo. 'Sorry, I don't think—'

'Oh, no, you wouldn't have overlapped,' Gill explained, failing to spot that the guy didn't seem to recognise either of them. 'She sort of left in our final year . . .'

'Oh!' Charlie's face lit up. 'You're Rebecca Ross! Oh, wow, I read about you in the papers.'

Jo nodded wearily. The conversation was clearly going the same way as all the others so far.

'Gosh, incredible. Nice to meet you. How's the memory?'

'It's all coming back, isn't it?' trilled Gill, stepping between Charlie and Jo. 'Probably good to be back in London, eh?' She turned to Charlie. 'She had a brief stint in the countryside. Quite a different life, I imagine . . .'

Gill prattled on about country living and her aunt's cottage in Dorset and an adopted sheep, masterfully weaving in her thoughts on the state of arable farming today and finishing with a story about paddy fields in Japan.

'So did you really not know your own name?' Charlie asked Jo when Gill had finished.

Gill leaned towards him and put a hand on Charlie's arm – something that Jo suspected she might have been wanting to do for some time – and said something in his ear.

'I'm so sorry,' Charlie said gallantly. 'I didn't realise.'

Jo waved away his apology. It occurred to her that Gill might rather enjoy having her here tonight, in the same way that school children enjoyed having broken legs so that they could show all their classmates the crutches. Jo was Gill's crutch. She was something Gill could show off, talk about – or rather, *not* talk about.

Jo sensed Gill's reluctance to move her hand off Charlie's arm, and decided to go with her instincts.

'Ooh, look, there's Gav. I've just got to . . . see him.'

Darting off into the darkness, Jo felt suddenly lost without her minder. She hadn't actually spotted Gav and didn't know what she would have said to him if she had. The bar seemed like the safest place to loiter.

'Treble?' repeated the barman. 'As in, three?'

Jo nodded. It meant using up all her cash, and she knew it wasn't a good idea for all sorts of reasons, but it was the only way she could see herself getting through the rest of the night. Ali's round had helped, but it would take more than a couple of measures to get her drunk. Her liver had become too efficient – or her kidneys, or whatever it was that did the job of getting alcohol into the blood.

She downed half of her drink and looked at the boisterous revellers around her. Gill, Ali, Gav and all the others whose faces looked semi-familiar, were enjoying themselves. And she . . . well, it wasn't that she was *un*happy, exactly; she just couldn't get excited about jumping around on a sticky dance floor or fawning over good-looking fops wearing Rolexes. Jo Simmons didn't fit in. Becky Ross, though . . . maybe she *would* have fitted in.

Becky Ross had been one of the ring-leaders; she knew that from what she'd seen on Facebook and what she now remembered. She had been the girl charging up to the DJ and requesting 'Come On Eileen' and making everybody dance. She'd been the one stealing traffic cones at the end of the night or climbing statues in Trafalgar Square. But Jo Simmons wasn't like that. Perhaps, in the eyes of Ali and her drunken friends, Jo Simmons was a bit of a disappointment.

Earlier in the evening, Jo had been concerned that once Gill wasn't around – and inevitably, there would come a point when she'd want to stop baby-sitting – then she, Jo, would have no one to talk to. It wasn't just the fear of 'looking like a lemon' that everyone had at social gatherings. She didn't need to worry about not knowing anyone; she had the opposite problem. She was worried about *knowing* them. She dreaded the awkward conversations with strangers who claimed to have once been her friend – and her concerns were quickly verified within minutes of Gill's abandonment.

'Hi, Becky!'

The fourth person in succession sidled up to her, this one a spotty-faced ginger guy in a checked shirt.

'Hi, um . . .'

The problem with being a minor celebrity, thought Jo, was that others knew more about you than you did them.

'It's Dave.' He blinked keenly at her. 'I heard about the, er, you know . . .'

'Yeah, so did everyone, it seems.' She smiled.

'So . . . what's it like? I hope you don't mind me asking. Can you remember stuff now?'

'Oh, I'm piecing it together thanks, Gerry.'

He gave an awkward laugh.

'No, really, I'm fine. The papers exaggerated everything – you know what they're like.' She rolled her eyes, hoping Dave wasn't a journalist, like the 'Dave' who had called her before.

'Yeah, I bet.' He nodded sagely. 'So, you were working at the, um, the Buffalo Club?'

'Oh *God*, no . . .' Jo laughed flippantly. 'The press completely made that up. I can't believe they get away with it! Sorry, I've just seen someone I need to speak to . . .'

And so it went on. Jo was getting quite keen on the idea of sloping off back to the flat, but she was reluctant to tap on Gill's shoulder as it was now sort of nestled in posh Charlie's armpit. She would have bought herself another vodka, but she'd used up all her money. It was typical, thought Jo, that of all the guys who'd approached her this evening, not one had offered her a drink.

'So, what's it like?'

Jo didn't even bother to turn round. She just sighed and picked up a glass from the bar that didn't seem to belong to anyone. 'Having memory loss, you mean?' She sniffed the drink. It smelled of tonic and she tipped it down her throat, enjoying the bitter gin aftertaste. 'Fucking annoying.' Maybe she was a bit drunk after all.

'I meant, what's it like having everyone ask you what it's like?' said the guy.

'Wh—' Her elbow slipped on the bar and she nearly dropped the empty glass. Standing next to her, one eyebrow raised, was Luke.

He was slightly skinnier than she remembered from the flashbacks, but she knew it was him. Everything else was the same: the white teeth, the leather jacket, the carefully crafted 'messy' blond hair. He looked like a poster boy for his ripped designer jeans.

'Hi, Becky.'

Jo closed her mouth. She was totally unprepared for this.

'It's been a while.'

He really did have the most fantastic set of teeth, thought Jo, and long eyelashes too.

'How is the back-from-the-dead stripper?' He was smiling, but there was a steely edge to his voice.

'So you saw the articles?' she managed eventually – not a very clever response.

'Is it true? About the amnesia?'

Jo was about to rattle off her stock answer about journalists being liars when it occurred to her that there was no point. Luke probably knew more about her than she did herself. 'Yeah,' she nodded. 'It's true.'

She clung to the bar, trying desperately to think of something appropriate to say, but her mind was addled and nothing she came up with seemed adequate.

'D'you know who I am?' he asked.

Jo gave a wan smile. ''Course I do.' She considered saying something about how the memory of their break-up had been one of the first ones to come back to her, and how it was still the most vivid and one of the most painful, but it all seemed wrong for the situation. 'You're the father of my two children.'

'Ha-ha. So the blast didn't damage your sense of humour then?'

'No.'

He smiled back at her. Jo wondered what he was thinking. Did he hate her? Surely he had every right to? But he didn't look as if he hated her. Did he understand why she'd broken up with him in the first place? Because she certainly didn't. Maybe he'd be able to tell her, she thought, although she didn't fancy having that conversation now. Perhaps they could swap numbers and meet up again. Perhaps . . . No. That was just unrealistic. She was thinking like a drunkard.

Luke started to say something, but as he did, Gill's face appeared at his shoulder. She was swaying and gripping Luke's shoulder for support.

'BeckyI'vegottagiveyousomething,' she said, transferring her weight onto Jo. She fumbled about in her handbag and extracted her keys, then dropped them, then picked them up and then pressed them into Jo's hand. 'Justincase,' she said, hiccuping. 'Water. Water. Must drink some water.'

She staggered off and then suddenly whirled round and stared at them.

'Oh.' She looked from Luke to Jo and then back again. 'Oh, right . . .' She looked at Jo, her mouth stretched tight and her eyes open wide.

Jo tried to convey the message, *it's OK, don't worry about me. I know I'm playing with fire*, but her facial muscles weren't up to it and nor, she supposed, were Gill's powers of deduction.

'Syoulater,' Gill mumbled, stumbling back into Charlie's arms.

'I guess she's pulled.' Luke nodded at the house keys.

'I guess.'

The conversation was not going well. Even Jo could see that, through her drunken fuzz. It was as though they had such monumental issues to discuss that it all seemed too daunting so they were saying nothing instead. Considering they had at one time been the Posh and Becks of the college, thought Jo, they weren't exactly exuding passion. Although . . . Jo let her eyes wander up to his. There was something. A spark. Or a glowing ember, at least. She looked away, annoyed, as the image of Matt's smile flashed through her mind.

'Where're you—'

A girl marched up to the bar and planted herself in between them, tossing her long, highlighted mane in Jo's face.

Jo was about to confront her but then realised the blonde was actually talking to Luke. He looked slightly taken aback. 'Er, a pint please,' he said, rather awkwardly. *Sorry*, he mouthed to Jo, over the girl's shoulder.

Pathetic! Jo nearly mouthed back, incredulous that Luke was going to curtail their conversation and accept a drink from this other girl. Then she stopped herself and thought about how a mature, sober adult would behave. One option was to walk away. Another was to ignore the blonde and continue the conversation behind her back, although that didn't look very feasible. The girl had quite broad shoulders and a mean-looking face, and she obviously had a thing for Luke. The third option was to find a drink on the bar and pour it over the girl's head.

Jo looked around and grabbed the nearest tumbler, then checked herself and put it back on the bar.

'See you around,' she whispered in Luke's ear, before serenely walking away. Unfortunately, she misjudged the step down to the dance floor and launched herself into a bunch of physicists, who were shuffling around to an old nineties dance track.

Maybe she would see him around, thought Jo, dusting herself down and retrieving her coat from the cloakroom. Maybe she wouldn't. Maybe it didn't matter either way.

As the night bus rattled into view, Jo found herself reliving the stilted conversation, reassessing her behaviour at the bar. She stepped aboard, wondering whether she should have been more assertive. Or decisive. It wasn't that she hadn't known how to get what she wanted; it was that she hadn't known *what* she wanted.

Leaning her head on the greasy, steamed-up window, Jo went through the conversation – such as it was – in her mind. It was all hazy and distorted by the alcohol. She'd made that stupid joke about children. Jo couldn't remember whether he'd laughed. He'd done that sexy lip-curling-up-on-one-side thing, she thought. They hadn't really talked about much. Or anything. Still, it had definitely been him instigating the conversation – he had sought her out. Shit, she really ought to have got Luke's number.

Idly, Jo pulled her phone from her bag and squinted at the display. There was the usual selection of missed calls and messages from Matt, all of which she deleted before she had a chance to think about them too much. One message remained in her inbox.

Jo, I love you. Please call.

Maybe Gill was right, maybe she did need a new phone. New life, new phone. All change. Yes, that was surely a good idea.

Another thought came to her as she drunkenly played with the buttons. She reached into her wallet and pulled out a well-thumbed piece of paper, grinning to herself. This was truly inspired.

Hey Luke, great seeing
you 2nite – let's do
coffee sometime. Bxx

Jo surveyed her handiwork, her thumb hovering over the Send button. Then she went back and removed the two kisses. She tried it with one kiss. Then she deleted the kiss and tried it with a space then two kisses, then reverted to the original message and pressed Send.

The screen displayed her inbox and once again, Jo was taunted by the message from Matt. She should have deleted it. Her thumb wavered over the red button, but she couldn't bring herself to do it. Locking the keypad, Jo stuffed the phone back into her bag and thought about the lovely, good-looking Luke who had struck up conversation with her tonight.

She cleared a patch in the steam on the window and squinted out at the London lights. Things were starting to come together. Tonight hadn't been as much fun as she would have liked, but it had been enlightening. She knew it wasn't going to be an easy transition, moving from Jo's life back to Becky's, but she would get there in the end.

Chapter Thirty-Nine

'That's great, thanks,' the receptionist glanced down at the security pass she'd just made, 'Rebecca. Just make yourself comfortable over there and someone will call you through in a minute.'

Jo crossed the barren room and perched on one of the remaining red cubic seats in the corner. *Make yourself comfortable.* How, exactly? There was a low glass table with about twelve copies of *The Economist* fanned out in a perfect arc that nobody had dared touch. In the corner was a large, spidery plant that was dangling down and tickling one of the candidates on the neck, and next to that was a water machine that looked like a spaceship. It wasn't really an environment conducive to comfort.

'It's the plant,' said Jo, nodding at the offending branch as the young man reached round and scratched his neck for the third time.

He stopped and looked up. The other two candidates surreptitiously peered sideways at Jo.

'I beg your pardon?' He had several chins, a middle parting and an accent that reminded Jo instantly of nice-but-dim Henry.

'It's the plant,' she said again. 'That's what's making you itch.'

Finally, the guy grasped what she was saying and looked up. 'Oh! Gotcha. Thanks.' He shuffled forwards on the little red cube.

An awkward silence reigned. Jo glanced at the girl on her left. She was small, with a narrow, pointy face and frightened-looking brown eyes that kept darting about. The other guy had such bushy eyebrows that he appeared to have caterpillars crawling across his forehead. He was whistling through his teeth at a volume just loud enough to annoy the other candidates. Jo tugged at the slightly-too-short sleeves on Gill's Zara jacket and concentrated on not looking nervous.

In fact, her nerves had died down a lot since this morning. She had already completed what she saw as the most stressful part of the day: the interview. It had gone surprisingly well. They had spent the first ten minutes talking about her 'excellent' results in the numerical test and then they'd discussed various things that Gill and Gav had warned her would come up: the economic downturn, the implications for various types of business, strategies to help companies improve their efficiency, market share, turnover, etc. Most of her answers were regurgitations from the internet, laced with bullshit. They had barely touched on her un-finished degree other than to say something about how universities these days were very open to mature and part-time students, which sort of implied that they thought she was continuing her chemistry course in her spare time – Jo hadn't bothered to correct them. Miraculously, there had also been no mention of her sordid past, implying that her interviewers hadn't read about Rebecca Ross in the press – or, if they had they hadn't made the connection. Fortunately for Jo, the photos of her in the newspapers had all been taken before the red streak had appeared in her hair, and the neutral makeup changed the look of her face quite considerably.

A shrill noise interrupted the young man's rendition of Handel's Hornpipe. On the fourth burst, Jo realised the ringing was coming from her handbag.

Withheld number. Shit. It was either Matt or one of the agencies she had approached for catering work. She had signed up to several in case the Flying High thing fell through.

Risk losing out on a job, or risk speaking to Matt? The choice that confronted her was a difficult one. Her phone continued to ring. Unemployment, or Matt. Fuck.

'Hello?'

Four sets of eyes stared at her head. The receptionist stopped typing and looked over.

'Jo, it's me. Please don't put the phone down.'

Wrong decision.

'I've gotta go.'

'No, please Jo. I just want to say one thing.' It wasn't the usual unruffled, chilled-out voice she remembered. Mat sounded frantic.

'Well, you can't,' she whispered. 'I'm . . . I'm busy.'

For some reason, she couldn't just lower the phone and press the red button.

'I only did what I did because I thought it would help you find out who you were,' he said quickly. 'I didn't want to hurt you. I love you.'

342

She tried to force her hand away from her ear, but it wouldn't budge. He had said it again. Jo tried to think of a suitable retort, still grappling with the possible implications. Would he really say that, if he didn't mean it?

At that moment a door opened and a skinny woman in a tight, beige trouser suit strutted towards them. Jo let the phone drop into her lap.

'OK, so . . . Dan, Germanicus, Rebecca and Susie, right?'

Jo slipped it back in her handbag and rose to her feet with the others. She had to focus. There was no point in wasting valuable brain power on a man she was trying to forget. Matt was a loser. He was just a country boy who thought he'd hit the jackpot when Jo had walked into his life back in summer and who now couldn't cope with reality. He didn't love her at all. And right now there were other things to think about. Like . . . Like . . . *Germanicus*? Was that a name?

The candidates followed the suited woman into a white-walled room with no furniture and no windows.

'So, this is the *final* part of the assessment. You'll soon be free to go,' she said, emphasising the last sentence as though talking to young children.

Three of the walls were adorned with large, square canvas prints depicting various forms of achievement: a sprinter winning a race, a handshake, two men high-fiving. All were printed in lurid pink, lurid green and lurid orange, the Flying High corporate colours.

Although there was no furniture of the traditional variety, there was plenty to look at around the room. A tripod stood at one end, its legs extended to maximum length, supporting a sophisticated-looking set of recording equipment. Then, in the middle of the room was a pile of branches – freshly chopped from a forest, by the look of them – and a bundle of blue rope.

'I'm sure I don't need to *remind* you that this is the *team* assessment,' she said, blinking rapidly at each person in turn. 'So all we're trying to do here is check that you can work *together*, as a *team*, just as you would do in the *workplace*.

'Some people are *alarmed* by the camera,' she said, 'but you should just forget it's there. We only record it so that other interviewers can see how you all *perform*. Don't worry, you're not on *Big Brother* or anything – ha!'

Nobody laughed.

'So, er, right. Your *instructions* are on the piece of *card* over there. I'll be observing, but try to forget I'm here. Imagine that this is a real-life situation, not an assessment.'

Jo couldn't help squirming a bit when she said that. She just couldn't envisage any real-life situations that involved six twigs, some string and a piece of card – and she was fairly well-versed in challenging real-life situations.

'OK, off you go.'

The first person to reach the card was Caterpillar Brows, whose name Jo assumed to be Dan.

'Jeez.' He stared at the instructions, shaking his head.

'Are you gonna read it out?' Jo suggested.

He didn't, so she reached over and extracted it from his grasp. 'You have ten minutes to build a chair that can support one person using the materials provided,' she read. 'The chair must raise that person to at least one metre above the ground.'

'A char?' echoed Germanicus, frowning at the sticks and rope. 'I say.'

'Won't be a very comfy chair!' whispered the mousy girl, Susie.

Dan was already picking up bits of wood and holding them up at various angles.

'OK, what have we got?' asked Jo, sensing that Dan had already forgotten about the team element of the exercise.

'It's not possible,' the young man declared.

'Well, let's have a proper think – we've got ten minutes.' Jo crouched down and helped to align the sticks, to see what lengths were available. 'OK, so we've got three long ones and three short. The three short ones are less than a metre long, so they won't be much good vertically.'

'Didn't you hear me?' Dan looked at her angrily. 'It's not possible. That's the answer. We've cracked it.'

Jo looked up at the others for support. Susie was chewing the side of her fingernail. Germanicus was still frowning at the sticks on the floor. 'I don't think there's an "answer", for something like this,' she said. 'I think they're expecting us to actually build something. Don't you?'

Germanicus nodded, looking again at the piece of card. 'Well . . . that does seem to be the implication.'

Susie shrugged nervously.

Jo reached across and started to unravel the rope. 'OK, so we've got five pieces the same, all about half a metre long.'

'Don't bother. We've already found the answer,' Dan said irritably.

At this point, the observing woman – who had remained silent until this point, only moving to jot something down on her clipboard – spoke up.

'Remember what I said. Try to imagine this is a real-life situation, not a test. What would you do in real life if you *had* to build this chair?'

'Phone a friend,' muttered Germanicus, pulling a silly face. 'Or get one of those Ikea chaps round.'

Susie nodded. 'I'd probably go get my boyfriend to do it while I made him a cup of tea!' She giggled softly and looked at the floor.

'Right, we've wasted too much time,' Dan announced suddenly. 'Come on. We've got to make this chair. OK. What have we got?'

'Three sticks that are longer than a metre, three shorter ones and five bits of rope.'

'A chair has four legs, though,' Susie pointed out, 'and we don't have four the same length.'

'I guess this won't be an ordinary chair . . .' Jo pulled the three long sticks upright. 'More of a seat.' She didn't want to use the phrase 'thinking outside the box', but it was clearly something they needed to be doing.

'We've got to think outside the box,' proclaimed Dan. The woman nodded and scribbled something on her clipboard.

'Hold this, will you?' said Jo, propping the three longest beams in a tripod shape and waiting for Germanicus – the only one tall enough – to grab the top.

'What are you doing?' asked Dan, eyeing the structure suspiciously.

'Well, I thought given that we only have three long bits, we'd have to make some sort of tepee, and use the short bits to hold it together.' Jo held two branches up against the construction to show what she meant.

Dan glanced over at the woman, who was busy scribbling something on her clipboard, then dropped to the floor and grabbed the one remaining stick. 'Here's what we'll do,' he said loudly. Actually, he was shouting. The woman

346

looked up from her notes. 'We'll do a tepee-type structure, yes, that's right, Germanicus, you hold that.' He slotted
the final beam into position. 'There. Susie, can you get
the ropes? That's it, now tie one around each of the joints,
yes . . .'

Jo opened her mouth, watching incredulously as Dan
proceeded to exploit her idea.

'Two minutes,' called the woman, as the wobbly A-frame
was fastened together.

'Right, come on guys,' said Dan, full of bonhomie. Jo
wondered whether he'd done exercises like this before. 'One
rope left, hmm. Does it say we have to use *all* the materials?'

Germanicus looked down. '"Using the materials
provided," it says. I wonder . . .'

Jo couldn't believe they were standing around discussing
the issue. It was obvious where the last rope should go –
other than round Dan's neck – and that was between the
two struts, to allow the seat to be mounted. 'Just do this,'
she said, demonstrating.

'That's right, Rebecca,' said Dan, quickly cottoning on.
'You secure that one. Tie it nice and tight. I don't want to
slip off!'

Jo turned to him. 'You?'

He tried to smile at her through his scowl. 'What d'you
mean?'

'Well, wouldn't it make more sense to have the lightest
person climbing up?' Jo tipped her head towards Susie.

'Thirty seconds!'

'I don't see it makes much difference,' argued Dan.

Jo finished fastening the foot-hold. 'It makes loads of
difference. Like, the difference between us succeeding and
us failing.'

347

'Gosh, d'you think it's safe?' whispered Susie, not helping Jo's case.

'See? She doesn't want to get up.' Dan hoisted up his suit trousers, ready to climb.

Jo was aware of the seconds ticking away. 'Fine. But just for the record, I'd say that given the smooth floor and our dodgy knot-tying and the brittle sticks, we should go for the lightest person.'

Dan looked briefly concerned by the logic in Jo's argument, but not for long. 'We haven't got much time. I'll do it.'

The annoyance bubbled inside her as Dan proceeded to climb, until, in one swift, beautiful, hilarious movement, everything – including Dan's trousers – came apart. The legs of the tepee splayed outwards and Dan plummeted to the floor with a ripping sound and a gratifying squeal.

The facilitator rushed over. 'Oh dear,' she flapped about ineffectively. 'Are you OK?'

Dan scrambled to his feet and felt around to the back of his trousers to where the ripping noise had originated. 'Uh, yeah. Fine. I'm fine. I think that counts though, don't you?' His face was dark red.

The woman hastily agreed that Dan's effort did indeed count, and that the team had succeeded in completing the challenge. They were ushered back into the reception area where one of the initial interviewers was waiting by the lifts.

'So! All done!' the woman beamed.

Jo sidled round to survey Dan's trousers. They weren't as badly ripped as she'd hoped, but she knew that the real damage lay elsewhere: not in the seams of his pinstriped suit but in his pride. If this young man succeeded in getting a job through Flying High, thought Jo, well . . . He wouldn't, surely.

'You'll be notified either way by phone in the next few days.'

Jo pulled out her phone as she stood in the lift, waiting to break free of her fellow captives, and replied to Gill's message.

> Went well I think. Up against
> 1 dickhead, 1 toff & 1 mouse . . .
> Dinner party sounds gd. C U
> l8r xx

She pressed Send and walked out into the weak autumn sunshine. The tower blocks opposite shone silver and blue, mirroring the sky, and somewhere nearby a church bell chimed. A couple of young men bustled past, looking suave and important on their mobile phones.

The city was beginning to appeal after all. Gill had been right. Waitressing *wouldn't* stretch her skills. If she had stayed 'on track' instead of veering off so dramatically two years before, she would have been here anyway, living this life, being a high-flyer – being Becky Ross.

Another message popped into her inbox as she strode along Cheapside, catching her leggy reflection in a shop window.

> Hi Becky, yeah gd seeing
> u 2. Coffee sounds gd.
> Name a time & place. L

A shiver of excitement ran through her. *Coffee sounds gd.* Her ex-boyfriend Luke was keen to meet up for a coffee. It was an omen, thought Jo. She had turned a corner. Becky Ross was making a comeback.

Chapter Forty

'You did *what*?'

'Got on a night bus.' Jo shrugged. 'I had to get away. I was . . . confused. There were people everywhere, asking questions, shouting . . . I dunno. I just wanted to get out of there.'

'Bloody hell, Becky.' Luke shook his head, smiling in amazement. 'No wonder we always said you'd be in Arsenal.'

'What?' Jo looked at him. The shirt and tie made him seem older, more masculine, and he had tamed his hair – or rather, messed it up in a more symmetrical way – to fit in with the city look.

'Oh.' He looked embarrassed. 'We had this silly conversation once about what football team we'd be most suited to. It kinda became a running joke. We agreed you were an Arsenal player because your life's like one of their games; you get the results, but you make it bloody hard for yourself along the way. I was more of a Palace player,' he laughed wryly. 'Mr Reliably Unpredictable.'

'Oh . . .' Jo wanted to say she remembered, but she knew she'd be lying. It was just a matter of patience, she told herself.

'So instead of going to the authorities and asking them to contact your family, like a normal person, you buggered off on a night bus at three in the morning and took your chances with where it was going.'

Briefly, Jo toyed with the idea of telling Luke the truth about her inexplicable feelings of guilt and fear, but her sense of preservation stepped in. She had already fallen into the trap of opening up to a man she thought she could trust.

Luke was laughing at her, shaking his head as he scooped the froth off his cappuccino. Jo thought back to their forced conversation at Barbarella's and allowed herself a little smile. Lying in bed the morning after Ali's birthday do, trying to nurse her head into action, she had worried that she might have blown her chances of ever speaking to Luke Johnson again, but here they were in the heart of London's insurance district, looking out over the Gherkin, drinking coffee together on a brown plastic sofa. Things weren't so bad.

'Enough about that,' said Jo, wiping the milky foam from her lip and breaking out of her reverie. 'Tell me how Crystal Palace is doing.'

Luke grinned. 'Like I said, reliably unpredictable.'

'You seem in pretty good shape,' Jo replied, casting her eye over his suited physique.

He smiled enigmatically.

Jo blushed. She hadn't meant it to come out like that. It had actually been a metaphorical reference to the shape of his team. A disturbing image of Stuart bending her over the fence, trying to kiss her, flickered through her mind.

'How come you're able to slip out of the office and spend

half your morning in Starbucks?' she asked, banishing the flashback.

'Ah.' He pulled a face. 'Well, officially you see, I'm seeing a broker right now.'

Jo smiled. 'I see. Hence the paperwork.' She nodded at the stack of official-looking sheets that sat between them.

'Oh, it's all right, insurance. Bit dull at times. Feel like I'm just playing for time, some days.'

'Right.' Jo caught his eye as they sipped their coffees.

She needn't have worried so much about today. Admittedly there was awkwardness; they were both being cautious about what they said and they hadn't confronted any of the real issues. It wasn't ideal that Jo remembered so little about their relationship. But she knew all she needed to know. She could sense how close they had been: the link was still there – albeit weaker now.

'So, if you're seeing a broker, does this mean you're expected to go back to the office with some sort of deal? Ooh – oh, sorry.'

Jo's phone was trilling away in her handbag. She lifted it out and read the ominous words: *Withheld number*. She was faced with the same dilemma as before, only this time the stakes were higher. She risked losing a *decent* job if it was Flying High calling, and she risked speaking to Matt *in front of Luke* if it was him. Shit, shit, shit.

'I'm expecting news on a job,' she gabbled, looking apologetically at Luke as the phone went on ringing. 'Some crazy strategy bullshit crap that Gill put me up to.'

'Shouldn't you answer it then?'

'Um, yeah. Right.' She watched it for a couple more seconds, then picked up.

'Jo, it's Sue.'

Her body flooded with dread.

'I got your letter.'

Jo swallowed. She could feel Luke's gaze wandering searchingly over her face.

'Jo? Are you there?'

For a brief moment, she considered hanging up on the woman. Then she could turn her phone off and delay this hideously awkward conversation about her resignation until another time.

'Jo?'

'Yeah,' she said eventually, remembering the promise she had made to herself. 'I'm here.'

'Oh, good. Now, Jo, I know you've been through a lot lately, and I can understand that you're a bit confused, what with the whole Jo-Rebecca thing and the newspapers . . . But, Jo – or Rebecca; which do you prefer?'

'Er, Jo. Beck – Jo.'

'But, Jo, decisions shouldn't be made in the heat of the moment.'

How ironic, thought Jo. Her decision to *join* Dunston's had been made in the heat of the moment – due to Jo Simmons' panic to settle into her new life. But her decision to leave had been perfectly rational – or at least, as rational as it was possible to be in the circumstances.

'You were good at your job, Jo. An asset to Fairmont House. I just wanted to make you aware of that, and to offer you the chance to change your mind. Don't throw everything away because of this little incident.'

Jo didn't know how to respond. She couldn't begin to explain to Sue how she felt. This was no 'little incident';

it was a revelation. It was a moment of enlightenment, a series of events that had shown Jo – Becky – who she really was, and why it didn't make sense for her to stay in Radley any more.

'Now, I'm assuming you need some more time, so what I was thinking was perhaps another week's compassionate leave starting from now, and then we can reassess the situation,' said Sue. 'How does that sound?'

'It sounds absurd,' Jo wanted to say. 'I've moved away. Moved on.'

Luke's searching stare was like a laser beam on her face.

'Um . . .'

She looked out of the window. A woman pounded past in a suit and white trainers and two security guards patrolled the glass building opposite, looking officious. A courier leaned against his bike, barking briskly into his radio. Jo strengthened her resolve. This was her home now. She was a city girl. Sue's offer was kind, but it was no longer appropriate.

'The kids are missing you.'

Jo felt herself waver and silently cursed Sue's tactics. Up until now, she had felt quite sure that she was making the right choice. Fairmont House belonged in her old life, along with the traitorous boyfriend, the china cats and the burned toast. Sue had thrown in the comment about the children deliberately, just to muddle her thinking.

'I've got to go.'

'You give me a call any time, won't you? You've got to be ready to come back. You've got to *want* it.'

'Yeah, bye.' Jo put the phone down on the table and stared at it for a couple of seconds.

Luke was looking at her, head on one side. 'Not the job offer?'

'No.' Jo sighed and tried to lose the mental image of Tim drawing Ferraris. 'The place where I worked before.'

'Where was that?'

'Oh . . .' She could see Kyle's artwork on the living-room wall, and his face – his mean, hardened face, a rare picture of concentration. 'Just this . . . place.'

'You're not going back, then?'

Jo rolled her eyes. 'Don't you start.'

'Oh. Sorry. I guess everyone's asking.'

Jo nodded. Not that Luke knew who 'everyone' was. He didn't know about Sue or Matt or Mrs P. He didn't really know anything about Jo Simmons.

'Well, if you will do your fancy footwork . . .'

Jo smiled and dismissed the memories. 'I'm doing a Ronaldo, aren't I?'

'Step-overs and extra turns when all you need to do is dribble in a straight line.'

It wasn't quite a fair comparison, thought Jo, although she could see what Luke meant. She *could* have opted to take the straight, single-track path, coming clean after the blast about her amnesia and slipping straight back into her old, albeit unfamiliar life. But there had been a reason for complicating things. It had been a conscious decision to divert from the main track and set off into the unknown. She'd been running from something – something she couldn't explain to Luke.

Her phone was vibrating again on the table, threatening to break into song.

'Maybe *that's* the job offer,' said Luke, raising an eyebrow at the flashing device, goading her to pick it up.

Jo watched it for a moment, then reached out and pressed the red button. Then she turned to Luke and fixed him with a meaningful stare. It was all very well passing the time with flirtatious football riddles, but they needed to talk.

'Woah.' Luke drew back his head in mock fear.

'Sorry, but . . .' She was still looking at him, wondering how to begin. 'Can I ask something stupid?'

'Er . . .' Luke looked uncomfortable.

'About us.' Jo hesitated. 'Why did we break up?'

Luke laughed timidly and shied away. 'That's not really one for me, Becky.'

She nodded awkwardly.

Luke's eyes flitted up to hers and then away again. 'But I'll have a stab, if you want.'

'Go on.'

Luke drained his mug and then looked at the table, not her. 'Well, basically, I didn't fit with your new lifestyle. You were all into money and cocaine and sleeping with random fuck-wits, and I was just . . . well, I wasn't even in the Premier League.'

Jo chewed on her lower lip, waiting for Luke to look her in the eye. Gill had been right. There was nothing more to it than that. She had been too busy messing up her life to let someone like Luke try to help.

He continued to avoid her gaze and focused on the empty cup. 'I think the thing with your parents kinda messed you up.'

Jo nodded, almost laughing at the scale of the under-statement.

'Um, I should probably head back to the office.' He started neatening up the pile of papers on the table.

She closed her eyes, wishing she hadn't brought up the subject of their split. 'Sorry.'

'No, it's OK. I just . . . Need to get back. You know. Show face, pretend to be working.'

'That's not what I meant.' Jo held his gaze. 'I meant, sorry. For . . . what happened.'

'Oh, right.' Luke stopped shuffling the papers. 'OK.'

Several seconds passed. It was only when Jo's phone started ringing that she realised she'd been holding her breath.

'Popular girl,' said Luke, gathering his notes and standing up. 'I'll let you get that. Keep in touch, eh?'

Everything was happening too quickly. Luke bent down and kissed her on the cheek, giving her a look that she couldn't quite decipher. Then, as she put the phone to her ear, he slipped through the door and sauntered across the road, casually lifting his paperwork in a goodbye gesture.

'You have *one* new message,' said the robotic woman. 'Received today, at eleven seventeen . . .'

Fuck. She had cut short being with Luke to listen to her bloody voicemail. *Fuck.* What a complete waste of time. Stupid phone. Why did it need to call her just to say she had a message? Just as they'd started talking about the things that mattered. They hadn't even said a proper goodbye. *Fuck.*

'Hi, Rebecca,' said a clipped female voice. 'It's Debbie here from Flying High. I'm pleased to say that you passed all the assessments and we've been able to find you a placement that starts *this Monday*, if that's OK? It's at one of the big city consultancies, P. Jefferson. I'll email you with the details. If you can call me back to confirm, my number is . . .'

Jo etched the phone number into her napkin with the

side of her spoon. P. Jefferson. Holy shit. That was a big name. They probably paid big money too. Her annoyance at Luke's premature departure abated a little, although it did seem like a shame he wasn't still here to share her excitement. She grabbed her phone again.

WAS job offer!
Gd 2 c u just now.
Spk soon. Bxx

Jo punched the numbers into her phone and listened while Debbie mechanically conveyed the details of the contract.

'I presume you're happy with all that?' she asked.

Trying to contain her excitement, Jo agreed that she was indeed happy. Happy was not the word. *Two hundred pounds*. That would be her day rate. It was absurd. Ludicrous. She doubted that even the Buffalo Club could have guaranteed that sort of money.

Glancing at the starched suits around her, Jo felt the elation give way to anxiety. She still didn't really know what people did in places like P. Jefferson. Gill had tried to explain, but it was as though she'd been talking another language. Leveraging synergies and pushing back on enhanced ROI strategies . . . Would she cope? Would the fact that she hadn't finished her degree hold her back? Jo breathed deeply and pressed the negative thoughts out.

Her phone buzzed again.

Like I said, Arsenal
always gets the
results. Xx

Jo smiled. Luke was right. She was a pro. After everything she'd been through in the last few weeks, pushing paper around or whatever they did at P. Jefferson would be a doddle.

Chapter Forty-One

'Becky, where's my hair dryer? Did you move it? And my brush – oh my God, I've spilt my tea!'

'It's all in the bathroom,' yelled Jo, spitting on the lapel of her nylon jacket and trying to rub off a dubious brown mark. She was standing in front of the full-length mirror in the hallway, trying to get used to her management consultant look.

'Becky! Where's my hair dryer?' There was a clattering noise.

'In the bathroom!' Jo yelled again. *Where you left it.*

'What's it doing there?' screeched Gill. 'Oh my God, I've cracked the mug!'

Jo gave the jacket a quick, final brush-down and got an electric shock. She reached for her three-pound handbag to complete the look and called up from the bottom of the stairs.

'I'm off – see you later!'

'Oh my God, another ladder!' screamed her flatmate, throwing her bedroom door open. 'What did you say?'

Sometimes – and she would never say this to Gill's face – Jo felt that her friend was a bit of a drama queen. Her lively nature was an asset, of course, but the constant fretting and flapping occasionally wore a bit thin. It was like having a fly buzzing around the flat.

'I'm off. See ya.'

Gill's head appeared, a brush hanging from her tangled hair. 'Ooh, look at you! Very smart. Oh God – look at these tights! How d'you feel? Any first-day nerves?'

Jo shrugged. Actually, she felt petrified, but she didn't think that stopping to chat to Gill would quell the anxiety.

'Cool as a cucumber,' Gill smiled admiringly as she tried to yank the brush through her mousy wet bob. 'You'll be great. See you later!'

Jo checked the time on her phone as she strode down the street, past the polished black Porsches and silver Mercedes. Eight fifteen. She had plenty of time. The website had told her it only took fourteen minutes to get to St Paul's.

Possibly, thought Jo as she jostled for a position in the queue for the ticket machine, the Transport for London website hadn't taken into account the other six hundred people wishing to make the same journey at exactly the same time on a Monday morning. The tube station was pandemonium: suited commuters ramming up against one another, indicator boards flashing, Tannoys blaring, barriers bleeping and the air laden with tension.

'It's not working,' said the lanky man at the front of the queue.

'Can you let someone else have a go?' asked the woman behind him, thrusting her chest out like a peacock.

The man started bashing the machine with his fist.

'I doubt that will help,' remarked peacock chest.

Another man jumped the queue to help clobber the ticket machine.

The walloping and cursing continued. Jo looked at her phone. Eight twenty-two. She was pushing it. Then, in the midst of the panic, she had a brainwave. She pulled out Joe Simmons' wallet and rifled through the pocket where she'd stashed all his defunct credit cards and gym membership passes. There, shining out at her in turquoise and white, was a top-up travel pass. If Joe Simmons had been walking past, she would have kissed him, there and then.

She approached the barrier and held out the pass. There was a satisfying beep and the grey plastic jaws sprung open.

'STAND ON THE RIGHT,' a man barked as she stepped onto the escalator.

Jo leaped sideways and watched as the man bulldozed through, his laptop bag banging against every shoulder he passed. She did know the rules – they were subconsciously engrained in her mind just like zebra crossing etiquette and high-street behaviour – she just hadn't been concentrating. She hadn't *expected* to have to concentrate. This was stressful. She felt more anxious than she had done on her first day at Dunston's.

The train doors opened and revealed what looked like a hundred suited mime artists, all pressing against an invisible surface, not changing their form in case the new arrangement left an arm or a head sticking out as the doors slid shut. Incredibly, though, people around Jo thrust forward and somehow levered themselves inside. Jo took a deep breath and did the same.

Squashed up against the rattling doors, Jo looked around and tried to identify the source of the techno beat and the powerful body odour. A man's watch said it was five to nine. Jo hoped he was one of those peculiar people who liked to trick themselves into being fifteen minutes early everywhere.

'Apologies for the slow progress this morning,' squawked a tinny voice from somewhere above her head. 'We're currently being held at a red signal while we wait for the track to clear up ahead. We should be on the move again shortly.'

Short was not the word Jo would have used to describe the agonising six-minute wait outside Marble Arch, but slowly, painfully, the train resumed its journey and eventually pulled in with a screech at St Paul's. Jo squeezed out and then ran like she'd never run before.

She flew up the escalator, through the barriers and into the grey morning light, then sprinted along Cheapside, dodging buses and taxis and angry men with umbrellas, thanking God that she'd memorised the map before she'd set off.

She arrived at the ten-storey P. Jefferson headquarters just five minutes late.

'Morning!'

Jo tried to stop her chest from heaving.

The tanned receptionist pointed in the direction of the Retail Division, where Jo found herself pushing through a series of glass doors.

'Rebecca Ross?'

A tall, wiry man with a well-trimmed triangle of hair on his chin held out a hand.

'I'm Ed Vesper. VP in Retail. Nice to meet you. The other analyst's already here.'

'The tubes . . .' Jo muttered as her fingers were crushed in the man's vice-like grip. The VP ignored her and turned on his heel. *Other analyst?*

They weaved through a large, open-plan office in which, wherever feasible, the furnishings were made of glass: desks, plant pots, even waste-paper bins. In a normal office there might have been cheap pin-boards dividing banks of desks, but here there were tall, blue smoked glass panels seemingly suspended from thin air. The floor was coated in a velvety layer that spelled out some sort of motto in green and blue. Jo felt as though she were swimming through a fish tank.

'These will be yours,' said the man as they hurried past a pod of four desks, one of which was occupied by a petite, busty blonde. He led her through to a meeting room at the end of the office. 'We'll just go through the task and then you can get going. After you.'

Jo nearly stopped dead in the doorway of the glass-furnished boardroom. There, sitting upright at the mirrored table like a schoolboy trying to impress the teacher, was Caterpillar Brow.

'Hi, Dan.'

'Oh, hi,' Dan said flatly.

'So you guys know each other, do you? From previous placements?'

'Yeah,' replied Dan, before Jo could say anything about how this was actually her first placement.

'Well, that's good. I'm sure you'll know all the tricks of the trade then.' The little brown triangle stretched across his chin as he smiled.

Great, thought Jo. Now the boss was under the impression that they were both whiz kids who had done this before and would work well as a team, when all they had done was tie bits of wood together with string. *Tricks of the trade*. What tricks? What trade, for that matter?

'So.' Ed looked from one analyst to the other. 'One of our clients is a large retail consortium with a loyalty scheme that allows data to be captured on customer purchases. As you can imagine, there are literally millions of transactions happening every day, which means gigabytes – actually, terabytes – of data rolling onto the system.'

With you so far thought Jo.

'I'm afraid this isn't going to be the most exciting task for you two. Basically, we need you to look at a month's worth of data, clean it, sort it, filter it, chart it and analyse it.'

They nodded again. Jo wanted to know how it was possible to *clean* data, but decided it was probably one for Google rather than a P. Jefferson VP.

'The database has been chopped up, if you like, into spreadsheets. How's your Excel?'

Jo continued to nod, marvelling at how a database, like some sort of vegetable, could be chopped up and cleaned. Then she realised that Ed was looking at her.

'Oh, um, fine,' she lied. Gill had reminded her of the basics, most of which she vaguely remembered from uni, and she had obviously managed to pass her Flying High test. She'd pick it up.

'Good! The agency said you were both very competent, so I'm sure you won't have any problems. Now, I know what you're thinking . . .'

Jo looked at him, rather hoping that he couldn't read her thoughts, because hers were focused on chopping up cabbages.

'You're thinking, why not write a macro?'

Jo nodded as though that had been precisely the question on her mind.

'Well, unfortunately it's not possible. Believe me, the data monkeys here have tried. Sorry – shouldn't call them that. Anyway, the instructions are in the same folder as the files on the system. Marie, your PA, will show you where everything is. I think that's all you need to know. Do you have any questions?'

They had a PA? Jo had lots of questions, but they all seemed too stupid to ask.

'How long do you anticipate this taking?' asked Dan.

Damn. That was a good question, thought Jo. Why hadn't she thought of that one?

'Well . . .' The bearded man drummed his fingers on the table. 'Each file will probably take you about five minutes, once you're up to speed, and there are about a thousand files, so . . .'

Jo's mouth fell open. *A thousand files?*

'Eighty-four hours,' said Dan, looking pleased with himself. 'So six days between us.'

'Well, there you go. Six days.' Ed closed his folder and stood up. 'And then I'll brief you on the next lot.' He smiled and pulled the door open.

Jo sat down at her shiny glass desk, punched in her temporary login details and waited for Marie, the elfin PA, to come over and navigate to the prescribed directory. There were one thousand and twenty-four files, to be precise.

'Shall I take the first half and you start from the middle?' She looked sideways at Dan, who was squinting at the instructions on his screen.

He turned to face her and frowned. 'What are you *talking* about?'

He asked this question very loudly, as though he wanted Ed Vesper to hear from across the office.

'What d'you mean?'

'Well, it doesn't make sense for *each* of us to do *all* the tasks, does it? I mean, that's like having a factory where every worker has to run along the production line doing everything. We should divide the *roles*. You do the data-cleaning and sorting and filtering – oh, and the charting. I'll do the analysis.'

Jo's laugh didn't reach her eyes. 'What?'

Marie, who was sitting opposite them pretending to read something, lifted an eyebrow.

Dan shrugged. 'You said your Excel skills were fine, so you can do the jobs that involve that, and I'll do the thinking part.'

Jo didn't know where to begin with her protest. Dan had proclaimed *his* Excel skills to be fine, too. And what made him more qualified to do the 'thinking'? And how was it fair that Jo had to do *all* the tedious tasks – assuming that cleaning data was tedious, and she thought it probably was – while he just did one?

'OK?' Dan blinked at her obtusely.

Jo sighed. Six days. Two hundred pounds a day. That was over a thousand pounds. Maybe it didn't really matter if her work wasn't stimulating.

'Fine.'

It was, she knew, going to be a very long week.

Chapter Forty-Two

'I love this song! Turn it up, Becks. Is it too early for a G and T, do you think? Oh, what the hell, it's five thirty. Want one? Come on, don't make me drink on my own.'

Gill pulled out two large tumblers and stuck her head into the freezer, without waiting for any answers. Jo turned up the radio as instructed and got back to hollowing out oranges, also as instructed.

It was quite undemanding, living with Gill. You didn't have to think much or express an opinion or make conversation; Gill did all that for you. In fact, Jo was beginning to learn, it was better if you didn't *try* to do any of that stuff. Going with the flow – rapid and turbulent though it was – made everything much easier.

'There you go!' Gill handed her a glass of gin and tonic in equal measures and danced across the kitchen to the Abba track. 'La-la-laaa, la-la-laaa, ah-haaaaah . . . Oh my God, look at my celebrity rolls!'

Jo abandoned her oranges and peered into the oven, where Gill's home-made bread rolls – each one supposedly shaped like a famous person's face – were beginning to brown.

'Oh, yeah! I can tell that that one looks exactly like . . .' Jo squinted into the heat, 'a bread roll.'

'Shut up.' Gill whacked her with the oven glove. 'You'll see. They'll be really distinctive when they come out.'

'Right.' Jo smiled, her eyes watering from the gin. 'How many Orange Surprises am I doing?'

'Six, assuming you like sorbet. I'm guessing the others will eat anything.'

Earlier in the day, Jo had almost plucked up the courage to ask Gill whether they could invite a seventh along, in the form of Luke Johnson. Almost, but not quite. She hadn't dared tell Gill about her coffee with Luke. It wasn't a deliberate denial; she just didn't want her friend to get carried away. Jo could see it now: Gill becoming all excited that 'Luke and Becks' were back on, organising double dates and soirées and, well . . . it just felt too soon for all that.

Her phone was buzzing its way along the kitchen surface. *Withheld number*. Again. Why did everyone have to withhold their number? Jo watched it, flashing, buzzing and whirring its way to the edge. It was Saturday, so it couldn't be Matt. Besides, he had practically stopped calling now, thankfully. Occasionally, Jo could go for a whole morning or afternoon without thinking about him.

'Hello!' cooed the familiar gentle voice.

Jo's heart sank. She moved through to the lounge, clamping the phone under her chin and wiping her hands on a towel as she went. She'd have to tell Sue that she wasn't coming back. She *had* to. It wasn't fair on the children to keep stringing them along.

'Hi, Sue. Look, I know—'

'How's it all going? Have you had time to do a bit of thinking?'

She would have to get the message across soon, or she'd lose her nerve. 'Yes. And I've realised that I fit in best in my old life, so I'm . . . I'm going back to that.'

'Oh,' said Sue. There was a pause. 'That is *such* a relief, Jo. I *am* happy. D'you think you'll be able to come back this week then?'

'No—'

'Oh, OK, maybe part-way through the week. I'll let you liaise with Clare. The kids have really missed you, you know. They've even dedicated a little section of the mural to you. Kyle painted a pole-dancer, would you believe!'

'No—'

'Oh, it's not that bad, really. Quite arty, in fact. And Charlene and Nadia wrote a poem. And Tim . . . well, he does like drawing cars, doesn't he?'

Jo tried to form an articulate protest, but it came out as a half-hearted grunt. The doorbell chimed and Gill darted across the room, then Charlie stepped into the lounge and there was some kissing and shrieking and then the doorbell sounded again and another man Jo half recognised walked in, and all the time, Sue was waffling on about murals and cake sales.

'. . . football without you, I must admit. We got someone in to cover for you this week, but I don't think they took to her. She's an ex-school teacher. Not much experience with kids like ours. I don't think she had a clue on the football front, and of course, there's only three weeks till the tournament . . . They'll be so glad to have you back.'

I'M NOT COMING BACK! Jo wanted to scream.

371

Instead, she took a deep breath and heard herself say, quite calmly: 'Sue, I'm sorry.'

'Sorry? Why?'

Then the calmness deserted her. The tears spilled out of her eyes and down her cheeks and her chest started heaving with thick, uncontrollable sobs.

'I'm sorry! I can't do it!' She ran, crying, into the bathroom and locked the door. Her carefully applied makeup was ruined. 'I'm not coming back. I tried to tell you but you wouldn't listen. I'm sorry about all the lying, and stringing you on, and confusing everyone.' She took a huge gulp of air. 'But I've made my decision. I'm going back to the life I *was* living – before the bomb.'

'Oh.'

'Sorry,' Jo said again, unable to bear the silence.

'Don't apologise to me,' Sue replied quietly, after some time. 'Apologise to the children. They're the ones who will miss you.'

Jo tried not to think about Sue's remark. She apologised a few more times, put the phone down, hastily repaired her face and re-emerged from the bathroom.

'Two more G and Ts, coming up!' cried Gill, haphazardly slicing a lemon. 'Charlie, can you get us some ice? Marcus, why don't you make yourself at home in the lounge – oh, here's Becky. Becks, d'you wanna go through to the lounge with Marcus?'

Dutifully, Jo accompanied the willowy young man through the flat, glad to avoid the kitchen. She hadn't relished the idea of standing around explaining her swollen eyes and bunged-up nose while Gill tried to flirt with Charlie.

Marcus was looking at her, clearly expecting some

conversation. Jo's mind was elsewhere. She had thought getting closure on her Radley existence would prompt a wave of relief. Finally, she had cut off her ties with Dunston's and Oxford and the village life. She had nothing more to do with her deceitful ex-boyfriend or any of his pitiable friends. She didn't need to supervise any more disastrous car-washes or outings. But she didn't feel relieved; she just felt horrendously guilty.

'So,' ventured Jo, sinking into the enormous sofa. 'Long time no see.'

Marcus nodded silently. Jo wondered where Kyle was living now. She should have asked Sue.

'D'you . . . d'you work in London?'

Her heart wasn't in it. She didn't care where Marcus worked. She wanted to know whether Kyle had been removed from his stepfather's care and whether Nadia had cut down on her spliffs – and who this teacher was who was taking the kids' sessions now.

'Yeah.' He turned the glass round nervously in his hand. 'In IT.'

'Right.' Jo nodded, not really listening. That was it, she decided. From now on, she wouldn't think about Fairmont House or any of the children. That chapter of her life was over. She would sip her gin and tonic, talk to Marcus and enjoy her evening.

The doorbell rang, signifying the arrival of Ali and Gav, and there followed a flurry of excitement in which Gill proceeded to get everyone's drinks orders wrong and then Ali nearly set fire to her top on a candle.

'OK, people, sit up!' the hostess cried, herding her guests to the table. Then she gasped. 'Oh my God! The celebrity rolls!'

She darted out, returning a moment later with a tray of what looked like black, smoking turds.

'Very hot!' she cried, circling the table and dropping a charred bun on each side plate as the smoke alarm went off. In her haste to restore calm, Gill knocked Gav's wine onto the floor. Ali grabbed the nearest thing she could find – the baking tray – and started frenetically fanning the bleeping device, sending a shower of burned crumbs all over the carpet.

The game of guess-the-celebrity didn't go down as well as Gill had probably hoped, and eventually the hostess resorted to microwaving some frozen bread and consuming the best part of a bottle of wine in an effort to forget about her landlord's upholstery.

Ali turned to Jo. 'So have you got over your mag – ag – abnesia?'

Jo watched as Gill poured red wine all over the table-cloth. 'I'm getting there.'

'But,' said Gill, mopping up her spillage with a slice of wholemeal, 'you haven't called your MUM, have you?'

She was drunk, thought Jo. She wasn't trying to be antagonistic. She was just doing that annoying let's-be-honest thing that people did when they were drunk.

It wasn't the first time Gill had brought up the subject of Becky's mother. For some reason, and it was something to do with the latest self-help book she had acquired, *Learn to Love Your Higher Self*, Gill had taken it upon herself to conduct an amateur psychological review of Jo's condition and had come up with a theory. In order for Becky to get back on track, she believed, she needed to confront whatever it was that had caused her to veer off the track in the first place. And that, apparently, was her mother's affair.

'Not now, Gill.'

Gill lifted an eyebrow and looked around at the other guests as if to say, *See?*

Jo started collecting the bowls.

'Her dad didn't even make contact!' Gill hissed as she left the room. 'She hasn't spoken to either of them!'

Jo returned with the four half-price Smoked Duck and Wild Mushroom pies that Gill had squashed together and reheated in an attempt to look home-made.

'Hope nobody's veggie!'

'Looks delicious,' said Gav. 'Did you make it, Gill?'

'Erm, mmm.'

'Really? In Cumbria?' Charlie held up the portion that Gill had gracelessly plonked on his plate. The pastry was stamped with a crest that quite clearly said Cumbrian Pies.

'Oh. Right.' Gill looked crestfallen, but not for long. 'Hey, did you hear about that trial thing in Yorkshire? That's in Cumbria, isn't it?'

There was a general mumbling indicating that nobody knew whether Yorkshire was in Cumbria, or vice versa, but that both were 'up north' so it didn't really matter.

'What trial thing?' somebody asked.

'You know,' Gill speared a chunk of meat and waved it about, 'that high-pitched wheeeeee . . .' She screwed up her face and did what looked like an impression of a sick mosquito.

'Oh!' cried Gav, somehow interpreting her actions. 'The high-pitched wheeeeee . . .'

Jo looked around the table, at a loss. She'd been taking it steady tonight, but she felt sure she hadn't drunk *that* much less wine than the others.

'The anti-social behaviour thing,' Gav said. 'The trial of

that wheeeeee noise that only teenagers can hear. Something to do with the frequency of pitch or whatever.'

'Oh . . ?'

People started nodding, slowly. They were referring to a local council initiative that had been all over the news in the last few days: a trial of some controversial new device that made a painfully high whining noise at young people.

'Weird, isn't it?' mulled Ali, swilling the wine around in her glass. 'I didn't realise that teenagers could hear different things. Like bats, or something.' She made antennae with her hands.

Jo said nothing. She was trying not to think about bat costumes or Hallowe'en.

'Good idea, though,' said Gav. 'Keep them out of the town centres and all that.'

'Yeah,' Charlie agreed. 'For sure. My father had the tyres slashed on his new Jag the other week – from right outside the restaurant!'

'Really?' Gill gasped.

'Shit.' Gav shook his head. 'The sooner the better, I reckon, with these bleeping things.'

There was a lull in conversation while people tucked into their smoked duck and wild mushroom pies. Jo was thinking about the kids. She couldn't help it. She was wondering how the bleeping devices would affect Kyle and Jason, and whether they'd ever deliberately vandalised anyone's car. They both hung out in the Westgate Shopping Centre during the week. If Oxford Council followed suit and adopted such a scheme then they'd have to find a new haunt. She could see them now, loitering in some old abandoned quarry, skulking in the backstreets with the addicts . . .

'Where would they go?' she asked. She hadn't meant to say it out loud, it just popped out.

'Who?' asked Gill.

Jo looked down at her forkful of mushroom and pastry. 'The young people.'

'The pikeys?' said Charlie, frowning.

Everyone looked at Jo.

'They're not pikeys,' she said quietly. 'They're just . . . kids, most of them.'

'Well, they can go where they like,' said Gav. 'As long as it's outside the town centres.'

Jo nodded silently, not meeting anyone's eyes.

'They should be in school, or at home doing something useful.' Charlie shrugged.

There was no way Jo could even begin to explain. That Kyle had been excluded from every school in the area, that he was scared to stay at home, that he loitered in shopping centres because it was the safest place he knew – these were concepts too alien for people here to grasp.

'Hey!' cried Gill. Jo sensed a change of subject coming. 'Did you hear about Becky's job? She's one of us now!'

Ali looked up. 'What, a management conslut— Fuck, I've had too much wine.'

Jo smiled meekly, grateful for the interjection but not really in the mood for any more scrutiny. 'It's just number-crunching,' she said modestly. It was true. She wasn't really being a consultant at P. Jefferson.

Gill was having none of it. 'It's a consortium loyalty scheme thing,' she enthused. 'To do with lean supply chain management.'

Remarkably, Gav seemed to know what she meant.

'Ha!' he cried drunkenly. 'Value stream mapping. Everyone's doing that in retail right now.'

The conversation went on in this way for some time, with Gav and Gill using phrases like enhanced bottom line, dynamic management and leapfrogging, and even Ali – who was an equity research analyst at Cray McKinley – making occasional garbled interjections. Charlie, who was doing a law conversion course at City University, nodded along wisely.

'So this associate on the Utilities desk,' said Ali, draining her glass and holding it out to be filled, 'he put down the previous year's e-bit-dah as the tangible assets on the balance sheet!'

Gav chuckled, shaking his head. Gill started giggling hysterically. 'E-bit-dah! Oh my God!'

Jo glanced sideways at Marcus who looked back at her blankly.

'I'll get the desserts,' she mumbled.

She returned a moment later, feeling even more sheepish and awkward.

'Um . . .' She pulled a face. 'I have an apology.'

'Not another spillage?' Gill pleaded.

Jo shook her head. 'It's the Orange Surprises. I got side-tracked.'

'So . . .'

'So I didn't fill them with sorbet. They're just hollowed-out oranges, and the sorbet's melted in the box.'

Gav snorted. 'That's the surprise, isn't it then?'

Suddenly, everyone was laughing, even though it wasn't funny and after a while nobody could even remember what they were laughing at.

'OK,' said Gill when the last few whimpers had died

down, wiping her cheeks free of mascara. 'No dessert. But hey, at least you all filled up on the frozen bread and half-price meat pie! Oh my God, stop, my stomach aches . . .'

It was only later, once the guests had staggered home and Jo was lying in bed, staring up at the slowly gyrating ceiling, that she stopped to think about her newfound – or old, depending on how you looked at it – friends. She was trying to decide, in a general sense, what the word 'friendship' really meant.

What it meant, she thought, was having something in common. Obviously there were other things like personality and doing things for one another and not being axe-murderers and so on, but mainly, it was about having common ground. She and Gill were united by their university years, Gill and Ali by their love of alcohol, Gav and Gill by the obscure language of management consultancy.

It wasn't just having things to talk about – 'old times', 'the other night', 'bottom-up strategies' and so on – it was having things that separated them from the rest of the world. Nobody else had been with them at the Horse Shed or Barney's or wherever Gill claimed they had been every Thursday night. Nobody else had been at the charity auction where Becks had met Luke. Their time at UCL was their glue.

So . . . Her brain felt overloaded with the complexity of her thoughts. Did that mean, given that she didn't actu-ally remember half of what had happened during that period, that their glue was weaker than it should be? Sometimes, when she was feigning familiarity, pretending to have things in common with people she barely knew, Jo felt as though she was hanging on by a thread – barely connected at all. But perhaps friendships could re-form, she thought. It seemed logical. The bonds would grow back, right?

Jo turned onto her side and closed her eyes. She wasn't sure. Maybe it would make more sense in the morning.

Chapter Forty-Three

'Busy, then?'

Jo looked up. Dan was peering sideways at her computer screen, raising one of his bushy eyebrows. She minimised the browser and highlighted some cells at random on her spreadsheet.

Working with Dan was like playing a game with a small child – you had to let him win all the time. He seemed to regard their six-week placement as an opportunity to prove his worth at P. Jefferson, which Jo supposed it was, but she didn't see why it had to be a competition between them.

'I think you're slowing down,' said Dan, loudly enough to catch the attention of one of the consultants walking past.

'Yeah, well, my eyes are going square,' Jo replied, changing the scale on the graph. 'Don't suppose *you* fancy doing the last few hours' grunt-work, do you?'

'No! That would mess up the consistency, wouldn't it?' He swivelled back to his screen. 'Just get on and finish them, then we can report to Ed.'

Right you are. Jo sighed and pulled up the browser again. She couldn't believe she hadn't done this before.

Here she was, ploughing through a task that could have been accomplished by a trained chimpanzee, and she hadn't even thought to relieve the boredom by logging onto Facebook.

P. Jefferson obviously didn't have a very strict policy on internet usage, thought Jo as she typed in the URL. The page loaded up instantly – a stark reminder of how slow the systems had been in the various libraries and internet cafés she'd used around Oxfordshire.

It occurred to her as she started to type Rebecca's email address that she still had two online identities. For some reason, she felt compelled to check Jo Simmons' account, just in case. She wasn't sure what she might find – in fact, she felt almost certain that there would be nothing there as she had only ever conversed with Saskia using that alias – but for the sake of completeness, she had a quick look.

The page appeared, white and empty, a sad reflection on Jo Simmons' shallow existence. There were no upcoming events or birthdays, no friend requests, no status updates except for a couple of meaningless comments by Saskia on the state of her finances and hangovers. One friend, thought Jo. That said it all, really. She went to log out, and then noticed that someone – Saskia, presumably – had sent her a message.

Hey, izat Jo frm Dunstons? Just wondrin wen u comin back – the techer is ok but her activitees r crap & it aint so fun without u. Nadia

Jo exhaled and noticed her breathing was shaky. She stared at the skinny face in the mugshot, then looked again at the words.

'How's it going?' asked Dan, glowering impatiently at her.

Jo moved so that her face concealed the screen and glared back at him. 'I'd be quicker if you didn't keep interrupting.'

He held his hands up in mock surrender and let out a sarcastic, 'ooOOOh', presumably for the benefit of Marie, whose attention he'd been angling for all afternoon.

Jo bit her thumbnail and tried to expel the guilt and frustration from her mind. She wanted to reach out and hug the skeletal thirteen-year-old. But she had to move on. Nadia and the other children were all in the past. Jo went to Account Settings and, with a trembling hand, forced herself to click on Deactivate.

Next to her, Dan started tapping his fingernails on the desk. She went back to the Facebook homepage and logged in as Becky. Her two hundred friends had been busy scribbling, updating and uploading. That was more like it, thought Jo. Most of their activities were of little interest, but she couldn't help noticing that Luke Johnson had updated his profile only six minutes before.

Arsenal is having a bad day.

There. It was a brief message, but it was enough. She minimised the browser and got back to her data.

'I'm saving the file on the system now,' she told Dan, minutes later. 'There's a weird spike in the data near the end of the month.'

He nodded patronisingly. 'Well done. I'm sure I'll find an explanation.'

Jo opened the next file and then quickly checked her inbox. Result. One new message.

Oh yeah? Why's that?

Jo carefully resized the browser on her screen so that the telltale blue borders didn't show, then tapped out a response.

Issues with a team mate.

She smiled, flicking back to the spreadsheet. Filter, sort, chart, format, copy, paste. She was like a machine.

'Pumpkins!' cried Dan, leaning back in his chair like a trader who'd just made a million pounds.

'Sorry?'

'The spike. It's just before Hallowe'en. The data's for pumpkin sales.'

'Oh, right. Good spot.' Jo nodded, turning back to her monitor and pulling up the browser. Beside her, Dan punched the air triumphantly. There was one new message.

Not passing the ball?

Jo grinned. This was much more fun than formatting graphs.

He's a glory-hogger. Wants to take credit for all the goals.

She continued with her mechanical task, slowly becoming aware of Dan's eyes on her again.

'What?' she snapped. 'Is there a problem?'

Dan's eyes widened. 'Easy! Just waiting for you to finish the next file.'

Jo noticed Marie look up to the ceiling – a sign of solidarity. 'Well, why don't you go and make us all a cup of tea while you wait?'

Dan seemed to notice something behind Jo's head. He waited a moment, then replied, 'OK, I'll go and make some tea WHILE I WAIT FOR YOU.'

Jo didn't need Marie's nod to know that someone – Ed Vesper, as it turned out – was passing behind her. Really, she thought, Dan's mental age couldn't have been much more than six.

At least you're getting goals, between you. Doesn't matter who shoots, does it?

Jo laughed silently, wondering how long they'd be able to keep this up. It did actually feel as though she were playing a very frustrating game of football.

I guess. We're getting paid good money, anyway :-)

Spreadsheet number one thousand and fifteen. Come on. Fewer than ten to go.

'I assumed milk, no sugar,' Dan said, stopping at Marie's desk. 'Sweet enough already.' He winked and dropped a custard cream on her mouse mat.

Jo exchanged a horrified glance with Marie and waited for Dan to bring round her tea. There was, she noticed, a small biscuit crumb lodged in his eyebrow.

Luke obviously wasn't having a very busy afternoon.

Sometime around spreadsheet one thousand and twenty-one, Dan threw his hands to his head and let out a strange, high-pitched screech. Jo and Marie looked at one another, then at Dan.

'Fuck!'

'What?' asked Jo, intrigued that the slick consultant wannabe seemed suddenly so frantic.

'Fuck!' He pointed at the screen hysterically. 'I just pressed Delete!'

'What? What did you get rid of?'

He looked at Jo, then replied in a strained, almost inaudible voice. 'Everything.'

Jo stared back at him in horror. *Everything*. Six days' work by two people. Gone. She didn't want to believe it was true. Sharing the glory when things went well was one thing – she was all for that – but sharing the *blame* . . . Marie was watching them nervously from beyond the smoked-glass divider.

'You mean, all your analysis and my charts and everything?'

'Well, no. My analysis is fine – I saved that to my desktop. But all your charts . . .' His voice petered out.

Jo started laughing as she shook her head, relishing the moment. This was what it felt like to be truly victorious. 'Because I was so paranoid about having to do all those fucking charts again, I saved each one to *my* desktop too.'

Dan let out a shaky sigh and wiped a hand across his faced. The crumb fell out of his eyebrow and into his tea. 'Oh. Uh, thank *God*.'

Jo smiled. 'Yeah. No worries.'

I just scored!

With renewed vigour, she got back to processing the last few files. Beside her, Dan sat, peevish, guilt-ridden and beautifully quiet.

What? With him? How could you?

Jo grinned as she planned her reply.

You know I wouldn't . . . I told you, we're not compatible. Can't play together.

'OK,' she said, clicking on Save and turning to Dan. 'That's the last one. I guess when you're done with that then we can go home.'

He nodded. 'And then start all over again tomorrow.'

Jo closed down her files and checked her inbox one last time.

Oh yeah? And who exactly *do* you play well with?

It was exactly the answer she'd been hoping for. All sorts of innuendos crossed her mind about making passes, keeping a clean sheet, making the first move.

I'll have a think. The whistle just blew. xx

Jo logged off and said her goodbyes, leaving Dan to email their boss. She knew there was a risk he'd take all the credit for their combined effort, but somehow she doubted he'd have the nerve after today's performance. And frankly, she was beyond caring if he did.

As usual, the tube platform was heaving with irritable commuters. Jo squeezed into the carriage and held her breath, trying to create her own private world amidst the damp coats and brollies. She couldn't decide which she hated more: the morning rush hour or the evening one. At least first thing, people smelt of shampoo and newspaper print. Now, the air was saturated with the stench of old food, bad breath and stale smoke.

She fell through the front door, exhausted and relieved to discover the flat in darkness. It wasn't that Jo disliked having her bubbly flatmate around – she could hardly begrudge the girl who had taken her in – but the incessant buzz that followed Gill around was . . . well, just slightly annoying.

Jo felt the tension drain from her body as the cold beer slipped down her throat. She closed her eyes and allowed the sofa to swallow her up. London was tiring. This new life of hers – or this continuation of her old life or whatever it was – was tiring. But she was getting used to it. It seemed like years ago, not just months, that she'd been pottering around in the Radley guesthouse, getting the quaint little bus into Oxford.

Sipping the lager, she switched back to the present and played through her flirtatious correspondence with Luke in her mind. Mmm. Luke. Lovely Luke with his ruffled blond hair and boyish looks . . . Jo hoped she was right about where that was leading.

She jolted upright as the front door burst open and her phone started buzzing.

'I'm home!' yelled Gill, as though there might have been any doubt.

Jo grabbed her phone and opened the message.

They haven't replaced
u yet. The kids need u.
Mx

Gill whooshed in, rifling through the mail as she went. 'How was your day? D'you want a drink? Oh, you've got a beer. Oh my God, the tubes were *rammed* tonight!' She frowned at something in her hand. 'Ooh. One for you.'

Jo pushed her phone away and reached for the letter. She *had* to forget about Matt.

'That's weird.'

'Mmm?' Gill tore at the envelopes.

'I haven't given anyone this address.'

'All I ever get is bills – it's so dull!' Gill flung the pile on the table and set off for the kitchen. Then she stopped, her hand resting on the back of an armchair. 'What did you say?'

Jo was already opening the letter. 'I haven't told anyone I'm staying here – apart from the uni lot, obviously. Hope the press haven't tracked me down.'

The envelope was clearly marked with her name and Gill's address, in neat, italic handwriting. Gill hovered nearby as Jo ripped the flimsy paper and pulled out a short, hand-written note. Then, as she read the letter, then read it again and felt the apprehension mount in her gut, she realised why Gill was loitering.

Several seconds passed. She stared at the letter, then slowly, up at her flatmate. Gill's eyes told her everything she needed to know.

'You spoke to my mum.'

Gill didn't reply immediately. She moved over and perched on the arm of the nearest chair, looking nervously at the letter and then at Jo. 'I meant to tell you,' she said. 'I didn't realise she'd get in touch directly. I thought she'd reply to *me*.'

'You thought . . .' Jo tried to piece things together. It was all too much. Her best friend had gone behind her back and talked to her mother, in order to . . . what? Why? What on earth could have possessed Gill to do such a thing?

'I had to do something!'

Jo looked at her, dumbfounded. 'What d'you mean?'

'Well, look at it from your mum's point of view! She didn't have any way of contacting you. She didn't even know you were OK. I mean, she's your *mum*, Becky.'

That was it. Jo leaned forward in the chair and screwed up the letter. The exasperation ballooned inside her. 'Yes, exactly. She's *my* mum. And if you'd listened to anything I've said in the last few weeks, you would've realised that I don't wanna see her. Not now, maybe not ever. I don't need your fucking psychobabble to help me decide what to do – and I *definitely* don't need you to do it for me!'

'Oh God, Becky—'

'This is . . .' Jo fought to find the words. 'This is no better than what Matt did, you know that? What *is* it with you people? Why d'you all think you can make things better?'

'I know, I just . . .' Gill shrugged helplessly. 'I'm so sorry, Becks. I really thought it would help.'

'Well, it didn't! It really fucking didn't! And neither did Matt's meddling, either. I thought you realised that?'

Jo continued to stare at the wall, shaking her head and trying to make some sense of the situation. Gill, of all people. Gill, who had stepped in and rescued her from an almost identical situation before, with such compassion . . . Maybe she *hadn't* understood. Maybe it had all been an act. Maybe Gill didn't really get her at all.

'What did she say, anyway?' Gill asked timidly.

'Nothing!' cried Jo, chucking the ball of paper across the room. That was pretty much the size of it; the letter hadn't said much more than Matt's latest text message. It was just a plea for her to come back.

'Well, maybe you could call her—'

'Gill!' screamed Jo, incensed. 'Why don't you get it? I *could* have called her. I've got her number – the number *you* used for calling her. I've had her number for weeks. But I didn't! I didn't want to! So what makes you think that I'll suddenly feel like calling her now?'

Gill opened her mouth to object but Jo carried on.

'Because I don't, in case you're wondering. I don't. I hate my mum. I hate her for doing whatever she did . . . pissing about with that guy in her office . . . splitting up with my dad . . . and I hate her for not giving a shit when I started fucking up my own life. OK?'

'Yep.' Gill nodded nervously.

Jo stood up.

'Where are you going?'

'Out.'

'Becky—'

It was too late. Jo didn't stop. The fury was ripping up her insides. She flew through the lounge, through the hall and through the front door. Once again, she was on the run. Once again, she had been wronged by someone she trusted. Maybe one day, thought Jo, storming onto the street and into the road, she would find someone who *didn't* betray her. But until then, there was only one person she could depend on, and that was herself.

Chapter Forty-Four

Jo turned the hot tap to full power. The pipes around her started hissing and spluttering, and slowly, a lukewarm trickle ran over her hands. A pile of cigarette butts floated in a puddle where the soap should have been.

As her hands warmed, Jo leaned forward and assessed the state of her face. Her cheeks were flushed – her own fault for coming out in November without a coat – and her eyes looked watery, partly from the cold and partly from the tears. Not that there had been many tears. She had cried, but it had been a sort of forced crying: a therapy, a means of expunging some of the pent-up emotion inside her.

It was hard to identify how she felt. The rage had subsided quite quickly once she'd left the flat, and had been replaced with something else. Despair, maybe. Loneliness. Confusion. Desperation. She didn't know. She ran a finger around each eye and gave her hair a quick shake. It was five to eight. He'd be here any minute.

The pub was one of those run-down establishments with unpolished brass and stuffed animals, which survived purely by virtue of the fact that it was in Soho. Jo ordered two pints and reluctantly handed over two five-pound notes. If it hadn't been so expensive, she thought, she might have ordered a chaser too, and maybe an extra beer for herself. Perhaps it was a good thing the place was so pricey.

He arrived half a pint later, his hair ruffled from the wind and his leather jacket looking wrong and flimsy over the pinstriped suit – although still somehow suave.

'Hi! How's things at Arsenal? Ooh, is that for me?'

Jo slid the beer across and waited while Luke unzipped his jacket and blew on his red, raw hands. She wasn't in the mood for football innuendos.

'I can't stop for long, I'm afraid – gotta leave at half-past.'

'OK,' Jo replied, disappointed. It was 8.10 already.

They sipped their beers in silence. Jo watched as he squeezed his hands together in his lap. She was procrastinating, she knew, but it wasn't going to be easy, asking such a huge favour in such a short time.

'I'm sorry for dragging you out at late notice,' she said eventually. 'I just . . . There was no one else I could call.'

Actually, that wasn't quite true. There were other people. There was Ali and Gav and the rest of the uni lot – although, to be fair, they would probably end up siding with Gill – and there was Saskia, if she could track her down.

'About what?'

Jo sighed. 'Well. You know how you left a message with the newspaper a few weeks ago, when you read the first article?'

He nodded.

'Well, so did Gill, and so did my mum, and . . .' she gulped down some beer, 'I still haven't called my mum.'

Luke frowned incredulously. '*What?*'

'I know, I know . . .' Jo shrank away, not wanting to have to explain herself again. Nobody seemed to understand. 'Don't ask. I just . . . I don't want to talk to her. I feel like she's kind of responsible for everything.'

'It takes two to—'

'Divorce, yeah, I know. But she was the one that had the affair. And, anyway, my dad didn't make contact. I don't know his number or where he is.'

'Oh. Right.' Luke still looked perplexed. 'So . . . your mum hasn't heard from you since she found out you were alive.'

'Well,' Jo gave a wry laugh. 'That's just it.'

'Just what?'

'Well, Gill got in touch with her. Told her where I was staying. So I got a letter from her today.'

'*Gill* got in touch?'

Jo shook her head, looking up at the ceiling where a moose stared back at her. It was odd, but she seemed to spend her whole life recounting to friends how other friends had betrayed her. 'Don't ask me why.'

Luke took several gulps of lager, as though suddenly aware of the time. It was twenty past. 'What did it say, the letter?'

She shrugged. 'Not much. Sorry. Come home. That sort of thing.'

Luke swigged more beer and pulled a face. He was drinking exceptionally fast, thought Jo. Perhaps he didn't like being lumbered with her problems. Perhaps she was being unfair, expecting him to share the burden like this. He had no obligation to listen. Maybe she shouldn't ask the favour after all.

'What are you gonna do?'

'I'm not sure,' she replied honestly. She couldn't ask. It was too much.

Luke finished his pint. 'Are you gonna carry on living with Gill?'

Jo hesitated. Luke looked at his watch. She knew she was running out of time. All of a sudden, the favour seemed too immense to ask. But then . . . who else could she ask? And surely Luke was expecting it. He must have assumed there was some reason for her asking him along tonight? It would seem odd to just walk away now.

Jo looked at his face. His eyes were darting around, meeting her gaze every so often but not settling. He knew what she was about to ask, thought Jo. She braced herself.

'I was wondering whether—'

As the words came out, a shriek filled the air and Luke disappeared beneath a sea of floaty fabrics. A powerful perfume descended on them and as the shriek died down, Jo heard the jangle of heavy jewellery.

'Hi! Hi!' cried the woman, when she finally finished kissing Luke's face.

Jo stared. Broad shoulders, blonde hair and a horsy face . . . it was the girl from the other night.

'Izzy.' Luke quickly regained his composure. 'You're early!'

'Well, nice to see you too, darling!' She rolled her eyes, wrapping herself around Luke.

Luke gave an awkward smile, then turned to Jo. 'Becky, this is Izzy, my girlfriend. Iz, this is Becky.'

Jo didn't know what happened after that. The walls of the pub suddenly seemed to be closing in on her. Everything went dark. She might have joined in with the small talk, she didn't know. All she could hear was the cursing and kicking going on in her head.

'Keep me posted, won't you?' she heard Luke say, through the fuzz. He slipped an arm around Izzy's waist. 'Hope you get things sorted out.'

Jo might have nodded. She couldn't think straight. There was only one certainty in her mind now, and that was the fact that Luke Johnson had a girlfriend.

Chapter Forty-Five

The place was in darkness except for an orange glow emanating from one of the upstairs windows. Jo pressed the doorbell and waited.

She still hadn't worked out what her opening line would be, or any other lines for that matter. She didn't feel convinced that coming here tonight was a good idea, but her brain was too tired to think of an alternative, and she'd come all this way, so she wasn't going to chicken out now.

Jo's thoughts were in complete disarray. A week ago, she'd been doing a pretty good job of picking up where Becky had left off – no, better than that. She had picked up from where she *would* have been if she'd stayed on the rails all along. She had reconnected with old friends, rebuilt her career, relocated . . . Everything had been coming together for Rebecca Ross.

But after weeks of hard work, of reconstruction, of forcing herself to do things because they were The Right Thing To Do, in the last twenty-four hours, her life had imploded. She was floating again: directionless, disorientated, alone.

There was a click, and then a sliver of light appeared through the shop window.

'Who is it?'

Jo moved round to the side door. The chain was pulled across and a silhouette blocked what little light there was coming through the gap.

'It's me. Becky. Jo.'

There was a pause, then the door clicked shut completely. For a moment, Jo stood on the doorstep, blinking hopefully into the night. The seconds ticked past. Gradually, she realised that the door was staying shut, and she felt the grip of desperation take hold. All she could think of to do was cry. She was *completely* alone in the world. Her only hope had just shut the door in her face.

The tears started streaming down her cheeks as she turned away and wandered back onto the road, not caring where she was heading. This was the consequence, she now realised, of thinking you could build a life from scratch. You couldn't. Jo Simmons was hollow and flaky – a rushed job. Her roots were shallow – non-existent, even – and the people she thought she knew, including Mrs Phillips, weren't real friends. She was on her own again.

There was a jangling noise from behind her. Jo turned round. She couldn't see properly through the tears but it looked as though the door was opening again.

'Blasted catch. So, hello again.'

Jo wiped a sleeve across her face. Even the ghastly cat-shaped slippers came as a welcome sight.

'Ug,' she said, trying to return the woman's greeting.

'Look at you! What on *earth* is the matter? Come on, get yourself inside.'

Without really knowing what she was doing, Jo stepped over the threshold and collapsed into the woman's bony arms. The emotional rollercoaster was too much. One moment she was plunging into the darkness, at her wits' end, and now she was crawling up the next hill.

'I see you've got a bag on your shoulder,' Mrs Phillips commented as they drew apart. She was smiling. Jo followed her up the stairs. She did indeed have a bag on her shoulder. She had gone back to Gill's and packed up all her belongings – something she'd done too many times – before catching the train out of London. Jo exhaled shakily and fell into the kitchen chair that had been pulled out for her. She didn't know where to start. There was so much to say, to explain, to apologise for.

'Mrs Phillips, I—'

'It's Pearl, I've told you.'

Jo managed a weak smile. 'Sorry. I . . .' She struggled to compose her first sentence. 'Pearl, I'm sorry. I'm *so* sorry.'

'I think we've been here before, haven't we?' Mrs Phillips looked mildly amused.

Jo nodded, propping her elbows on the kitchen table and sinking into her hands. Mrs Phillips was right. They had been here before, only the last time had seemed trivial in comparison. The last time, Jo had crawled back after an alcohol-fuelled row, with a plastic watering can as a peace offering, and all had been forgiven. This time, her wrongdoing was more severe, her desperation more absolute.

'I've been – I've had . . .' Unexpectedly, the tears started flowing again. Her body shuddered and her throat became choked by a wave of desperate sobbing. 'Ug,' she said again. The words just wouldn't come out.

'I'll make us both a hot chocolate,' said Mrs Phillips. The kettle gurgled, cupboards opened and shut, teaspoons chinked and slowly, Jo found herself sniffing away the tears.

'There you go,' said the woman, setting a mug down in front of her.

Jo inhaled the sweet-smelling steam and felt her composure returning.

Mrs Phillips pulled up a chair. 'Why don't you tell me what happened?' she asked softly.

The shopkeeper listened in silence as Jo recounted everything that had happened since she'd stormed out of the guesthouse six weeks before. She talked shamefully of her rationale for assuming Mrs Phillips had leaked the story and of her subsequent discovery that it had been her Perfect Boyfriend – and then broke down in tears again as she begged forgiveness for not making amends before now. She described the new life she had made for herself in London with the help of Gill and Ali and all the other people she had foolishly, *idiotically*, assumed to be her friends. She hung her head as she told Mrs Phillips about her deluded plans to win Luke back, cursing her own naïvety as the words left her lips.

'So I came back,' she concluded, 'because I didn't know where else to go.'

'Gosh,' said Mrs Phillips, stirring her drink, eyebrows raised. 'What a journey.'

Jo nodded. She hadn't realised how heavily everything had been weighing down on her. All the facts and opinions and theories and doubts had been colliding in her head, conflicting and running out of space, and now, having laid them all out in some sort of order and relayed them to the landlady, they seemed . . . well, manageable. Daunting, but not insurmountable.

'I really thought I was doing the right thing,' she mulled, sipping her drink and letting the steam rise up over her face. 'But I guess not.'

Mrs Phillips looked at her. 'Right for whom? For Jo, or Rebecca?'

Jo frowned.

'Well, you have to decide who you really are, don't you?'

Jo sighed wearily. She didn't have the energy for a philosophical discussion about who she was.

'Don't look at me like that,' said the woman, replacing the lid on the milk bottle and giving her drink a vigorous stir.

Jo propped her head up on the table and sighed. Deep down, she knew that Mrs Phillips was right. She had to work out for herself whether she was a bubbly, middle-class Londoner who talked about e-bit-dah and value chain analysis over expensive dinners, or whether she was an unqualified but optimistic care worker living in sleepy Radley and kicking footballs around with the lads.

A few weeks ago, Jo thought she had solved the conundrum. The 'real' Jo was, of course, Rebecca Ross: the girl who had been moulded by a million little incidents, events, experiences and people over the last twenty-four years. Jo Simmons was just a name. It was a shell of an identity that had tided her over while she found her feet.

But now, sitting with Mrs P, surrounded by plastic cats at a quarter to midnight, Jo was beginning to think more carefully about the question. It seemed implausible, but she was beginning to wonder whether her true self – without taking into account the millions of events and people and so on – was actually more like Jo Simmons. Perhaps *this* was the real her. She rubbed her eyes. It was too late to be contemplating such things.

'I thought you weren't gonna let me in,' said Jo, working her way up to an apology.

The woman smiled weakly. 'Silly girl.' She looked at Jo. 'The truth is, you helped *me*, in a way.'

'What d'you mean?'

'Well.' She shrugged. 'I miss all this.'

Jo tried to work out what exactly she missed. Presumably it wasn't being woken up half-way through the night to make hot chocolate.

'The guesthouse. I miss running it. And if you hadn't stumbled in off the street that day, I might never have realised.'

Jo nodded. 'But . . . you can't run it any more, can you? The council . . .'

The woman's grey head danced from side to side. 'Well, I've been thinking. I might have another go.'

'Really?'

'That's my plan. I'll have to comply with some new regulations and whatnot, and I'm sure there will be hoops to jump through and so on. And I'll have to think about getting help in the shop. But hopefully the beastly council members who closed me down in the first place will have moved on by now – or died, perhaps.'

Jo laughed. It was comforting, being back in the guest-house – like coming home after a long time at sea. She was noticing little things about the place that had previously passed her by: the sphinx doorstop, the colourful placemats, the paw-print curtains. For all the time she had lived here before, she had taken for granted its cosy warmth and quaint, pastel tones, never stopping to think about how Mrs Phillips had welcomed her into her home – her home; not just a B&B. Then she saw her chance. 'I can work in the shop.'

'Oh, now don't you start that again.'

'No, really. I want to. That seems like a better "sorry" present than a watering can shaped like a cat.'

Mrs Phillips shook her head stubbornly. 'I very much liked my watering can, thank you very much. But anyway, I don't think you came all this way tonight to talk about my plans for the bed and breakfast, did you?'

Jo looked down at her drink, feeling ashamed and awkward. Mrs Phillips was right, again.

'Now I know you'll object when I say this, particularly in light of the way you reacted to your friend, but . . .' Mrs Phillips paused, 'I think you should talk to your mother.' She looked at Jo expectantly.

Despite her rage at the way Gill and Luke and everyone else had expressed their opinions on the matter, Jo didn't scream or shake her head or tell Mrs P she didn't know what she was talking about. She just looked at the woman and waited.

'You may have already guessed this, but I'm a divorcee myself.'

Jo didn't say anything. She knew that Ted and Pearl were no longer together. Which implied that Mrs P was a divorcee. She just hadn't stopped to think about what it meant. She hadn't made any connection between Pearl and her mother. The divorce was all they had in common, unless . . . Jo looked at Mrs Phillips, wondering whether she had any children.

'There were no children, if that's what you're thinking. Only cats. Well, one cat, by the time we split up. Poor Ronald. Yes, I know – we found him picking through scraps at the back of a McDonald's. But my point, Jo, is that going through a divorce is . . .' she waved her hands, searching for words, 'it's like nothing else on earth. People talk about it all the time – too much, really. There are books and TV programmes and statistics and news features, but unless you've actually experienced it for yourself, I don't think you'll ever know how it feels.'

Under different circumstances, Jo might have felt riled by the frankness of Mrs Phillips' words. But she didn't feel riled. She felt terrible.

'It's worse than an ordinary break-up,' Mrs Phillips said, looking into space. 'And it's not just the material things – the who-gets-what and the court proceedings and so on. It's the fact that you're ending something that you both agreed was to be for ever. In our case, we'd made it last thirty-nine years.'

Jo didn't know what to say. She could see the pain in Mrs Phillips' eyes – a pain that she now realised her mother had felt too, or perhaps still felt now. Clearly that was the point Mrs Phillips was trying to make.

'When you're in the middle of it all, it consumes you. It takes over your thoughts every minute of every day, and your dreams too – you never escape. You forget that there's anything else – anyone else – in the world. It's just you, and him, and everything crashing down around you.'

The way she was talking, it was as though she had divorced Ted yesterday. Jo wondered how fresh it would feel for her mother. She felt embarrassed and guilty for not having looked at the situation through her mother's eyes before. It was so obvious, now Mrs P was spelling it out to her, how crippling the pain of divorce must have been. And now, to add to it, along with the guilt she probably felt for causing the break-up and the worry of her daughter going 'off the rails', that same daughter had decided to fake her own death, make a surprise come-back, then refuse to communicate in any way. What a despicable thing to do.

'I'm not saying she forgot about your feelings,' Mrs Phillips went on. 'I'm just saying . . . well, she had a lot on her mind.'

Jo nodded. She got it now. It had taken too many months and too many explanations, but finally, she understood why she had to speak to her mother. She needed her Becky back. She needed someone.

'Who did you have?'

'Sorry?'

'Well, who helped you through? Ronald?'

Mrs Phillips smiled sardonically. 'No. Ted took him. I had the shop and the guesthouse. They kept me busy.' She paused, still looking at Jo. 'And I had my sherry.'

Slowly, the fog cleared and Jo understood. *That* was why Mrs Phillips had been so intuitive about the drinking. She'd been there herself.

'So! What are your plans?' Mrs P asked brightly, padding across the kitchen in her ridiculous slippers and piling things up in the sink. 'Start all over again and embark on a completely new life?'

Jo smiled and allowed her mug to be whisked away. 'No. I think I'm done starting new lives for now.'

It was a good question, actually. Jo meant what she said about not starting any new lives, but the fact remained, she had two on the go, and she wasn't really living either one. If the P. Jefferson contract worked out and she patched things up with her uni mates, she had a job and a social circle in London. If Matt and the Abingdon lot forgave her for abandoning them and she explained her actions to Sue, then there was a chance she could come back to Radley. It all depended on which path she chose. She felt like a piece of flotsam caught between two diverging streams.

'You should sleep on it,' said Mrs Phillips, wiping down the kitchen surface and dimming the lights.

Jo followed her across the landing and into her old bedroom. The sight of her neatly made bed made her want to cry with gratitude.

'Good night. Sleep well.'

''Night.'

Just as Jo was drifting off, there was a faint tap on her door. It opened and Pearl's head poked round.

'Sorry, I meant to give you this before. It's from your boy.'

'My . . .' Jo hauled her brain into gear. 'What?'

Mrs Phillips reached inside and dropped something on Jo's bedside table.

'He came round a few weeks ago. Wanted to see you but obviously I told him you'd gone. So he came back with this. Good night again.'

Squinting, Jo switched on the light and tore open the envelope. She looked at the jagged, blotchy handwriting and felt a swell of guilt course through her.

Dear Jo,

I hope this reaches you – Mrs P told me you've moved back to London.

There's loads of stuff I want to say, but I guess there's no point in saying most of it if you never want to see me again – and there's no point in saying it if you *do* want to see me again either, because I can just say it when I see you. Fuck, this isn't making much sense. I don't usually write letters.

I just wanted to explain why I did what I did. It might sound weird but hear me out.

I won't pretend to know how it feels to have amnesia, but I do know what it's like to be drifting. Everyone else seems to have these anchors – parents, friends, home, whatever, but you just have yourself. And you can't tell which direction you're heading in because you have no points of reference. You're just kind of going wherever the wind blows, feeling frustrated and angry and alone. Or at least, that's how it was for me.

It's the same for the kids. That's why they're like they are, and that's why you're good with them. (I know you say you're not, but you are. All the shit they give you is their way of showing affection – believe me, Kyle Merfield would *never* put his arms around anyone.) They're drifting too, and they need you to give them direction.

I know now that I did things the wrong way. But I was trying to help you find some anchor points of your own. Sorry if I messed everything up.

Good luck with your new/old life in London.

Love, Matt

PS. I'm moving to Manchester soon – got a job in Marketing at the Red Cross. So I guess we won't cross paths again.

Chapter Forty-Six

Two days had passed since Jo's return to the Radley guesthouse, and still the images of Matt – Matt playing football, Matt on top of her in bed, Matt cooking pizza – kept popping into her head, leaving her with a sense of frustration and loss. It was like throwing something into the fire, only to find later on that it was the ticket or banknote or letter that was your passport to a better life.

He was moving to Manchester. She had to forget about him. But it wasn't that easy. In her head, she kept going through all the things that she could have done differently to change the course of events. If she'd thought about why he'd done it . . . If she'd returned just one of his phone calls . . . If she'd come back and apologised to Mrs P before now . . . It was too late. Ironically, after weeks of *trying* to shrug him off, get him out of her life, he really had gone, and she wanted him back.

For short periods, Jo was able to fool herself into thinking she could get on with her life. On a practical level, she was doing fine. She had called Fairmont House and left a message for Sue, asking whether there was any chance of her old job back. She had spoken to one of the singsong girls at Flying High and told her she wouldn't be going back to P. Jefferson. She had spent a morning online, explaining to various friends that she was moving back to Radley – not Gill; she hadn't quite plucked up the courage for that exchange yet – and she had called her mother, whose answerphone had informed her that Mrs Ross would be in Spain until mid-December, which was odd, thought Jo, for someone supposedly racked with guilt and despair at her daughter's refusal to make contact.

The biggest question of all seemed to have answered itself by virtue of all the other, smaller ones. It now seemed obvious which path she would take. She was choosing Dunston's and the village life over the bustle and stress of the high-flying city career. And this time, it was for ever. Finally, she had made a decision that wasn't a consequence of a row or misguided loyalty. She had considered her options on the basis of who she really was. And she was Jo, not Becky. She was staying put.

Jo sipped her coffee and drew a cross next to the Regulations section in the 'How to Run a Guesthouse' pamphlet she had downloaded from the council's website. Mrs Phillips appeared at the top of the stairs.

'There's a young man in the shop, demanding to see you.'

Jo looked up. 'Is it . . . ?' She didn't need to say his name; he was the only young man who knew where she was living. Matt must have got wind of her return through Sue Meads. Jo felt panicked and – stupidly – a little hopeful as she slipped on her shoes.

'No.' Mrs Phillips retreated again with an anxious look on her face.

Jo took one more sip and rose to her feet, apprehensively. The only other young men she knew were Matt's friends, and they wouldn't be here on a weekday. Jo thought through all the people she had encountered since living with Pearl. Stuart, after another date? Trev, wanting his waitress back? Geoff? Surely he didn't count as young. She hurried down the stairs.

Jo knew who was lurking behind the magazine rack, even before he turned round. Dressed in a black hooded top and baggy jeans, the boy was hunched over as though bracing himself for a whack on the head.

'Kyle.'

He grunted, hands staying firmly in his pockets.

'What . . . What are you doing here?'

The boy shrugged and looked warily at Mrs Phillips, who was eyeing him equally suspiciously from her checkout post.

'D'you wanna . . . Shall we go for a walk?'

He lolloped out, letting the door swing shut in her face. Jo took this as a yes.

Kyle hadn't changed in the weeks since she'd last seen him – or at least, not as far as Jo could tell. But in her mind, he had. He seemed older. Wiser – if a twelve-year-old could ever be described as wise. In a strange way, Kyle had taught her things while she'd been in London. He would never know it, of course, but the boy had played a critical part in her decision-making.

The sky was a perfect blue, but a coating of frost lingered on the pavement where the sun hadn't shone and Jo wished she'd brought a coat.

'How did you know where I was?'

'Heard Sue talkin'.'

'But . . .' That wasn't actually what she had meant. 'You knew where I lived?'

'Followed you home once.'

'Oh.' Jo wasn't sure whether to be flattered or worried. This, presumably, was what had led to her inadvertent involvement in Kyle's late-night disappearance that time. 'Why did you do that?'

'Dunno.' Kyle pulled his hood up over his cap, so that no part of him was visible whatsoever. No wonder old ladies got scared, thought Jo.

They turned left at the end of the street, onto the road that led to the park where the lads played football.

'Is everything OK at home now?' asked Jo, remembering the scene in Geoff's office with Kyle's deranged mother.

The boy didn't answer. He might have shrugged inside his top but Jo couldn't tell.

'You haven't . . . run away again, have you?'

There was a slight movement inside the hood.

Not for the first time, Jo wished she was qualified to deal with situations like this. She wished she knew what you could and couldn't ask, how you steered this thing, what buttons you pressed or handles you turned to get the results.

'It's not the answer, Kyle.' She was treading on thin ice, she knew. Talking about Kyle's tendency to erupt and storm off could cause him to do exactly that: erupt and storm off. 'Running away. It's not the answer.'

'Uh?'

Jo was stumped. Not because she didn't know why running away was not the answer, but because Kyle had just made something abundantly clear to her. The twelve-year-old, with his inarticulate grunts, had opened her eyes to something that should have been obvious to her a long time ago.

She was a hypocrite. It was wrong of her to tell Kyle to stop running away, because she had done exactly that – several times. She had fled the scene of the explosion. She'd stormed out of Mrs Phillips' guesthouse. She'd tried to quit her job. She'd run away from her life in Radley, and Matt. And now, after fleeing to the greener pastures of London, she was turning her back on *that* and grovelling her way back to the life she'd abandoned. Jo had no right to preach to Kyle about running away.

'Sorry,' she said. 'I didn't mean that, exactly. Sometimes it feels like you just have to run away. I know. Like, when there's something you have to run away *from* . . .' Jo looked at Kyle, remembering his domestic situation. 'And I guess, if you can't think of any option but to run away, then that's all you can do, but . . .'

'*What?*'

'Um . . .' Jo suddenly realised that she'd been talking about herself and not Kyle. 'Sorry. Um . . . why did you come and see me today?'

The boy pushed on the park gate and barged through, leading the way to the small children's playground. Jo squeezed onto one of the swings, which gripped her rather tightly around the buttocks.

'Kyle?'

He leaned self-consciously against one of the roundabout handles, pulling a face, which was just visible beneath the cap and hood, that said, *work it out for yourself.*

'Kyle, I'm not psychic,' she said after several seconds of silence. Her hands were freezing.

It really did seem as though Kyle was trying to tell her subliminally. He fidgeted, kicking the hard ground with

413

his heel, then crossed and recrossed his arms. He shifted his weight from one foot to the other.

Jo ran through Kyle's history in her mind, in case she had missed something. He lived with his mother – a recovered heroin addict – and, until recently, his stepfather, who had almost certainly been the perpetrator of the red marks on his neck two months ago. After that incident, Sue had called Social Services. Presumably they had stepped in between Kyle and his stepfather. He was obviously still going to Fairmont for activities . . . What was the matter? And why was he coming to *her*?

Finally, there was a muttering from inside the hood. 'Colonel Megan girder risen,' it sounded like.

'What?'

'Colonel Megan go to prison.'

'Who's Colonel Megan?'

'Me dad!' he snarled angrily. 'They're *gonna make him go to prison*.'

'Oh.' Shit. This was serious. Jo tried to seek out Kyle's eyes, which were lost in the shadow of his cap. 'Why?'

Kyle shook his head impatiently. 'Because o' the bruises, innit?'

'Sorry . . .' Jo realised she sounded dense, but none of this was making any sense to her yet.

'You gotta stop 'em.'

'Stop the bruises?'

'No!' he yelled. 'Sue an' that! Stop 'em reporting me dad to the pigs!'

'Oh.' It was becoming clearer now, but Jo still didn't have the full picture. 'So . . . can you just explain to me what's going on here, exactly? Is this about the bruises on your neck that time?'

'*Yeah.*' (Delivered in a way that made it sound like 'duh!')

'Did your dad do that?'

'Yeah,' he said, much more quietly.

'And Sue reported it to Social Services?'

'Yeah, an' now we ain't allowed to live wiv 'im an' stuff.'

'So you're . . . you're living with your mum, away from your dad?'

'Yeah.'

Jo wrapped her hands inside her sleeves for warmth, thinking about the episode in Geoff's office. 'He's not your real dad, is he?'

Kyle stretched sideways and crushed a cider can with his foot. 'No.'

'Are you . . .' This was the difficult part. This was the bit Jo wasn't trained to do. 'Are you ever scared of him? I mean, when he gets violent?'

Kyle didn't answer. He ground the can into the hardened mud with his heel, then kicked it away. Jo cursed her inadequacy. What a *stupid* question. When was the last time a twelve-year-old skinhead admitted to being scared?

She rephrased the question. 'Is it better, not having him at home?'

Kyle finished denting the turf around his feet and looked at her. She could just about make out his eyes now. They were like slits of black ink. '*You ain't listening,*' he growled through gritted teeth. 'If they send 'im back to prison it'll be *my fault, innit!*' He raised his voice several notches. 'YOU CAN'T LET 'EM SEND 'IM BACK TO PRISON!'

The words echoed in Jo's ears. Finally, the situation made sense. Kyle was worried about taking the blame if his stepfather got sent to jail. She felt for him. She knew all about feeling guilty and wanting to run away. She wanted to reassure him, to tell him everything would be OK. But suddenly, she couldn't speak.

It wasn't just the fact that she didn't know the laws on what would happen to a man accused of nearly strangling his stepson. It was something else, something huge and ugly and sinister, blotting out everything else in her mind.

Kyle's outburst had triggered it. Prison. The paranoia. They were connected. The fear inside her – that sickening feeling of dread that she'd had ever since she'd come round from the blast – was something to do with prison.

'You gotta tell 'er,' said Kyle.

'Who?' Jo was clutching at memories that were just out of her reach.

'*Sue.*' He shook his head, kicking the roundabout as he walked away.

Jo tried to refocus. She slipped off the swing and rubbed her numb, squashed backside. All of a sudden, she felt anxious and fraught, just as she had done after the explosion. Her hands were shaking, not just from the cold, and there was a pressure building up in her head. It was exactly the same feeling, the same need to get away.

'I will,' she said, catching up with him at the edge of the park and desperately trying to sound convincing. 'I'll talk to her.'

He grunted and shoulder-barged his way through the gate.

'Kyle?'

He was already sloping off up the road.

'I'll do what I can!' She watched helplessly as he ignored her cries and shuffled towards the bus stop. She would speak to Sue to find out what the hell was going on in this poor boy's confusing, horrendous family life. But her mind kept flickering across. Like a car radio caught between two local stations, it was toggling between Kyle's situation and her own.

All the way along Radley Road, it flickered, but by the time she climbed the stairs of the guesthouse, she was temporarily out of range of Kyle's problems. Her mind was preoccupied by the ominous feeling. It hung, dark and heavy, like a layer of lead on her brain. She couldn't get any more clarity. She didn't know why Kyle's words had sparked it. It was just *there*, this obstacle that prevented her from thinking about anything else.

Her phone was lying on the kitchen table where she'd left it. With numb digits, she scrolled through the names.

'Hello?'

'Hi, Saskia, it's J— Beck— Roxie.'

'All right, Jabeckroxie! How's it goin'?'

'I need your help.'

'Nice to hear from you too. What is it this time?'

'Well . . .' Jo hesitated. 'This is gonna sound strange, but . . . Well, something weird happened today. Someone mentioned prison and I got all spooked out, like, scared. For some reason, I've got this feeling it's something to do with the club.'

There was silence at the other end.

'Saskia?'

After another short pause, Saskia replied, 'Fuck.'

'What?'

Saskia sighed. 'Fuck. I was waitin' for this.'

417

Chapter Forty-Seven

'I wasn't gonna tell you,' said Saskia. 'Fought you'd forgotten.'

Jo clamped the phone tightly against her ear. 'Tell me what?'

'Well . . . It was this thing that 'appened.'

'What? When?'

''Bout a year ago. When the old manager was running the club. Remember Pervy Pete?'

'Vaguely,' Jo scoured her memory. The flashbacks and the facts were all mixed up in her head.

'An' you was goin' out wiv Poncho.'

Jo pressed her finger and thumb into the corners of her closed eyes. *Pancho*. She hadn't really made a start on that part of the jigsaw.

''E was a dealer,' Saskia explained. 'I never met 'im. Colombian or something. Sounded like a bit of a twat to me, but you seemed to rate 'im – until he started fuckin' around. Anyway . . .'

Jo thought back to the scene that had popped into her mind when she'd been on the disastrous date with Stuart, reliving the feeling of hurt, of betrayal.

'Cocaine?'

'An' the rest. 'E got you supplyin' to all the girls in the club.'

While her university friends had been embarking on lucrative careers in the city, hosting dinner parties in Notting Hill, she had been stripping and sleeping with some promiscuous Colombian drug dealer. Jo recoiled at the depth to which Roxie had apparently sunk.

'Then one night there was a drugs bust.'

Jo's hands trembled as she waited for Saskia's next words.

'You 'ad a massive wad of the stuff in your bag. I mean, like, way too much. Enough for like ten girls or whatever. So you hid it.'

Jo was gripping the phone so tightly her fingers were starting to ache. 'Where?' There was a pause. 'Where did I hide it, Saskia?'

'In the manager's office. In a drawer.'

Jo didn't respond. Her brain was too full of questions and thoughts and emotions.

'But it was all cool,' Saskia went on. 'You got away wiv it. They 'ad dogs an' all, but they didn't find nothin'.'

'Oh. So . . .'

'But then the police came back. You hadn't shifted the stuff, an' they found it. Pervy Pete got taken away. Got four years for supplyin' Class A – although 'e's probably out by now.'

Jo couldn't speak. She couldn't allow herself to believe what Saskia was telling her.

'Rox?'

'Uh . . . ?'

'Rox, it's OK.'

'What?' Jo said weakly. *OK?* It wasn't the least bit OK. For a start, she had been dealing cocaine. But far worse, she had framed someone else for a crime she'd committed. A man had gone to prison because of her actions. It wasn't OK; it was unspeakable.

''E deserved it.'

'No!' Jo yelped, still reeling from the hideous revelation. Jesus, no wonder she'd been feeling paranoid for the last four months. 'No, nobody—'

'Shuddup!' yelled Saskia. 'Yes 'e *did*. 'E was well into the coke, too.'

Jo didn't reply.

''E 'ad it coming,' said Saskia, with venom in her voice. ''E was a bastard. You must remember.'

'I . . .' Jo didn't remember.

'Tried it on wiv all the girls an' that.'

'But . . .'

'No,' Saskia said forcefully. 'I know what you's thinkin'. But don't. No point. Nobody else knows, so just keep it like that. Only me an' you in the whole fuckin' world, Rox. Just keep your gob shut.'

Jo tugged her hand through her windswept hair, overwhelmed and not able to think straight. Part of her wanted to revert to her previous state of ignorance. Another part of her wanted to run to the police and own up, let them throw her into jail where she belonged. But the rest – the part of her that was all about self-preservation and survival – was already following her friend's advice.

'You OK?'

Jo jumped. She was so lost in her world of cocaine, paranoia and prison cells that she'd almost forgotten she was still on the phone.

'Yeah.'

'You're not gonna say nothin', are you?'

Jo hesitated. If she *was* going to say anything to anybody, then she wouldn't be doing it on a whim. She needed to let it sink in first, then consider her options. 'I guess not.'

'You *guess*?' echoed Saskia, perhaps taking her response a bit too literally. 'Fuckin' hell, Roxie, what're you on?'

Jo smiled faintly, putting aside the gigantic, eclipsing revelation for a second.

'I should be askin' for hush money,' Saskia laughed. 'I fuckin' need the cash.'

Grudgingly, Jo dragged herself back into the conversation.

'It ain't easy, going back to proper work after this long. You got work, where you are?'

'Er, sort of.'

It was no good. She couldn't think about anything else.

'Lucky you. Shout if there's anything spare going, eh?'

'I'll keep my eye out,' said Jo, half-heartedly. Then, somehow, she poked her head up out of the despair and thought of something. 'You wouldn't consider moving out of London, would you?'

'What for?'

'Well . . . a job in a shop, and maybe, like, other things too.'

'Er . . .'

'And a reference that would cover you for the last few years.'

'Oh, right. Fuck yeah, for *that*, I'd consider it.'

'I'll ask around.'

'Thanks, hun.' Saskia paused. 'Hey, look, Rox, you be careful, OK?'

'What, you mean like don't accidentally walk into any police stations and tell them what happened?'

'Well, no,' replied Saskia, again missing the sarcasm. 'Just . . . take care.'

Jo managed a smile. No matter how different they were, or how quickly their lives were converging and diverging, one thing was for sure about Saskia: she was a good friend.

'I will.'

Jo lowered the phone and let her head drop onto the table. The door opened behind her.

'Jo? Are you there?' Mrs Phillips poked her head in. 'Ah. I've got someone on the phone for you downstairs. She says she's your *mother* . . . ?'

Chapter Forty-Eight

'You have *one* new message,' said the voicemail android. 'Received today, at two thirty-two.'

'Hello!' It was Sue. Jo pressed the phone to her ear, blocking out the loud, unintelligible station announcement as she bleeped through the Finchley Road barriers. 'I got your message. That's wonderful news. I was just talking about your role with Geoff. He's, er, he's got some ideas . . .' She said this in a tone that suggested the ideas weren't necessarily very good. 'I think he's going to call you to discuss them. Oh, and I'm sure you haven't forgotten, but the kids have their tournament next Saturday. I think . . . I think it'd mean a lot to them if you went along. Anyway. Bye for now.'

Jo was about to delete the message when Sue's voice came back on the line. 'Ooh, one more thing, sorry. Are you still there? Er, no, obviously not *there*, um, sorry . . . It's about Kyle. I got your message. I think things might have blown a little bit out of proportion in his head. His stepfather hasn't been charged with anything, so nobody's going to jail. I'll have a word with Kyle. OK, talk soon!'

Jo's stomach flipped. *Nobody's going to jail.* Except maybe her, if she turned herself in. She hadn't decided what to do. She was still coming to terms with the fact that she was a criminal.

Her phone bleeped again as she turned into Broadfield Gardens.

From: Kieran
Indeed. I know all about council
guesthouse regs – did a
placement in Licence &
Permit Dept. Hit me! K

Jo's smile, ignited by the concept of Kieran in a position of authority, was short-lived as she realised that her friend's eccentricity was just another one of the things she'd have to do without for the next four years if she turned herself in.

She forced the thoughts into a faraway corner of her mind and breathed in the cold night air. It smelled faintly of spices and log fires. Some of the houses had Christmas lights on display. They were more subtle than the gaudy, full-colour LED affairs she had seen along Radley Road: beads of white lights, bauble-hung trees, Nativity scenes. On top of the nerves and the fear, Jo felt a little nostalgic.

The road was strangely familiar. Very familiar. Jo looked down at the pavement and realised she knew where to expect the tree roots to poke through. She knew which part of the street had good kerbs for football. She knew where to find the little clearing with its miniature climbing frame and slide. It felt familiar. It felt . . . it felt like *home*.

In her pocket was a scrap of paper that told her the house number and directions, but she didn't look at it. Her instincts led her straight to the red-brick semi that was number nine, where, pausing with her hand on the rusty gate, she looked up at her old family home. Her mouth felt like cardboard.

Her childhood had been a happy one, she knew that much. The details were hazy; she could only vaguely remember the climbing frame, the football, the family next door. But she remembered the feeling of security, the warmth and the safety. It was a far cry from the apprehension she felt now.

Her finger hovered over the doorbell. This was it. She was about to face the woman who, in some ways, was responsible for all the devastation in her life, and who, up until a few weeks ago, had assumed her only daughter to be dead.

She suddenly felt overcome with terror. This was big. She was meeting her mum. The last few weeks had been difficult enough, meeting old friends, acquaintances, colleagues . . . but this was far more important. Jo wasn't sure how it would go. On the phone, her mother had seemed, well, *placid*. She hadn't given much away. But then, it was different on the phone—

'Rebecca!' The door nearly swung off its hinges.

Jo stood, hand raised, mouth open. Her mother was tall, like her, with a graceful physique and a surprisingly youthful complexion. Her shoulder-length brown hair was faintly streaked with white. This was all Jo managed to take in before she was swept off the step and whisked inside.

'Oh, Rebecca, you *silly* girl!'

Jo's head was squeezed against her mother's chest, which started to heave in time with the sobs.

Up until this point, Jo had been so preoccupied

worrying that her mother wouldn't let her in, or that they would row and Jo wouldn't have answers to her accusatory questions, or that her mum would describe how ashamed she'd been of the sordid details she'd read in the papers, that she hadn't stopped to think about how this might feel. But now she was here, in her mother's arms, it was like . . . well, it was like being a child again; she felt secure, warm and safe.

Finally, her mother released the pressure on her head and they pulled apart.

'Look at you! You've still got that ridiculous red thing!' Her mother tugged fondly at the lock of hair, then wiped her teary eyes.

Jo held her gaze, and to her surprise, found herself crying too.

'Hi, Mum.'

They hugged again. Jo leaned against her mother's warm body, crying and laughing at once, her mother's perfume bringing back faint memories of childhood hugs.

'I'll make some tea,' said her mother, when they could hug no more.

Jo followed her into the kitchen. Small, neat and functional, with a little fold-out table in one corner, it felt immediately familiar.

'I presume you still love chocolate digestives?'

Jo smiled as a family-sized pack was pulled out of the cupboard. Then she watched her mother add a handful of what looked like twigs to the pot of tea and the air filled with an overpowering aroma of cinnamon. *Cinnamon. Special tea.* Jo smiled.

Together, they loaded a small tray with mugs, milk, biscuits and tea, and Jo carried it through to the lounge.

426

She stopped on the way in, surveying as if for the first time the place where she had spent much of her childhood.

She set the tray down and wandered across the room, scanning the photos that were dotted about the place. In some, she was on her own: Jo the baby, all chubby and pink, Jo the freckle-faced girl, Jo the lanky teenager. Her mother featured in a few, as well as a man with thick glasses and receding hair. He had a soft, smiling face and dark eyes that she recognised as her own. Jo smiled at the image of her dad.

He looked like a soft, caring type. Perhaps a little scatty, she thought, seeing that in one photo – a group shot of a dozen girls and their parents at some sort of ceremony – he was dressed in a checked shirt and corduroys whilst everyone else was wearing a suit. Jo put the picture down and looked around.

The individual items of furniture weren't immediately familiar, but the place was. Jo remembered its warmth, its cosiness. She knew she had spent lots of time here. The thick-pile carpet under her feet, the smell of pine cones coming from the basket on the hearth, the sound of the little clock, the—

'What's *that*?'

Jo stared at the incongruous item. She felt sure it didn't belong on the mantelpiece.

'Oh, Pedro?' Her mother walked over and squeezed the plastic reindeer's belly.

Jo stared as the grotesque ornament started flashing and emitting a high-pitched noise that sounded vaguely like a Christmas carol. It had a giant sombrero wedged over its antlers.

'Lovely, isn't it?' Jo's mum had a glint in her eye. 'It's

427

my Christmas present from your dad.' She poured the tea.

'Wh—' There were so many questions vying for space in her head, Jo couldn't speak.

'He's in Spain,' said her mother, passing Jo her mug. That answered one of them, then. 'Costabella. Near where we used to go every year.'

Jo nodded, grasping her tea and picturing a white-washed villa in the sun, with a rug on the patio and lots of toys . . . Costabella. Then her mind flipped forward to the moment outside the tourist information office and she remembered the ease with which she'd translated the guidebook title.

'How much do you remember?' asked her mum. 'Your friend told me you had quite bad amnesia.'

Jo smiled awkwardly and thought of Gill. That was another person she still had to see. 'She's right. I do. But I've pieced stuff together. I know you and Dad split up because of . . .'

'Roger,' her mother inserted. 'My colleague, whom I was briefly seeing when things weren't so good between your dad and me.'

'*Roger?*'

'Yes, I know, I know. Please don't lecture me. I've tortured myself enough in the last eighteen months, believe me.'

'No, I just mean . . .' Jo screwed up her nose. She already knew about the affair. It was the name that alarmed her.

'Anyway,' her mother went on, 'that blew over.' She stirred her tea furiously. 'But the damage was done. Your father and I separated last year and he moved to Spain.'

'Oh.' Jo nodded, wondering whether her dad even *knew*

about his daughter's exploits. 'So he's been there ever since?'

'Well, you know what he's like . . .' Her mother stopped. 'Or maybe you don't. But I'm sure you can imagine the appeal: sun, sea, a little villa with a pool and a maid that cost about three pounds . . . The most stressful thing he has to do every day is put up the parasol.'

Jo took a chocolate digestive. She didn't entirely remember her dad, but now she had seen the photos and heard her mother talk, it felt as though she knew him, vaguely. 'Doesn't he work?'

'Occasionally. Bits and bobs. A week's over-paid consultancy lasts him about a year out there.'

'Consultancy?' Jo tried to visualise her father in the glass-walled P. Jefferson office.

'Telecoms.' The image disappeared. 'You really don't remember, do you?'

'Well . . .' Jo dunked the biscuit in her tea. It was hard to explain. She did and she didn't. Once she heard the answers, it all made perfect sense. She just couldn't summon the answers herself. It was like the difference between having general knowledge of a subject and knowing the material well enough for an exam. Hearing her mother describe things, well . . . She'd been avoiding it for months, but it was exactly what she needed.

'So your father was fortunate enough to miss all the paraphernalia that went with the Buffalo Club bomb.'

'He doesn't know?'

'Well, he does now. But he didn't for a while. I hadn't told him about your chosen "career path", you see.'

Jo looked guiltily at the carpet.

'Even after the bomb, I didn't tell him initially. Not till

I knew for sure. But then when they listed the survivors and you weren't on there, and your phone was dead, and you didn't make contact . . .'

Jo could hardly look at her mum. When she did, she noticed her eyes were filling up again. '*Sorry,*' she whispered.

After all the time spent mulling things over, all the conversations with Mrs P and opinions from Gill et al., it was only now that she realised the full extent of her selfishness.

'It was unbearable,' said her mother, choking on the last word. Jo moved over to the sofa and squeezed in next to her. 'You just . . . disappeared. I thought, well, I *wanted* to think you were still alive. I persuaded myself I had some sort of mother's gut feeling, but . . .' She shook her head and reached for a tissue. 'Anyway, that's when I told your dad.'

Jo didn't speak. Neither of them did for a minute or so. They sat on the sofa, thighs touching, listening to the sound of the ticking clock. Eventually, Jo's unanswered questions got the better of her.

'What happened?'

'Oh.' Her mother wiped her eyes. 'Well, I suppose it was a good thing what happened, in the long run. I went out to see him and we did lots of talking and crying. Somewhere along the line I suppose we sort of patched things up.'

'You suppose?' Jo looked at her mother hopefully.

'Well, we didn't rush out and get married all over again, if that's what you're thinking.' She forced a little smile. 'We're still divorced. But at least we're speaking again. We're on good terms.'

Jo smiled too. 'So that's where you were last week?'

Her mother nodded. 'I went out again, once I knew you were OK. Once your friend told me you were OK.'

Jo winced. *Gill* had made contact, not her. And then, once she had, Jo hadn't thanked her; she had stormed out in a rage. Jo couldn't believe how misguided her reactions had been. If it hadn't been for Gill and Matt and Mrs Phillips and all the other people who had stepped in against her will, she wouldn't have been sitting here clutching her mother's hand.

'I'm an idiot,' said Jo, flatly.

Her mum laughed and shook her head. 'You're just . . . Rebecca.'

'I'm mean and inconsiderate and thoughtless and—'

'Oh, shh!' She looked up to the ceiling and then back at her daughter. 'You could say the same about me, anyway. Perhaps it runs in the family.'

Jo shook her head. This had been her line of thought for the last few months. She had convinced herself that her mother had been to blame for her own downfall. But equally, the converse was true. Perhaps they were as bad as each other.

'And the resilience,' said her mother. 'That's in the genes too. Your friend told me about how you'd bounced back.'

Jo lifted one corner of her mouth. Gill, again. Gill, with her endless zest and enthusiasm. Jo had mistaken all that for phoniness; she had seen her need to get involved as an intrusion. Now she realised; she'd been trying to help.

'I can just imagine you, wandering around with amnesia, determined not to go to anyone for help. Anyone else would've held up their hands, walked into the nearest police station and explained the problem. But, oh no, not *my* daughter. *My* daughter decides to jump on a bus and start a *new* life in Oxfordshire on her own!'

Jo couldn't quite bring herself to laugh. Clearly, Gill had brought her mother up to date on the events of the last few months, and her mother was – among other things – proud. But her mother didn't know *why* she had fled the scene of the bomb, why she had been so desperate to get away. She didn't know that her daughter was a criminal.

'You always were resourceful. D'you remember when you were four, when we went to the New Forest to try out our new tent?'

Jo shook her head. Of course she didn't remember.

'Your dopey father had forgotten to pack the tent poles. So you went foraging in the forest and found us some sticks, you did, without anybody telling you to! At four!'

Jo thought back to her Flying High assessment day, and chuckled.

'Was Dad always dopey?'

Her mother smiled wistfully. 'I suppose he was, yes. Chilled out, that's probably how he'd prefer to be described. That was what drew me to him in the first place.' She laughed quietly through her nose. 'And what drove me away, in the end.'

Jo said nothing. She could imagine the household dynamic: her mother, rushing around, sorting things out, being pragmatic and organised, Rebecca following closely in her footsteps at a hundred miles an hour, and her father, sitting calmly in the eye of the tornado, reading a newspaper or humming a tune.

'Is he planning to stay out in Spain?'

Her mother took a sip of her lukewarm tea and turned her nose up, putting it back on the tray. 'He's not sure,' she said, shrugging. 'He's never sure. I think it suits him out there, though.'

'Leisurely pace of life, I guess.' Jo nodded.

'*Leisurely?*' She snorted. 'Leisurely would give them a heart attack! Static, more like. Nothing moves at more than a snail's pace. It's like trying to live your life in treacle over there!' She shook her head impatiently, then gradually, the corner of her lip turned up. 'He said he might come back for Christmas, but who knows.'

Jo watched her mother's expression and felt something shift inside her. The wound that had been raw for months was finally beginning to heal. 'I'm so glad.'

Her mother squeezed her hand. 'Me too, actually.' She reached round and hugged Jo closer. 'I guess we've got you to thank for that. Amazing how a death brings people together!'

Jo's smile was fake. She felt awful for what she had done.

They stayed like that for a while, Jo's head nestled in the crook of her mother's neck, their shoulders pressed up against one another.

Eventually, her mother sprang into action. 'More tea?'

They stacked the tray and moved into the kitchen.

'Your friend told me about the boy you were seeing.' She dried her hands and leaned back on the counter. 'Have you forgiven him yet, for leaking your story?'

Jo was slightly taken aback by her mother's apparent knowledge of her love life. The answer, of course, was yes. She had forgiven Matt for doing something that, on reflection, had helped her in so many ways. But it was too late for forgiveness.

'Rebecca, we all do things we regret,' she added, mistaking Jo's contemplation for uncertainty.

'Oh, I know.'

That was true. Her mum didn't know quite how appropriate her comment was; she had no idea what her daughter had done.

'I mean, I had a fling with a man called *Roger*, for God's sake.'

Jo smiled. She stepped forward and allowed her mother's arms to wrap around her, her chin to nestle against her shoulder. She shut her eyes, still smiling, and felt a warm, wet tear of relief trickle down her cheek.

Chapter Forty-Nine

Jo sat on her bed, staring anxiously into space and thinking about all the things she would miss: Mrs Phillips' home-made marmalade, the elderly Radley residents . . . she'd even miss Nadia's sniffing and Kyle's prolific use of the C-word. She leaned over and picked up the grey card from her bedside table. Her hands were shaking.

She forced herself not to think about the enormity of what she was about to do. For two long, lonely nights, she had grappled with the options, making lists, pros and cons, conscience versus survival, tossing and turning, feeling crushed by the fear. She had wanted to scream. Last night, the anxiety had gripped her so tightly that she'd had to stuff her face in the pillow and let out a muffled whimper of panic.

There was so much she wanted to blot from her mind: what Bronzefield Women's Prison was like inside, how much of a four-year sentence she'd be likely to serve, how her mother would react when she found out, whether she ought to tell anyone the truth before owning up . . . she was fighting a losing battle.

The fact was, she couldn't live in this thick, black cloud of guilt all her life. She had to confront her actions, own up to them, and stop running away. The sooner she picked up the phone and arranged to meet DI Davis to tell him the news, the sooner she'd be tried and sentenced and the sooner – in however many years – she'd be let out. Jo had made her decision.

'Metropolitan CID, how can I help?'

'Um . . .' Jo was thrown by the woman's voice. For some reason she had envisaged getting straight through, like they did in the films. 'I need to speak to Detective Inspector Michael Davis.'

'And your name is . . . ?'

'Jo – Rebecca Ross.'

'Rebecca? And can I ask what it's regarding?'

'Um . . . the Buffalo Club . . . thing. Well, sort of.' She wavered. 'Something that happened at the Buffalo Club.'

'The bomb investigation, then?'

'Um . . . yes.'

'Hold on one moment.'

The moment stretched out for what seemed like hours as a tinny voice reeled through tips for personal safety and warned of the dangers of identity fraud. Jo switched the phone to her other ear and wiped a sweaty, shaking palm on her jeans.

'Rebecca? It's Detective Inspector Davis. How are you?'

The fear surged up in her throat like bile. She needed to swallow but her mouth was dry. Every part of her body was willing her to put the phone down, but her conscience wouldn't allow it.

'I . . . I have some information.'

'Regarding the Buffalo Club bomb?'

'Well, not exactly. It's to do with the club, but not, um, the bomb.'

'OK . . .' The uncertainty was apparent in his voice.

'It's about a crime that happened a little while ago in the club.'

'Riiiight . . .'

'The arrest of the old manager. Pete—' She broke off, realising that the only other name she had for him was Pervy.

'OK. And what is the nature of your information?'

The nature? Jesus. Why couldn't he just ask what it was? Her imminent admission was bearing down on her.

'It's drugs related.'

'Right. Well, sounds like one for Narcotics. If you don't mind, I'll get one of my colleagues to give you a call back. Is that all right?'

I'M A CRIMINAL. The words were burgeoning inside her, begging to come out.

'OK.'

'And if anything does come to mind about the explosion or anything else, do call again, won't you?'

Jo was deaf to the man's parting remarks; she was too busy trying to come to terms with the fresh surge of fear in her throat. She still had to do the deed. She still had to talk to Michael Davis's colleague. But for now – and this was the frustrating anticlimax – for the next few minutes, or hours, or however long it took, she was a free woman.

She jumped. The shop phone was ringing.

'Radley Convenience Store,' she said, the words just tripping out of their own accord while her mind continued to tie itself in knots.

'Don't put the phone down, don't put the phone down, don't—'

'I won't. Who is this?'

'Phew! It's me, Gill. I wasn't sure whether it'd be you or Old Mrs Miggins picking up. God, you wouldn't believe the problems I've had trying to track you down!'

'Mmm . . .'

It was too much to cope with at once. This wasn't going according to plan. Jo had intended for Gill to find out about her wrongdoing *afterwards*, once she had owned up and it was too late to be talked round. She couldn't chicken out now.

'Are you OK, Becks?'

'Yeah, fine.' Jo tried to blot out the emotions and say something sensible.

'You sound a bit weird – oh, you're in the shop, of course. I'll be quick. I just wanted to say sorry for being a nosy parker and getting involved in things that are none of my business, and to say that I hope we can still be friends.'

'Cool.' Jo tried to focus, to think of the right thing to say. Gill was apologising.

'Did you go round?'

'Round where?'

Gill tutted. 'To your *mum's*. I gave her this number. She did call, didn't she?'

'Oh, yeah. Yeah, I went round.'

'And?'

'Well . . .'

Under different circumstances, Jo would have relished the opportunity to thank her for building the bridge with her mother. She would have told her about going round to Finchley Road and she would have said sorry, too, for rejecting Gill's kindness and storming out. But her mind

438

was so crowded with worry and fear that she couldn't form a sentence.

'You're obviously busy,' said Gill. 'Call me back when it's a better time, eh?'

'Mmm.'

'You are OK, aren't you, Becks?'

'Er, yeah.'

'Sounds like you're stoned or something. You haven't slipped back into the world of drink and drugs and shagging strip-club managers, have you?'

Jo forced a little laugh, and then stopped. 'What did you say?'

'I was joking. I didn't—'

'No, I mean, about shagging . . .'

'Strip-club managers? Oh, I dunno. It was just something I heard on the grapevine ages ago – probably nothing. Sorry, shouldn't have said it.'

'No, it's . . .' Jo trailed off. In her mind, she was holding one of the jigsaw pieces above the puzzle, trying to work out where it fitted. *She had been shagging the manager?*

'OK then, speak soon!'

Jo mumbled goodbye and scrabbled around for her mobile.

Saskia wasn't picking up. Jo tried again, her knee jiggling nervously to the sound of the monotonous *brrr, brrr* and then Saskia's chirpy voicemail.

'Hey! This is Saskia . . .'

Jo left a quick, desperate message and then sent a follow-up text, just in case. Staring at the handset, she wondered whether there was anything else she could do – any other way of getting hold of Saskia, or finding out more. *Facebook*. That was the answer. She frantically started pressing buttons, wondering how to log on using her phone. Raj would know.

Then it rang. *Withheld number*. Jo snatched it up.

'Hello?'

'Ah, hello there,' said a jovial male voice. 'Is that Ms Rebecca Ross? This is Sergeant Reynolds from the Metropolitan CID. I understand you have some information for us?'

Jo froze. Gill's comment had muddied the water. She no longer felt so sure about turning herself in. And, she thought, if she *did* turn herself in, she wanted to work a few things out beforehand. Like whether she'd been sleeping with Pervy Pete when she'd got him arrested.

'Anything you tell us, Ms Ross, will be treated as confidential, of course. We have very strict rules on non-disclosure and if you're informing on someone then I can assure you that your identity will remain anonymous . . .'

Sergeant Reynolds went on, but all Jo could hear was the beep-beep-beep that informed her she had a call waiting.

'Sorry,' she said eventually. 'Could you just hold for a second?'

'No problem.'

'Hello?'

'Rox, it's me. What the fuck's going on this time?'

'Oh, thank God. It's all a bit confusing.'

'As ever.'

'I've got someone on the other line – let me just tell him to wait. Er . . . Mr Reynolds?'

'*Sergeant* Reynolds, yes, hello.'

'Oh, sorry. I've just got to speak to someone quickly. Do you mind holding?'

'Depends what the information is you've got for us.'

'Um—'

'Go on, I'm joking.'

'Right. OK . . . Saskia?'

'Yes, ma'am.'

'I have a question. It's a bit . . . random.'

'What a surprise.'

'Was I sleeping with Pervy Pete at any point, d'you know?'

'Gyheugh!' she spluttered. 'I hope not!'

Jo felt her hopes plummet. She wanted there to have been some truth in Gill's remark, so that somehow, maybe, in some way, she could say that she hadn't been entirely to blame for the cocaine incident – that Pervy Pete had been involved after all.

'What gave you that idea?'

'Oh, nothing.'

'What, *nothing* made you suddenly wonder whether you'd been knockin' off some twat-faced pervert?'

'Yeah, look, I'd better go—'

'Anyway, you'd never've got away wiv it if you had. Poncho woulda killed you.'

'Right. Thanks. I should go—'

'Mind you, dunno which woulda been worse . . .'

'See you later, Saskia. Um, Sergeant Reynolds?'

'Ms Ross.'

'Sorry about that.'

He grunted in acknowledgement. 'Do you want to start by telling me which case your information relates to?'

Her jaw was shaking uncontrollably.

'The case of Pete – er, the manager of the club getting caught with, um, a certain amount of cocaine, about a year ago.'

She sounded clueless. It was a wonder that Sergeant Reynolds didn't put the phone down on her there and then.

'Are you talking about the arrest of Francisco Gonzalez Quesada in October last year?'

'Wh— Er, no, I don't think so. Was there . . . was there another case involving the Buffalo Club, around that time?'

There was a rustle of papers at the other end.

'No. That's the only narcotics case in the last four years. And I should know – I headed up the investigation.'

Jo frowned. The nerves were still fluttering in her stomach, but she tried to get a grip. Assuming Saskia's sources were accurate, Pervy Pete had been arrested and charged with supplying Class A. And according to Sergeant Davis, the only case on file had involved a man called Francisco, not Pete.

'Could you just, er, run me through the details of that case?'

The sergeant laughed sarcastically. 'You want me to read out the case file?'

'No, just . . . What he was accused of. And sentenced to.'

He sighed. 'Possession with Intent to Supply, and four years.'

'OK . . .'

The information swam around in Jo's head. The only conclusion she could draw was that Pervy Pete *was* Francisco What's-his-face. Which didn't make much sense.

Sergeant Reynolds cleared his throat noisily. 'If I may, Ms Ross, I'd like to suggest you have a think about the facts and then get back to me when you have a clearer picture.'

'Right,' she said, nodding to herself. 'Yeah.'

She had just worked something out. Or at least, she thought she had. She had an idea about where the jigsaw piece went. And if she was right – and it was a big 'if' – then the sweating palms, the dry throat, the sleepless nights and the horrible, dark feeling of paranoia that had troubled her ever since the explosion would have all been for nothing.

'Saskia, it's me again.'

'What now?'

'Just quickly. Can you tell me: did I stop seeing Pancho at around the same time that Pervy Pete got put away?'

'Er . . . I guess. Can't really remember.'

'Try.'

'Ooh, I know,' said Saskia, suddenly excited. 'It was around then, yeah, 'cause I made a joke. When the new bloke took over an' got all those new customers in, I said something about you needing a poncho 'cause it was raining men – ha! Get it? Poncho . . .'

The jigsaw piece *seemed* to fit, thought Jo, almost not daring to ask her next question in case the response thwarted her theory. She took a deep breath.

'Did Pervy Pete have any sort of accent?'

'Well, 'e never spoke, hardly ever.'

Jo waited, hoping, willing Saskia to remember.

''E sort of grunted, and snarled, like. And perved.'

'But when he did speak?' Jo prompted. 'Occasionally?'

'Ummmmm . . .' Saskia seemed to be meditating or something.

Jo waited, biting her lip, trying to contain her urge to scream.

'Actually, now you mention it . . .' She sucked on her teeth. Jo held her breath. 'Yeah. "Go ghome," 'e used to say. If we pissed 'im off. Not, "Go home." "Go ghhhh-home."'

Jo exhaled and found herself smiling. It was as though a massive weight that had been crippling her for months had finally been lifted.

'Is that it for now? No more random questions?'

'Thanks, yeah. That's it for now.'

Jo dropped the phone in her lap and lay back on the bed, the smile spreading across her face. She felt light, all of a sudden, as though someone had come along and relieved her of a heavy load.

It all made sense. There was no mysterious Colombian drug dealer called Poncho or Pancho; that had just been the name she'd used to avoid people – including Saskia – finding out that she was seeing the manager.

She, in true, misguided Roxie style, had been sleeping with Pervy Pete – or, to use his real name, Francisco Gonzales Quesada. She had been his drugs mule; his pawn. That was why she'd felt betrayed by the guy in the flashbacks – not because of another woman. And then, perhaps deliberately, perhaps simply out of sheer desperation, she had ended up framing the man who'd been guilty of the crime all along.

Jo closed her eyes, hearing the chink and clatter of Mrs P's dinner preparations through the wall. She was still a criminal, legally speaking, but morally she was clear. And she had changed, anyway. She was Jo Simmons now, not Roxie.

Another piece slotted into place in the still-incomplete jigsaw puzzle. And as it did, something else happened too. The cloud lifted. The sense of foreboding that had plagued her for over four months was gone.

She stared up at the ceiling, trying to make sense of this last realisation. The paranoia had gone. Which seemed to imply, she thought, that it had had something to do with the cocaine incident. But it couldn't have, because the girl who had crawled away from the site of the bomb would have known about Pancho's culpability, and would have felt no guilt. So . . .

Jo closed her eyes and took a long, steady breath, inhaling the smell of Mrs P's roast chicken. There seemed to be only one explanation: It wasn't the cocaine incident that had forced her to flee the scene, that had hung over her ominously ever since. It was her old life.

She'd been running away from Roxie's life.

Chapter Fifty

'I don't mean to sound rude,' said Mrs Phillips as they worked their way along the aisle, 'but is she *trustworthy*?'

Jo smiled anxiously. It was a bit late for asking that, she thought, but it was a fair question. As someone who had survived for the last few years by dealing low-grade cocaine, forging documents and taking her clothes off, Saskia wasn't the most obvious choice of assistant – not that Mrs P knew all the squalid details.

'She's very loyal,' Jo replied truthfully, thinking about the huge, ugly secret that Saskia had faithfully guarded.

'Hmm. And how long do you think she'll stay?'

That, thought Jo, was another good question. Given Saskia's track record, or lack of, in gainful employment, it was possible she wouldn't even see out the week. But, having heard her friend's earnest intentions to clean herself up and get 'a real job', Jo was quietly hopeful that the arrangement might work out.

'If you give her the incentive of a reference that goes back, say, two years,' Jo reached to the back of the shelf for a stray can of plum tomatoes that looked like a relic from the Second World War, 'I reckon she'll stay a few months.'

The door of the shop flew open and hit the magazine rack with some force.

''Ello! Anyone in?'

Jo looked at Pearl, who raised a thin eyebrow apprehensively. Then they both hurried to the front of the shop.

The sight that greeted them was unusual, to say the least. Saskia, wearing bug-eye sunglasses, spray-on jeans, furry boots and what looked like an inflatable polythene jacket, was standing in the doorway surrounded by bags, one hand held out at right-angles to stabilise the magazine stand.

'Hey!' She broke into a movie-star smile and pushed the shades up into her hair. The rack clattered to the floor. Saskia cast a quick backward glance and then hopped over the self-made barricade, throwing herself at Jo. 'Good to see ya!'

'You too.' Jo smiled as she was engulfed in the squeaky fabric, her eyes wandering to the pile of bags and the magazines all over the floor.

'Sorry 'bout that,' said Saskia, jerking a thumb over her shoulder at the carnage. 'God, you look shit, hun.'

'Thanks.' Jo stepped back to catch Mrs Phillips' eye. She looked rather tense. 'This is Saskia. Saskia, this is—'

'Mrs P! Yeah, I've heard all about you. Nice to meet you, Mrs P.' She leaped forward and hugged the old woman – a greeting that clearly Mrs Phillips hadn't been expecting.

'Oh! Oh, nice to meet you too, Saskia.' She extracted herself with a nervous smile and looked over at the landslide by the door.

'Don't worry about them, Mrs P. I'll sort it out. Think you might need a new mags rack.'

Mrs Phillips smiled politely. 'That one's lasted me ten years.'

'Well, there you go!' said Saskia, clearly missing the point.

Jo laughed awkwardly. Suddenly, this idea of hers seemed like a very dubious one.

'Shall we get your bags put away? I'll show you upstairs. Pearl, you're all right to watch the shop for a mo, aren't you?'

'I have done in the past,' she replied tightly.

'Um, right.' Jo hauled three of Saskia's bags over her shoulder. 'Jeez! I think you're gonna need an extra bedroom for all your stuff!'

Saskia stomped up the stairs behind her. 'Nah, I fink I'll be all right.'

Jo smiled. 'Right, are you OK to come back down and talk shop with Mrs P before you unpack?'

''Course!' Saskia chucked her sunglasses onto the bed and looked around. Her eyes met with the shelf of porcelain cats and then roamed over the collage of cat prints and the Top Felines poster. 'Is Mrs P into cats?'

'I suppose she is!' Jo gave up on the irony.

'Ah, cute.' Saskia picked up a small, tortoiseshell thimble and then plonked it back down again. 'I love cats.'

They made their way back downstairs, Jo dreading the moment when she would leave the two women alone together. Really, she thought, aside from their mutual adoration of cats – which could only sustain conversation for so long – they had nothing in common.

'You do look shit,' Saskia told Jo as they re-entered the shop.

'Thanks. You said.' Jo led them back to the counter where Mrs Phillips was sitting primly, having restacked the magazines.

'Your eyes are all poky and pink. What's up?'

'Just tired,' she lied. Now was not the time to explain that she'd spent the last two nights wrangling over whether to go to the police over a crime that turned out to be an affair with their sleazy ex-boss.

'She's been busy,' explained Mrs Phillips from her rickety checkout stool.

'Oh.' Saskia looked at Jo, then back at the shopkeeper. 'Doin' what?'

'Meeting up with old friends and family.'

'Oh, right.'

Jo watched incredulously as the conversation proceeded to go ahead without her.

'Why's that tirin', then?' Saskia frowned at the old lady.

'Well, it's emotionally tiring, isn't it? Jo hasn't seen her mother since before the explosion.'

Jo held up her hands and waved theatrically. 'Er, hello!' Suddenly, the tide had turned. Instead of being the link that was desperately trying to bind the two women together, Jo was now fighting to break them apart.

'Who's Jo?' asked Saskia, looking puzzled.

'Me! Hello!' Jo looked from Saskia to Pearl and then back again. 'I am *here*.' She danced about in an attempt to attract their attention. As she did, the shop door opened and the magazine stand toppled over in the breeze.

'Oh, heavens!' cried Mrs Phillips as a man with a Russian military hat and thick gloves walked in.

'Sorry I'm late,' he muttered, stamping his feet on the door mat and removing the ridiculous headwear. 'Ooh. Oh dear. You need a new magazine rack.'

He pushed the door shut with a large black boot and

made his way towards them, clutching the monstrous hat and a bundle of papers.

'I'm Kieran. Nice to meet you.'

Jo hadn't had a chance to warn the women properly about the third member of the team today. If she had, she might have explained that whilst holding a relatively senior position in Oxfordshire County Council and allegedly having extensive knowledge of local guesthouse regulations, Kieran *was* known for blurting out facts from his head that bore no relation to anything.

'Um . . . right.' Jo looked around, introductions complete. 'Well, I guess I should leave you all to it.'

Nobody moved. Jo cursed herself again for being stupid enough to expect these unlikely characters to get along. It had been awkward with just Saskia and Mrs Phillips, but now with Kieran in the mix as well . . .

It was too late to be having second thoughts.

'Come on, out you get!' She barged into the checkout area and gently shepherded Mrs Phillips onto the shop floor. 'Go upstairs and start scheming. I'll look after the shop.'

'Careful,' cautioned Kieran. 'Sixty-year-old bones can take up to twelve months to mend.'

'Oh, yeah?' said Jo, shooing the party away. 'And how long do twenty-three-year-old bones take?'

Kieran looked back, biting his bottom lip. 'Hmm. I'm not sure.'

Perhaps Kieran and Saskia had something in common after all, she thought: their ability to take everything literally.

Hovering above the uncomfortable stool, she watched the slow-moving customers drift around the shop and made small talk as they passed through the checkout. She was unsure as to whether the Saskia–Pearl combination would be a successful one, or whether Kieran's input would be a help or a hindrance, but either way, she thought, at least she could say she had tried. In as much as she could, she was making amends to Mrs Phillips for all her wrongdoing.

The radio was on low and Jo turned up the volume as an old Abba track came on. She found herself smiling, picturing Gill's animated face as she danced around her kitchen, getting excited about her celebrity bread rolls. The whole Notting Hill episode seemed such a long time ago now – as if it were a temporary transportation into someone else's life. It was ironic to think that, back in London, she had been so convinced that it was the right place for her, that Becky Ross was the girl she should strive to be. Yet now, it seemed obvious that she'd simply been trying to shoehorn Jo Simmons into someone else's life.

Earlier, Jo had called her old lab partner to apologise. It was a conversation she'd been putting off for days, but in the event, she needn't have worried. Gill understood – in fact, not only did she understand but she insisted on taking some of the blame for what had happened.

'I was so fixated with getting you back on track that I never stopped to think about *which* track you were aiming for,' she had said. And in those few words, she had summed up the problem. The track Gill had laid for herself would have suited her old friend Becky, but it was no longer right for Jo.

Her phone vibrated against the checkout.

Dear Rebecca, Dad
coming home in
time for Christmas.
Will you be coming
over?
Mum XXX

Jo's smile stayed with her as she pictured her mother preparing vegetables and turkey, draping tinsel around the lounge and hanging sprigs of holly on the door of the family home. Gill had been right about one thing, even if her rationale had originated in a book called *Learn to Love Your Higher Self*. Jo *had* needed to confront the source of her turmoil. Meeting up with her mother had been a turning point. If she hadn't followed Gill's piece of advice, the cloud of remorse would still be hanging over her now, the guilt still rearing its head at every little reminder of her cowardice. And if she hadn't gone to Finchley Road then all the other questions, like the mystery of her childhood and her father and all the little things like the smell of cinnamon tea, would still be unanswered.

Slowly, Jo's life seemed to be coming together. It may have taken the threat of prison to make her realise, but she had a lot to be happy about here in Radley. She was living an honest, guilt-free existence, and the paranoia – along with all the other hang-ups from her days as Roxie – had finally lifted. She didn't keep a bottle of vodka by her bed any more, and she no longer broke into a sweat in the presence of uniformed men. Mrs Phillips was probably right when she said that the slow pace of life was doing her good.

Jo looked up as another customer hobbled towards

the till. The only uncertainty now, she thought, was her job. She had been playing phone-tag with Geoff for two days now, so she still didn't know what his 'ideas' entailed, but by the tone of Sue's voice in her message Jo suspected that they wouldn't be entirely to her liking. She tried to remain optimistic that they wouldn't signify the end of her career at Dunston's. If they did, she reasoned, then surely Sue would have conveyed such a message herself.

'We're back!' Mrs Phillips called brightly as the door at the back swung open.

'We got a plan!' cried Saskia, stomping up beside her in her giant boots.

The women smiled sideways at one another, almost as if . . . Jo frowned. They almost looked like *friends*.

'And Pearl's gonna have Saskia's pussy,' Kieran piped up from the back.

Jo nearly exploded all over the broccoli as she rang it up. 'What?'

'Fluffy,' said Saskia, straight-faced. 'I left 'im wiv a mate when I came 'ere. But Mrs P says 'e can live upstairs an' all!'

'Great!' cried Jo, composing herself. 'That's six pounds twenty-two. So, d'you think there's hope for the guesthouse yet?'

They all nodded earnestly.

'A few regulations to comply with, but I don't see any reason why it can't open after Christmas,' declared Kieran, patting his pile of papers. He looped his giant hat in an arc so that it landed squarely on his head. 'See you soon. Goodbye, all.'

Saskia flashed a provocative smile and waved. 'Nice to meet you, Kieran!'

453

Chapter Fifty-One

The sound of high-pitched voices carried across the frosty car park as Jo raced along. She pushed on the gate that led into the labyrinth of tall, metal cages.

'That's it! Put the pressure on! Turn the screw!' yelled an agitated man in a tracksuit.

Jo hastened past and found herself in an open-air, Astro-Turfed corridor surrounded by raucous supporters, all clinging to the metal enclosures like apes in a zoo. Above her, a plastic banner hung crookedly between two flood-lights: 'Centrepoint: Giving Homeless Young People a Future'.

She squeezed along the gangway looking left and right. On the first pitch, a team jogged into position and embarked on an elaborate warm-up. Jo weaved through the bodies. All the players looked significantly more mature and organised than she imagined the motley Dunston's gang to look. The words 'lamb' and 'slaughter' crept ominously into her mind.

She reached the end of the enclosure and stopped. On pitch five, play had yet to start. The referee was poised, whistle in mouth, hand in the air, ready for kick-off. Five players in red were jumping up and down on the spot, their bodies steaming in the cold. Jo realised, with a sinking feeling, that they were waiting for their opposition.

'Well, you can do wivvout me!' yelled a voice that Jo recognised immediately. 'I ain't takin' it out!'

The pink fashion trainers and scraped-back red hair confirmed the girl's identity as Charlene's. She was leaning against the pitch door, arms crossed, staring sullenly at a woman Jo didn't recognise. Either side of Charlene, like henchmen, were five scruffy teenagers wearing a mixture of Primark and fake Nike in various styles and colours. Jo sighed. Her fears had not been unfounded; Team Dunston's didn't stand a chance.

'Hey!'

Out of the commotion, a familiar, round face appeared.

'Boy, am I glad to see you.'

The tension in Jo's body ratcheted up a notch as she was enveloped in Clare's enormous bosom. She hadn't expected anyone to feel glad to see her today.

'What's going on?'

Clare rolled her eyes and glanced at Charlene. 'It's this ref. He's more strict than the others. Says she can't play with the stud in her lip, but she's just had it pierced and won't take it out in case it heals over.'

Jo nodded and looked across at the flame of red hair. Like a hamster's, Charlene's face was distorted by the swelling on one side of her mouth.

'Why don't you just tape it up?' Jo wasn't sure where the idea had come from; maybe some distant memory from her footballing days. 'Use a plaster or something.'

'Oh, right. OK.' Clare re-entered the ring and after a few last-minute protests from Charlene, covered the offending metalwork and bundled the kids into the enclosure.

Jo felt a surge of affection as she watched Kyle lead the others to the halfway line with a menacing swagger. She wondered whether anything had happened since their little chat in the park. At least he was here – without any bruising, as far as she could see.

'READY?' yelled the referee as the reluctant team shuffled into position.

'Not in the slightest,' muttered Clare, under her breath so that Tim, the team's sub, couldn't hear. 'They lost the first two games, by the way.'

The match kicked off. Poking her fingers into the mesh, Jo felt a pang of guilt. She should never had entered them into the tournament.

'Oh, sorry, I don't think you've met.' Clare stepped back to form a triangle between her, Jo and an older woman. 'Jo, this is Maggie. She's been running the kids' activities for the last few weeks while you've been . . . away.'

'*Trying* to!' the woman laughed. She was in her forties, Jo guessed, with lank auburn hair and an earnest face. This was the ex-school teacher Sue had mentioned.

They watched as Kyle and Jason made a charge for the man with the ball, who deftly passed it back to a team mate, only to find his legs being kicked from under him.

'PENALTY, REF! PENALTY!' shouted the man standing next to them. He was wearing a red sports jacket that matched the T-shirts of the players on the pitch. The referee ignored him.

'I think some people are taking this all rather seriously, don't you?' Clare remarked as the opposition scored their first goal and the man started banging his fists against the meshing.

Jo pulled her fingers away as the metal grated against them. 'Where's Charlene playing?'

Maggie frowned. 'She's over there.' She pointed to the stationary figure.

'No, I mean, where on the pitch? What's her position?'

Clare looked awkwardly between Maggie and Jo.

'Oh. Er, well, I just suggested that the girls have a pop if the ball came towards them, you know . . .'

Jo nodded, slowly. She wasn't sure whether to step in. Clearly Maggie had tried her best to prepare the kids for today.

'GIVE IT SOME WELLY!' The man whacked the fence again, this time in exasperation as one of his players tapped the ball straight into Taiwo's arms.

'Good save, Taiwo!' screamed Jo, clapping her hands.

Then the opposition scored again.

'THAT'S WHAT I'M TALKIN' ABOUT!' bawled the man. Jo glared at his bristly chin.

'Nadia, get involved!' she shrieked, burning up with frustration and guilt. Why had she left the kids like that? What had she been thinking, running off to London?

It was so important that the children had something to aim for. That was the reason she'd entered them into the tournament in the first place. But now, watching them flounder about under the guidance of poor, clueless Maggie, Jo realised that she might have done them more harm than good.

'I don't think she likes running,' Maggie observed. 'She's asthmatic.'

'Unfit,' Jo muttered, watching helplessly as the girl's dark hair swung sideways and one of the androgynous beings dribbled past her and scored. 'Shit. How many is that?'

'Three,' Tim replied. 'Will I get to go on soon?'

'Maybe,' she said ambiguously.

The noisy supporter looked over. 'One minute to go. THAT'S THE STUFF, REDS! FINAL MINUTE!'

Jo tried not to let her disappointment show as the kids let in two more goals and then ambled off the pitch, heads down.

'That was . . .' Jo tried to catch someone's eye as they passed. 'That wasn't too bad!'

They shuffled past her in silence, eyes fixed on the worn, fake grass.

'GREAT WORK! FANTASTIC!' cried the annoying man, slapping various members of his team on the back and handing out drinks.

'Fuck off,' muttered Kyle as he passed.

Jo couldn't suppress a little smile. 'How many games left?' she asked.

'Well . . .' Clare waited for the youngsters to disappear into the crowds. 'There's only one more in the groups stage, and I think, judging by the scores so far, that'll be it for us.'

'I think I might go and see how they're doing,' said Maggie, pulling a face.

Jo slumped back against the metal fence. She had bullied them into doing this tournament, and then left them to fend for themselves. Now, not only did the children feel vulnerable and angry, they felt like losers too.

'You OK?' asked Clare.

Jo smiled faintly. *Her* being OK wasn't really the point.

'Sue said you might be coming back,' Clare prompted cheerily.

Jo nodded. 'If anyone wants me back.'

Clare laughed softly. 'Hey, stop beating yourself up. Of *course* we want you back. By the way, don't feel you have to hold back on coaching them – Maggie won't mind. I think she might appreciate it, actually.' Clare looked up and flashed a broad grin at the kids. 'Hey! So, last game! Er . . . of the groups stage!'

Jo allowed herself a small, cautious rush of joy at the fact that they *hadn't* managed fine without her, then attempted to buoy the ramshackle team into something that resembled action. She put Tim on the pitch, removing a very indignant Jason, and explained to Kyle the concept of tackling in a way that didn't involve knocking the opponent unconscious. Then she had one last go at persuading the girls to exert some energy.

'Good luck!'

They trotted – *trotted*, not wandered – onto the pitch and resumed their positions. Jo glanced at Clare, who gave her a quick, feeble smile. The opposition didn't look nearly as menacing as the last lot, Jo noticed. There was a slim possibility, she thought, that Dunston's might even score a goal.

'So, where are you living?' asked Clare, as play commenced and the ball bounced randomly from player to player.

'Back where I was, between Radley and Abingdon.' The teams were evenly matched, Jo noted hopefully: equally crap.

'I guess you'd come back after Christmas? Ooh! Good tackle – did you see that?'

Jo nodded, gobsmacked. Kyle had won the ball off another player without knocking him over. 'Yeah, I guess. I'm waiting for Geoff to call.'

'Well, you're not missing much,' said Clare, eyes widening as Nadia moved for the ball. 'Just tinsel and mince pies and terrible music. Oh, and the Christmas party last week.' She raised her eyes heavenwards.

A person of indeterminate gender took the ball from Nadia's feet and started zooming down the wing.

Christmas party, thought Jo, finding herself daydreaming wistfully of Matt and mistletoe and darkened corners of the dance floor late at night. She tried to override her imagination and think of a subtle way of asking Clare about his move to Manchester without offering any information about their relationship – or lack of.

'How is everyone in the office?'

'Oh my God!' Clare gasped as Charlene made a nervous attempt to get in the way of the ball, and, perhaps because of her pink footwear or the lumpy blue plaster on her face, managed to put the player off his or her stride. 'Er, everyone's fine, I think.'

Tim intercepted the ball and dribbled it carefully around several sets of feet, then took a shot at goal.

Clare shrieked. Maggie threw her hands up to her face. Jo watched in amazement as the keeper fished the ball out from the back of the net.

'He's scored!' Clare cried breathlessly.

Play resumed and, inevitably, the opposition scored an equaliser within the next few seconds.

'Shit,' muttered Clare. 'Oh, you heard about Matt?'

Jo tried to sound blasé. 'Er . . .'

'Heard what?' asked another voice from behind them. Jo whirled round. Matt was looking straight at her.

Chapter Fifty-Two

'Are they winning?'

Jo didn't know what to say. She hadn't expected to see him again, hadn't planned for this ever to happen. After all the weeks spent trying to expel the memories and images from her mind, here he was in the flesh, asking her about the football.

She wasn't prepared for this. All the conversations she'd run through in her head flooded back: the confessions, the explanations, the justifications . . . she could even remember some of the lines she had used, but none of them seemed appropriate now he was here – not least because in her daydreams, they hadn't had Maggie and Clare and Jason standing between them.

'One-all in their final game.' She smiled tentatively. 'How are you?'

'Not bad,' he replied in a monotone. 'They're doing all right then?'

Jo tried to catch his eye but he was being evasive, his gaze fixed on a spot straight ahead.

Clare spluttered and glanced sideways. 'Not exactly.'

Jo leaned closer, trying to get his attention. 'They lost their first three games.'

He nodded mechanically.

Jo tried to think of another way to engage him, slightly distracted by the white T-shirt that showed off his arms and the day's worth of stubble on his jaw. She was about to explain how imperative it was that they win the match, when suddenly Clare started leaping up and down.

'Ooh, look! Tim's got it again! Come on, Tim! *Come on.*'

They watched tensely as Tim weaved past one player, then another, then –

'Ow!' cried Clare in sympathy as one of the larger members of the opposition kneed him in the chest.

The whistle blew.

'Shit,' muttered Jo, watching in horror as a crowd gathered around Tim's limp body. 'Where's the first aid?'

To her relief, a few seconds later, the ten-year-old emerged from the group and started hobbling towards the exit.

'OK, Jason, you're on,' she instructed. 'Last minute or so. It's a penalty. Tell Kyle to take it. Good luck!'

The referee placed the ball on the yellow line. Kyle stepped forward and glared menacingly at the goalie, then the ball. The tension mounted. Even the girls, chewing their fingernails together at the edge of the box, seemed to understand the significance of the moment. *Don't fuck it up,* prayed Jo.

And, miraculously, despite the pressure, the lack of training, despite everything else going on in Kyle's head, he didn't. The ref blew the final whistle and declared the game a win for Dunston's. *A win.* Jo jumped up and threw her arms around Clare, and then almost without thinking, around Matt. Stiffly, he returned her embrace.

She stepped away, feeling self-conscious and uncomfortable. They watched as Kyle sauntered off the pitch, closely followed by his four disciples, who, had there been branches and grapes to hand, would have been fanning and feeding their hero. They had won. It was only one game, and it wasn't the Champions League, but they had won.

Eventually, the excitement died down and the group splintered into twos and threes on the way back to the clubhouse. Jo strategically hung back and timed her stride to match Matt's.

'So,' she said. 'Red Cross, eh?'

'Mmm.' He nodded vaguely.

'Is that it? Mmm?' Jo frowned. 'Aren't you excited?'

Matt shrugged. Maybe he loathed her so much, she thought miserably, that he'd taken a job he didn't even want, just to get away from her. Secretly, Jo had been hoping that he'd come here today to tell her that the Manchester thing was all off; that he'd changed his mind and wanted to go back to the way things were. Now, seeing his expression, she realised just how misplaced and naïve her optimism had been.

They walked on, accompanied by the whoops and screams of the victorious players around them.

'When do you start?' she asked as they neared the clubhouse.

'January.'

They were getting nowhere, thought Jo. She couldn't go on like this, asking pointless questions, getting one-word answers. *She had to tell him how she felt.*

'Look, Matt.' She stopped, and Matt finally turned towards her, his face still blank. 'I just . . .' She couldn't start. There was so much inside her, waiting to spill out, but Matt was all cold and vacant, and she couldn't even be sure he was listening. Jo looked imploringly into his lifeless eyes and forced the words out.

'I need to tell you something. I know it's pointless – you're going to Manchester and I'll probably never see you again – but I just want to say . . . I understand now why you did what you did. And I'm sorry I reacted so badly at the time, running off to London, and . . . well, I made a mistake. I realise that now. You were helping me all along, and . . .' She trailed off. It wasn't coming out as coherently as she had hoped.

'The thing is,' she went on, determined to tell him everything, albeit inarticulately, 'I was confused. I didn't know who I was, but . . . well . . .' She took a breath and exhaled slowly, looking at Matt. 'I know who I am with you.'

There was an almost imperceptible change in his expression: a slight tilt of the head, a narrowing of the eyes. He was with her now, she could tell – she just wished she could decipher his reaction.

'And I have to ask,' she added hesitantly, 'did you mean what you said in your text message and on the phone that time?'

She was actually shaking, she realised, as she waited for Matt's response. There was a look in his eyes that seemed almost . . . almost like the warmth she was used to. Jo suppressed her hopes. It was probably just her imagination playing tricks.

'Jo-oh! Telephone!'

Her heart plummeted as she saw Clare pushing through the crowds, waving a mobile phone. Jo glanced quickly at

Matt, who gave a slow blink of despair. She wasn't going to get an answer now.

'It's Geoff!' Clare explained breathlessly. 'Here you go!' She thrust the phone into Jo's hand and edged back the way she had come.

'Hello?' Jo said cautiously, still looking at Matt. It felt as though, by maintaining eye contact, she could put their conversation on hold, cryogenically freeze it, so that they could pick up where they left off once she'd finished the call.

'Jo, it's Geoff. Finally, we speak! I hear the football was something of a success, eh?'

'Mmm, er, could I call you ba—'

'Congratulations all round, I say. Now, about your job. I think Sue mentioned, I have a proposition for you. There's a role that's just opened up in one of the other homes. It's an activities coordinator function, same as the one you've been doing, but at a bigger centre. You'd be looking after several sets of kids. Similar stuff, just more of it, basically. How would you feel about that?'

'Er . . .' Jo didn't know how she felt – about anything. Holding Matt's gaze, her thoughts were drawn to the momentous, unfinished conversation that hung in the air between them. It remained impossible to interpret his expression.

She tried to focus. It was a relief, in a way, that Dunston's was willing to take her on in any capacity after all that had happened. And it was flattering that they wanted to entrust more children to her care. But at the same time, Jo felt uneasy about the prospect of moving away. She had only recently decided that Radley was her home and her future. She had just started to feel like part of the team at Fairmont House – and now, it seemed, she was being asked to tear up all that and step back into the unknown.

'Where would it be, this role?'

'The Chapel Street centre in Manchester.'

Jo tried to respond, but the words got caught in her throat. Matt was frowning slightly, clearly wondering what had triggered her incredulous reaction. She didn't remember how the conversation ended. Her head was elsewhere. At some point, she told Geoff that she'd like some time to mull it over, but her thoughts had already moved well beyond mulling. She was seeing herself unpacking boxes with Matt, ordering takeaway pizza, wandering the northern quarter in his arms . . . Jo lowered the phone and tumbled back to reality, her smile fading fast. Matt was looking solemnly into her eyes.

'Yes,' he said.

Jo wondered for a moment whether he had heard both sides of the conversation and was pre-empting her decision.

'What?'

'Yes,' he said again, smiling as he stepped towards her. 'In answer to your question before – I meant what I said.'

She closed her eyes, letting Matt draw her in and feeling the tension drain away as his lips met hers. It was like another one of her daydreams. She caught the familiar scent of his skin as his stubble lightly grazed her cheek, and she realised, with absolute certainty, that she was on the right track.

'Jo-oh!'

The kiss came to an abrupt end.

'Have you got a minute? Kyle wants to speak to you. Oh, you're – oh, oh.'

466

'It's fine,' Jo replied, glancing at Matt, who grinned back at her.

Apprehensively, she followed Clare through the clubhouse and out into the car park, where the Dunston's children were arranging themselves around a plastic trophy that someone had presumably awarded them for turning up.

The possibilities spooled through her mind as she sought out the hooded figure at the edge of the group. His stepfather had hurt him again . . . Kyle had committed a crime . . . His father was going to prison after all . . . Jo felt terrible. She had been so obsessed with planning her *own* perfect life that she had forgotten all about the person who needed her most – and who, in a way, had helped her to get this far.

'Are you OK?'

Kyle shrugged, hands in pockets, his face veiled by a cloud of his own breath. 'Fought I'd tell you. I ain't gonna be comin' to Activities no more.'

'Oh – oh right.' Jo nodded anxiously. 'Why's that?'

'I'm gonna go to a school.'

'What . . . sort of school?' asked Jo, picturing a bars-at-the-windows detention centre. She was terrified to ask what had happened.

'An academy.'

Jo's mouth fell open. 'Oh my God. As in—'

'An art one.'

She didn't know what to say. She wanted to throw her arms around him and squeeze him, but she knew he'd be mortified. She did it anyway.

He wriggled free with a grunt. 'Fought I'd just say. Anyway. See ya.'

Jo watched speechlessly as the boy ambled across the gravel towards the exit.

'Hey, Kyle!' she called. 'Aren't you going to stay for the award ceremony? You won Player of the Match!'

He stopped and turned, yanking the hood down over his face.

'Horseshit,' he muttered, sloping off through the gates.

In conversation with Polly Courtney

What inspired you to write The Day I Died?

A few months ago I attended a dinner with my university friends, many of them engineering graduates, like me. Almost without exception, they had followed the well-trodden path into the Square Mile and were earning huge salaries in the City, as I had once done. I was the odd one out, for having broken free from the pack to become a novelist instead of a 'high flyer'.

It occurred to me, as I listened to their tales of long hours and monotony, that too many of us are constrained by the expectations of our peers and of society. Instead of doing what we *want* to do with our lives, we do what is expected of us. I wanted to write about the conflict between the two: a sort of nature versus nurture debate.

A good friend of mine works for a charity that helps vulnerable young people to get back on their feet: the complete antithesis to the heartless financial district inhabited by many of my contemporaries. I decided to highlight the difference by challenging Jo to fit into both worlds.

How do you write? Do you have a regular routine?

I lead something of a double life. As well as writing, I have a career in web development – partly so that I can keep my novels 'real' but also because I enjoy working with numbers, not just words. For two or three days each week my web projects take priority, which means that my 'writing days' are precious.

On a typical writing day I start by running round the local park or playing football if it's the weekend. I'm only creative in the afternoons, which means that before midday

I'm free to work on other ventures – the main one at the moment being Girls in Football.com.

I tend to write one chapter per day, and I plan my novels quite carefully so that when it comes to sitting down at my laptop, I'm not staring at a blank sheet – it's all mapped out for me. I have to shut out any distractions, including my phone and email – and my boyfriend!

Do you draw upon your own experiences with family and friends as you create characters and plots?

I don't knowingly use personal experiences or acquaintances in my novels, although I have a feeling that they creep in without me realising. I draw on society for inspiration; people-watching is a key pastime when it comes to planning a new novel. I do a lot of wandering, watching and listening, sometimes making notes. I have become an expert in taking photos on my mobile phone whilst pretending to make a call.

How did it feel to place yourself in Jo's shoes? Do you think that you could create a new identity if you were placed in similar extraordinary circumstances?

Being in Jo's shoes was challenging and exhausting – but exciting. She's a resourceful, resilient girl and I enjoyed thinking up ways for her to get out of tricky situations. I suppose there's a bit of me in Jo – and in Becky, too. When I first moved to London as a graduate, I was full of the joys of the rich City life, but when I became disillusioned and discovered my passion for writing, I saw that there were other, less conventional paths I could take – in the same way that Jo found Dunston's.

In a way, I have several identities already – we all do.

When I'm on the football pitch I'm a very different person to the one who sits quietly in the office thinking about online strategies. In the evenings I change from being a solitary novelist to a sociable pint-drinker, and occasionally, when playing violin with the girls in my string quartet, I become a performer. But I'd find it hard to create a whole new identity from scratch and to leave everything else behind. I'd miss my friends – and I'd be a terrible actress.

Who are your literary influences?
I always have several books on the go, so I can pick up the one that suits my mood. For humour, I like Nick Hornby and John O'Farrell. For inspiration and reality, I enjoy autobiographies – the latest one being Richard Branson's. I also love P.D. James and Ian Banks for their twisted plots. As a child, I always read adventure books, mainly ones with a female protagonist. Nancy Drew was my idol.

Which person, alive or dead, would you most like to swap identities with for a day?
I'd be Queen Elizabeth I. She was a feisty, no-nonsense monarch who ruled in the 1500s, not only defeating the Spanish Armada during her reign but also passing several new laws including one that forced people to wear flat caps on Sundays and another that put a tax on men's beards! I'd like to have her job for a day – although I'm not so sure she'd take to mine.

What's next?

Tell us the name of an author you love

| Polly Courtney | Go |

and we'll find your next great book.

www.bookarmy.com